To
Tommy, Gayle, Polly and Sarah,
the best chapters in the pages of my life.

R.M. Clark

IF THE WORLD IS YOURS

AUSTIN MACAULEY PUBLISHERS™

LONDON * CAMBRIDGE * NEW YORK * SHARJAH

Copyright © R.M. Clark (2021)

The right of R.M. Clark to be identified as author of this work has been asserted by the author in accordance with section 77 and 78 of the Copyright, Designs and Patents Act 1988.

All rights reserved. No part of this publication may be reproduced, stored in a retrieval system, or transmitted in any form or by any means, electronic, mechanical, photocopying, recording, or otherwise, without the prior permission of the publishers.

Any person who commits any unauthorised act in relation to this publication may be liable to criminal prosecution and civil claims for damages.

This book is a work of fiction. Any reference to historical events, real people or real places have been used fictitiously. Other names, characters, places and events are products of the author's imagination, and any resemblance to actual events, places or persons, living or dead, is entirely coincidental. Space and time have been rearranged to suit the story.

A CIP catalogue record for this title is available from the British Library.

ISBN 9781528921008 (Paperback)
ISBN 9781528921015 (Hardback)
ISBN 9781528969529 (ePub e-book)
ISBN 9781398418264 (Audiobook)

www.austinmacauley.com

First Published (2021)
Austin Macauley Publishers Ltd
25 Canada Square
Canary Wharf
London
E14 5LQ

Thank you to the writers, aspiring writers and poets in the Migratory Words Writing Circle for your valuable feedback. To Canmore's Georgetown Inn for offering your Snug Room for the writing circle meetings. To Wilma Rubens for your encouraging writing classes. To Brenan Dewar Jones for reading my first draft and fostering my confidence. To Rosemary Nixon, Georgia Bell and Pat Hjorleifson for your support and input. To the Alberta Writers Guild Manuscript Reading Service for your guidance and direction. To Polly Clark-Abbi, thanks for badgering me to start this book. To Sarah Clark-Pickett, thanks for urging me to finish this book. To the Fairmont Banff Springs for the use of your vintage photograph (book cover). A special thanks to Gayle Bories. Through countless dinners, you unwearyingly nodded, chewed, swallowed and smiled while I voiced my imaginary characters and plotted my tale. And last, but not least, Austin Macauley Publishers for believing in my work.

Alberta Strong: The colours of the Alberta tartan (spine of book) represent the green of our forests, the gold of our wheat fields, the blue of our clear skies and sparking lakes, the pink of our wild rose, and the black of our coal and petroleum. The tartan was designed by Alison Lamb and Ellen Neilsen, two ladies from the Edmonton Rehabilitation Society. It was adopted as the official tartan of Alberta in 1961.

A chronicle of the lives of the rich and their servants during WW1
Not centred around 'that' great English estate but an equally magnificent
place, Canada's Banff Springs Hotel

Chapter 1

Afternoon, June 21, 1914

Below Stairs, Banff Springs Hotel

Banff, Alberta

A door in the beamed high-ceilinged kitchen opened setting forth a stream of light into a little room two steps lower: a clay sink, a slop sink, an overhead pulley laden with kitchen linens. Above a little window, misty with condensation, the plank sign read, *'A new broom sweeps clean but an old broom knows the corners'.*

The sudden fearsome sound of a train whistle obliterated the cheery domestic sounds and muffled voices. Ethel Finch plucked at the fob watch dangling from the bib of her apron. Glanced up at the Canadian Pacific Railway clock, clanking, struggling, and striking half past two. "Oh me nerves. Another blinkin' shipment o' mollycoddled toffs." She adjusted her timepiece and wound its crown tight. "Every-*body!*" she bellowed across the small beehive of organised labour. "We need this scullery sorted! 'Fore we're invaded!" A cold wind of chaos blustered through the room. A stench of castile soap rose from a tub of boiling washcloths. Ishbel McColl wiped her hands down the sides of her pinny, grabbed the rough pulley cords, and leaned all her weight into the slab stone floor. The cumbersome frame of damp linens made a harsh high-pitched squeal as it hiked towards the ceiling. Her lungs thawed with confidence when the contraption reached its maximum.

"Wassgoin'on in here?" The bristly supervisor pushed an escaped wisp of wiry hair up the front of her mop-cap. "This scullery's for dippin', rubbin' and scrubbin'!" She jabbed the hulky canvas sack with the point of her boot. "It's for all the jobs that involves water *not* flour! Ya, over there—"

Ishbel, stiff as a wary deer. "Me?"

"Yar name?"

"Oh. My name." Her flesh raised into goose bumps. "My name is Ishbel."

Ethel raised her voice and waved her hands about. "Well get crackin'! Move this bloomin' bag ter the kitchen. But mind ya secure that blinkin' clotheshorse first."

Ishbel turned and took an undignified tumble over a jutting-out oil jar. She struggled to her feet. Chest tightening, breath speeding, she wound the cords around the wall cleat.

The supervisor gave a little laugh. "Come day go day God send Sunday. Ya must be the new one sent up from thc Laundry?"

"Yes ma'am. I was hired on yesterday as maid-of-all-duties. They said to take down the fine linen for straining soups. Hang up the working linen for drying dishes. Then report to a Miss Finch."

"Well, *I'm* Miss Finch." Ethel pointed to her bosom with her thumb. "The one responsible for whippin' this scullery inter shape. What's yar name again?" She screwed up her broad face. "Queen o' Calamities?"

Muffled conspiratorial giggling resonated across the scullery.

She sucked in her cringe. "No, ma'am. It's Ishbel."

"Well, Isabel, it's about time ya got a blinkin' move on."

"Ma'am, my name isn't Isabel," her heart pumped. "It's I*sh*bel."

Ethel's rage rose from her toes to her cheeks. "Yar takin' a helluva time movin' that blinkin' sack!" She gripped Ishbel's elbow. "If ya can't handle the work, girl, plenty'll take it off yar hands."

A heavy layer of dread settled over Ishbel. She wiped her forehead with her sleeve, grasped the top end of the pack and pressed her fingers into its coarse threads. Blood pumping. Stomach churning. For the life of her, she couldn't budge the stupid thing. She felt the overseer's stare on the back of her neck. Her heart sank. She was out of a job.

"Gimme an end."

The voice brought a little hope. Ishbel looked up and relief flooded through her. A tall maid, uniform blazing white against her auburn hair, was already hauling up one corner. "Oh, whut the duck!" She dropped it. Looked at Ishbel. "Try placin' yir hands like I've got mine on yir end." She waited. "Righty-o! One two three. Pu-*uuull*!"

The colour rose in their cheeks. The cumbersome weight began shifting. "Keep it goin' keep it goin'—" The two young maids dragged the solid pack up two steps through the door past fifty cooks cheffing in the well-equipped kitchen. The weighty sack tugged at their spirits. A whiff of batter assailed their noses.

"Keep it goin' keep it goin'—" Their shoes clattered across the glazed-brick floor dappled in afternoon sun until they reached a white-washed wall where piles of flour sacks caressed the ceiling. The bag dropped with a thud from their hands. The obliging maid grinned at Ishbel. "Sweet cheeses, yi look knackered."

Pearls of perspiration surfacing on Ishbel's forehead and beads of sweat budding on her back. "I'm fine. Now. Thanks. Thanks a lot."

"Thanks a lot me arse!" shrieked Ethel Finch, hovering like a hunting hawk. "Pull out that blasted bin. Heave up the stupid sack. Rest the bloomin' bag on the blinkin' brim!" The two young maids grabbed the flour pack, hoisted it up with all their might, and eased its middle onto the edge of the big container. Ishbel glanced sideways at Miss Finch who was now lifting the lid off a tub boiling washcloths. The vinegar stench assaulted her nose and the lid clattered back down. She turned her head and glared at Ishbel. "Have ya got that damn flour in that damn bucket yet?"

Ishbel's fingers grappled for the tiny end of twine. Hand trembling. She couldn't seize hold of it.

"Yar makin' me some vexed." Miss Finch pushed passed Ishbel, snatched the bit of string and gave it one almighty tug. The thread flew from the hem of the sack and the contents whooshed out plummeting forcefully into the container billowing high into the air coating everyone and everything in floury dust. Ethel, dizzy and completely white, staggered blindly about the kitchen until she tripped over the oil jar and caught her balance against the washtub. "When I get my hands on that little strumpet." She coughed and swiped the air.

"But, I—" Ishbel splurting white particles.

"Isabel," Ethel snorted with rage. "Ya'd be wise ter hold yar blabberin' tongue."

"But my name isn't Isabel." Ishbel's hand flew to her mouth.

The supervisor's eyes, big, red and flashing, shone menacingly through her ghostly face. "Why ya *ya* uppity little madam!"

The tall maid's hands stopped mid-air at supervisor's thunderous voice. "Oh, Missus Finch," she cried, a buffer between them, "surely it wuz an accident."

"An accident!" Ethel snatched up a dishrag and waved it about like a flag. "Get this damn mess cleaned up 'fore I skin the pair o' ya alive. And when yar done doin' that, get yar scrawny carcasses ter the 5th floor. All those sash windows need closin'. 'Fore that bloomin' Tallyho comes rollin' in blowin' its blinkin' dirt ter kingdom come."

"Missus Finch, are all the rooms occupied on the 5th floor?"

"Oh me nerves. Where does ya think they're puttin' the next shipment o' spoon-fed toffs?" She twisted the dishrag with imprisoned energy. "Only one mothball space is occupied. Room 520. The 1st Duke o' Connaught moved in this mornin'. He's a son o' late Queen Victoria. But they're callin' him the governor general o' Canada now. So mind ya keep invisible and noise-*less!*"

2 pm, June 21, 1914
Canadian Pacific Railway Station
Banff, Alberta

Thick smoke blew from the chimney of the magnificent train, circled the pungent fragrance from surrounding pine trees, and rode the spring breezes. In the first-class carriage, a sharp-featured governess turned stiffly in a deep-buttoned seat. "Winston, wake up, child. We have reached the end of our journey." She shook the boy's slight shoulder. "Banff. Alberta. A remote corner of the world. Sit up straight like a little gentleman and tell me. When did Alberta become a province?"

Winston opened his eyes, face crumpled with sleep. Squinted at the brightness. Stared dumbly at the stationary landscape then popped into life. "Wow! The Rocky Mountains!"

"Indeed they are." His father, Lord Randolph Fairfax, turned the page of his newspaper with crisp irritation. "Now answer Nanny's question."

"September 1, 1905," he replied, tapping the tubular-metal foot warmer with tip of his shoe.

"Correct, child. And who was it named after?"

Winston slid his spectacles over the bridge of his nose. "Princess Louise Caroline Alberta. The daughter of Queen Victoria and Prince Albert." He had an overwhelming need to look out of the window. "Oh, Nanny Patterson! Can I climb to the top of one of those mountains tomorrow?"

"Lo-*wer* your voice, child." Nanny turned sideways to yank up Winston's elastic garters and straighten the turnovers on his socks. *"Your father will decide if and when you attempt a summit. I can assure you it will not be tomorrow. Now. Before you extricate yourself from that seat, may I remind you, we are English. Renowned across the world for good manners, socially appropriate behaviour and excellent posture. Straight back chin up chest out. And don't forget to square those shoulders."*

But Winston had already bolted to the opposite side of the varnished-teak carriage. He pressed his nose flat against the glass and stared into the kaleidoscope of activity bustling in the humble station platform: Trolley-pushing porters with flat caps and shiny shoes dodging between weary passengers pouring from the train, its hiss subsiding. A group of urchins with dusty boots doling out newspapers, their cries going up:

"Crag & Canyon! Crag & Canyon!"

"Banff News!"

"All the News That's Fit to Print!"

A coin was placed in a sticky palm. "Thanks mister!"

"Crag & Canyon! Crag & Canyon!"

"Banff News!"

Nanny Patterson poked a vicious-looking hatpin into the crown of her felt hat to hide her excitement. "Winston, we are about to disembark. Stop daydreaming and put on your cap and jacket. And be mindful of those steep and narrow steps. Winston! Come back here at once! Now. Take hold of nanny's hand."

The wind, channelling across the busy platform, whirled the gravel and blew the dust. Lord Fairfax turned up his collar against the cold, drank in the glorious air, and watched his son from the corner of his eye. The English school cap, a solid grey, hid a pair of curious eyes scanning a mountain of luggage.

Nanny Patterson followed the gaze of her employer. "Children have the capacity to adapt, sir." She straightened her spine. "You will be pleased to know your boy is maintaining a stiff upper lip."

"Oh the stiff upper lip," he groaned inwardly. "A British plaster for a broken leg, a broken heart and everything in-between."

Nanny's narrow lips disappeared into a grim pin-line. "Children who are encouraged to display fortitude in the face of adversity, sir," she enunciated each word slowly, "are better prepared for life."

Lord Fairfax nodded in agreement. "You of all people should know," he said, his voice gentle. "You have nurtured three generations of Fairfax children to lead the noble line."

A cheery porter approached. "Here you go, lad!" He placed a wicker container at the boy's feet. "Suspect you're lookin' for this, eh?"

One short-sharp bark and Winston's eyes sparkled with anticipation. He knelt down, pushed two fingers through a hole in the rattan container and wiggled them in front of his dog's nose. "Do not worry, Bobby. Nanny is coming."

The governess, exhaling exaggerated annoyance, unlocked the box and the Yorkshire terrier stepped over a slobber puddle and exited his smelly sanctuary. Ruff! He shook his luminous black and tan coat. Ruff! Yawned and stretched. Ruff! Ruff!

Winston beamed a huge smile and pressed his cheek against the warm body. "Bobby, we are here now. You do not have to go back in that awful prison."

Outside the train station, a pungent smell of horses filled the air. A street-trader with a neck strap supporting her tray spotted Lord Fairfax in the crowd. "A toffee apple for your boy, sir?" she asked but the important-looking man shook his head.

A rosy-cheeked girl eyed Winston vigorously. "Red Rope Licorice! Peppermint Humbugs! *Only* a Penny a Bag!" The rich scent of sugar caught his nose and her bold stare brought a flush to his face. He delved in his pocket to pull out a coin but Nanny Patterson whirled around.

"Such things both cloy and weaken the stomach!" She gave Winston a look of sour disapproval and shuffled him away. Bobby trotted behind, the tip of his little tail beating the air.

Horses hitched to carriages and wagons were lined up on both sides of the street and all the drivers were calling out for their share of business. "Climb on Up for a Ride to The King Edward Hotel!" hollered a jowly chap with flourishing whiskers. "The Cleanest Rooms on Main Street!"

A red-haired lad, holding a pair of snorting ponies, roared, "Who Wants the Cheapest Lodgings on the Banks of the Bow?" A young couple raised their hands. "Then climb *on* up! Make way, folks, skoosh along the bench. That's the way that's the way."

"All Aboard for the Cascade Hotel!" The man, thumbs down his waistband, winked at a potential customer. "I've got a comfy cushion in my wagon for a lovely lady to sit on—"

Nanny Patterson moved her hand in short motion. "Shoo! *Away* with you!" she shrieked and Winston laughed quietly.

Then it appeared. The largest, most splendid coach of all. The Tallyho. Harnesses clinked and hooves clanked against the stone as four splendid horses, flicking their tails and tossing their manes, pulled up at the station entrance, a privilege kept by special arrangement. The carriage driver, a top-hatted gent, rose from his seat. "Lad-*ies* and Gentle-*men!*" He rang a brass bell and the clapper inside sounded a clear musical note. "Lad-*ies* and Gentle-*men!* If your confirmed destination is the esteemed Banff Springs Hotel, please make your vouchers visible as you board our Tallyho."

Winston looked up at the driver. "May we ride up front with you?"

The driver glanced down at the eager-looking lad with a Yorkshire terrier tucked under one arm then switched his gaze to the gentleman. Lord Fairfax nodded his approval. "Hop up then," said the driver, and Winston pulled himself up by a handrail and slid, grinning, onto the straight-backed wooden bench, squishing poor Bobby who yelped a sharp protest.

Nanny Patterson regally ascended the high metal steps to take the very front leather-clad passenger seat. It was a little higher than the driver's, giving her a superb view of the road ahead, and a splendid view of Winston's gleaming locks below, 'Hmm, I wonder if Canadian soap is perhaps I should have packed a bar of Wrights Coal Tar.'

The driver called across his shoulder, "Is everyone ready?"

All the passengers responded with a resounding, "Yes."

"Then prepare for a ride to the grandest hotel on the North American continent!"

Neeeiiiaaaahahahaha! A flock of whiskey jacks fluttered up and the weighty vehicle with curved springs and leather straps, jolted into motion. The horses with high heads and hollow backs clip-clopped away from the station, their hooves providing a percussive rhythm until they reached the busy thoroughfare of Banff Avenue. Winston's eyes scanned the appealing structures through a blur of stony dust: a Dutch colonial building with a painted sign, 'Cascade Dancehall' above the door. The Paris Tea Room window, jam-packed with pies, profiteroles, and polka dot dandies. A young woman scrubbing the entrance to the Byron Harmon Photography shop. She stopped to wring out her cloth and the fresh-cheeked boy riding high on the Tallyho gave her a royal wave.

Arf!

"Shush, Bobby!" he snapped at him.

Nanny Patterson's nose peaked, "Winston. Do you have full control of that unruly animal?"

Bobby wriggled and kicked. "I do I *do*," Winston retorted.

The governess sat upright, needlepoint bag on lap, eyes fixed on the road ahead. "Gracious me. This thoroughfare is in appalling condition. And there is a frightful-looking bridge lying ahead." She leaned over the top of the driver's head. "It would behove you to proceed with caution."

"Ma'am, you are in safe hands," was his assured reply.

The Tallyho rumbled and bumped over a chuckhole. Nanny Patterson clung on for dear life to the sides of her seat. "How very dreadful. Is it not? To expect this higgledy-piggledy bridge to sustain the weight of this dubious contraption."

"Ma'am," the driver cleared his throat. "This sturdy link over the Bow River is as strong as the one you have over the River Thames."

"Driver! Sure-*ly* you are not suggesting this this tie-together is as safe as the iconic London Bridge?"

Unexpectedly, the whistling tune, *'London Bridge is Falling Down',* hit the air. Nanny Patterson's eyes popped with indignation and she flicked him off like she would a bothersome bee.

The driver chuckled inwardly then began his effortless spiel. "Banff is situated above the Bow Falls, near the confluence of the Bow River and Spray River. It is surrounded by mountains thrusting their peaks into the sky. Notably. Mount Rundle. Sulphur Mountain. Mount Norquay. Cascade Mountain."

The breath bounced from the chest of an elderly passenger. "Gracious me!" she gasped. "It is all quite thrilling!"

"Quite thrilling," echoed Lord Fairfax.

Winston pointed straight ahead to the impressive-looking building where two nurses, their cloaks blazing red, were pushing cane and rattan perambulators past a bed of showy blooms. "Is that your hospital?"

"Aye," replied the baggage handler, sitting to Winston's right, "they call it the Brett Sanatorium. 'Alf is a private 'ospital. The other 'alf is a 'otel." Slowly, laboriously, the powerful horses turned left until the carriage was brought into line on Spray Avenue. A thought occurred suddenly in Winston's mind, 'Spray Avenue because the sun sprays through the branches, dappling shadow patterns onto the dirt road.'

"Almost there," announced the driver.

Nanny Patterson patted her forehead with her lightly-starched handkerchief. "Oh my giddy aunt," she cried expansively, "this clippity-clopping reverberation is driving me positively batty." Winston groaned quietly.

The driver concealed his thoughts but 'spare-me-your-hoity-toity-English poppycock' was written all over his weather-chapped face. "Ma'am," he adjusted his reigns. "I would have thought your English horses would make similar sounds on your cobbled lanes."

Nanny Patterson's hands tightened around the Bakelite handles of her needlepoint bag. "My dear fellow," lips pursed, "horses, quintessentially English, are stealthy on their hooves. More genteel."

"Well, I'll be darned." The Tallyho rolled along merrily. Great stands of Douglas fir lining the way building anticipation fostering entitlement.

The tall maid poked her head around the kitchen door. "Are yi ready?"

"Nearly." The skin on Ishbel's throat tingled as she readjusted the stud on her stiff-starched collar. "Thanks again for helpin' me with that flour bag. That Miss Finch was ready to murder me."

The apron-clad bosom heaved. "As long as that bizom's at the helm, there's gonna be chaos in the kitchen."

"I cannae believe a grand hotel like this would hire a supervisor who uses that sort of language. She cusses like a dock-walloper!"

"Ooh, it wuz a complete fluke she landed that job."

Ishbel's eyes huge in her pale face. "A fluke?"

The girl smoothed out the skirt of her apron. "Missus Robertson, a long-standin' employee, ran this kitchen so well she deserved a mehdul. But, approachin' a month ago, her elderly mum took a turn the same mornin' the new assistant manager arrived. He's called Mistur Ross."

"So what happened?"

"It wuz orful. The new chief, it bein' his first day and all, was distracted by all the commotion. That's when Ethel Finch moved in for the kill. 'Jeez b'y,' she said, smilin' like the darlin' buds in May. 'Ya've got a lot on yar hands, sir. Let me take the burden off yar shoulders 'til ya get on yar feet. Ya concentrate on the guests, sir, and I'll run this kitchen.' 'Fore we knew whut wuz happenin', the temporary supervisor's position wuz bestowed on Ethel."

Ishbel shoved her hands into her pinny pockets. "I'm glad to hear it's only temporary."

"Well, it started orff as temporary," said Lily, rolling her eyes. "But 'taint now. Missus Robertson's no comin' back."

Ishbel let out a long, deep audible breath.

"Yi'll just have t' keep out of her way. When Ethel rose in the world, it went t' her head. Yi think she'd know better at her age."

"How old is she anyway?"

"Twenty-four."

"She's *not,*" Ishbel splattered.

"She is."

"You'd never think it," Ishbel replied bluntly, "she carries on like Granny Muchy."

Lily laughed and gazed around the kitchen, wiped, waxed and polished. "Sweet cheeses, yi've got everythin' spick and span. Wuz it not for my orful hair it took me *ages* t' brush out the flour."

"Your big curly bun's lovely. Mine's horribly straight by comparison."

"Oh no! I like yir straight hair. 'Tis shiny."

"Thanks." Ishbel pointed a finger at the cornet on top of her head. "Wish we didn't have to wear these though."

"Yir tellin' me! Whut with the robust aprons, scratchy black stockin's, clodhopper shoes and all, 'tis a wonder we get any work done. By the way," she smiled broadly, "I'm Lily Saunderson."

The girl's friendliness warmed her through. "I'm Ishbel McColl," she replied.

"Well, I'm right pleased t' meet yi, Ishbel. Gimme a few days and I'll teach yi the ropes. Learn by doin', eh."

"Thanks."

"Well, work half done is worse than wasted. Time t' shut the windows."

The wood creaked as they climbed the numerous back steps. When they reached the top, Lily opened a small door and stepped onto the landing. "Prepare to be surprised by its grandeur," she said, adjusting her cap. "This is the 5th floor."

"Wow!" Sparkling crystal chandeliers hung the length of a hall enriched with huge carved-crown mouldings and glossy baseboards the height of an under-butler's boot. Dainty chairs, resplendent in wine plush velvet, lined the walls. Gilt-framed oil paintings hung from ornamental picture rails. Ishbel slowed her pace: an image of a peasant tilling the soil; fairies in a fairy-tale setting; a poor widow, child in arms, another by her side; a train blowing around a mountain like a great iron monster; a huge portrait of an important looking man. Her eyes moved to the description, *'Cornelius Van Horne'*. Oil on canvas.

"Ishbel, we've no got time t' waste."

"Sorry, Lily, I couldn't help but notice the paintings."

Lily moved ahead. "The swankiest rooms are on this floor. They're kept for the really rich and famous."

"Did Ethel tell you that?"

"No. Bill Peyto did." She met Ishbel's eyes. "No that he'd take his hat off t' any of them."

"Who's Bill Peyto?"

Lily walked to the window. "Him over there," she said, pointing to a man wearing a tilted sombrero and a fringed buckskin coat. His heavy belt held a row of cartridges, a hunting knife and a six-shooter. "They call him Wild Bill Peyto. He's a legend around here."

"What?" Ishbel screwed up her eyes. "*That* old geezer smoking a pipe under the tree?"

Lily looked at her with an uncertain expression, but grinned in the end. "Sweet cheeses! He's no an old geezer. He's a real man no afraid t' speak his mind. He's got all those fancy ladies eatin' out of his hand. Look. They're all standin' around patiently right now just waitin' for him t' take them hikin'."

"They are?"

"Aye. They're drawn t' him like a cluster of bees around a honey pot. He makes them laugh, helps them forget about their stuffy husbands."

"Lily, you'll get the boot talkin' about the guests that way."

"Oh, whut the duck, they'll have t' catch me first." She folded her arms and said, "Ishbel, whut would yi do if yi wuz a proper lady?"

"Oh let me think." Ishbel bent down to remove a speck of dust from the rug. "I'd sit on a cushion and sew a fine seam and feast upon strawberries, sugar and cream."

"I'm *serius*!" Lily picked up the hem of the heavy silk drape and twirled it around herself, its luxurious fabric swathing her head and shoulders. "Oh, Ishbel, try t' imagine 't," her pretty face peeking out. "A social life sparklin' with balls and concerts. And compliments and curtsies. And I'd get t' dress up six times a day."

"Six times a day!?"

"Aye. The ladies here have different dress codes for breakfast, lunch and dinner. Then there's the ridin' outfits; the hikin' outfits; the payin'-a-call outfits. No t' mention the beautiful ball gowns!" Her work-scarred hands fell from her hips. "If I wuz a lady, Ishbel, I'd have t' learn how t' speak, eat and sit properly."

Ishbel gave a ghost of a chuckle. "And communicate with your groundskeeper."

"Aye. That too. It would all be worth it though. Coz my days would be wrapped in bonnie pink bows and like in my dreams," an exaggerated sigh heaved itself up from beneath the bib of her apron. "Wild Bill Peyto would worship the ground I walk on."

Ishbel gazed up at the tall window. "So what's the best way to close these heavy panes?"

Lily promptly dropped the curtains. "I'll show yi the quickest way. We both climb ont' the sill and hold ont' that overhangin' thingamajig." She shot Ishbel a glance. "Sweet cheeses, stay put 'til I open the nib in the middle. Now put yir hands the way I've got mine, on yir end. I'll count: one two three. Then we'll let window slide down gently. Keep it steady 'til it lands. If the glass breaks, 't'll come out of our wages."

Winston, enthusiastic and eager, breathed in the air, pure as pine. Marvelled at the mountains, bronzed by sun. Inhaled with an open mouth at the turrets and towers, rising from the forest. "Look!" he cried with pointed finger, "A castle in the Kingdom of Canada!" The Tallyho made a sharp left-turn and the imposing Banff Springs Hotel, British Union flag flying from its topmost terrace, shimmered into view. "Indeed, a stately pile," announced Lord Fairfax. "As impressive as the rumours back home led me to believe."

Another Tallyho was unloading in the porte-cochere so they pulled to a halt in the courtyard. The driver squared his shoulders, "Lad-*ies* and Gentle-*men*! Welcome to the castle in the Rockies." The weary travellers, adhering to a time-honoured code of upper-crust behaviour, deliberately regained their good postures. Nanny Patterson demanded the driver's hand to help her down the steps.

Winston tucked his Yorky under one arm and together they vaulted from the Tallyho.

"Winston Fairfax, conduct yourself with decorum!" Nanny's voice was sharp and strong but the boy's attention was drawn to a high-up, tall, narrow window. Under its pointy arch, behind a glass panel, two maids were smiling down at him and the two worlds met: servants and guests; British and backcountry. When Winston raised his other hand to wave, Bobby's leash rushed through his tightly clenched fist. "Merciful heavens!" wailed Nanny Patterson. "The frightful animal is chasing a ghastly rodent!"

The two young maids pushed up the moving glass panel and Lily began to laugh. "Ishbel, look at that lad chasin' after a Yorky that's chasin' after a chipmunk," she chuckled. "'Tis causin' havoc. Oh sweet cheeses! Here comes the poker-faced nanny. Lord, she'll stand no foolin'."

"There!" triumphantly, "he's caught his dog!" Then Ishbel's voice grew louder than before, "Oh *no!* The wee scamp's off again!"

"'Nuff entertainment. Better finish these bluddy windows. Are yi ready, Ishbel?"

"I am."

"Right. One two three. Let it down. *No!* Stop!"

"What? Why?"

"I see a famous person." Lily stretched her neck further. "Look! 'Tis Mary Pickford, herself! She's talkin' t' that American whose picture wuz in all the newspapers."

Ishbel looked down. "Oh, Roosevelt."

"Not the past president of America? Is it?"

"No. The younger one. He's related but he's not a president."

Lily gave Ishbel a head nod and they lowered the pane.

"How old are yi?"

"Fifteen. You?"

"Fifteen too. Where are yi from?"

"Scotland. My dad and I immigrated to Canmore last year. We thought it'd be a new start after my mother passed on."

"I'm sorry t' hear yi lost yir mother." Lily respectfully waited a moment before adding, "Canmore's full of rowdy coalminers. Wuz it hard livin' there?"

Ishbel's back straightened. "No. When you immigrate, you learn to bloom wherever you're replanted."

"S'pose. Well, yi'll no be lost for company coz Scottish folk are pourin' in here. Sweet cheeses, they've even named Banff after a Scottish town."

"And Calgary's named after a Scottish beach." Ishbel tightened her apron straps. "And Canmore's named after Malcolm of Canmore, the ancient Scottish King who turned a fort on a rock into Edinburgh castle. That was surely a lucky omen for us 'cause the mornin' after we arrived in Canmore, the sun turned the clouds pink and my dad got a full-time job in Mine Number Two. And the very same day, we found a place to rent. Partially furnished it was."

"Duz yir dad still live there?"

"He does."

The two maids joined in step on the way to the last room. "You know," Ishbel continued, "I once saw a picture of Malcolm of Canmore in a history book. He had curly red hair. A bit like yours, Lily."

Lily stopped in her tracks. "Duz yi think there's a chance I might be a descendant of Scottish Royalty?" she asked, clearly serious. "My grandpa wuz a Plesberteriun."

"We-*ell*," said Ishbel, not wanting to impinge upon her daydream. "Where are you from?"

Lily told her.

"Where's that?"

"Fort McMurray. 'Tis in a valley surrounded by forest, halfway t' nowhere in northern Alberta. My father paddles and portages for the Hudson Bay Company." Her smile dropped. "No paid-work for women up there. But, sweet cheeses, there wuz plenty of God-bless-you jobs."

Nanny Patterson rifled in the depths of her handbag. "When manners are forgotten—" She popped the cork on her trusty bottle of smelling salts. "Virtues are in question."

A short, round, neckless man in an impeccably tailored suit, strode towards them. He presented a cordial grasp, "Lord Fairfax. Welcome. I am Mister Dimbleby, the manager of the Banff Springs Hotel." Before relinquishing his grip entirely, he added, "At your service."

The imposing structure drew the eyes of the nobleman to its soaring tower. "I must say you have a sumptuous affair here. Hardly what one expects to find in the western wilderness?"

Mister Dimbleby clasped his hands behind his back and joined in the critical observation. "Indeed, sir, a luxurious symbol of Canadian hospitality. The brainchild of Sir William Cornelius van Horne, an aristocratic railway builder of the Canadian Pacific."

"I must say this Scottish Baronial style certainly captivates the mind."

"And, if I may add, rejuvenates the soul, sir. Now, if you and your party care to step this way—"

Lord Fairfax contracted his brow. "I am afraid our Yorkshire terrier bolted. Problematic behaviour. Causing quite a stir by the looks of it."

"Rest assured, sir," Mister Dimbleby, ultimate host and fixer, pulled out his much-thumbed notebook. "My capable staff will retrieve your pet and deliver it to your suite in a timely manner."

"In that case," Lord Fairfax responded with a smile of satisfaction, "I will summon my group of two. Nanny Patterson! Winston!" He motioned for them to follow.

Winston stopped in his tracks. "But, *Bobby*—" he cried, staring in every direction.

The governess was quick to grasp his elbow. "Come along, child!" she shrilled, and they stepped over the threshold of the stately castle in the Rocky Mountains of Alberta. Winston glanced back with troubled eyes.

"Phew, the last bloomin' window. Ready?" Lily waited. "Right. One two three. Let it down." She clambered off the sill and shook out her skirt. "We're done. Time for our midday meal. Vegetable soup."

"How do you know?"

"Coz that's whut the guests ate yesterday."

"Oh." Ishbel wiped her brow with the back of her hand.

"Well, get a wiggle on. We've only got half an hour t' eat. We don't want Ethel Finch flying off the handle again." Lily licked her thumb and rubbed a small mark off her white starched apron. "Follow me, I'll show yi a shortcut." She pulled on a knob and a small door, covered to blend in with the wallpaper, opened. Ishbel followed Lily and they wound around and around, all-the-way-down to the very bottom of the spiral staircase.

Ethel sprouted from thin air and grabbed them by the crooks of their arms. "'Bout time too! Thought the pair o' ya got lost." She tightened her grip on Lily. "Ya can start on those greasy pots." She let her go and turned to Ishbel. "Ya, girl! Take these blinkin' flowers up ter the Fairfax suite. It's not our bloomin' job but the bellhop forgot this bunch." She raised her head higher. "And don't forget ter tell the guest it's a welcome present from Napoleon Bonaparte."

Disbelief crossed Ishbel's features. She picked up the arrangement. "From Napoleon Bonaparte?" she echoed faintly.

Ethel inhaled through gritted teeth. "The hotel m-a-n-a-g-e-r!"

Early-afternoon sun spilled through the tall windows of the grand room. Nanny Patterson was casting on a brown shooting sock when a knock came to the door. She stabbed her knitting needles into the ball of wool and placed it on the highly-polished end table where it looked totally inappropriate. "The return of the pesky rapacious mutt, no doubt," she whinged, and rose to her feet.

"Ma'am," the little maid curtsied and held up a floral arrangement, "this is a welcome gift from Mister Dimbleby, the manager of the Banff Springs Hotel."

"Flowers?"

"Yes ma'am. Where would you like me to put them, ma'am?"

Nanny Patterson clasped her tiny hands to her tiny bosom. "I would like them over there." She pointed. "By that window."

Ishbel set the heavy crystal vase on the gleaming mahogany table then took a step back. Nanny Patterson stuck her nose into the colourful array. Sniffed in several different spots. Resurfaced with a wrinkled forehead. "They do not smell like English flowers."

Ishbel was taken by surprise. "'Cause they are Canadian flowers, ma'am."

"Um Canadian flowers."

In a brave attempt to lift the mood, Ishbel added, "Fresh-cut Canadian flowers never fail to delight the eye or touch the soul." She stood there waiting. "Will that be all, ma'am?"

"For the time being," Nanny Patterson harrumphed.

Around the back of the Banff Springs Hotel, outside the kitchen door, old Donald Duncan stood, hands in his pockets, watching the darkness carry him into daylight. Almost 6 am and it was hot already. He lifted his crumpled face to the sun and rolled the little pebble between his finger and thumb, a behaviour pattern regularly followed, now almost involuntary.

The sound of hoofs and wheels on gravel made him open his eyes. "Well, I'll be darned," he declared with a crooked, snaggle-toothed grin. "If it ain't Wild Bill Peyto, himself!"

"Hullo, Donald!" The outdoorsman controlled his horse by pulling on the reigns. "Allowin' the mornin's tender breeze to tickle yar jowls, are ya?"

"Aye. I'm tryin' to catch a bit of a youthful colour while the goin' is good."

"Well, don't overdo it." The man climbed down from his wagon. "Ya don't want that snout of yars gettin' any rosier."

"You cheeky bugger!" Donald Duncan reached to wallop the side of his head but the mountain man ducked, avoiding the blow. "So what brings you up here at the crack of dawn?"

Peyto rubbed his chin, "I've somethin' in my cart that needs storin'. 'Tis too big for my hut."

"Well now. That's the thing." Donald's eyes danced with mischief. "The Banff Springs cellar is gettin' mighty cramped all these townsfolk comin' up here and takin' advantage of my good nature."

The mountain man dug into his trouser pocket and held up a Dominion of Canada two-dollar note. "All I need is a bit of space, eh?"

Donald took the money and slipped it into his pocket. "Right lad, show me what you've got."

Peyto spat out his chew and motioned for the old man to follow him to the cart. He placed a hand on the tarp and drew his brows together. "I'm just hopin' yar heart can take it."

"Oh stop takin' the piss and show me what's under your bloody cover," Stooped and tottery, he moved closer.

Peyto whipped back the sheet.

"Blimey!" Donald almost lost the grip on his bladder. "Where the hell did you get it?"

"Aw, that's a secret, eh."

"Oh. Right. I'll no ask then." He teetered around the cart to scrutinise it further. "Hey, I bet you'd make a few bucks if you sold it to them in Ottawa. Or even them Americans. Oooweee! It's a gobsmacking wonder o' the world."

"Ain't it just." Peyto's chest increased. "I know it's worth a bob or two but it's not for sale."

"You're keepin' it then?" The wrinkles in old Donald's brow deepened. "And do what with it?"

"Look at it."

"Like, like a big decoration?"

"No. Like a piece of, um, art." Peyto removed his sombrero and used his fingers to push back his springy black hair. "Well, that's what you do with art. Right?" He put his hat back on.

"Aye. I suppose." Donald scratched his head. "I didn't think you were the type, lad. Never mind. Get yourself into the kitchen. The coffee's brewin'."

"First, show me where to put my fossil. I'll find a couple of lads to help me take it down."

"No, Peyto, there's no time. The maids need help loadin' the coffee urns. Then I've to run like hell to the other end of this bloomin' fortress with my bloody pole!"

"How?"

"'Cause Dimbleby had a newfangled idea to put a high-up window above the circular staircase. Now it's throwin' a draft onto the wall candles and everyone else and their dog on their way to the Oak Room." He shook his head. "Sometimes, I think I'm working for Bertram Mills Circus. All these changes addin' to my work."

"Away ya go! It keeps ya young."

"Well, let's just say, it keeps me on the hop." Donald pulled a square of fabric from his pocket to mop his brow, and a pebble with a hole in the middle tumbled to the ground.

Peyto stooped to pick it up. "Whut's this?"

"Nothin' that would interest you, lad." The old man reached to take it back but Peyto closed his fingers over it.

"Whut is it?"

Donald shook his head ever so slightly. "Go cover your fossil and unhook your cart."

Peyto's grin grew bigger. "Not until ya tell me what it is."

He marshalled his words, "It's a simple token of affection."

"Ya cunnin' old codger. Ya've got a girlfriend!"

Donald's face grew red. "Gimme the bloody thing!"

He tossed him the stone. "Keep yar shirt on, man."

"Oh, Mister Duncan," said Lily, arms folded and leaning against the heavy trolley, "we wuz wonderin' where yi were." Old Donald shambled into the room, too distracted to give her much attention but her heart exploded with joy when she saw Wild Bill. *"Hullo*, Mister Peyto," she said coyly.

The mountain man turned his head. "Oh, 'tis Lily. The belle of the Banff Springs Hotel," he replied, his eyes sparkling with tease.

"Don't be foolin' Mister Peyto." A faint blush warmed her cheeks; she choked back an embarrassed laugh, and turned to her new friend. "This is Ishbel. She just started."

Ishbel flashed a smile.

Peyto doffed his sombrero.

"Ishbel's never been t' the dancin' before so I'm takin' her on Friday night."
The chimes on the Canadian Pacific Railway clock sounded her out.

"Right girls, push your carts over here." Donald's reedy voice rose up.
"Peyto, when you finish your smoke, I wouldn't mind a hand with these urns."

Ishbel moved her gaze from the weight-driven pantry clock to the pipe-sucking man. "Mister, would you mind hurryin' up?" Her brow puckered. "The Alhambra Room is openin' for breakfast and we're supposed to be up there with this coffee."

"Blimey," said Donald, "we've got a keener here."

Ishbel shoved her hands into her pinny pockets. "A keener? It's just it's just that I don't want to cross-the-line with that Miss Finch."

"Oh me neither. Sweet cheeses, I'm scared stiff orf her."

Peyto, laughing, heaved the coffee urn onto the trolley. "Ethel Finch might be blessed with a voice that carries across the Dominion of Canada to the Colony of Newfoundland, but she'll do ya no harm," he said, helping himself to a hotel napkin, wrapping it around his gun finger and tying it off in a buckaroo knot. "Believe ya me. Her bark's worse than her bite."

Lily, wide-eyed with astonishment, turned to Ishbel. "Easy for him t' say, eh?"

The Alhambra Room's tall sculptural doors opened setting forth a stream of light onto a sweeping-carpeted staircase leading down to a vast dining room where music swirled from the fingers of a pianist, partly hidden by a soaring parlour palm. A towering fruit and flower centre piece, set on an enormous solid-oak table, surrounded by an assortment of silver dishes with revolving lids: smoked bacon, steak sausages, devilled kidneys, scrambled eggs and poached eggs. Hard-boiled eggs perched on cruets with silver-hoop handles. Freshly-baked buns in silver bread baskets. Hot-buttered toast under heavy linen napkins. The tantalising aroma making hotel guests politer to strangers.

At the marble-topped beverage table, Lily buffed a smudge off a silver-plated urn and placed a fresh cup and saucer under its spout. "This Loysel's a scunner. Taps are too slow pourin'," she grumbled.

Ishbel was sorting the cups. "How come its CPR and not BSH?" she asked, once the embossed letters were facing in the same direction.

"Coz Canadian Pacific Railway owns the Banff Springs Hotel."

"Oh. Right. Daft question."

"So just remember. If the waiter says, 'café au lait', put 1/3 coffee from this urn into the cup then fill with a hot milk and cream mix. If yir asked for a con panna, top it with whipped cream. Donald puts less grounds in the other urn for the American guests. They take less milk too. The waiters'll keep yi right."

Ishbel turned at a tap on her shoulder.

"Excuse me, I am Winston Fairfax." A boy about eight-years old, pushed up his spectacles. "Have you seen my Yorkshire terrier?"

"Not today," she answered, "but I saw you and your nanny chasin' him yesterday. He's a wee handful, eh?"

"Indeed, he is." The boy's face showed mild frustration. "Nanny said if she finds Bobby first, she is going to send him to a sausage factory so Banff Springs Hotel can serve him for breakfast."

Lily's head jerked up. "Sweet cheeses!" she retorted. "The toffee-nosed nanny is partial t' dog meat."

Ishbel tried to hold back her laughter but her hands were shaking and the full cups of coffee were rattling in their saucers. Lily took a stumbling step to grasp the noisy crockery. Too late, all of it crashed to the floor, violently breaking into pieces, brown liquid flowing freely. All heads turning towards them. Winston flying back to his seat.

"Oh. My. Lord." Ishbel dropped to her knees to scoop up the wreckage.

"Oh. Sweet. Cheeses." Lily grabbed the tea towels and tried to blot up the stain.

A sudden shadow fell across them. Ishbel, a broken saucer in one hand, and a handle less cup in the other, looked up with the wariness of the guilty. Lily sat back on her heels, sodden tea towels scrunched up in each hand. Mister Dimbleby's chest swelled with disapproval. He tried to keep his voice low but his anger beat the air. "What are you?" He looked from one to the other. Silence. "You two are worse than useless! What are you?"

"Worse than useless," they mumbled.

Ethel Finch approached with vigour. "Mister Dimbleby, I knows how ter handle disaster recovery," she said, her tone clipped. "I'll have these two clean up the mess. And I'll make sure the damage comes out of their wage packets. And I'll get two competent ones ter come up from the kitchen." Her eyes darting to take in his fuming face. "Anythin' else, sir?"

"No. That will be all, Miss Finch. Thank you." He slipped his notebook into his pocket and with a short sharp nod turned on his heels. An air of calm and conviviality returned to the dining room.

"Oh dear," Nanny Patterson uttered. "In England, we train our staff from a position of knowledge."

Chapter 2

"Lily," Ishbel paused on the half-landing below stairs to catch her breath. "Lily, if we're late after what happened this morning. She'll she'll have our guts for garters."

"Sweet cheeses! We'll likely get the boot. *Cumon*, hurry up!"

The two maids scrambled up the remainder of steps and Lily turned the handle of the discreet door that led onto the back lobby of the hotel. Lengthening their strides, they ran along the corridor, up the staircase with speed, and through the kitchen. A dry, soft whisper, "Here goes nothin'." Lily turned the handle of the scullery door and a stream of light fell upon the overseer standing under the Canadian Pacific Railway clock sounding the hour.

Ethel Finch fixed the two of them with a fierce stare. "About time!" she shrieked, grabbing their elbows and propelling them across the room. "Adorn yarselves with those comely pinnies. Then shuffle across ter the utility table."

The cumbersome hemp aprons had extra-long straps for neck and waist. 'Life's too short to wear an ugly apron,' popped into Lily's head but she bit her tongue. They quickly tied the straps and stared down at the assortment of labelled bottles.

Ethel rested her coarse hands on her hips. "Now girls, 'fore we start, I've a warnin'. There'll be no more blunderin'. For if there's a blunderin'. There'll surely be a firin'. Get me meanin'?"

Ishbel and Lily nodded their heads, their smiles not reaching their eyes.

"Fair enough." Ethel snatched up a bottle marked 'Linseed-oil'. "Now, unclog yar ears 'cause yar gonna learn how ter make Banff Springs magical furniture polish. First, ya determine the amount of ingredients that's always a good start." She poured some into a tin measuring cup. "Watch closely I'm only showin' ya once." The yellowish substance was transferred to a ceramic bowl. "Now add half a pint of vinegar, two ounces of spirits of salts, one ounce of muriatic antimony. And mix." Ethel beat the mixture, her mouth pressed thin. "See. Easy-peasy!"

"It smells orful." Lily shifted her weight to her other leg.

"Well, ya better get used ter it. Ya'll be usin' it ter mop and polish the Oak Room this afternoon." Ethel poured the concoction through a funnel into a jar then screwed the lid on. "And fore ya put it on, remember ter shake it thoroughly. Like this. Easy peasy! And mind ya spread it sparingly. Not thickly. Muddle makes more muddle."

"Do we need rags?"

Ethel's breathing turned heavy and laboured. "Why don't ya just use yar mop-caps, eh? There's a nice bit o' cloth in them ter buff and polish."

Ishbel's eyes opened wide, her gaping mouth speechless.

A crease appeared between Lily's eyebrows. "Do we get new caps after then?"

"Oh me nerves the pair o' ya've got me drove." Ethel grappled in her apron pocket for a hanky to dab her moist forehead. "The bucket o' rags is under the blinkin' sink!"

"Yes." Ishbel stifled a choke. "Under the sink." She ran across the room and grabbed a handful.

Lily snatched up the jar of polish and tossed her head at Ishbel to indicate they should leave.

"I knows the pair of ya!" Ethel cried after them. "So there better be no yackety yakin'! Get that elbow grease goin'!" She strangled the dishrag. "If that Oak Room has a blinkin' mark on it! By jings! Ya'll be hearin' from me!"

Ishbel waited until Ethel was out of earshot. "What a bloomin' relief to get away from her." She followed Lily up a steep set of narrow-stone steps and along a lengthy, dimly-lit corridor. Under a plastered segmented arch, opposite a circular staircase, was the door to the Oak Room. "Wait 'till yi see this, Ishbel. 'Tis oozin' with opulence." Lily turned the cast-iron knob and pushed the door wide open.

Ishbel gazed into the buttery-kissed chamber, looked up at the coffered ceiling and down at the herringbone floor. Walked inside and ran her fingers over the curved-oak panels. "Looks and feels like folded linen."

"Aye. And needs plenty of buffin' and polishin' t' prevent 't from worpin'. Well, we'd better get at it." Lily unscrewed the jar and dribbled some mixture onto two cloths. They began their buffing in compatible silence.

Then Ishbel reflected. "That Ethel Finch has a bloomin' cheek bossin' us about like she does."

They traipsed along the opposite wall.

"'Taint right. The cocky so-'n-so gets away with it coz she's got the power t' hire and fire us." Lily bent down to rub a scuff off the skirting board. "That's why we've got t' toe the line."

"Lily," Ishbel's polishing became slow and deliberate. "What's that in the corner?"

"Whut? Where?"

Ishbel stood up and tiptoed across the room in her heavy black shoes. The dog's eyes opened and his short tail beat the air.

"Aww!" Ishbel scooped him up and cradling him like a baby. "You must belong to that English boy. Lily, do you mind if I nip upstairs and hand him back?"

"Yi won't be long, eh? If Ethel comes and yir no here—"

"No, no, perish the thought."

Ishbel opened the servants' door and stepped onto the 5th floor, surprised to see Winston sitting cross-legged in the hallway. "Here's your wee scamp," she said, and the boy came rushing towards her. "Have you got a good hold of him now?" she asked, tipping Bobby into his outstretched arms.

"Oh, *yes*," his tone jubilant and the dog licking his face. "Thank you very much for bringing him back."

Ishbel's brow creased. "What are you doing out here all by yourself?"

"I have to stay here until I learn my collective nouns. By heart." He looked up at her. "Can you help me practice?"

"Winston, I can't. I'm supposed to be—"

"Please."

Against her better judgement, Ishbel slid onto the floor, reached for the sheet of paper, and curled her knees up beneath her skirt. "Okay. Nanny Patterson's List of Collective Nouns. *If labour is the collective noun for a group of moles,"* she read and grasped it mentally, *"what is the group noun for penguins?"*

"A colony."

"Parrots?"

"A company."

"Hawks?"

"A kettle."

31

"Sparrows?"

"A… a dole?"

Ishbel pointed to the line. "It says 'host' here."

Winston hands flew to his cheeks. "I remember now."

"Okay. Next one. *What is the group noun for doves?*"

"A dole."

"*Owls?*"

"A parliament."

"*Hens?*"

"A brood."

"*Hedgehogs?*"

"A prickle."

Ishbel chuckled. "You're great at this."

Winston beamed. "Do you want to see a picture of Bobby when he was a puppy?"

"Okay. But be quick," her face in worry, "I need to get back to work."

Winston reached inside his jacket pocket and pulled out a sepia-toned photograph. "My mother is holding Bobby. I took the photograph with my box Brownie," he said, bending down so their heads touched.

She studied the picture: a smiling lady wrapped in a white fox-fur embracing a black puppy. Beside her, a large travelling chest. Behind her, a limestone building with classical architectural details. "Your mother's pretty. Is that your house?"

Winston was quiet for a second. "Yes. That is Duncraig House. My home in England. Bobby's coat was all one colour. See. Because he was a puppy."

"He has all his Yorky colours now!" Bobby's short tail beat the air enthusiastically. "*Yes you do!*" she giggled.

Winston screwed his eyes shut. "My mother gave me Bobby because—"

Behind them, the door flew wide open. "Hah! Caught the pair of you!" Nanny Patterson's face was red with rage. Bobby flew between her slippered feet and bounded towards his water bowl.

Winston sprang up. "No. I I was just showing Ishbel a picture of Bobby," he said, tucking his photograph into his pocket.

The eyes of the governess, sharp as pointers, switched focus.

A scarlet hue rose in Ishbel cheeks. She stood up and brushed off her apron. "When I brought Bobby back, I should not have sat down."

"You should not have, you slothful servant! Be on your way before I lodge a complaint."

Ishbel exchanged a glance with Winston then hurried off.

Nanny Patterson poked a finger at his chest. "Do. Not. Fraternise. With. The. Servants."

"Why not?" Winston's voice slight.

"Because we are uncertain as to their habits and principles." She nudged him inside. "How are those collective nouns coming along?"

Lily slid down the wall and sat on the floor with her back wedged into the corner. "Sweet cheeses, where is she? If Ethel comes in, she'll murder the pair of us." The door creaked open. Lily breathed a sigh of relief. "'Bout blinkin' time!"

"I'm sorry, Lily."

"Whut the duck. Yir back now." She scrambled to her feet and picked a bit of fluff from her woollen-clad legs. "I bet Winston wuz as happy as a bumble bee in flower time when he saw that dog."

Ishbel grabbed her cloth and set to a ferocious rubbing.

"Okay. Okay! Stop with the pinny power." She yanked the cloth from Ishbel's hand. "Whut's up with yi?"

"Oh, Lily—"

"Whut?"

"I gave Winston his puppy and I was comin' down the servant's stairwell when I heard a murderous yell. I knelt down and looked through the railings. On the landin' below, Mister Peyto and Mister Dimbleby were havin' it out. And it was no namby-pamby argument either. Our big boss was splatterin' threatening words when, all of a sudden, Mister Peyto picked him up and propelled him through the air. Then he walked off, leavin' Mister Dimbleby sprawled across the floor."

"Whut!?"

"Our manager cried after him, 'I will have you thrown in jail!' And Peyto grinned back at him, 'Good luck findin' a witness.'"

Lily began to laugh. "Oh, 'taint our bizness."

"You're right, none of our business."

It was three o' clock on a Tuesday afternoon. Nanny removed her plain bonnet and set it beside the bowl of pot-pourri. "Well done, Patterson," she said, praising herself in the hallway mirror. "You survived the copious amounts of cages, stinky-putrid ponds, and dens full of the oddest-looking creatures one would prefer not to cast eyes upon."

"Nanny."

Her chest swelled. Through the reflective surface, her eyes met those of Winston. "Another question?"

"Nanny, I just want to ask. When you were my age, did you like the zoo then?"

His governess would not be drawn. She sat down in a chair by the fire, the embroidered screen halting its shooting sparks. "That is a brazen inquiry into my past." She picked up her knitting. "I did not go to the zoo. I was content with food on the table and a uniform designed to prepare me for work that lay beyond the walls." Nanny Patterson pointed an accusing finger. "Feet! Feet! Feet! We do not curl like a cat on a seat!"

Winston straightened his legs, his slippers now barely touching the footstool. He crinkled his nose, "What walls?"

"Pert and useless questions are the germs of vanity and affectation." She pursed her brow. "And do not sit with your back to the fire. It softens the spine and predisposes one to influenza."

Ishbel slid open the hatch of the dumbwaiter and pulled on the cable rope until it reached the 5th floor landing. She made sure the two manual locks were clipped in place before transferring the tea paraphernalia onto a two-tier mahogany tray with brass-cap castors. "Oh, no, it is already 4 o'clock." She quickly unclipped the brakes and wheeled the cart towards Suite 522.

Nanny Patterson bristled. "Since the Duchess of Bedford introduced afternoon tea in 1840, it has been served promptly at four!"

A discreet tap on the door. Winston slid off the chair. "Can I—"

Nanny gave him a stare. "You may answer the door. But do not fraternise with the servant. We are uncertain as to her habits and principles."

Winston smiled up at Ishbel who smelt like butter and milk and was drowning in a big white apron. She pressed a quietening finger to her mouth. Winston nodded and stood back so she could push the piled-high rattling-cart into the room.

Nanny Patterson lifted her chin. "Black from Ceylon?"

"Yes, ma'am. It was purchased from Taylors of Harrogate as per Lord Fairfax's instructions."

"Devonshire clotted cream? Strawberry jam? English scones?"

"Yes to all three, ma'am. And thin-cut cucumber sandwiches, cakes and pastries."

Bobby wagged his tail and trotted towards Ishbel.

"Do not touch that animal before pouring my tea."

"No, ma'am. I will not do that."

The door opened and Lord Fairfax bounded in. He strode towards the desk, pushed aside the backgammon board, the newspaper, his smoking materials, and sat down. "Girl, scoot that trolley over here; save me the trouble of getting up. We shall serve ourselves. You may go."

Ishbel offered a slight curtsy and gave Winston a smile before closing the door.

Nanny Patterson looked over the top of her glasses. "What is the rule, child?"

There was a flash of rebelliousness in Winston's eyes. "I only upturned the corners of my mouth at her." He moved his face to demonstrate. "Like Prince Arthur does."

Nanny drew her eyebrows together. "I was referring to the afternoon-tea rule."

"Oh. Savouries first. Scones next. Sweets last." He inspected his sandwich and took a large bite.

A clear afternoon light streamed in through an opening in the brocade drapes, blazed the stained cups, and enhanced the crumbs on the tea plates.

"Blast!" Lord Fairfax threw down his newspaper. "The projected dividend growth a paltry 1.6%!?"

Winston looked up from his stamp collection and pulled a face. His father was talking to himself.

Rrrrrr! Rrrrrr! Rrrrrr!

Nanny Patterson's knitting slid off her lap and her eyes opened wide behind her glasses. "Good grief, sir!" She sat upright in her chair. "It is that that contraption. It permits two users to conduct a conversation when they are not in the same place."

Rrrrrr! Rrrrrr! Rrrrrr!

"Sir, I think you are obliged to respond to the wretched instrument."

Lord Fairfax looked fixedly at the telephone. "I would rather not. I agree with Western Union. It has too many shortcomings to be seriously considered as a means of communication."

Rrrrrr! Rrrrrr! Rrrrrr!

"Drats!" Lord Fairfax picked up the candlestick phone and held it at arm's length. "Hello! *Hello!* HELLO!"

Nanny stared at him. "May I suggest you remove the earpiece from its cradle and hold it to your ear," she said, more sharply than was necessary. "And bring the bakelite mouthpiece closer to your face."

He stamped his foot angrily. "What a pile of piffle! HELLO! Yes! This is Lord Fairfax. I cannot hear you! Talk up, man!"

Winston blinked hard. His father's face had turned blood red.

"The, the Duke of Connaught! My my most humble apologies, your your Royal Highness! Yes, it would be both a privilege and an honour to fish with you from a canoe. Tomorrow. Yes, if you wish, I will bring my boy along."

Woof!

"Yes, I have a dog too." Beads of sweat dotted Lord Fairfax's brow. "Yes, if if you wish, I will bring the dog too. Thank you. Goodbye your Royal Highness." Lord Fairfax inhaled deeply and put the phone down.

A hardness entered Nanny's voice. "That animal cannot mingle with royalty."

A spasm of dread overcame Lord Fairfax. "Tell me why not."

Nanny Patterson squeezed the bridge of her nose. "Because Yorkshire terriers are bred to eradicate the rat population in coal mines."

The nobleman's shoulders stiffened. "The dog will remain behind."

"But Father," meekly, "His Royal Highness told you to bring Bobby along. It is our duty to obey him."

Bobby heard his name and thumped his short tail.

"The dog will go." Lord Fairfax paused for a moment. "One cannot have a proper fishing trip without a dog in tow."

"Twaddle."

"Twaddle?" Lord Fairfax was pop-eyed with surprise.

"*Paddle*," Nanny Patterson responded, "the maps of Canada were rewritten with every stroke of the paddle."

Shafts of early-morning sunlight fell between the white spruce, aspens and Douglas fir. Jim Brewster secured his sturdy animal to the slimy fence post, its base walled by dense moss. He checked the quick release knot then scratched his horse's forehead. "Wish me luck, Whiskey."

Heeeiiiaaaahahahaha! The horse's steamy breath circled the air above his cowboy hat.

Jim threw a satchel over one shoulder and set off along the popular but arduous hiking trail shaded by a verdant tunnel of shrubbery. His breathing laboured. His neck moist. He had taken this path since he was ten years old. In those days, his five brothers, even his little sister, Pearl, had helped deliver the milk to the swanky Banff Springs Hotel. Jim smiled at the memory. Years later, with the help of his native friend, William Twin, he and his brother, Bill, had become expert mountain men, skilled in camping, hunting and exploring the mountain terrain. They had taken a chance when they opened their outfitting business but with preparation and opportunity, it had flourished. And today he was going to take a Duke, the brother of the King of England, to fish from a canoe. The end of the path narrowed onto grass and he gazed up at the imposing building rising from huddles of gold anthers and star-shaped blossoms with indigo petals.

Jim approached the rustic steps. 'Don't wait for the day to be gone before you find the charm in it,' he chuckled inwardly and all his misgivings fell away. He leapt up the steps two at a time and rapped twice on the kitchen door.

The energetic little man answered immediately. "Well, if it's not Jim Brewster, himself! Come away in, lad," he beckoned to the fellow dressed in a long-sleeved flannel shirt and a pair of canvas pants tucked into his boots. "Have you come to fetch the royal feast?"

"Aye, Donald. I got my orders to pick up the hamper."

"Well, you'll have to give us a minute," he told him. "It was too heavy for the girls so they went to get a trolley from the main kitchen. Oh, here they come now with a picnic for a party of four." He eyed the huge basket. "Or maybe it's forty-four."

Jim bent his knees and lifted the cumbersome wolf-willow container. "Right, Donald," he adjusted his grip and groaned. "I'll be on my way."

The old man, stooped and tottery, pushed the kitchen door back as far as it would go. "Allow me to lift the bascules," he giggled. "Um try turning sideways, Jim. Aye, that's better. Now mind you don't drop it. The royals are known for chopping heads off."

Beads of sweat surfaced on Jim's brow as he struggled to submerge his laughter.

Jim Brewster walked around the full-size birch-bark canoe built in the old-form Algonquin style. Royal crowns had been painted on both sides of each end, and a Union Jack was flying from a flag pole attached to its bow. He checked the traditional Indian paddles, and plumped up the bright-red cushions on the four wood and cane seats. He was buckling down the food hamper when the sound of footsteps made him turn his head. The Duke of Connaught, in a Homburg hat and tweed jacket, was striding towards him. "Good morning Brewster!"

Jim stood up and lifted his cowboy hat, revealing more of his weathered face. "Good morning, Your Grace."

The Duke turned to his companion, a man in his mid-forties wearing a Panama boater. "Lord Fairfax, this is Jim Brewster," his chirpy demeanour set the tone. "He will be our guide for today."

"Pleased to meet you old chap."

Jim lifted his hat again. He didn't think of himself as an old chap. He moved his gaze to the lad who looked typically English in short trousers and knee-high socks.

"And this is young Winston," said the Duke.

Winston's right hand was engaged with the dog. "Excuse my left hand, sir," he said, as evidence of respect.

"That's a fine-looking dog you have there."

"Thank you, Mr Brewster. His name is Bobby."

Jim grinned. "Do you know anything about canoes, Winston?"

"Um, you need a bowman. A sternman. And you never give up I mean stand up."

They both laughed.

"And you keep an eye on your dog at all times," he replied with a wink. Bobby jumped from Winston's arms to zestfully lap at the water's edge.

Jim Brewster and Lord Fairfax moved to the centre of the canoe on opposite sides. Spreading their hands a distance apart, they gripped the gunwales, bent their knees and lifted the canoe. Crossing hand over hand, they gently eased it into the water.

Jim scooped the fishing tackle into the canoe. "Go ahead, Winston. Bobby too. Keep your weight centred and low," he urged, steadying the vessel. "Now, who's our bow paddler?"

The Duke stood, chest out. "I will decline the paddles. Go ahead Fairfax. Climb in."

"Your Grace, the middle seat?"

"Yes, Brewster. That will do." The Duke settled down and pulled a folded newspaper from his inside pocket. Bobby found a comfortable spot behind Winston's ankles.

Jim pushed the boat out and called to Lord Fairfax, "First we'll let her float with the current," he said, before leaping inside the vessel. "Now plunge the blade into the water on the right side and draw it towards you. When the paddle reaches the canoe, take it directly out of the water and repeat the process. We will advance when you get the hang of it."

"What a topping way to spend a morning!" The Duke filled his lungs with the earthy smell of woodland then pulled out his binoculars, pressing them to his eyes. "Listen to that birdsong, most evocative."

"Indeed, Your Grace," replied Lord Fairfax then added, "Winston and I are honoured to be here today."

The important man drummed his fingers on the yoke. "Well, it has been quite some time. Three years or more—"

Lord Fairfax kept a bright ring in his voice, "I believe we last crossed paths just before Lloyd George gave his Mansion House speech."

The Duke closed up his binoculars. "Fairfax, not putting too fine a point on it, what is your opinion of that up-and-comer, Lloyd George?"

Wrinkles framed Lord Fairfax's eyes. "Regarding his social welfare system?"

"No, regarding Germany."

"Well, he made it clear to Germany that France is not isolated. That Britain would not stand down."

"And now Germany is shoring up its alliance with the Austro-Hungarian Empire. Building up its force in preparation for its next move, no doubt." His troubled gaze sought a response.

"Your Grace, I believe a global war is becoming an increasing possibility."

A moment passed. "Fairfax, do you fancy an evening of cards and whisky?"

"Indeed I would, Your Grace."

"Spot on! I look forward to you joining me."

The narrow-pointed boat made steady progress through the crystal waters until the Duke of Connaught pulled out his heavy gold pocket watch. "I am feeling rather peckish, Brewster. Are we close to pulling in?"

"I am about to steer into a prime fishing spot, Your Grace."

Bobby's ears popped up at the creak of the lid. The Duke pulled out a thermos flask labelled, 'Cream of Barley Soup'. "Hmm, rather unappetising," he murmured, "what else do we have; a roast chicken, a lobster salad, asparagus-in-a-pastry-crust, a French loaf, an assortment of cheeses, butter in a covered jar, a pot of mustard, two bottles of Banff Springs famed house wine, plenty of juicy-looking plums and lashings of ginger beer. What? No smushables? There *has* to be a smushable! Aahhh here it is, a toothsome Victoria sponge cake, oozing with strawberry jam and named in honour of my dear mother. A compliment, or not?"

Everyone laughed along with him.

The Duke soothed the dazzling white napery across his knee. "Well, tuck in chaps."

Winston unfolded his napkin and placed it across his lap. A poem from Nanny Patterson's little book floated through his brain as he buttered his bread: *'Cut your meat both neat and square, and take of both an equal share. Also, of bones you'll take your due, for bones and meat together grew. Don't pick your teeth, or ears, or nose.'* He looked down at the little dog's tongue dripping saliva all over his well-polished shoes and slid his feet under the seat. "Lie down, Bobby. I will give you a tidbit when I finish eating." The terrier scuttled behind Winston's ankles and licked the exposed flesh above his socks.

When the meal was over, the Duke opened his newspaper then closed it to take a second look at the front page. *'The Banff Springs Hotel Welcomes the Duke of Connaught'.* "Hmph, where did they dig up that ancient photograph?" He partly closed one eye in an attempt to see more clearly. "Aaah, yes. The Foundling Hospital in Bloomsbury, an age-old charity founded by Coram, Hogarth and Handel."

Winston stared at the picture, his curiosity peaked. "The boys are dressed like soldiers and the girls are dressed like maids."

The Duke gave a thin smile. "Prepares them mentally for a life beyond the hospital walls."

"Do they all want to be maids and soldiers?"

"Of course! They are given skills that will help them earn a living; punctuality, honesty and hard work. Hard work is the currency that ensures their survival." He brushed crumbs from his lapels and pulled out his pocket watch. "Brewster, time to fish!"

Bobby settled down to bask in the sun, and the three men and the boy simultaneously dropped their fishing rods into the water, clear and running.

Apart from an occasional breeze tugging at their clothes and ruffling their hair, all remained comfortably silent for the remainder of the afternoon. The clouds were drifting eastwards when a trill of a wood frog startled the Duke. He gave his head a shake, looked up at the sky, and pulled out his pocket-watch. "Brewster, time to pole upstream!"

Jim plunged his oars into the water and they paddled back along the riverbank, passing many horizontal trees on the brink of splitting and dropping into the water. They were coming into the clearing just below the hotel when Winston spotted a row of Royal Canadian Mounted Police. Bright, chilly sunshine streamed down upon the familiar representation, and the Duke said at length, "I think I know what this is about."

Jim pulled the boat in. The nobleman got out, shallow waters rushing around his boots as he walked toward the highest-ranking member. The officer gave him a distinct salute then presented him with an official-looking document. The Duke broke the seal and read the contents before looking up. "Gentlemen, I regret to inform you, Great Britain has declared war on Germany. God Save the King."

"God Save the King," echoed all the voices.

The Duke turned to face Lord Fairfax. "We have been summoned by the Secretary of State to return to Whitehall immediately," his voice weakened by the burden.

Lord Fairfax's brows gathered in. "The War Office will be making top-level military decisions. Your Grace, I—" But the Duke was already scaling the path to the hotel.

"But but I do not want to go!" cried Winston, railing against life's injustice. He hurled a stone into the water and it rippled in wrathful circles. "I want to stay *here!* Forever!"

Lord Fairfax rested a hand on his son's shoulder. "England expects this day that every man will do his duty. Fetch your dog. I have no time to waste."

The wind was blowing with a degree of gentleness as Jim Brewster, with heavy heart, pulled the canoe onto dry land. Little pebbles, polished and gleaming from years of rushing waters, crunched under his feet. He stopped at the river's edge and looked up at the low-hanging summer clouds skimming the mountain tops. Thoughts of war rifled through his mind. "Will this world ever right itself?" All of a sudden, a massive raven with shiny-black plumage and a bowie-knife beak made a large curve above his head then swooped down to settle on a near-by branch.

Caw! Caw! CAAAWW!

A chill ran through Jim's veins at the symbol of folklore immersed in his Irish roots. Morrigan, the goddess of battle.

Nanny cried, "Winston! Into the tub!" And then it started. Armfuls of books gathered up higgledy-piggledy. Trunk lids flung wide open. Wardrobes emptied onto the beds. Shoes stuffed into shoe bags. Toys tossed into the toy chest: a teddy bear, a spinning top, a big bag of marbles. Nanny tried to close it sat on it knelt on it climbed on top of it. By the time Winston emerged from the bathroom, every latch and catch had been closed with a snap.

"But I do not want to go! And neither does my dog!"

Arf!

"Winston, we have no choice."

"But my mummy will not be there."

Nanny stopped in her tracks. "A boy with a stiff upper lip displays fortitude in the face of adversity."

Winston broke down and sobbed. Bobby growled at Nanny Patterson.

"Horrid dog! How dare you bare your teeth at me!"

Grrrrrr! His dog language was specific and direct.

Nanny picked up her shawl and swiped the Yorky across the nose. "You are a beastly, greedy, spoilt animal! How dare you steal the Royal chicken!"

"Bobby did not steal the Duke's chicken!" he yelled at the top of his lungs. "He only passed his tongue over it!"

"Winston!" Nanny's face screwed into a knot. "As a future leader, you must exercise self-restraint in the expression of emotion," she pointed out, sighing windily. "Thank goodness we are returning to England where an advanced state of civilisation exists because you, dear boy, are turning you into a little savage."

Winston's voice wobbled. "But England is at war."

Nanny Patterson sucked in a deep breath. "This conflict will be over in the blink-of-an-eye, and we will be celebrating the glory of England's worldwide colonial possessions and our mighty heritage. Winston, I think a rousing British patriotic song is in order. Sing along with Nanny." She faced him, positioning her arms as if she was preparing to conduct the Philharmonic Orchestra. "One. Two. Three. *Rule, Britannia! Britannia, rule the waves. Britons never, never, never shall be slaves.*"

A knock at the door. "Oh *please!*"

"Madam," announced the elderly porter from behind the door, "You requested another luggage trolley—"

Lord Fairfax slipped his arms into the sleeves of his jacket and snatched up his briefcase. "Come along now," he urged. Nanny Patterson stuck a vicious-looking hatpin into her bonnet and grabbed her Bakelite-handled bag. With a tear rolling down one cheek, Winston picked up his Yorky dog, and they all hurried out of the room and moved with haste along the hallway. A maid was coming in the opposite direction, her face partially hidden by an armful of fluffy white towels.

Winston hung back. "*Ishbel*," he whispered tensely.

Ishbel was caught off guard. She swirled around and caught sight of Winston, his father and his nanny taking great strides towards the elevator. "Enjoy your day," she responded.

"Do *not* fraternise with the servants." Nanny Patterson grabbed the boy's free hand. The doors of the ascending room opened. The doors of the ascending room closed. The Fairfax party were gone.

Ishbel walked onto a large room with an unmade bed. "I wonder where they're off to?" she said, transferring her pile to Lily's outstretched arms.

"That's them gone. The porter hauled their luggage. An orful lot. Mister Duncan wuz called t' bring up another trolley."

"What?" Ishbel's brow furrowed. "But Winston told me yesterday he was staying for another month. Oh, I wish I'd gotten a chance to say a proper goodbye. I was fond of that wee lad and his dog."

"He wuz fond of yi too." Lily chuckled to herself. "Hey, yi missed the Punch and Judy Show. Nanny Patterson had a go at Mister Duncan regardin' the luggage placement on the trollies. Sweet cheeses, they looked like two peas in a pod, argy-bargyin' in that same daft way."

Mister Dimbleby waited at the front door of his hotel with a shaky hope in his eyes. "Your Grace! I hope you are so well pleased with your visit to the Banff Springs Hotel that you will be glad you came, sorry to leave, and eager to return."

"Yes to all three," replied the Duke as he passed by.

Lord Fairfax was next. "Much obliged for your assistance, Dimbleby."

The two high-ranking officials climbed aboard the first coach. Winston, Nanny Patterson, and Bobby took the second coach and both horse-drawn vehicles set off, rumbling across the Bow River Bridge and riding passed the zoo. Winston waved to Buddy but the bear did not see him. "I wish Buddy did not have to wear that awful metal collar and chain. It must be cold and heavy around his neck."

"He is a polar bear," Nanny replied. "Do you want him to gobble you up?"

At the train station, the visiting dignitary inspected the guard of honour by walking down and looking at the row of polished and gleaming Royal Canadian Mounted Policemen. Then, he leaped aboard a boxy-long wagon. Lord Fairfax followed him inside. Nanny Patterson nudged Winston up the steep and narrow steps and into the second coach, whereupon Bobby jumped out of his arms and landed on a plush seat, stretching to rest his front paws on the ledge of a half-open window. The porter closed the carriage doors. The stationmaster checked his chronometer. The Royal Canadian Mounted Police prepared to give their final salute. All of a sudden, a hefty hare actually shot across the platform. In the blink of an eye, Bobby was up and out of the window. He jumped down onto the rail tracks, paws pounding joyously through the haze of the heat rising above the metal. The marauding hare plunged into a thicket of powder face willow.

"Bobby! Bobby!" Winston threw himself at the window. *"Bobby! Bobby!"* He streaked down to the door of the car. "Nanny Patterson! *Help me*! This door will not open!" He rattled the handle in its metal casing. A whistle blew. The engine jolted him forward. The carriage floor juddered under his feet. Winston's heart pounded inside his chest. "Let me out! Let me *out!"* He banged the sides of his fists against the heavy metal door.

The steam locomotive burped smoke and the grunting wheels began to turn.

Nanny Patterson scrambled along the aisle, grabbing backs of seats to steady herself. "Winston Fairfax! Stop this childish behaviour!" she cried, seizing him by the back of the collar and giving him an almighty shake.

"No! No! Stop the train!" Winston cried above the rush of sound. "We cannot leave Bobby behind!"

"Child, conduct *yourself* with good taste and propriety! You know full well trains cannot turn back once they leave the station."

"But Bobby Bobby is only a *little* dog!" Winston gazed in horror at the quickly-passing landscape, cupped his hands over his face and choked back the tears that were burning his eyes. "Who *who* will care for him?"

Nanny Patterson dragged her charge back along the aisle, his flaying arms and legs banging against the wood, leather and metal. "Oh my giddy aunt," she breathed, "you are behaving like a member of the working class! If I had my way, you would be properly relegated to an inferior station in life!"

The train, roaring and hissing, travelled full steam ahead towards the prairie grass land. Rain slopped across the window pane. The mountains faded into the distance and the landscape flattened. The spruce trees in due course disappeared. Clutching her lace handkerchief to her chest, Nanny Patterson sat rigid and aloof. "Winston. Bobby has gone to seek his future in the big-wide world and I warmly applaud his decision." She fanned herself with her printed ticket. "Believe me when I say. Your dog is more suited to the wilderness of Banff, Canada than to the civilised society of London, England. No more moping, boy. Sit up straight and sing along with Nanny. *"God save our gracious King. Long live our noble King. God save the King. Send him victorious, happy and glorious."*

Silhouetted against a shaft of evening sunlight, Winston rested the side of his achy head against the window. He had trusted his Nanny all his life. He felt her hand reaching out for his and he sat beside her, hurt and betrayed.

The two maids pranced into the kitchen where old Donald was pressing candles into candlesticks. Lily spoke first, "Miss Finch sent us up t' see yi. She said y' have a speshul job for us. Is it t' do with the war effort?" Her hands slipped from her hips as she waited for his answer.

"What are you blabberin' about?" He flattened a wisp of his white hair with the palm of his hand.

"The war *effort*," Ishbel added. "Onwards and upwards with the greatest of vigour'. 'Keep calm and carry on.' Miss Finch is knittin' dickies for the troops."

"Dickies?" Donald replied, a hint of agitation in his voice. "What the flying fig are dickies?"

"A dicky is a chest-warmin' turtleneck." She noticed a subtle shift in his expression. "Mister Duncan. You don't look yourself today. Is everything alright?"

"Oh, Ishbel, I've been a ten million kind of fool." He shook his head and rose from the spindle chair. "You two were sent up to do a special job. But it's nothin' to do with the war effort." He removed his jacket from the hook and covered his yellowish-brown waistcoat. "Follow me," he said picking up two unlit oil lamps. They left through a side door and entered a deserted servant's corridor. "I'm carrying a burden of guilt that I don't care to talk about," he grumbled. They rounded a corner and descended into a steep and narrow steel-stairwell, the only light coming from a tiny window high up. The old servant stopped in front of a rudimentary door and rested his lamps on the stone floor. "The bowels of the grand hotel, eh." He pulled a clunky metal ring from his trouser pocket and the keys clinked and clanged in his twisted fingers until he found the one that turned in the lock. "Wait here until I light these lamps. And watch your step," he said, blowing out the match. "There's three of them."

Lily pinched her nose. "Ugh, smells like a musty old washcloth in here!"

Ishbel wrapped her arms around herself for warmth, her mind taking in the exposed brick and thick timber. The old man suspended one of the lamps on a curly-iron wall bracket, hung with cobwebs. Stooped and tottery, he crossed the room and hooked up the other. The green-tinted light served to make the cellar more bleak and lonely.

"Ewww! Whut whut's that?" cried Lily, her hollow laugh breaking the silence.

Donald pulled a square of fabric from his pocket and flicked a scuttling spider off the rough object. "'It's an incredible wonder of the world, Lily. A very special fossil." He blew and wiped his nose. "Oh the forehead slap of hindsight! If I had given him permission to bring it down. When he wanted to. None of this would have happened."

"What happened?" asked Ishbel.

"I don't wish to talk about it." His face ravaged with grief. "I get enough pain when I lay my head down at night and get a verdict of disapproval from the judge within."

Ishbel leaned towards him, her brow furrowing. "My dad says if you give pain a voice and let someone listen, it lifts a weight off your shoulders. Please, Mister Duncan. Tell us what's troublin' you."

Donald rubbed his bony hands through his sparse white hair. "Wild Bill," he heaved a weary sigh, "Wild Bill Peyto trusted me to take care of his fossil *that* fossil." He directed his gaze at the boulder. "But instead of taking care of business. There and then. I put it off. Low and behold, Mister snooping Dimbleby decided to take a stroll around the back of the hotel. He *never* comes around these parts," his voice on the defence.

"Try not to get your dander up, Mister Duncan."

Old Donald shook his head. "The interfering blaggard pulled out his little leather notebook and asked what Peyto's cart was doing on CPR property. Before I could think up an answer, he whipped off the cover. Well, it was obvious the rascal had already taken a peek because he didn't look the least bit surprised. *'This object will be of great interest to my guests,'* he said in that snooty tone of his, '*Donald, make arrangements to have it cleaned. I want to display it in the front lobby.*' Well, when I heard that my heart sank."

"Taint his t' keep!" cried Lily with spirit.

Old Donald held his chest. "I tried to explain so, but he said any stone resting on the grounds of this hotel belongs to the Canadian Pacific Railway. When Peyto came back for his cart, I had to tell him what happened. Well, they don't call him Wild Bill for nothing, eh. He was madder than a bag of frogs!" Old Donald sat down on a rickety old stool, the only seat in the room, and covered his face with his hands.

Ishbel's voice was soft. "Don't go upsetting yourself, Mister Duncan."

"No. Just tell us whut happened next."

"Peyto insisted. I didn't want to. But he told me to find Mister Dimbleby and tell him it was very important so he would come down."

"Sweet cheeses. Did he come down?"

"Aye. And one thing led to another, and the two of them had it out on the back stairs. Well, of course, Peyto was fired."

"Fired!" Lily's hands flew to her face. "Jusslikethat?"

"Aye, lucky he didn't land in jail. And I've only myself to blame," he moaned, his face the picture of misery.

"'Tis orful," said Lily. "So where's Peyto now?"

Donald moved his shoulders with a twinge of unease. "He's gone to cool off in his cabin in the wilderness."

"Oh, sweet cheeses. Whut will become of him?"

"Lily, don't go worryin' about Peyto. He's well-liked and well-placed to take advantage of all the opportunities this town has to offer. Not to mention that Park Warden's job. They're always pushing him to take that."

"Peyto's speshul. I heard Conrad Kain and Walter Wilcox have a great respect for him."

"Aye, they do indeed, Lily. Mountaineers and explorers will always seek Peyto out for his skills and abilities. But that's no the problem. No. The problem is *I* was the man who helped our greedy manager covet Peyto's property under false pretences. Oh, the whole incident makes me sick to my stomach. I can hardly keep my mind on my job."

"I'm gonna miss him terrible, Mister Duncan. Why didn't he—"

"Oh, I'm wound tight, Lily. Don't ask me anymore questions. The top and the bottom of it is. The big boss man wants this fossil cleaned and you two were given the job."

Lily's shoulders slumped. "So that wuz the speshul job sloggin' away on this bluddy big boulder."

"Aye. And he wants it shinin' like a precious gem."

Ishbel shivered. "Do we have to clean it in this gloomy place?"

Donald nodded. "I hate to tell tales but you can blame that Ethel Finch. She told Dimbleby you two are a rambunctious pair and working in a place as cold as charity would calm your high jinks. Put a damper on your shenanigans."

"Whut a bluddy cheek!" Lily's voice soared in righteous indignation. "Who duz she think she is?"

"Oh, Lily, let's just get it over with."

"Aye, put some pep in your step the water's getting' cold," he pulled a paper bag of lozenges from his pocket. "Here. Take two each. They'll stop your teeth chatterin'."

Old Donald left the two maids sucking on their medicated candies. "Sweet cheeses," droned Lily. 'This tomb's givin' me the heebie-jeebies."

Ishbel carried the pail of water closer to the fossil. "It's like somethin' out of the Pit and the Pendulum."

"The whut?"

"That scary Edgar Allen Poe story."

"Duz yi think Ethel Finch is tryin' t' scare us?"

"Maybe. But she won't if we keep our minds occupied." Ishbel wrung out the cloth. "Mister Duncan is a nice old man. He sounds like he's from London."

"Dunno. Duzn't talk about his past." Lily picked up the bar of soap and plopped it into the bucket of water. "I'm frozen t' the bone. Are yi?"

Ishbel wasn't listening. "Wow! Come look at it from this side, Lily." She ran her frigid fingers across the stone's hushed shades of crimson and muted violet. "It's like lookin' at the passage of time."

Lily knelt down and set about scrubbing. "Sweet cheeses, Peyto must have done some chippin' 'n chisellin' 'fore he got this bluddy thing down the mountainside. Have yi ever climbed a mountain, Ishbel?"

"Aye. I climbed up the back of Cascade with my dad. The natives call it Minihapa, 'mountain where the water falls.'"

"Did yi manage t' reach the top?"

48

"Aye. But it was a long slog. We started off at dawn and didn't take a break until we reached the tree line."

"Then whut?"

"Then we met an upside-down chickadee. He stopped plucking seeds from a cone to laugh at us."

"I'm *serius*!"

"*I'm* serious! After the rest, we started on the rock face. Thank heavens for the tumblin' waters. We drank it. Splashed our faces. Cupped it over our heads. Anythin' to keep us goin'. By late afternoon we were up on the scree, slippin' and slidin' every which way. Eventually we reached the top and that's when our adventure revealed its sweet reward three-hundred and sixty degrees of astonishment and admiration. 'Dad!' I cried, the howling wind battering my clothes and blowing up my hair. "The world is mine!'. And he yelled back, 'Mas leat an saoghal, is leat daoin' an domhain.' It's Gaelic. My grandfather's tongue." Ishbel wiped the sweat from her brow with the back of her arm. "Translated, it means: 'if the world is yours, the people of the world are yours too'." She glanced at Lily's puzzled expression. "What?"

"That would be an orful responsibility," Lily replied, a rag hanging from her hand.

"Aye. Anyway. Ever since that day my dad has called Cascade *my* mountain. Whenever he looks up at it, he says: 'Indeed lass, that's your mountain.'" She smiled at Lily. "Are you a mountain person?"

A few moments passed then Lily said, "No. I think I'm a river person. The town I grew up in has five rivers: Athabasca, Clearwater, Horse, Snye 'n Hangingstone."

"Is that in Fort McMurray?"

"'Tis. They all freeze over in winter 'n the sun makes them glisten, glimmer 'n flicker. Sweet cheeses. 'Tis a sight t' feed the soul."

"Hey, what's this?" Ishbel picked up a little stone with a hole in it.

"'Tis Mister Duncan's. Must have dropped from his pocket when he pulled out his rag to blow his nose." Lily attacked the great fossil with the boar-bristle brush and her cheeks flushed with annoyance. "'Tis gonna take all day t' clean this blinkin' boulder."

Ishbel wrung out her cloth and trilled, *"With a scrub scrub here. And a scrub scrub there. Here a scrub. There a dub. Everywhere a—"*

"Ishbel! Shut yir mouth up!"

"Sweet cheeses, 'tis done!" Lily stood up and brushed off her apron. "Come take a look round this end."

Ishbel studied the beautiful rock. "Oh, Lily, it looks amazin'. I wonder how old it is."

"As old as Mister Duncan."

They did not hear his footsteps descending the stairs. The door opened. "What's so funny?" He looked around the dimly-lit space. "I think I might have dropped my token in here."

"Here it is!" Ishbel removed it from her pinny pocket. "It was on the floor. Do you keep it for good luck, Mister Duncan?"

"I do." He dropped it into the pocket of his yellowish-brown waistcoat. "Now," he said, straightening his back. "How did the work go?"

"Tickuty-boo!" Lily cried with delight.

"And hunky-dory," Ishbel added.

He looked at their grinning faces. "Your sunny dispositions are worth more than a fortune. But the time has come to inspect your work."

Lily called attention to the big stone. "Ta-da—"

"By gum, by *golly*." He nodded his approval and his chest loosened. "You did a grand job, girls. *"*

"'Tis a shame Mister Peyto can't see it."

Donald sighed with despair. "Oh Lily, it would only rub salt in his wounds."

"So where's the fossil goin' now?"

"In the front lobby of this grand hotel. Right beside the stuffed and mounted parakeet." Donald blew his nose and wiped his forehead. "The carpenters made a fancy cabinet for it."

Lily looked at old Donald expectantly. "Are we done for the day then?"

Clattering footsteps made them turn their heads

"Wassgoin'on?" Ethel Finch, huffing and puffing from descending the stairs. "Ya knows I've not done *my* inspection yet. Move back!" Her jaw dropped when she saw it. "G'wan! Is that?"

"The fossil, Miss Finch. Lily and Ishbel did a grand job, eh?"

"Hmm, 'bout time."

"Duz that mean we're done?" Lily beamed with girlish enthusiasm. "Coz we need t' get ourselves dolled up for the Cascade dancehall t'night."

Donald Duncan drew down his brows. "That's no place for respectable young women isn't that so, Miss Finch?"

50

Lily folded her arms and lifted her chin. "But Miss Finch goes there too."

The old servant looked slightly alarmed. "Of course she doesn't." He turned to Ethel. "You don't. *Do you?*"

"Don't ya worry, Donald." A snort of derision flew from Ethel's nose. "I never howdy 'fore I shake."

His eyes and mouth were frozen open.

Ethel shook her shoulders. "I never 'comes familiar 'til I'm formally introduced."

"Ooh, Mister Duncan," cried Lily, "all the maids go to the Cascade dancehall. Even ladies of gentle birth go there."

"Oh, gobbledygook!"

"Jeez b'y! It's *only* a bloomin' dance."

Donald's skin folded into a scowl. "It's obvious my opinion carries no weight round here." He unhooked the lanterns. "Right! Everybody *out!*"

Chapter 3

"This is it!"

Ishbel put her hand on the crown of her blue-ribboned bonnet and tilted her head back. The building on Banff Avenue had a broad-gambrel roof, large-flaring eaves, and a big sign, 'Cascade Dancehall'. She smiled at Lily and they quickly joined the crowd hurrying up the steps towards double doors, painted the same colour as old Donald's Sunday waistcoat.

A little woman with a silver bun peered at them through a hole in the kiosk. "Good evening. How many?"

"Two, pleez." Lily adjusted her gossamer wrap. "I'm treatin' my friend t'night. She's never been t' the dancin' before." The girls exchanged an excited giggle.

Her hands moved quickly in her fingerless gloves, tearing two numbered-squares from a roll of tickets. "Two at a nickel each. That will be a dime, dear."

Lily slid a Dominion of Canada twenty-five cent note across the counter.

"You don't have the right change, deary?"

Lily shook her head.

"Tut, tut." The elderly lady's face knitted. "Wait here. I'll go see if there's change in my tin."

Lily tapped the toe of her Mary Jane shoe. "Sweet cheeses! Heaven help the old biddy if she gets a rush."

The old woman returned. "I was filling in for five minutes. Should have locked the blinkin' door." She shakily counted the money out. "You'd better count out the fifteen pennies in case the *old biddy* got it wrong."

A blush crept up Lily's cheeks. She scooped the change into her purse.

The ticket lady turned her attention to Ishbel. "That's a lovely hat, dear. The prettiest blue-ribboned bonnet I've ever seen."

Ishbel turned her head to show off the back. "It belonged to my late mother," she revealed.

The ticket lady's face softened. "Your mother had very good taste, dear. Very good taste indeed."

The Ladies Room was big and bright and covered in rose-patterned wallpaper. Ishbel fidgeted with the folds in her frock. "Oh, Lily, I don't think this dress is right. I ran it up from a six-cent dress pattern."

"'Tis lovely. The colour suits yi."

"Thanks." Ishbel hesitated. "You know I've only ever done the Scottish country dancin' at the primary school."

Lily studied herself in the mirror then pinched her cheeks. "Don't worry. Just let the bloke lead."

"But what if I stand on his fumbs?"

"His *whut*?"

"His large toes," she replied and Lily howled with laugher.

"Forget the fumbs. Yir here t' enjoy yirself," she said, nudging her friend out of the Ladies Room and into a dimly-lit hallway. Folks were leaning against the walls, smoking, laughing, and shrieking.

"Whoo wee!" A cowboy with slicked-back hair and an embroidered silk shirt looked Lily up and down, "Hey pretty lady, I'd be mighty pleased to have this dance."

Lily's gaze moved from the cowboy to Ishbel.

"Oh, don't worry about me. I'll be absolutely fine."

Before Lily could toss her hair off her face and award him a demure smile, he grabbed her arm like it was a pot handle and pulled her through the double-hinged doors.

Ishbel waited a moment then followed them into a big hall where a band was playing to a room already heavy with smoke. Nice-looking couples were moving in time to the music and the Union Jack was flying, fluttering, and flopping above the swinging doors as merrymakers came and went. She turned her head. Woe and ruin, Ethel Finch was making a beeline for her. "Jeez Isabel," she said, a glass of something in one hand and a Fatima cigarette in the other, "ya look like a great bloomin' wallflower."

Heat rose in Ishbel's face.

"No worries, girl. I brought ya Mister Poppy. He'll dance ya around the hall, eh." Ethel stepped aside to reveal a man, his pallor worsened by a gray sack suit, his hair exacerbated by an oily dressing. He made brief eye-contact with Ishbel. "W-would you c-care to d-dance, Miss?" he asked with sticky apprehension.

"Uh—" The breath was sucked out of her.

"Just a d-d-dance, miss," he wheedled, his smile apologetic.

"Er—" The words clogged in her throat.

"Oh me nerves!" Ethel's bosom heaved under her rosy-pink bolero. "Girl, aspire ter inspire 'fore ya bloomin'-well expire!"

Ishbel took a deep breath. 'The man stinks of Brilliantine. But he is nice enough to ask me. Better than bein' a great bloomin' wallflower. I think.' She gave him a flicker of a smile. At that moment, a strapping lad in buffalo-plaid shirt pushed in and knocked the timid man to one side. "Come here often?" he asked, his boyish smile inviting her to like him.

"First time," she replied.

"Can I have this dance?"

"Er yes, thank you."

Slow-Slow-Quick-Quick-Slow. Ishbel was just getting the hang of it when a man in uniform cut in. "Goodness me!" she laughed, letting him take the lead as she counted the steps in her head. The night progressed. Soon there was no shortage of dance partners. From time to time she glanced across at Lily, twirling and swirling; her face radiating joy and fun: The Tango. The Cakewalk. The Grizzly Bear. The Foxtrot

"Come on and hear, come on and hear,
Alexander's Ragtime Band.
Come on and hear, come on and hear,
It's the best band in the land"

Half-way through the night, when the band took a break, Ishbel stood on her tiptoes and looked over the shoulders of the crowd in search of her friend. Lily snuck up behind her. "Fancy a ginger ale?" she whispered and Ishbel jumped in fright. Laughing and linking arms they walked out of the hall with the Union Jack flying fluttering and flopping above their heads. They passed by the cloakroom then stepped into an open area where bottles lined a wall behind a long counter. The sound of a violent quarrel made them stop dead in their tracks.

A heavily-built cowboy was grappling a young man around the throat.

"Stop!" Ishbel shrieked.

"*Ishbel!* Keep out of it!" yelled Lily.

"You goddamn filthy hunky!" cried the big angry man, pulling back an arm and knocking the lad to the floor. "Get the hell outta Banff! *Now!*" He kicked him hard when he was down. The lad screamed in pain. Blood poured from his mouth and nose. In an instant, rapid knife-like colours flashed in front of their faces. Flying tumblers flying bottles flying chairs tumult chaos wild uproar. A barman with a curly moustache jumped the counter. "Oi! You gals!" he yelled with a belch of whisky breath, "Get the 'ell outta 'ere!"

Outside, the cold night hit their faces. Lily put her head down against the wind. "Sorry yi had t' witness that drunken brawl."

"Oh, I've seen a bare-knuckle fight before. I grew up in a mining town, remember." She hurried to join in step. "What's a hunky, Lily?"

"A Ukrainian. The Ukraine's at war with us," she said and they continued up Banff Avenue in silence.

"Lily, where did you learn to dance like that?"

"My dad taught me." She grinned at the memory. "My mum would sit at the kitchen table and yell, 'Jack! Concentrate on the reversin'! She needs help with her reversin', Jack.'" The two friends laughed and quickened their step, staying close to the buildings where the path was less travelled. They had just crossed Buffalo Street when the wind carried a pitiful whine towards them. Ishbel put a finger to her lips, "Shhhh, did you hear that?"

"A cougar?"

"Oh don't be daft, Lily. It sounds like a wee dog. It's comin' from that entryway." She pointed.

"The Imperial Bank of Canada?"

"Think so."

"Don't go over there." Lily hung back. Her voice rose to a squeak, "It might pounce out of the shadows."

Ishbel stopped outside the covered doorway and squinted into the darkness. At first, the shape of a small creature was barely visible but when it moved towards her, her whole being jolted. "Bobby?" She dropped to her knees and scooped him up. "Lily!" she cried over her shoulder. "It's Bobby! Winston's dog!"

"Are yi sure? They went back t' England."

"Lily, they left three days ago! This poor wee soul must be starvin'." She looked down at him through a fuzz of tears.

Lily put her hands to her face. "Ishbel, look at yir frock! 'Tis covered in muck."

"I can wash it," her voice tangled in the wind. "Lily, I need to clean Bobby up and feed him."

"But dogs are forbidden in the servant's quarters. Yi'll lose yir blinkin' job—"

Now that Bobby was washed, fed, walked and well-hidden, Ishbel felt enormous relief and a tweak of fear. She pushed her squeaky-wheeled trolley down the steep and narrow corridor and stopped outside the laundry room, tightened her grip and shoved it through the hinged-metal doors. The air, dense as thick-pea soup, obscured her vision and the stench of foul water made her gag. She put a spring in her step and hurried passed the row of leather-aproned washerwomen, standing on slotted planks, scrubbing sheets hard against metal washboards. Bypassed big box mangles, the hissing press irons, and the goffering machines. The air began to clear. The noise subsided. Shelves upon shelves of folded crisp-white linen rose up to greet her.

Lily finished counting pillowcases. "Did yi hand the dog over?" she asked before writing the number in the Laundry Book.

Ishbel moved her gaze from the sock driers to the ledges. "Look at all those protrudin' lavender faggots. Don't they look pretty markin' the half-dozens?"

Lily responded with crisp irritation. "Ishbel! Dogs are not allowed in the servants' quarters. Yi need t' take him t' the manager's secretary right *now*!" She dropped the pencil and it bounced on the string attached to the spine of the register.

Ishbel reached for her elbow, "Lily, you saw the state of the wee mite. He was cold and starvin' so caked in mud we couldn't see the colour of his coat. If I hand him over now, he'll be shoved into a crate and shipped off."

"Good Lord! Yir no thinkin' of keepin' him?" Her manner was a mixture of disapproval and alarm.

"Of course I'm not *keepin'* him." Ishbel's chest swelled. "I'm just gonna fatten him up and all that. And when he's happy and healthy, hand on heart, I'll hand him over to Mister Dimbleby's secretary." Ishbel sneezed and her face reddened. The supervisor was waltzing towards them.

"*Come on and hear, come on and hear, Alexander's Ragtime Band,*" crooned Ethel, her cheeks pink and moist. "Jeez, it's mausey in here." She glared at them. "Well, wassgoin'on?"

"We're just collectin' our linens, Miss Finch," Lily replied.

"Well hurry up 'fore I assign ya washerwomen jobs! A hundred-turns-per-load with a peg-dolly in a fat-bellied tub that would sort the pair o' ya out."

Lily waited until Ethel was out of earshot. "Ishbel McColl, I'm no helpin' yi harbour *that* dog."

"Right then."

"Right then whut?"

"Can I borrow your big basket so I can sneak him in and out?"

At quarter to eleven the next morning, Ishbel left the servants' quarters and wheezed her way up the steep and narrow steps. "Bobby, you're heavier than a flippin' Dundee fruitcake." She rested the covered-basket on the stone slab, secured it with her knee and felt inside her pocket for her hanky. 'Drats Lily's key. She'll be in Mount Stephen Hall settin' tables for that weddin'. Suppose I could run by.' Ishbel filled her lungs with air, lifted the creel and puffed her way up the rest of the stairs. Opening the discrete door, she looked left, right and left again. All clear. She hurried along the carpeted lobby and was just about to pass the Oak Room when strains of music reached her. She immediately stopped in her tracks and gave her attention to the sound, *Veni Creator Spiritus*.

"And where do you think you are you going?" The usher's sharp-dark eyes looked her up and down.

Bobby stirred in his basket; Ishbel's face flushed. "I'm on my way to Mount Stephen Hall." A slight quiver in her voice. "But if your bride's comin'. I'll I'll just go the other way."

"Stand behind that marble column," he ordered. "Once she has passed, you can continue on your way."

Ishbel put the basket down and rested her back against the towering cold stone. She was admiring a portrait of King George V in his coronation robes when curiosity got the better of her. She stepped from behind the column. At the top of the circular-staircase a beautiful bride, tiara sparkling with jewels, bouquet spilling with Alberta roses, myrtle, and lily-of-the-valley. Ishbel couldn't help but smile up at her. The bride lifted her chin and stared down her nose. Ishbel backed her way behind the column.

Then, an ear-piercing shriek.

Ishbel swung back around. A flame was rising from the sleeve of the bride's dress. The woman's feigned indifference now a blood-curdling scream for help. Alarmed beyond measure, Ishbel's throat caught with panic. She snatched the heavy apron from the basket. The Yorky shot out. "Bobby!" Nausea arose inside her. No time to think. She scrambled up the marble staircase, unfurling the pinny as she went. Candlewax nipping her arms, she flung the protective garment across the bride to douse the flame but the woman's foot slipped.

"AaaaaahhhhhhhHHHHHHHHHH!" A whirling bouquet. Limbs tumbling loosely. Skull striking every rise and run. Flowers scattering in every direction.

Ishbel gawped in horror. "Oh. My. Dear. God."

Three ushers bolted out of the Oak Room: "What happened?"

"Get help!"

"Someone call a doctor!"

"Is she going to be alright?!"

"Has someone called the doctor?!"

Guests began pouring from the Oak Room: confusion feeding their need to know what happened.

"Stand back everyone! Give her some air!"

"*You*, girl!" A man pointed a finger at Ishbel. "Get Dimbleby! *Now!*"

Violent butterflies flapping in her stomach, she ran as fast as she could, turning a corner and almost bumping into him. "Sir, sir! You must come at *once*!" She shut her eyes in anguish. "There's there's been a terrible! A *horrible* accident!"

"Pull yourself together, girl!"

"Oh, Mister Dimbleby!" Her mind reeling. "She's she's dead!"

"Dead!? *What?!* Who?!"

"The bride! Her dress caught the flame! She she fell down the staircase!"

Together, they ran towards the tragic scene.

"Everyone, move back! Move back!" ordered Mister Dimbleby.

"Let me through!" cried a guest. "I am a doctor! Let me through!"

"Is she going to be alright?" Mister Dimbleby rubbed his hands.

The densely packed crowd held its collective breath until the doctor closed the bride's eyes and the horrified expression was gone from her face.

A shocked silence then a man pushed his way through the throng and gaped down at her but seemed unable to speak. The doctor grasped his stare. "Richard," he uttered in helpless appeal. "I am so very sorry. Geraldine. Her neck is broken."

"But this cannot be." The man's eyes welling up. "What caused this tragedy?" He fell to his knees and drew his bride gently into his arms.

One of the ushers came forward. "A small dog shot passed my feet. That's the likely culprit."

"No!" Ishbel cried out in fright. "The sleeve of her dress caught on the wall flame!"

"Perhaps not surprisingly," the usher held his fist to his face. "If the dog tripped her? If she threw her hands up in alarm?"

The groom reached for his handkerchief to wipe his whole face. "Is is that what happened?"

Ishbel rubbed her arms as if to expunge the usher's statement. "No! Sir, I *swear* the dog didn't cause her death! When I heard the bride scream, I ran to help her. I lifted my apron from the basket and Bobby flew out!" She pointed to the empty container by the marble column. "I *swear* he went nowhere near the stairs!"

Mister Dimbleby ignored her remarks and turned to face Mister Ross. "Locate the offending animal." He handed over his keys. "There is a handgun in the top, right-hand drawer of my desk. Under the circumstances, we should dispose of the dog at once."

Ishbel was bereft of speech. She turned on her heels and fled the scene, not stopping for a breath until she reached Mount Stephen Hall. The sun shone through the high-up, stained-glass windows, heightening the Gothic architecture. Carved oak banisters swaged in satin and vines. Panelled walls graced with garlands of white roses on feathery palms. But worst of all: a table set for a bridal breakfast that would never be eaten. The sudden sound of footsteps echoing behind made her swing around. "Oh, Lily. Thank *goodness* it's you!"

"Of course, 'tis me. I got the speshul job of turnin' bluddy serviettes int' pyramids. Remember?"

"Oh, Lily, there there's been a horrible accident," she explained in a breathless rush. "And now now they're goin' to shoot Bobby!"

"Whu-*uut?*"

"The usher said he ran this way. *Lily*, we have to find him first!"

"Sweet cheeses, he's right behind yi!"

Ishbel whirled around and Bobby leaped into her waiting arms. "Oh, what a relief!"

Lily reached under a table. "Here, put him in this napkin box."

They fled from the hall. Lengthening their strides until they came upon a meandering guest. They immediately slowed their pace.

Arf!

The woman's eyes were showcased behind the turned-back brim of her hat. "I believe you have a little doggie in there?" She came closer. "Do allow me a tiny peek."

Ishbel tightened her grip on the box.

"He's contagious!" blurted Lily.

"Contagious?!" The lady's eyes widened.

"'Tis essenshul we remove him from this hotel. *Immediately*."

The woman's chin dropped. Ishbel and Lily broke into a run, not stopping until they turned the corner and spotted Mister Dimbleby walking towards them with Mister Ross. "Sweet cheeses, Ishbel! Jump int' the elevator!" Lily pressed the button but it was already going to the 5th Floor. An elderly gentleman stepped aside to let them out. "I say! I say!" His monocle fell from his eye orbit. "No need to rush!" he cried, but the maids' minds were whirling and their box was juddering as they made a beeline for the concealed door at the opposite end of the hall.

Madame Mistinguett's heart-shaped face peeked out of Room 526. "Qu hest-ce que c hest?" she squeaked.

Lord Proby turned his key in the lock of Room 521. "Two maids with a large carton ran right passed me! Their conduct was appalling!"

Madame Mistinguett's brow creased. "Sacré bleu."

A full head of ringlets popped around the door of Room 522. "What is causing all the commotion out here? Ugh maids! In England, we train our staff to remain invisible and they use the *back stairs*!" harrumphed the Dowager Countess.

Back on the ground floor, Ishbel took advantage of the shadows and peeked around the flock-wallpapered corner. "All clear," she inhaled and they made a dash for the small back door that took them outside. Keeping close to the stone façade, they hurried towards the woodshed. Thankfully, it was unlocked. Winded, Ishbel placed the box on the floor. "Now what?"

"Arf!" Bobby pushed his head through the flaps. His chocolate-drop eyes, momentarily blinded, blinked repeatedly.

"Oh, Bobby," Ishbel gently stroked his little face. "If only you'd stayed in my blinkin' basket."

Lily rubbed her forehead. "Let's head to the Bow. We can hide in the reeds 'til we think of something better."

The foaming waters of the Bow River tumbled between the wooded cliffs and quaint trails winding through the brushwood. Ishbel, Lily and Bobby rounded a bend and navigated their way towards the thick, tall grasses. There, they hunkered down. The sound of buzzing insects. The noise of chirping crickets. In the far-off distance, the crack of a gun. Then two more quick to follow. Two birds, sleek and plump, abruptly rose from the ground, their wings flapping. A bubble of hysteria rose in Ishbel. "They're tryin' to flush Bobby out."

Lily's eyes locked on her friend. "Shhhh." She placed a quieting finger over her mouth. "Listen—"

Restless branches of white birch rustling in the wind. Twigs cracking and snapping. The ominous sound of dead leaves squelching underfoot. Then a dark shape falling between them and the sun. Lily looked up. "Sweet cheeses Miss Finch."

"Wassgoin'on?" she squawked.

A wind blew up and skittered dust around the clearing. Ishbel, holding Bobby tightly in her arms decided honesty was the best policy. "We're tryin' to hide him 'cause, 'cause they're goin' to shoot him for a crime he didnae commit."

Bobby gazed up at Ethel and thumped his tiny tail on the ground.

For what seemed a long time she said nothing then she said. "Count yar blessings I've a soft spot for animals follow me." They all loped behind her, along a jagged path that turned and twisted. Prickly offshoots bit through their stockings; big leafy branches swept across their faces, and Bobby's fur collected burrs and stickers. When the track narrowed, Ethel came to a sudden stop and clambered up the side of a jutting rock. "Yar in luck! It's still there!"

"Whut's still there?" asked Lily as a crow's grated cry sliced through the air.

Ethel was back beside them. "Keep yar eye on me and I'll show ya," she said, scrambling down the bluff towards the gushing and milky-foam waters then doggedly scuttling along the shore line. She stopped in front of an abandoned boat and looked up at the two maids. "There's even a fishin' basket for him ter sleep in!"

Ishbel stared at Ethel, disbelief blaring inside her. "You can't mean? I can't put Bobby in that boat by himself!"

"No. Orff course yi can't!" uttered Lily.

Ethel, water lapping around her ankles, was already untying the rope.

"Oh, this is pure folly!" Ishbel's forehead crinkled in a frown. "I can't put him in that boat. By himself. I don't even know if he likes the water."

"Jeez girl, all dogs like water Lab Retriever's pull fishin' nets outta the bloomin' Atlantic."

Bangbang! Bangbang!

Ishbel's indecisiveness rose to a fever-pitch. Heart drumming in her ears, she looked hungrily at Lily for reassurance but Lily's expression was one of bewilderment.

Bangbang! Bangbang! More startled birds taking to flight.

"Mudder in heaven!" Ethel filled her lungs with restoring fresh air. "Yar runnin' outta time."

The two maids clambered down the cliff.

Tears blinded Ishbel. She knelt down by the boat. "Be a good boy, Bobby." She gently placed him inside the lidless basket and stepped away. The little dog, trusting her voice, obediently settled down but under his mishappen fur there was a growing puzzled look. Sadness, emptiness flooded through Ishbel.

Ethel began dragging the small vessel out of the marsh. "Can one o' ya lend a blinkin' hand!?"

Lily looked at Ishbel crouched in numbed silence and obligingly sloshed into the water.

Ethel stopped to catch her breath, fist against her breathing bosoms. "Is ya ready?"

Lily nodded her head yes.

"This bloomin' boat needs ter catch the blinkin' stream so when I say push, give it one almighty shove. *One two three. Pushhh!"*

Lily stood up. "Sweet cheeses. There it goes!"

"Tooraloo, Bobby!" Ethel waved to the dog. "Oh me nerves. It worked for Baby Moses so I hope it works for him." In next to no time, the tiny craft caught itself up in the fast-flowing waters, rapidly disappearing into the far-off distance.

Lily splashed her way back to land. "I knows when the boat passes through Canmore, Bobby'll take his chance. He'll jump out and somebody'll take him in coz Yorkies are good at catchin' vermin."

Ishbel's face florid, she shielded her tear-filled eyes. Water rushed over the rocks and ridges and a Great Blue heron cruised over the riverbend with slow, deep wingbeats. Other birds squealed and swooped from the mountainside, luminous in the strange half-light.

"Oh, Lily, I curse myself for not listening to you. If only I had given him back. Straight away. When I had the chance." Her face crumpled at the mass of dark clouds rolling in.

Lily's voice was low. "Yi didn't know this wuz goin' t' happen."

Ishbel stood on the edge of the alpine crag. "I won't I can't rest until I put this wrong right," she cried, her hands fluttered to her skirts, her hair, squeezed themselves tight. "I'll pour my heart, blood and soul into finding him. I'll get Bobby back to Winston. I will. I swear."

"Hang on a minute!" Ethel stopped cupping up handfuls of water to clean her hands. "Yar no sayin' that bloomin' Yorky belonged ter the grand Lord Fairfax?"

Ishbel nodded and drew her shawl against the moody grey mountains.

"Ishbel yar as stunned as me arse." Ethel stepped onto dry land and her feet felt like stone. She bent down to pour water out of her shoe. "If that old fart, Dimbleby, knew the dog belonged ter that rich and powerful man, he never would have shot it. Hell no!"

"*But* I tried to tell him! I tried to tell them! The gunshots!" Ishbel choked.

"Well, ya've no one to blame but yourself for putting that dog into the boat." Ethel shook her head and shoved her foot into her sodden shoe. "That young lad lost his mudder on the Titanic and now thanks ter yar blinkin' meddlin', he's lost his furry companion."

The words were like a thump in Ishbel's stomach. 'The Titanic!" Suddenly it all made sense. Winston's photograph. His mother posing with the black puppy beside a pile of travelling chests.' Ishbel's heart turned as heavy as the sky. "She gave her son Bobby to comfort him in her absence." The wind rushed through the pine trees and across the dark surface of the water.

Ethel plucked at her fob watch. "Aye, it's an uncertain world. Isabel your shift starts at five. Mind yar in that kitchen 'fore the pantry clock chimes the hour. As for *you*, Saunderson. No shillyshallying! Head back ter the kitchen right now."

"Sweet cheeses, my shift's finished. I wuz goin' t' have forty winks."

Ethel stared, open mouthed. "Forty winks me arse. Ya have ter make up for yar lost time."

The afternoon breeze freshened, lifting a strong scent of moss to their noses as they made their way back along a creeping carpet of toothed leaves and stinging hairs. Above them, the Banff Springs Hotel. Eerily quiet. Ishbel reached inside her pinny pocket and handed Lily her key.

Lily looked up at the pantry clock, struggling, clanking and striking the midnight hour. She wiped the draining board and rolled down her sleeves. "Our beds are callin', Ishbel."

The two maids hurried along the hallway, temporarily quiet. They slipped through the Oval Room, soothing blue tones and guilt-edged moldings. They entered the Riverview Lounge, barrel ceiling and heavy columns. Lily stopped at the first massive window and beckoned Ishbel into its small recess where a colossal piece of glass was confronting the pelting rain. Wind howled down the chimneys, thrashed the stone walls and assaulted the turrets. In the distance, a long low rumble a thunderous roar a deafening boom. Then a flash of lightening illuminating the universe. "Sweet cheeses, I've never seen the river as black as this."

"Oh Lily, I coulda I woulda I shoulda—" Ishbel's crumpled features betrayed her fear. "If anything happens to that wee dog, my life will be ruined totally ruined!"

"'Tis a dog's nature t' find shelter." Lily grasped Ishbel's arm, "C'mon—"

High up on the wall, the glass-eyes of a colossal buffalo head followed the two maids as they hurried down the picture staircase and turned the handle of the discrete lobby door.

The sun had not yet shifted from behind the lofty mountain peaks so it was cold and damp when Bobby gave a huge yawn, stretched and shook himself. The wild ride over. The shattered vessel impaled on a sharp rock, jutted out from the riverbank. The sonsy wee terrier was gazing up at the magpies darting back and forth above his head when a squeaking gopher drew his attention. He perked up his ears, wrinkled up his snout, and took a flying leap across the gurgling waters. Heart beating and paws scrambling, he pounded around the woodland floor, awash with wild flowers and scarlet berries, until a pointy-branch of a mangled tree slid underneath his collar and brought him to an abrupt halt.

Rain drummed onto the river. Day turned into night. The forest created new shadows. Eyes watching. Wolves howling. Owls hooting. A wailing wind. A bewitching hum, dark and curious, remote and close. Branches creaking. A hostile squawk. A chilling screech. The stench of rotting wood. The tang of spongy moss. Bobby's barks, raw and primal, continued until the dawn broke over the timberland and the sun edged its way above the horizon. He lifted his muzzle to its warmth. Objects became distinguishable again and the cheerful sounds of chirping birds and buzzing insects returned. The bedraggled Yorky was licking the dew off the grass when he heard the crunch of twigs and the vibration of heavy boots. Curling himself into a tight ball, he hid from the creeping dark-shadow etching across his body.

"Whut the—" a scrap of surprise in a man's voice.

Bobby bared his teeth and growled. He was only a little dog. Very small.

The man began to laugh. "Relax. I ain't gonna hurt ya." He removed an egg biscuit from his satchel and stooped to crumble it under the terrier's nose. "A hungry stomach has no ears, eh." He poured water from his canteen into his cupped hand and the Yorky drank with gusto. "So yar name's Bobby," he said, noticing the elaborately engraved docket attached to his collar. "Hold still 'til I free ya from this branch. There ya go, ya lucky little bastard."

Wild Bill Peyto searched the entire area, finding nothing more than an empty smashed-up boat and a lidless fishing basket. With a grave expression, he tucked the bedraggled dog under one arm and set off for his cabin deep inside the forest.

A wax melt-yellow sun in a bright-blue sky, and a red-breasted nuthatch chirping monotonously. Peyto picked up a rock and smashed it off his cabin door. Listened for two ear-splitting snaps: the click of a trigger, the clank of a falling-lock mechanism. Bobby flew from his arms and hid behind the woodpile. "No worries, Bobster," he said, ejecting saliva forcibly from his mouth then grinning across at the little dog. "I'm only tryin' to catch a fat-headed bastard. Except, I'm shit out of luck again." Peyto stretched his arm down inside a hollow tree. Felt for his chunky key. "Every time that moron, Boris Klumpenbovur, goes on a bender, he breaks into my place, pinches my grub and drinks my booze. Hell, I even caught the suckin' insect playin' on my banjo ukulele!"

Rrrrruff!

"Ya, Bobster, a man's gotta do what a man's gotta do." Peyto pushed the door wide open and the hinge on the log frame squealed. The little dog paused on the doorstep to the dark and musty interior: a battered chair, a rough table, a metal bed with a bare mattress. Smells of furs and skins. "Home sweet home, Bobster. Come on in." Peyto walked across the room with a singleness of purpose and dust rose up from an ancient rug. "I was plannin' on restin' my great fossil right there," hands out, imagining it against his wall, "but the dick who runs the Banff Springs nicked it off my wagon."

Rrrrruff!

"Ah, no worries. 'Tis only a minor setback in my brightly-coloured life." He took off his fringed buckskin jacket and threw it over the chair. "When the opportunity presents itself, I'll show that authoritarian bastard the error of his ways. I'll rip his fat head off his neckless body and reclaim my property." A beam of light from the open door fell upon a crescent saw hanging on a masonry nail. Beside it, a cobwebby window. Below that, a little square table with a yellowed photograph set in a tin frame. Peyto picked it up and a rush of love closed in on him. "My wife and son, Emily and Robert. We were on top of the world when this photograph was taken." He fell silent, fingers tenderly touching the image of their faces. "We had big plans for our outfittin' business. Hell, we'd yak on about it day and night." He let out a chuckle. "Whenever my glance fell upon her, her gaze was always waitin' for mine."

Bobby stretched his body down flat, eyes looking up, examining the expression of the man who was giving his head a sad, slow shake.

"A year later," Peyto's voice low, turned into a whisper, "in the last hours of her life, I held her in my arms and we listened to the wind thrashing against the walls. Our plans for the outfittin' business well, they didn't matter anymore." He put the picture back on the table and the shaft of late afternoon sunshine fell upon it. "When the dawn broke, Emily turned her head towards the window. There was a blanket of fog rolling towards us across the Bow and for a dreamlike moment, it thinned. I felt her grip my hand. A moment later, she was gone." Peyto got down on one knee and wadded up an old newspaper lying by the hearth. "I covered her over and walked to our lad's room. He was barely three. Sorrow despair panic rushed through my veins. Hell, Bobster, I've no words for the anger I felt." He made a mound in the centre of the hearth. Crisscrossed the kindling around it and placed a log on top. "Emily's family asked if they could take Robert in. I knew he'd have a good life with them he needed a mother figure. So I made the right decision to take him to Armstrong. 'Tis a sprawling town about 250 miles west of here. He's well settled now. So it was the right decision." He paused. "Hell, 'tis all ass-backwards. But it was the right decision, eh." Bobby watched the flames lick around the kindling and, in no time at all, a big log was burning brightly in the stone grate and the aroma of mouth-watering rabbit stew was seeping from the kettle.

With the little dog shaking his tail against his legs, Peyto spooned the tasty morsels onto two tin plates. Placed one on the floor. Bobby used his sniffing sense to deem it safe then slurped and licked until the squeaky-clean dish flipped into the air and clattered back down.

Arf!

As well as the floor-to-ceiling books, the Duncraig House library boasted a sliding ladder, an aspidistra in a bronze pot, and an elaborately-carved writing desk.

Nanny Patterson curled the wire loops of her glasses behind her ears and loomed over the top of Winston's head. "Tut-tut. A missing tittle." Winston quickly dotted the 'j' in 'justly'. "And I spot another error." She stabbed at the offending word with the tip of her finger. "'Nice' is a non-descriptive word for a dog. State the breed and describe the docket that will be sufficient. And be respectful in requesting the Mister Dimbleby's help. Now begin again."

"But Nanny!"

"Do not argue, child. The English language is the richest in the world; five hundred thousand words." She pulled a thesaurus from the bookshelf and plunked it on the writing desk. "Look up a few. Express yourself."

"But my hand is sore."

"Diligence and determination, boy! The wisdom of it will come as you age."

Master Winston Fairfax, Esq.
Duncraig House
35 Duke Street
London
England

August 21, 1914

Mister Dimbleby, Hotel Manager
Banff Springs Hotel
Spray Avenue
Banff, Alberta
Canada

Dear Mister Dimbleby,

On a recent visit to Alberta, my father, Lord Fairfax, and I lodged at the Banff Springs Hotel. I trust you will remember us.

Regrettably, on the morning of our departure, I was separated from my Yorkshire terrier at the train station. I am writing to respectfully ask that you inquire into his whereabouts. My dog is wearing a tag: 'Bobby' engraved on the front and the Fairfax coat of arms embossed on the back. Father says whomever finds our family pet will be justly rewarded.

Sincerely,
Master Winston Fairfax, Esq.

Nanny Patterson gave Winston a boost up and he pushed the envelope through the slot in the red pillar box. It fell to the bottom with a gratifying plop.

"Done!" said Nanny. "Now we have to catch the tramcar, Winston. Somewhat of a burden, I must say."

"Where are we going, Nanny Patterson?"

"We are going to Kensington Gardens. First, to Round Pond then we will take a stroll through the wealth of autumn-plant life. And if you behave yourself, we will visit the Peter Pan statue." She gripped his hand. "Oh, here comes a guardian of the peace to assist us."

The truckmen and horse-car drivers slowed down and stopped.

"Keep together! All safely cross!" announced the man in custodian helmet and brass buttons.

"Round Pond! Can we hire a rowing boat, nanny?"

"Hmm, no more than thirty minutes."

"Whoopee! Nanny—"

"Yes."

"The last time I was on a boat Bobby licked the back of my legs. I think he was telling me he loved me."

"I think he was telling you to pull your socks up."

Winston's stomach clenched. "I wonder what has become of my little dog."

"I am sure he is curled up in front of someone's fireplace," she replied with a sharp intake of breath.

Nanny Patterson and her charge left Round Pond and walked briskly along the path, the air fresh with the perfume from carnations, crocuses and chrysanthemums. "The rowing boat was fun," said Winston, his mind filled with Banff memories he thought best not to mention.

"Look, child! A horse chestnut tree. Completely absent in Banff, Alberta. Why?"

"Because it is too cold there."

"Correct. Now look closer. What do you see?"

"Oh, I see a little owl, nanny."

"Yes, indeed. What is he looking at?"

Winston's gaze followed her pointed finger. "I, I am not quite sure."

Nanny Patterson's nose turned up like the corner bit of a stale bread. "It is looking at a bad-tempered Gadwall attacking a stocky Pochard. See—"

"Yes! Yes! I do!"

"Shoo, shoo, you horrid bird!" she waved her umbrella and both birds scattered. "Now listen. Listen, Winston. What do you hear?"

"A singing bird."

"Correct! A Blackcap. Is it melodious to your ears?"

"Oh, yes."

Nanny Patterson reached inside her jacket to check her fob watch. "Time to make our way to the Peter Pan statue. Tell me, Winston, who wrote the delightful story of Peter Pan?"

"Sir James Matthew Barrie."

"Correct. He is a Scottish author. And who is Peter Pan?"

"A mischievous boy who never grew up."

"Yes and, in a few moments, we will see a statue of him blowing his pipe on the stump of a tree. The animals of the English countryside and delicate winged good heavens!" Nanny Patterson stopped in her tracks. A sinking feeling griped her stomach. Two women she would prefer to avoid were sitting on a bench enjoying the gentle warmth. Before she could escape, plump Nanny Dutton's eyes flew in her direction. "Yoo-hoo Patterson!"

Skinny Nanny Brighton shuffled along the bench to make room. "Haven't seen you, nor your apple-cheeked darlin' for a while." She drew back her lips, revealing a row of little peg-like teeth. Winston took a step back to avoid being eaten.

Caught without a plausible excuse, Nanny Patterson sat down on the wooden slats and rested her Bakelite-handled bag on her lap. "Run and play, child. Nanny must visit with members of her profession."

"Us girls are overdue a chinwag, eh?" said Nanny Dutton, twisting in her seat. "So. Tell us about your trip to Canada. Utterly exhausting was it?"

Nanny Patterson emitted a long, deep audible breath, "We travelled First Class."

Nanny Brighton doubled her arms across her bosom. "First Class, eh. Well, doesn't matter how much they tart up them coaches, they can't get rid of the stink, the noise and the dirt! Hours and hours of boredom. Draughty too. Can't imagine how you managed."

"I don't know where you got your information," Nanny Patterson said tetchily. "Our train was luxurious. The journey was sheer heaven. And all the hotels were delightful. Utterly ostentatious. Terribly wasteful. But delightful none the less. And when we reached Alberta, we stayed at the magnificent Banff Springs Hotel." She remembered Mister Dimbleby's spiel. "A place to dream, cultivate relationships, and craft memories. The food was scrumptious! The service stupendous! Did I mention Prince Arthur was there?"

Nanny Brighton's eyes grew round. "Prince Arthur?"

"Yes, the Honourable Prince Arthur, the Governor General of Canada and the son of the late Queen Victoria on the same floor as our party. Oh, he's ever so friendly took young Winston on a fishing trip. And everyone but *everyone* was dressed to the nines. Even the cowboys were charmingly outfitted. And they had an amazing zoo; it was wonderful to see it through a child's eyes. And, the

Canadian flowers absolutely delightful. And the mountains even more so. You know, it is true what they say."

"What," Nanny Daulton held her gaze, "do they say?"

Nanny Patterson smiled a dreamy smile and said, "*All you touch and all you see is all your life will ever be.*"

Winston's head popped up from behind the bench. "But Nanny Patterson, you—" he said with surprise in his eyes. "You hated—"

His governess maintained a fixed expression. "Yes, Winston, I hated to leave. But with the war on and all. Well, we had no choice, did we?" A strutting peacock stopped in front of the three pokerfaced nannies. The bird began to spread its tail. The nannies held their sniffs. The peacock changed its mind, tightened its feathers and walked away. Nanny Patterson looked at her wristwatch. "You will have to excuse me now, I have more pressing business young Winston is in need of tweeds and wellingtons." She rose to her feet. "Come along, child. James Purdy & Sons closes at five-thirty." She seized and held Winston's hand firmly and, firmly enjoying the effect she had on them, chimed over her shoulder, "Good day to you both."

Nanny Brighton's neck cranked to look at Nanny Dutton. "Well now. What did you make of *that*?"

"Hmm, showing off about her trip to Canada. Snooty bizom."

"I don't know what she has to be snooty about. She began life as a foundling."

"A foundling?" Nanny Dutton felt herself grow more interested. She stretched her mouth, "Get away with you!"

"'Tis true. Nanny Patterson was trained as a nanny in the Foundling Hospital. Worked all her life for the Fairfax family. Brought up three generations of them. Now she thinks she's one of them." Heat rose in Nanny Brighton's cheeks. "The luck o' the white ball, eh."

"The luck of what? A white ball?"

"You've never heard of the white ball?"

"No."

"Well, I'll tell you," Nanny Brighton sucked in her breath. "In the old days, way back when, many womenfolk were too poor to care for their infants. Of course, the Foundling Hospital couldn't take them *all* so a lottery system was put into place. If a mother picked a black ball it meant her child was turned away. A red ball, her child was put on a reserve list. If she picked a white ball and the child was healthy, it was admitted. In a bag of 80 balls, only 16 were white."

"So Nanny Patterson's mother must have picked a white ball."

Nanny Brighton adjusted her hat. "Well, let's hope her luck holds out. She's getting up in years and when the apple-cheeked darlin' goes to boarding school, they'll not be givin' her another. She's too old. She'll be out on the street."

"She can always hock fish at the Smithfield Market."

"Can you imagine?"

Both nannies howled with laughter.

Nanny Dutton opened her bag and retrieved her handkerchief. "Joking apart," she dabbed the corners of her eyes. "Just because she's a foundling doesn't mean she's no family."

"Well if she has, the Foundling Hospital will never tell. They have a strict policy: rechristen the bairns; change their names; protect the innocent." Nanny Brighton looked intently at her colleague. "At least they get a roof over their heads."

A noisy woodpecker ended their conversation.

The late afternoon was warm and sunny. It was rush hour so Nanny Patterson kept a tight hold of Winston's hand. "Child, what is the largest city in the entire world?"

"London."

"Correct. It is a great centre of trade, industry and banking. It has palaces, towers, bridges, churches, and theatres."

"And a store with a moving staircase."

"Yes. The continuous leather-belt contraption in Harrods allows one to admire the painted cherubs on their pretty dome ceiling. Oh, I *do* love the city of London."

"You told the other nannies you loved Canada too."

"Did I? Hmm. Well. I suppose the majestic Rockies have their own beauty. And the flatness of prairies are serene. As for the wilderness of the northern forests, well they are similar to the remote Scottish isles of Rum, Eigg and Muck but on a much larger scale. Now, what shall we do tomorrow? Perhaps a trip to Hyde Park Corner is in order. We can seek out the statue of the 1st Duke of Wellington. Winston, tell me, when did the Battle of Waterloo take place?"

"October 21, 1805."

"Wrong!"

"June 18, 1815"

"Correct. The Battle of Waterloo." Her voice sharpened, "Our guns blazed. The French fleet was sunk. And the statue of the 1st Duke of Wellington was made from a melted French cannon."

Afternoon, September 22, 1914
The Manager's Office, Banff Springs Hotel
Banff, Alberta

Mister Dimbleby ran his eye over the letter and turned pale in the face which made Miss Pidgeon's mouth twitch slightly. "Is there a problem, sir?"

"Goodness gracious! I almost shot Lord Fairfax's family pet!"

"You had every right to," his secretary replied in a soothing voice. "The appalling dog caused the horrific accident."

"Did he?"

Miss Pidgeon twisted her fingers. "Well, it might have been Donald Duncan's fault. I told him to remove that candle wall sconce straight away."

The manager looked at her properly for the first time. "Miss Pidgeon, the renowned Banff Springs Hotel would not lay itself open to such an appalling accident. Everyone knows it was the dog. I was trying to clarify if it was the *Fairfax* dog."

Miss Pidgeon's face turned scarlet.

Mister Dimbleby handed her the letter. "You know the drill, Miss Pidgeon. Follow protocol. Posters. Flyers. The Lost & Found column in the newspaper. Etcetera. Etcetera. Six weeks have elapsed. I do not hold much hope of recovering the animal. It is just a matter of formality."

"Yes sir. And sir—"

"Now what?"

"The raft of complaints is growing, sir."

"Raft of complaints? What raft of complaints?"

"Reports of eerie music coming from the Oak Room, sir. And regarding that Donald Duncan, sir sir—"

"Spit it out, Miss Pidgeon!"

"Mister Dimbleby. I hate to be a snitch. But that Donald Duncan is frightening all the maids. He is telling them the bride's spirit is still lingering."

"That old fool. Leave it to me."

The bride's death had shaken the hotel and ever since that fateful day, hair-raising tales of hauntings swirled around the servants' quarters. Lily stood nervously at the door of the Oak Room. "Whose idea wuz it t' draw straws?" she asked Ishbel who was busy brushing the lobby.

"Ethel's. No one wanted to clean in there."

"Sweet cheeses, I'd like t' see her doin' it."

"Don't think about it, Lily. Just get in there and do it."

Lily slowly turned the handle and peeked through the crack in the door. "Oh, gone are the merry voices that made this room alive, but now left eerily empty." She quickly closed the door and turned to face Ishbel. "The dead bride's spirit is in there. And and somethin' much worse is surfacin' from the ashes in that fireplace."

"Oh, don't be daft, Lily. Can you imagine what the poor groom would say if he heard you?"

"'Tis no daft." Lily's face a sheen of sweat. "*Even* the Vanderbilt's put the legs of their beds in dishes of salt water t' ward off evil spirits."

"You shouldn't believe everything you hear in the servants' quarters."

"Oh, Ishbel—"

"What?"

"*Pleeeeez!* Can yi do it for me? Yi has spades of courage."

Ishbel, her mind filled with self-reproach, guilt and grief over Bobby, had no time to worry about a ghost. She was running her brush along the tongue-and-grove mopboard when Mister Dimbleby walked into the Oak Room. "Toccata in D Minor." His eyebrows knotted together. "Where the hell is that organ?"

Ishbel tightened her grip on the handle of her broom. "Not in this room, sir."

Mister Dimbleby rotated his eyeballs to give himself a field vision of 270-degrees. Gothic Revival tapestries adorned the walls. A classic herringbone floor underfoot. A magnificent fireplace with a trundle of cold ash trickling through the grate. He turned his attention to Ishbel. "Girl, be fleet of foot. Get the Housekeeping Department to stoke up this fireplace, immediately."

"Yes, sir." She lifted her broom and set off down a corridor with openings to many parts of the Banff Springs Hotel.

Mister Dimbleby was prodding the dying embers when the old servant arrived with a bucket in each hand. "Oh, it is *you*, Donald. When did they move you to the Housekeeping Department?"

"About thirty-two years ago, sir," he replied cordially, "I was here with the old structure."

He nippily changed the subject. "Have the chimneys been swept?"

"Chimney sweeps pencilled in for the third week of September, sir," he replied.

Mister Dimbleby looked down at the servant who was lowering his rickety knees onto the hearth. "Donald, I was meaning to have a word. I little bird told me you were spreading ghost stories, frightening all our maids."

The old man shook the ash from the glowing embers. "If that little bird was a pigeon with a face like a prune, she should learn to keep her beak closed."

The manager's eyes expanded. "I hope you are not referring to our lovely Miss Pidgeon?" Suddenly, without warning, a raging fire whooshed up the chimney and old Donald struggled to his feet as fast as he was able. "'Tis the spirit of the dead bride causin' it!" He pulled a square of fabric from his pocket to dab his brow.

"What nonsense!" The manager could hardly draw breath. "Get out of my sight! *And* get yourself a decent handkerchief!"

The old servant grabbed his buckets and hightailed out of there faster than any man of his age could move. Mister Dimbleby turned his back to the fireplace which was now burning nicely. "Ghosts and ghouls!" The back of his legs warming. "Starting Monday, I will smarten them all up. I will fire one employee per week until this hogwash ends."

The door banged shut.

The gas lamps flickered.

The heat was gone. Mister Dimbleby turned around in time to see the glowing embers disintegrate into cold grey ash. His skin prickled with annoyance. He strode to the door and turned the brass handle. It rattled violently in his hand then fell to the floor. His fear unleashed in a temper tantrum and, red faced, he shouted, "Jammed doors! Faulty lights! Sloppy maintenance!" A sudden ruthless timbre whipped around him. Then worse. A square in the panelled-wall began to evaporate. Mister Dimbleby put his deathly-cold fingers on his cheeks and watched in horror as a ghostly-veiled woman floated out of the wall. Vaporous flowers began teeming from her hands: myrtle, lily of the valley, Alberta wild roses. Never-ending. Falling faster and faster until the words fell from his lips, "The dead bride." He swallowed hard and shook his head. "It was Mister Ross who let that Yorky get away with your murder! Mister Ross!

Not *meee!"* He wheeled around and banged on the door with the sides of his fists. "Help! Let Me Out!" The door began juddering then it flew wide open and the manager of the Banff Springs Hotel skyrocketed through the air, landing face-down on a flagstone floor made crooked by wear. He opened his eyes to Mister Ross's highly-polished shoes.

"Mister Dimbleby! Good gracious! What on earth happened, sir?"

"Nothing. I I suffered an optical illusion. Just just help me to my feet."

The assistant manager reached for his boss's elbow. "An optical illusion, sir?" he asked, apprehensively dusting down the front of his superior's jacket.

"Yes, damn it an optical illusion! That Vinho do Porto. Must must have swallowed it far too fast." He took a huge gulp of shuddery air and grabbed Mister Ross's shoulder, clinging on like a great floppy puppet.

"Sir, I think we need a wheelchair for you, sir—"

The important man spread his fingers tautly on the rim of his desk and looked across at his assistant. "Mister Ross, I want you to make arrangements to seal off the circular staircase where the tragedy took place," he said, the decision anchoring him. "I would like a solid wall of marble blocks built around it."

"A solid wall of marble blocks?" Mister Ross tried to hide his sharp breathing. "Built around the staircase, sir?"

"Yes. That will not be a problem it is but one of many staircases."

Mister Ross's words were drawn out, "Yes. Very well." He coughed into his fist. "Will that be all, sir?"

"No." Mister Dimbleby lifted his head from his dog-eared notebook. "I want you to gather our workforce together make sure that enfeebled Donald Duncan is present. Then threaten to fire him, or any other mumpish fool caught talking about that that silly ghost."

And so, the very next day, workmen arrived to seal off the limestone staircase across from the Oak Room door. And never again was a word spoken of the eerie happenings.

A stillness before the dawn. Then the upper-edge of the sun became visible from behind the imposing Banff Springs Hotel, and life in the mountains, valleys and streams emerged from a state of sleep. On the hotel estate, a tiding of magpies swooped above the bronze head of Sir William Cornelius Van Horne and an unkindness of ravens pecked at his yellowish-brown feet. Lily threw down her scrubbing brush discoloured with soot from the chimneys. "I hate this orful job!" The wind whipped at loose strands of her hair. "Whut duz a front door step need brightenin' for anyway? 'Tis a load of fiffle-faffle a waste of bluddy time."

"It is not." Ishbel swapped her scrubbing brush for the donkey stone. "It is essential."

"Essenshul! How?"

Salty beads of sweat ran down Ishbel's forehead as she scoured the step. "'Cause a slovenly doorstep is the first sign of a slovenly castle."

Lily howled with laughter and pushed up her cardigan sleeves. "Yir funny, Ishbel," she told her. "Hey, I meant t' tell yi. I saw a poster in the lobby, 'Reward for Lost Yorkshire Terrier."

The cold cut through Ishbel's clothes. "I know," she said quietly. "I watched Mister Dimbleby's secretary put it up. She told me it is coming down in seven days to avoid attracting unscrupulous owners of Yorkshire terriers."

Lily wrinkled her brow. "But the real Yorky would have the Fairfax coat of arms on his tag."

"If he's still wearin' it."

One of the magpies landed on the statue and preened its feathers. "Whut's a coat of arms anyway?" asked Lily, inspecting her red-raw knuckles.

Ishbel heaved the bucket onto the next step. "The symbols on a coat of arms depicts the identity and values of a family. It goes back to medieval times when knights wore them on their shields."

Lily pushed a strand of sweat-dampened hair behind her ear and gazed at her friend admiringly. "Whut are yi? The mother of all knowledge?"

"I read the pamphlet." Ishbel wiped her brow with the back of her sleeve. "If you look up at the stained-glass windows in Mount Stephen Hall, you'll see the coats of arms of past and present leaders of the great Canadian Pacific Railway."

Lily gasped. "Let's go look at them tonight."

"I can't. I have to write a letter to Winston. I got his address from the manager's secretary."

"Get away!" Lily squealed. "'Tis a wonder Miss Pidgeon gave it t' yi."

"Only 'cause I promised her the whole reward if I found Bobby."

"Whut? Are yi daft in the head?"

Ishbel's crumpled features bore witness to her life in guilty shambles. "Lily, the young lad lost his mother on the Titanic and now, thanks to my meddlin', he's lost Bobby. If I canny find that wee dog, my life will be ruined totally ruined! Oh, I coulda I woulda I shoulda—"

"Shoulda listened t' me!" Lily bristled with annoyance. "But yi didn't! So hush up 'fore I stot this scrubbin' brush orff yir noodle."

Ishbel opened her mouth to speak but stopped. All that mattered now was finding Bobby. That evening, before she went to bed, she picked up her pen and paper.

Dear Winston:

I am hoping you will remember me. I was a maid-of-all-work at the Banff Springs Hotel when you were a guest there. I am writing to tell you I found your little dog a few days after you left but, I am ashamed to say, he is lost again.

I only wanted to spoil him for a bit before he was put into a crate for the long journey home. But when he was in my care.

Summer was over and all the guests had departed. A few maids were kept on, scrubbing, mopping and polishing, and counting the days until the hotel closed for the season. Finally, that day came. The small group of maids, their sibilant voices echoing off the stone walls, waited at the bottom of the grand staircase for Mister Dimbleby.

Ishbel set her carpet bag and a much-used hatbox on the floor and rested her back against the bannister how different it felt now. The tropical plants all gone. The stuffed and mounted parakeet hidden under a dust cover. Marble busts of Lord Mount Stephen, Queen Victoria, and Cornelius Van Horne stacked in a corner. Her eyes moved to the magnificent plaid rug, gracing the entrance. The colours had come up grand, despite their ordeal with the fangle-dangle, ball-bearing vacuum and Lily uttering colloquial profanities. Her mind wandered back to her first day. *'Hold yar blabberin' tongue, Isabel!'* Ethel covered in floury dust. *'But my name isn't Isabel.'* She laughed at the memory and watched the dappled sunlight dance on the wall of armour. The sound of squeaky shoes. It was Mister Dimbleby and Mister Ross in black wool coats and bowler hats, the brims resting on their brows. "The time has come to bid farewell to another successful season," said Mister Dimbleby. "So gather up your possessions and follow me out." When everyone was assembled in the portico, the important man ceremoniously turned the big iron key and the Banff Springs Hotel slipped into hibernation for another long, cold, Canadian winter.

Their leave taken, Ishbel and Lily hurried down the front steps. The air crisp. The sun brilliant. Spray Avenue simmered under their feet and the mountains glimmered like new pennies until they came to the parting of ways. "Ishbel, I wish yi were comin' with me t' the Brett Sanatorium. Yi'll be workin' all on yir own in Canmore."

"Lily, I can't search for Bobby if I'm workin' in Banff."

"Oh, I know. Well. Don't go workin' yirself int' a swivet in that Mine Director's place."

Ishbel hooted. "Says you with fifty beds to make and twelve tubs to clean. Oh, did I mention Ethel?"

Lily's face flushed. "But she's not the supervisor no more. 'Tis lucky she's got a job after getting' caught in the woodshed with the delivery man and a case of hooch."

A leaf fluttered to the ground. "Lily, I want to say thank you for bein' a great friend when I needed one most."

Lily opened her arms wide and immediately banged her suitcase off Ishbel's carpet bag and hatbox. "Bluddy nuisance that hatbox. Duz yi want me t' store 't under my bed? Save yi takin' it t' Canmore and back."

"Oh, you're the best, Lily." She passed over the bulky container. "Well, I'd better get goin'. I've an errand to run before I catch my train." They hurried off in opposite directions, Lily calling over her shoulder, "Remember write me *every* week!"

Dave White's Groceries & Dry Goods on Banff Avenue smelt of furniture polish and paraffin heaters but it held a solid reputation for fair pricing and quality goods. Ishbel waited her turn to be served amid the noisy tourists, crying babies, and products showcased in long, narrow spaces. Her eyes wandered to the pressed-tin ceiling. Its silvery metallic design looked very avant-garde.

"Next please."

Ishbel presented herself at the highly-polished counter.

The assistant pushed up her puffy leg o' mutton sleeves. "What can I get you, Miss?"

"A bottle of Bayer's heroin, please. They've stopped sellin' it in Canmore."

"We haven't got it either. Bayer Pharmaceutical stopped making it. Apparently, folks were getting addicted. And it was the best cure we had for whooping cough. I pity those poor mothers," her mouth quirking. "They'll not get a wink of sleep if the fairies replace their bonnie babies with sickly changeling children." She adopted a winning smile. "Maybe you'd like to try a carbolic smoke ball? Pricey. But everyone from the German Empress to the Duke of Edinburgh are recommending it."

"I'll have to ask my dad first."

"Well, would you like anything else, dear? We have our Kellogg's Cornflakes on for 8 cents a pack today."

"No thanks."

A croaky male voice came from behind, "Is that a wee Scottish lilt ah'm hearin'?"

Ishbel swung around. An elderly gentleman in a tweed jacket was smiling at her through a soft white beard. Ishbel's face lit up like the sun showing its first rays in the morning. "Are you Scottish too, sir?"

"Aye, lass. Ah'm Doctor Macpherson fae the auld grey toon o' Aberfeldy."

Ishbel's eyes were immediately drawn to his black and yellow diced-hose socks.

He reacted with a twinkle in his eye. "A subtle way o' expressing ma personality."

She laughed reached for his hand. "My name's Ishbel McColl. From Cowdenbeath. It's north-east of Dunfermline. My dad and I immigrated to Canmore last year."

"Cowdenbeath tae Canmore," the elderly man shook her hand warmly, "then yer father's likely a miner?"

"He is. Unfortunately, he's not keeping well. He asked me to pick up a bottle of Bayer's heroin but they don't sell it anymore."

The old man nodded. "Ah heard ye ask for it. Has yer father been tae the doctor?"

"Um, my father doesn't," the words came out awkward and pale, "doesn't believe in doctors."

Doctor Macpherson laughed. "Och, miners can be like that. Never understood it, masel. They think if they put it tae the back o' their heid, they'll see aff their ailments."

Ishbel picked up her faded bag. "Well, it was very nice meeting you, Doctor Macpherson but I have to go now. I'm catching the six o'clock to Canmore."

The old man lowered his voice. "Listen lass, if ye can keep it tae yerself, ah'll give ye a bottle o' Bayer's heroin. Ma hoose is on the road tae the train station."

His offer took Ishbel by surprise. "Oh, thanks thanks very much. I won't breathe a word of it. Except to my dad."

Doctor Macpherson and Ishbel stepped onto Banff Avenue. "Let me tak yer bag, lassie," he said as they set off down the road, walking until they reached a Queen Anne style house with delicate-turned porch posts on Lynx Street. "Ah bide here, Ishbel."

"What a pretty house, Doctor Macpherson."

"Aye, no bad. Could dae wi a lick o' paint."

The rusty hinges shrilled on the metal gate. They walked up his path and Doctor Macpherson opened his front door. "Stand inside, oot o' the wind," he said and Ishbel waited in his dimly lit lobby, thick with stags' heads and portraits of Scottish kings and Scottish clansmen. Stacks of books alternating high and low were lined up against one wall. The plaque above read, 'A room without books is like a body without a soul.'

A few minutes elapsed before the old man reappeared. "Ah had twa bottles left. There ye go," he said with a crafty wink, "hide them inside yer bag noo."

Ishbel quietly expressed her thanks. "This will cheer my dad up no end," she said, opening her purse. "How much do I owe you, Doctor Macpherson?"

"Och, away and catch yer train, lass. If yer father asks where ye got it, tell him it's a wee present fae a man fae Aberfeldy."

Ishbel leaned out the window, feeling the reverberation of the train wheels under her feet, and the wind blowing in her face. A gust of soot purged from the firebox. A shriek erupted from the cast iron brake shoes. The train powered onto the Canmore spur line, subsided into a gentle roll then came to a complete stop but the airbrake pump continued to pant. Ishbel spotted her dad through the window. He was moving haltingly, his eyes scanning every carriage.

"Dad!" She pushed out the cumbersome door and hurried down the metal steps. Through twirls of wet steam and invasive odour of smoky grit, she threw herself into his waiting arms and hugged him like she hadn't seen him in a hundred years.

Finally, he pulled back. Looked at her face. "Ahh lass, lass, 'tis great to have you home and you looking so well! Here, let me take your bag." He slung his other arm around her shoulders, giving her another squeeze. "I have your supper ready and waitin'. I canny wait to hear all about your life in the grand hotel."

"And I canny wait to tell you. Oh," she remembered, "I got you two bottles of Bayer's Heroin."

"*Two* bottles!"

"Yes. But when it's gone, Dad, you'll have to switch to a Carbolic Smoke Ball. They're not making the Bayer's Heroin anymore."

"A Carbolic Smoke Bomb? Sounds like a booby trap to me."

They were still laughing when they left the station. "And you'll never guess where I got the Bayer's heroin."

"From Dave White's."

"No. From an old doctor who told me he was from Aberfeldy."

"*Aberfeldy* well I never!" he replied with a rumbling cough. "Tell me, lass. When do you start at the Mine Director's cabin?"

"In two days."

He nodded his head yes. "Then we'll get up with the lark tomorrow. See if we can track down that wee lost dog. You never know, lass, someone might know somethin'."

***

The gaping mouth of Lily's mailbox, forsaken and forlorn, today contained a personal letter, written and addressed just to her:

Miss Ishbel McColl
c/o Mine Director
The Mine Director's Cabin
Canmore, Alberta

Thursday, October 5th, 1914

Miss Lily Saunderson,
The Servant's Quarters
Brett Sanatorium
Spray Avenue
Banff, Alberta

Dear Lily,

I hope this letter finds you well and happy and settled into your new job at the Brett Sanatorium. As promised, here is all my news:

The Mine Director's cabin is hidden from Bridge Road by a screen of mature trees. It is on two levels with a door in the middle and windows on either side. It faces a lawn sliding down to the Bow River and when the wind blows up, the water smashes off the rocks and casts up white foam and spray. It is full of material wealth and humble elegance in the explosion of furnishings and brightly-patterned wallpaper. On weekdays, it's geared to the pleasures of the Directors of the Canmore Mining Company. On weekends, the Mine Director's family take the train here from Calgary. The little back garden, surrounded by berry bushes, has the remains of a flower border and a vegetable patch. Behind a trellis, little stone steps lead from the kitchen door to the washing line.

Alas, I don't have a room to myself. I have to sleep in a settle-bed partitioned off from the kitchen by a folding screen. But I was given a lovely Witney blanket (practically new) and a small blanket box to keep my things in. The kitchen has a fancy ventilating Kitchener range. It roasts, bakes, boils, steams and provides constant hot water enough to supply a bath every single day (but I'm only allowed one on Monday nights.) From the kitchen, it extends in a long wing into a dining room with a table that seats twelve. If you continue through the dining room, you come out in a tiny square hall with a long case clock flanked by two doors, one leads to a big sitting room with a large stone fireplace. The other leads to the Mine Director's small office. Upstairs, there's three bedrooms. One faces west, so when I clean it in the morning, I can admire my Cascade Mountain. I work 16-hour days and report to the Mine Director's wife. She's pinned my list of chores to her kitchen wall (painted haint blue to repel flies) and I have to tick them off as I go: wash/hang/iron the clothes and bedding, polish the windows, dust the furniture, scrub the floors, apply blacking to the grates, apply blacking to the stove, set the table, wash the dishes, whiten the doorstep, Brasso the doorknobs I'm rushed off my feet. On my first day, she looked me up and down and said, 'Ishbel, your watchwords are: no pilfering and no lollygagging!' I felt terrible. What kind of person does she think I am? Anyway, thankfully, she makes the meals for her own family, and hires a cook when they entertain. The cook is called Mrs Bloxham. I haven't met her yet. I hope we get along 'cause she's the only company I've got. I'm not allowed visitors.

The day after I arrived in Canmore, Dad and I went to the Northwest Mounted Police cabin on Main Street to report Bobby missing. The officer who lives there said he would keep an eye out. Dad, bless his heart, surprised me with a tin of black paint and a roll of paper so I could make 'REWARD' posters. I try to do five a night. They are so time consuming I have an ache in my wrist. Tomorrow is my half-day off so we're going to hang them all over Canmore. The weather is getting colder. I worry about Dad being outside for too long, but he says the fresh air is the best cure for his black lung. Well, that's all my news for now.

Miss you lots,
Ishbel xx

PS: It looks like the miners are going on strike again. Hopefully, it won't last long.

***

Back in London, England, the butler of Duncraig House ascended the wide, brightly-carpeted staircase. Sunshine filtered through an enormous stained-glass window and bounced off the silver tray in his white-gloved hand. His other hand clutched the mahogany handrail until he reached the top landing where portraits of Fairfax ancestors adorned the walls and an Azerbaijani carpet ran down the centre of a gleaming wood floor. The scent of polish hit his wide nostrils, forcing him to pull out his spotless handkerchief and blow his nose. He stuffed the rumpled linen back in his pocket and knocked on Winston's door. As usual, the one opposite flew wide open.

"Yes Webster?" Nanny Patterson's voice was curt.

He raised the small silver tray, an envelope peeking over its edge. "For young Master Fairfax."

The door creaked open. Winston stuck his head out and pushed up his glasses. "A letter! For me!"

The elderly man smiled down at the fresh-faced child. "Quite so, Master Fairfax, and the postmark tells me it came *all* the way from Canada."

Miss Ishbel McColl
c/o Servants' Quarters
Banff Springs Hotel
Spray Avenue
Banff, Alberta
Canada

Friday, September 11, 1914

Master Winston Fairfax, Esq.
Duncraig House
35 Duke Street
London
England

Dear Winston:

I am hoping you will remember me. I was a maid-of-all-work at the Banff Springs Hotel when you were a guest there. I am writing to tell you I found your little dog a few days after you left but, I am ashamed to say, he is lost again.

I only wanted to spoil him for a bit before he was put into a crate for the long journey home. But when he was in my care, a terrible accident occurred and Bobby was wrongly accused. I thought his life was in danger so I made a foolish decision that I'll regret to my dying day.

When my job here finishes, I'm movin' to the nearby town of Canmore so I can search for your little dog. (For reasons I'd prefer not to mention, there's a good chance he's in or around that area.) My dad is goin' to help me and we are committed to searching every nook and cranny until we find him. Winston, I'm so very sorry for what has happened. I hope all's well, and you're happy to be home. As soon as I have some news, I'll write again. I promise.

Sincerely,
Ishbel McColl

PS: I'll be gone from the Banff Springs Hotel by the time you get this letter so I've enclosed my new address: Miss Ishbel McColl, c/o Mine Director, The Mine Director's Cabin, Canmore, Alberta, Canada.

Winston clutched the correspondence in both hands and somersaulted across his bed. "Nanny Patterson, Bobby is alive!"

***

A pithy smell of disinfectant hung in the entrance hall of the Brett Sanatorium, wafting under the ceiling and along the buttermilk-coloured walls leading to the bright and pristine hospital wards to the right, and the tastefully-decorated private residence to the left. Lily pulled back the temporary screen to inspect the small geometric floor tiles. The boiled linseed oil had dried nicely. Time to give it a wax polish.

Ethel wrapped the straps of her rubber apron around her waist. "Jeez," she heaved a sigh, "I've gone from playin' the boss at a fancy hotel, ter skivvyin' in a blinkin' sanatorium."

"The rise n' demise of the infamous Ethel Finch."

"Aw, shut yar face, Saunderson, and pull that bloomin' screen. I hate folks gawkin' at my bum when I'm tryin' ter work."

"Sweet cheeses, Ethel, yi wiggle yir big bum at the Cascade dancehall every week."

"Better a big bum tha a boney wee arse like yars!" Ethel drew the partition herself, just as the front door was opening

The rhythmic tapping of Mrs Brett's shoes lured Ethel and Lily to kneel down and peek under the room divider. "Home at last, dear!" She greeted her husband with a little peck on the cheek.

"Yes, thank goodness." The bright hew on Doctor Brett's face increased as he laboured out of his bulky jacket. "I will never understand," his elbow nearly knocked the giant aspidistra off its pedestal, "why Rutherford made Edmonton the capital. Growing a province is hard enough without trailing up there all the time."

"Hmm," Mrs Brett's eyes twinkled with mischief, "perhaps Rutherford did it to annoy you, dear."

The doctor grimaced.

The 'invisible' maids stifled their giggles.

"Oh, I am only teasing the Lieutenant-Governor of Alberta." Mrs Brett kissed him again. "You make us all very proud, dear."

Doctor Brett took a closer look at his wife. "Forgive me, Louise, but you do not look yourself today." Suddenly, the double doors of his private residence flew wide open and Doctor Brett was taken aback by a well-dress lady bustling into the entrance hall.

"Er," Mrs Brett's expression changed from bland to frosty. "This is Lady Clementine Victoria Corrinwallis, dear. From New York. She arrived this afternoon."

Doctor Brett's smile involved his whole face. "I am delighted to meet you, madam. Your father and I shared many a happy—"

The attractive visitor threw up her hands. "*Please.* I simply cannot bear another account of father's schoolboy years."

The maids stared at each other with saucer-sized eyes.

The important man rose above the woman's rudeness. "Lady Clementine, you obviously know more about me than I do about you. I hope we can rectify that during your stay."

Lady Clementine shook her curls no. "It is inappropriate for a lady to stay in a hospital-for-the-incurables."

"Madam, our establishment is sizable, encompassing a hotel and a hospital. The hospital part promotes health-restoration and rejuvenation. And most patients walk out on their own two feet."

"Actually, I would pre-*fer* to stay," she stretched her lips in a condescending smile, "at the Banff Springs Hotel."

"Unfortunately, it is closed for the winter." Mrs Brett's hands gripped her husband's jacket. "We are the only year-round one in Banff."

She flashed them a hostile glare "But I cannot possibly write to my friends in Europe and America from *this* place?"

Doctor Brett straightened his back. "May I ask why not?"

"Your stationery! It is embossed with the awkward word, 'SANATORIUM'. Everyone would think I have a chronic disease. Or worse a mental disorder."

Doctor Brett's posture relaxed and he turned on his warm, professional manner. "I understand your predicament. There is a train to Montreal in one hour. I will have my stableman bring the horse and buggy to our entrance, right away."

"Actu-*ally,*" Lady Clementine made a little face and patted her pearls. "It is an utterly inconvenient and totally unsuitable. But I plan to stay."

Mrs Brett gulped. "May I be so bold to ask why?"

"If you must know. The reason I came to Banff is to reconnect with a lost suitor."

Being the wife of the Lieutenant-Governor of Alberta, Mrs Brett was skilled at listening to all sorts of nonsense without flinching. "A lost suitor?" She smiled benignly.

"Quite," replied Lady Clementine. "He is a man of purpose and fortitude. Conservative. Cultured. Refined. A Princeton graduate of independent means who moves in the higher echelons of society. We have known each other frightfully well since childhood. Our families were part of a close-knit, upper-class set." Lady Clementine touched her forehead with the back of her hand. "The pong of your disinfectant and the reek of your floor polish are making me quite queasy."

Mrs Brett maintained the formal courtesy that distinguished her marriage to Doctor Brett. "Then let us go and be comfortable in my parlour, my dear." With an eye roll to her husband, she ushered Lady Clementine towards a room with heavily-patterned wallpaper. Robert Brett beat a grateful retreat.

Lady Clementine was offered the palmetto-green brocade chair. Mrs Brett took the one opposite and for a few moments they played pass-the-frosty smile. Then Mrs Brett said, "Perhaps you will feel better if you get the whole story off your chest. Be assured it will go no further." A heavy-net curtain stirred from an open window and an oriental floral fragrance drifted from a vase of Casablanca lilies. Lady Clementine tucked her vertiginous heels slightly to the rear, and began pouring her heart out. The maids remained gleefully silent listening in.

"It was a delightful east-coast summer's day and I was wearing my new sparkly high-heeled shoes and a dress with a skirt that whirled when I twirled." Lady Clementine's voice took on a softer tone. "We, my gentleman suitor and I, were strolling hand-in-hand down 5th Avenue on our way to an afternoon tea dance at the Waldorf-Astoria when we accidentally crossed the paths with his ghastly friend horrid Hussey." She touched the tip of her nose with her lace handkerchief. "The cad is an interfering rapscallion! He was completely certain we would enjoy. Of all things. The Sportsmen's Exposition! Before I could put my foot down, I was hauled off to Madison Square Garden."

Mrs Brett's eyebrows rose in genteel astonishment. "Oh you poor dear your sparkly high-heeled shoes—"

"Oh, it gets worse. The pair of them ended up in cahoots with two toughies from Western Canada the Brewster boys." She drew a deep breath and exhaled audibly to express her despair. "One thing led to another and, before I could stop it, they were all off on a silly horse trip out west. Horrid Hussey returned a year later but, alas and alack, my handsome suitor did not. I have not seen nor heard from him in *years*."

"Before he left, did he tell you he loved you?"

"Well, he never exactly used the 'L' word but he did everything to make me happy and content."

"Are you still in love with him?"

"My desire to say 'no' interferes with my 'yes'. So whatever love means, I rather think I am." Lady Clementine clutched her throat with both hands and stared at Mrs Brett with wide eyes. "His impudence makes me fume. His ambivalence makes me bristle. But I refuse to consider myself spurned and rejected. No, no, no."

"So you have come to Banff in the hopes of reconnecting with him?"

"Yes." She flexed the muscles on the sides of her mouth. "And rest assured he will not slip through my fingers a second time."

Lily Saunderson
The Servants' Quarters
The Brett Sanatorium
Spray Avenue
Banff, Alberta

October 9, 1914

Miss Ishbel McColl
c/o Mine Director
The Mine Director's Cabin
Canmore, Alberta

Dear Ishbel:

It wuz great t' get a newsy letter from a cabin where the windows gleam and the doorknobs are brasso'd bright. Ha-ha. Apart from yir pernickety boss, sounds like yi landed yirself a half-decent position thank goodness.

Sweet cheeses, I'm not so lucky. I got stuck sharin' a room with Ethel and she snores like a banshee. Between her and the terrible cold last night, I couldn't sleep a wink. Yir lucky yir beside a fancy Kitchener range. I have t' fill my stone piggy with boilin' water and wrap my nightgown round it 'fore I can put it on. Then I put on: 2 pairs of knickers, 2 pairs of socks, and my pink woolly cardy. 'Tis murder. That aside, 'tis been fun 'and games around here (where wealthy folks come t' take the waters). Yesterday, this posh woman arrived from New York. Her name is Lady Clementine Corrinwallis. She's on a mission t' track down a missin' suitor. She is pretty as a picture but as ill-tempered as they come. She wanted t' go ridin' after breakfast and took a hissy fit 'cause the stable lad couldn't produce a horse with an 'enchanting' trot. She has him all confused. Ha-ha.

Changing the subject, I read Mine #2 went on strike yesterday and I thought about yir dad. I hope they won't be out too long. And I hope yi find Bobby soon. I always say a little prayer for yi when I'm buffin' the tiles.

Miss yi lots. Write soon.
Lily

Morning, October 10, 1914
Wild Bill Peyto's Cabin
The Wilds of Alberta
A bowl of burning tobacco jutted from Peyto's lips as he rattled open the latest copy of the Dominion Illustrated:

TOURIST ATTRACTION
AT THE BANFF SPRINGS HOTEL

During the CPR Annual General Meeting yesterday, Mister Dimbleby, the manager of the prestigious Banff Springs Hotel, talked about the astounding fossil exhibited in his hotel lobby. "This half-billion-year-old wonder-of the-world is guaranteed to attract the paying public when I open for the season in 1915," he told the delighted Board of Directors.

Keep on top of upcoming events and a lot more with the Dominion Illustrated.

Peyto, foaming and seething, balled up the newspaper and hurled it across the room. "Bobster, keep the hell away from my feet," he yelled then promptly tripped over his dog. "O.F!" He hauled himself off the floor and stuck his pipe back between his teeth. "If I had any sense, I would kick yar little ass outta that door."

The little dog stared up questioningly.

Peyto immediately felt remorseful. He rubbed his brow until his eyes focused. "Sorry, Bobster. Just keep the hell away from my feet, eh." Intense black clouds rolled across the sky. A cutting north wind tore at the trees. The heaviest branches creaked and cracked. Peyto advanced up the mist-covered mountain, his boots chomping into the icy surface and his Yorky bounding at his heels. "Time for a break, Bobster." The mountain-man stopped in his tracks, threw down his sack and plucked the pipe from his pocket. "For a little dog, ya've no trouble keepin' up, eh?" He picked up a twig and waved it in front of Bobby's nose. "Go fetch, Bobster!" he commanded.

Bobby toed and froed, lifting bits of twigs with his teeth and dropping them by his master's feet. When Peyto had a satisfactory pile, he struck a match. The sparks spat and the flames took. "Haah haaah *choo!*" He looked up from scooping snow into his empty syrup tin. The wind was licking at Bobby's fur.

"Bobster! Come! Sit by the fire!" he hollered, straightening the bent-wire handle before setting the can on the heat. The shivering dog came towards him. "Atta-boy!" Peyto held his breath against the wafting smoke and cut a shaving from a square of cheese. "Are ya lackin' the cold-weather adaptations of yar wild ancestors?" he asked, holding the titbit under the little dog's nose.

Bobby shook his coat and licked it up.

Peyto added cured leaves to the steaming liquid then pulled out his knife. "I think ya need a coat, Bobster." He yanked at his heavy trouser leg, ripping off a piece of twill, revealing a cleaner pair of trousers underneath. Pipe still between his teeth, he scooped up the little dog and bound his middle twice before tying off with a bit of string. Bobby's eyes peeked out from underneath the haphazard covering. Peyto grinned down at him with his whole face. "Are yar a lucky little bastard, Bobster?"

Arf!

Peyto patted his dog's back with a comforting rhythm then turned his attention to filling his mug. "Bobster," an intense smell of stewed-tea permeated the air, "next week, I'm headin' into Banff to see my mates. If we throw back a few too many, we'll spend the night in my storage hut. Don't worry. 'Tis prime real estate I put a window and a stovepipe in it last year." Peyto's cheeks bulged with a hunk of bread. "I'll clean off my cobwebby chair and open a bottle of moose meat for ya. Can't stand that tripe myself so ya can have the lot." He looked up at the sky, lifted his foot, and pressed a log further into the flames. "Okay, pal! Time we got goin'."

By the end of that day, Peyto had checked all his trap lines. Pelts taken during the winter, after the big-game season, were thick, furred and sure to fetch a pretty penny. Happily, they headed for home. The forest was thick with trembling aspen and Engelmann spruce. "Bobster," Peyto's breath frosted the air, "'tis likely the eyes of curious wildlife are following us so keep close to my heels, eh." Branches failed threateningly and blue-green foliage danced wildly on woody-stemmed shrubs. Bent against the elements, man and dog moved on in a forceful way until Bobby halted under a tree that was weakened by ice and riddled with termites. *Come on*, Bobster!" A swift blast of wind gave rise to a stinging spray of dust. Peyto stretched forth an arm to grasp his dog. A deafening crack. An almighty splinter. The disfigured whitebark pine came crashing down. Bobby clambered towards his master circled, licked and tugged on his sleeve. The moaning man opened his eyes and shook his woozy head. A hoarse whisper, "Go, Bobster, go."

He pushed away a fractured branch then threw a twig as best he could. Then another. "Go. Bobster. Go."

Arf! Bobby sat down to watch them fly across his head.

Peyto looked up at the moon, melting to nothingness behind a ghostlike cloud. "Life sure chooses its moments to shove a man to the g-ground." Then far off and faintly, the sound of barks snatched up by the wind. The Bobster was gone. Gagging at the pungent smell of pine, the injured man hoped against hope his little dog would return with help.

Defying bitter wind, pellets of frozen snow and biting hunger, Bobby bounded down trails, sprinted across streams, and scurried over rocks until he was stopped in his tracks by a pair of enormous boots. The thick-bearded man gawped down at the little dog with teeth clamped solidly to the hem of his pants. He shook his leg vigorously. "Piss off *you* rat-faced mongrel!" he cried but Bobby held on rigidly. Tugged and pulled vigorously. Repeatedly. Bizarrely.

All of a sudden, the big man began to laugh. "You win. Lead the way. Goddamn stupid mutt."

Fractured moonlight falling between the clouds. Winter foliage rustling in the wind. A panting dog against his brow. Peyto's eyelids flickered open and his heart sank to the pit of his stomach.

"Well, well, well. Look what we have here!" Boris Klumpenbovur tweaked his slouch cap with the black-cock feather, and tapped Peyto's head with the tip of his unlaced boot. "You goddamn cross-eyed lousy rat-faced bastard you goddamn blood-suckin' son of a bitch!" Peyto spun his head barely avoiding Boris's spit. "You nearly done me in with that goddamn stupid trap!" He made an obscene gesture with both hands. "You're a good-for-nothing &%%#$#*@!!! If you think I'm here to save your scrawny carcass, you're shit outta luck, mate!"

The night's whisper rustled the treetops. Cold wind nipped at his cheeks. Peyto strained to lift his head and bled a stream of sweat his only hope was walking away. "Boris, Boris! Stop! Gimme a chance, m-mate. *Boris!*" he cried, a jagged breath escaping his lips. "Help me now and I'll *I'll—*"

The big man, shoulders hunched inside his coonskin jacket, stopped in his tracks and turned. "You'll what?"

Peyto's heart banged like a hammer. He looked up at the man with the bulbous and bumpy nose. "I'll g-give ya," his voice frail but determined, "my my banjo ukulele."

The offer was enough to make Boris walk back. "Your banjo ukulele!? Hell, man. You must be shit scared."

"Shit scared of whut? Dyin' out here or listenin' to ya playin' my my m-musical instrument?"

"Yar takin' the piss."

"Boris, give me a chance, mate. Haul this log off my leg and g-get me into Banff, eh?"

The grizzly neighbour's chin came up and he scratched his wiry bristles. "I've always dreamt of ownin' a ukulele." A hunting owl hooted in the distance. He squatted down. Eyeballed the load. Wrapped his burly arms and great paws around more than half the tree trunk. Breathing agitated. Anger rising

"Boris. Yar doin' g-great, man."

"Shut your pie hole!" The great big fellow gripped the load with all the pressure-power of jaw-locking plyers. Drew air into his stomach. Locked his abdominals. Paused then pushed through both legs. Grunting. Creaking. The weight began to lift.

Peyto's spirits soared. He grabbed his gammy leg with both hands, dug his good heel into the ground pushed dragged shuffled. A bloodcurdling cry broke above his head and he forced a painful turn at the same time the tree trunk and branches came crashing down. Dirt and twigs flew high into the night sky and debris rained down upon Peyto and his dog, both yowling like howler monkeys. Boris ran his sleeve down his face. You're a helluva a lucky bastard," he uttered, scooping Peyto up and slinging him over one shoulder. Bobby bounded gleefully ahead.

A fresh blanket of snow hushed the mountains and soothed the landscape, and a pattern of teeny-weeny paw prints and great-big boot prints grew and glistened on the trail as they all headed for Banff, iced and sparkling.

During the weeks that followed, Wild Bill Peyto came to realise his storage hut in Banff was better suited to storing sling-ropes and pack-saddles than housing himself and his dog. He was gazing up at the patch of damp on his ceiling, now the size of a pantry-clock face when he was roused by a knock on the door. He tucked his shirt into his trousers and tried to flatten his hair that was up like a haystack. "Who goes here?" he cried.

"'Tis me Pearl! I've brought a dish from Ma."

"Ah, Mrs Brewster-Moore!" Peyto's head fell back on the chair. "Come away in."

The woman in her mid-thirties opened the door, stared at the mess and gagged at the stink. "Peyto your kettle. It's boiling mad!" she exclaimed through the steamy space. "Here let me get it for you." She shoved her mother's cast-iron dish through the pile of junk on the plank table, lifted the hem of her woollen skirt, and hopped over Peyto's bad leg resting on an empty crate. "I need a cloth I *need* a cloth!" She looked around the room. "*Peyto* I need a flippin' cloth to lift it off the blinkin' stove!"

"Keep yar hair on keep yar hair on." Peyto yanked at the frayed hem of his pant leg and ripped off a piece of fabric, exposing another pair of trousers. "Here ya go!" he cried, tossing the coarse cloth at Pearl's head.

"For the love of mankind do you not own a tea towel?" She lifted the kettle and looked around for a place to put it.

Peyto stretched his neck, rough with stubble. "Is that Bella's Irish stew?" He ogled the dish.

"It is." Pearl rested the kettle on a trivet and pulled a square of paper from her pocket. "I got my orders to read this aloud," she said, rolling her eyes.

Dearest Peyto,

'May the good saints protect you, and bless you today. And may troubles ignore you, each step of the way.' That's an Oirish blessin' from Ma Brewster. Enjoy yir stew, lad. It'll save yi a day o' chuckin-it-all-in-the-pan-and-seein'-what-happens. Keep oyt av trouble and get better soon.

Love from Ma Brewster

"Bless her. Here, pass me that note," he chuckled, folding it into a square and slipping it into his shirt pocket. "The ladies of Banff sure are spoilin' me rotten with home cookin'. But nothin' compares to my Bella's Irish stew. Yar family's fair good to me."

Pearl laughed. "And you to us."

"Well, we share a bit of history, eh. I finished my cabin the day ya were born."

"So you keep tellin' me." She picked up the Crag & Canyon from the dirt floor and threw it onto Peyto's lap. "Were you readin' this?"

"Aye. I was readin' the obituaries. Strange. Everyone is dyin' in alphabetical order."

"Very funny." She unbuttoned her coat. "Seriously, how are you doin'?"

Peyto lifted his leg off the crate and slid the other heel back to bend his knee. "I won't flaunt my troubles. No doubt ya've plenty of yar own."

"Right. Then I'll brew us a cup of tea." Pearl removed the chipped lid from the teapot. "You like it strong, don't you?" She scooped a heap of leaves out of the caddy.

"Strong with a wee nip." He smiled up at his visitor. "To cheer my little heart up."

"Hell, my little heart can do with a bit of cheerin' too. Where is it?"

"Behind the syrup tin."

Pearl examined the half bottle of Old Fitzgerald. "It's got a caution label on it."

"It's harmless, tastes like juicy fruit gums."

"If you say so." Pearl added a splash to both mugs. "You know Philip left this morin', eh?"

Peyto whistled. "His conscription came quickly."

"And they've only just extended it to married men." She gave a shaky groan. "The train's takin' him to the boat that'll take him to France and the brutal trenches."

What could he say to make her feel safe and less worried? He slurped his tea. "Together, we'll all get through this."

Pearl was silent for a moment. "My heart aches so bad." Her tears welled quickly. "I might never see him again." She wiped her eyes with the backs of her hands but the hot tears came back fast and burned her cheeks. "And and before he left I I made it worse." She grappled inside her pocket for her handkerchief and blew her nose, but the tears came again.

Peyto's pupils dilated. "Pearl. 'Tis the first time I've seen ya bubblin'. Sit down. Drink yar tea, woman."

Pearl sat down, unsure of the rickety crate collapsing under her weight.

Peyto touched her arm in a kindly way. "Ya said ya made it worse. How?"

"We," Pearl sucked in a large noisy breath, "Philip and I. We were on the station platform. He, he looked so brave. But I sensed what he was feelin' so I hardly dared look at him." There was a small silence. "Then without warning the train whistle blew. Sniff. Philip threw his canvas duffle bag over one shoulder." Her eyes misted over. "He put his hand under my chin and tilted my face towards him. 'Pearl,' he whispered, ever so gently. 'Will you miss me when I am gone?'

Oh, *Peyto*, I wanted to tell him I will hurt like hell. I wanted to tell him I will miss him with every fibre of my bein'. I wanted to tell him I love him ever-so-much. But our clasped-hands fell apart and I I—"

"Whut?"

Pearl took a deep defeated breath. "Thumped him with my fist." Her chin wobbled. "You've gotta blinkin' cheek,' I told him, 'hoppin' off to war and leavin' me with all these blinkin' chores. But don't worry, Philip, I'll be nicely occupied. Thanks.' Peyto, before I could eat my words, I was cut off by the stationmaster's whistle. A moment later. He was gone. I let him go without a proper kiss, a last wave of farewell." She buried her face in her hands.

"'Tis bad luck to wave a man off to war."

Pearl looked up, hoping it was true. "You said that to make me feel better?"

Peyto laughed a little and nudged her arm.

She covered her hot cheeks with the palms of her hands. "Oh, what the hell's wrong with me?"

"Ya grew up with six of the rowdiest brothers in Alberta." He took a thoughtful puff on his pipe. "Stands to reason yar lackin' in the lovey-dovey department." He gave her a very direct look. "And the things we feel most deeply. Well. That's the hardest stuff to say."

Pearl nodded but her expression remained forlorn.

"The days'll fall off the calendar and yar man'll be back 'fore ya know it. Hey, remember when ya threw him outta the house?"

Pear's smile was tremulous. "And what's that got to do with the price of eggs?"

Peyto chuckled and accidentally slapped his bad leg. "Ouch!"

She hid her amusement. "Are you okay?"

"Yeah, yeah. Give me a laugh. Tell me again what happened that day."

She gave a slight involuntary grimace and reached for her tea. "Well. I was bathin' my mucky wee nephew in the kitchen sink when a knock came to the door. I opened it to a bloke with a city-boy haircut and a silky cravat." She giggled at the memory. "Said his name was Mister Moore and he had come to see my brothers. Well, Bill and Jim were due back so, of course, I let him in. I was goin' about my business, givin' the bairn a hasty wash, while the man with the 'cultivated-qualities' sauntered around like he owned our place the next thing I knew, a great swoosh of sudsy water flew from the basin and landed all down the front of him! Oh, *Peyto,* if you'd seen his expression the little lad and I were

98

squealin' with laughter. I threw him a dishrag so he could dry himself off." She let out a broken laugh. "And he said."

"Whut?"

"'Miss Brewster,'" he upped his posh-plummy accent, "'dishes are washed in the kitchen. Children are washed in the bathroom.' *Cheeky* monkey! I put the bairn down, picked up my broom, and chased him outta that door and right down that path."

"Then, if I remember rightly, yar Ma arrived." Peyto masked a blade of humour. "Ignorant to what had happened, and him bein' yar brothers' biggest and best business partner, she invited him back in for dinner."

"And by the time the figgy-duff reached the table," Pearl's face shone with rapturous joy, "I was head-over-heels in love with the bloke with the city-boy haircut and a silky cravat." She slid a look at Peyto who seemed preoccupied with his pipe.

"I'm listenin'," he said with a grin.

Pearl's eyes sparkled. "After that, Philip and I spent all of our free time together. Horse-back rides on the mountain trails and moonlight nights around the campfire. I'd never felt so alive. I was drunk on love."

Peyto's eyes glazed over. He leaned across the arm of his chair and lifted the lid off the Irish stew. It looked thick and meaty and the aroma was highly pleasing. He swept his trigger finger around the rim and drew up tiny drafts of gravy as Pearl continued to share her memories.

"Philip would walk me home and we would linger on the doorstep." She cupped her hand to her mouth to hide her smile. "No word of a lie, Peyto, the minute he swooped in for a kiss, Ma would pop her head out of the window. 'Pearl Brewster cum inside dis pure minute!' she would yell because she was worried I'd get my heart broken. I was only seventeen. Philip was ten years older. I was workin' class. He was rich and well-educated."

"Well-educated in books maybe," Peyto struck Pearl a thwack on the knee, "but ya've always had the smarts to hold yar own, girl."

Pearl nodded. "Oh, but it was a bloomin' awful time. When he asked for my father's permission to marry me, Dad said no. I said yes. And Ma said, 'Mark me words, lassie, you'll suffer de repercussions av marryin' outside av yisser class!' I replied, 'Class My Arse.' I'd heard my brothers sayin' it. Well Ma took a hairy fit. She chased me around the kitchen, wallopin' me at every chance with her dishrag." Pearl doubled up with laughter. "But thankfully they came to trust him, and Philip Moore and I got married on a snowy day in the January at St. George's-in-the-Pines."

"I know. I was there." Peyto ripped off another piece of trouser leg and blew his nose with the harsh fabric.

"Oh, right." Pearl smiled. "And the followin' year, our Edmée was born."

"How old is that Brewster baby now?"

"Eight." Pearl moved to the window and gazed out with her elbows on the sill. "Hey, what's that flappin' above your door?" she asked, the sun shining on her skin.

The mountain man pushed himself out of his chair and hobbled towards the little window. "Oh, that. That's my *'Ain't it Hell'* house plate."

"I like it. Better than *Rose Cottage* danglin' from two brass chains. That wouldn't suit ya." Then she remembered, "Hey, did you know Jim was out fishin' with the brother of the King of England?"

"Aye, I heard he was hobnobbin' with royalty."

"He was present when the Duke announced the war. A witness to history." Pearl rested her back against the wall. "Hey, Peyto, you must be dyin' to get back to work?"

Peyto shuffled back to his chair. "Goin' back a week on Monday." He unfolded the foil inside the flat tin of tobacco and the earthy smell crept up his nose. "Said I'd help out the Park Warden he's got a big grizzly sayin' no to hibernation."

"So the pair of you are gonna catch him, tuck him up, and sing him a lullaby?"

"Somethin' like that," Peyto tittered, pressing a pinch into his pipe with his thumb. "Then I'm takin' up arms for the country. I've signed up for the machine gun brigade."

"You've got to be kiddin' me! Peyto, you're nearly fifty."

"Well. An old man's gotta do, what an old man's gotta do!"

"S'pose. Hey, there's another old man takin' stock of his life. Canon Harrison. He's joined up as Army Chaplain."

"Strewth! One dronin' sermon from him and all armies will run for the hills."

Pearl stifled her giggles. "Oh, Peyto, you'll never get into heaven."

Bobby head sniffed around the side of the chair. Arf!

"*Oh!* Dear Lord!" Pearl jumped from her seat. "I didn't know you had a dog in here." The Yorky swept a soft welcome against her legs.

"This is Bobster. Now I've signed up, he's lookin' for a good home." A lightbulb went off in Peyto's head. "His needs are simple and easily met. Would ya like him?"

"Hell no."

"I'd eat my hat if he gave ya any trouble."

Annoyance sharpened Pearls voice. "I said. No."

Bobby yawned, fur dishevelled. His little black nose twitched. Pearl bent to stroke his fur and the little dog leaned into her ankles for more. "You're as cute as a bug's ear, Bobster, but I share my house with a crusty old cat."

Peyto's expression reflected his dashed hopes. "Um, maybe ya could ask around town. I'd sure appreciate it, Pearl," he said, pipe between his teeth.

"Would you like me to start with the Banff Springs Hotel? They'll be needin' a dog to guard that fancy fossil."

Peyto looked up, his dark eyes animatedly alert. "Ya heard then?"

"God, yes. When the most-popular, long-standin' guide gets fired from Banff's grandest hotel, news travels fast. You gave the town somethin' to chew on, believe you me."

Peyto snorted. "That pig-faced, dumbass-sod stole it from me but the arrogant bastard won't be keepin' it!"

"Oh, don't get yourself all fired up." Pearl squeezed his shoulder. "You can't take your relic to France, so you might as well leave it up there. 'Til the war's over."

Peyto felt himself relax slightly.

"Hey, it's gettin' a bit dark in here. Let me light this rusty old lamp 'fore I go." She took a match to the wick.

Peyto turned in his chair. "I like my rusty old lamp and there's plenty paraffin in it." The flame surfaced under the chipped-glass shade and threw a pool of light around the small space.

"That's better," said Pearl. "Bright and cheery. Now, you'll need a shave. I'll fill your ewer."

Peyto ran his hand over his stubbly chin. "Naw, woman. I'm fine."

"Then what's this?" She passed him a chipped bit of mirror. "A baby bear attached to your jaw?"

"Okay. Okay. Ya win. I'll shave in the mornin.'"

"Well mind you do." She rested the pitcher back in its bowl and buttoned up her coat.

"Thanks for droppin' in, eh. And I much appreciate yar offer to find Bobster a good home."

Pearl rolled her eyes and closed the door against the pipe-smoking man and the yawning Yorky. Outside, the stroppy wooden house-plate swayed in the breeze and she could hear Peyto talking to his dog, "Ma Brewster always had a soft spot for me, Bobster. I'll read ya her note. *'Dearest Peyto,'* he chuckled. *'May the good saints protect you, and bless you today. And may troubles ignore you, each step of the way.'*"

Morning, November 2nd, 1914
The Mine Director's Cabin
Canmore, Alberta

There was snow on the mountain tops and a sharpness in the air but the sky was blue and cloudless. The temporary Park Warden with a mindset of promoting professionalism, straightened his hat, pulled back his shoulders, and wrapped his knuckles on the solid door.

"One moment, please." The sound of the bar latch. "Mister *Peyto!*" The young maid looked him up and down, "You're dressed in a Park Warden's uniform?" Her shocked expression drew laughter from the mountain man.

"Ishbel McColl! Whut are ya doin' here when all yar pals are workin' at the Sanatorium?"

Ishbel's face flushed. "I came to Canmore for the winter 'cause—"

"'Cause ya wanted to be near yar dad. And rightly so," he said with a knowing nod. "Ishbel, I need a quick word with the Mine Director."

"He's not here. He's in Calgary." Then quickly added, "but I'm glad you're here 'cause there was a big grizzly in our back garden."

Before Peyto could respond, a fair-haired lad walked briskly around the side of the cabin. Ishbel noticed he'd removed his sweater and rolled up his sleeves. She glanced at the muscles on his forearm. "Peyto, this is Joe, Joe Ukrainec," her face turned bright red, "he was crossing the bridge when he spotted the bear so he leaped over the fence and chased it out of the garden."

"Glad that worked out for ya, son," he grinned and extended his hand, "I'm Bill Peyto." The lad's grip had a good feel to it.

Joe turned to Ishbel. "I found the quilt and fixed the clotheslines so you're good to go." He threw his sweater over one shoulder and touched his cap. "Nice meeting you."

A pang of loss took Ishbel by surprise. "Nice meeting you. Too. And thanks." The abrupt sound from the whistling-kettle brought her back to the present. "Oh, just a minute, Mister Peyto." A split second later she was back. "Do you like your new job?" she said, eager for more information so she could update Lily.

"I'm only fillin' in." He lifted his hat, pushed back his hair and grinned. "Once I chase that grizzly back to his den, I'm off to fight for King and country. I signed up with the Twelfth Mounted Regiment & Machine Gun Brigade."

Now she was bursting to tell Lily. "Can I make you a cup of tea, Mister Peyto?"

"No thanks." He smiled at the gentle girl, too fragile for her workload and thought of his mother who had worked as a domestic from the age of twelve. "Mind you take a rest when the Mine Director's away," he said with a crooked grin.

Ishbel watched him walk across the gravel towards his horse. She waved when he turned and tipped his hat. Then she closed the door.

Neighhhhh! Smokey gave himself a shake and Bobby jiggled about helplessly in the bag attached to the saddle. "Sorry, Bobster." Peyto, the cold against his face, worked nimbly to untie the straps. "Can't have ya runnin' around when there's a bear in the vicinity." Once freed, Bobby bolted for the cabin. "*Whoa!*" Peyto caught him in the nick of time. The little rapid heartbeat pounded on his fingers. "Bobster, what the heck's the matter with ya?"

Woo-OOOF! Woo-OOOF!

He glanced across at the log building. "I wonder if the Mine Director would like a soon-to-be-homeless pooch."

Bobby's tail wildly beat the air.

Peyto roared with laughter. "Naw. Ishbel would likely call me a hard-necked opportunist. No worries, Bobster, Pearl's gonna find ya a good home."

***

Ishbel McColl
c/o The Mine Director
The Mine Director's Cabin
Canmore, Alberta

November 3rd, 1914

Miss Lily Saunderson,
The Servant's Quarters
Brett Sanatorium
Spray Avenue
Banff, Alberta

Dear Lily,

Guess who came around here WILD BILL PEYTO! He's a Park Warden now, guardin' game, nabbin' poachers, and chasin' big grizzlies back to their dens. Not for long though. He's signed up with the Twelfth Mounted Regiment & Machine Gun Brigade. (I bet you're swoonin' imaginin' him in uniform?)

Changin' the subject. There's a lot of hardship around Canmore right now. The miners' strike draggin' on. Dad is fillin' his days searchin' for Bobby. On the upside, you will never guess what happened to me today.

It was a blowy mornin'. The Mine Director and his family set off for Calgary early so I thought I'd tackle the beddin'. By ten thirty, I had it all done, the tubs emptied and everythin' was through the mangle. I was runnin' a damp cloth along the washin' lines and it set me thinkin' about my mum. 'Make sure you hang the sheets on the outside so our knickers are hidden from public view,' she would say and 'when you take the washin' in, never leave the clothes pegs danglin'. That's a sure sign of a sloppy housekeeper.' Ha-ha.

Anyway, I had the first row hung up and I was bolsterin' the line with the clothes prop when I heard some rustlin' in the bushes. I looked over. I could see nothin' so I started peggin' up the next load. (Nifty tip: I put a scarf around my neck and clipped the pegs to it. Much quicker than dippin' into the peg bag.) Anyway, more rustlin'. Peg between my teeth, I cautiously turned my head. And there he was. A BIG-SNOUTED GRIZZLY! I gulped. It snorted. I quaked. He turned back to munch on a berry bush. Cautiously and quietly, I backed up until I reached the kitchen door. Thankfully it was open so I rushed inside and slammed it shut. I took a deep breath and put the kettle on, hopin' he would leave once he'd ate his fill.

By the time I finished my tea, I couldn't see out of the window 'cause the steam from the kettle had settled on the glass. I gave it one wipe and nearly fainted his big damp nostrils were pressed hard against the pane, snortin' and sniffin' and coverin' my clean windows with sticky sludge. I banged on the glass and he bounded off towards the washing lines. Horror of horrors, everything came crashing down a whole morning's work lying in the mud the mistress's prized-quilt draped across his back. I was madder than a wet hen! I threw the kitchen door wide open and screeched like a fishwife. Picked up a pot and hurled it at him. I was in the middle of throwing its cover when somethin' made me look up at the sun. And there he was. A strikin' lad standin' in a blaze of luminosity. Pale yellowish-brown hair. Blue eyes so appealin', I could hardly meet their glance. He wore a checked shirt under a pleasin' woolly sweater. His broad back straight. "Good on you!" he laughed as my lid stotted off the tree.

I forced myself to meet his gaze. "A bear," I whimpered. He nodded. "Go inside," he said in a strong grainy voice.

From the safety of the kitchen, I watched out the window. He picked up a bucket and stick and began hollerin' and bangin'. The bear scampered off into the forest. I went outside to thank him. Lily. He gazed at me. And I at him. I could feel the heat of a sudden blush, but he quickly dispelled my awkwardness. "I'm Joe Ukrainec," he smiled.

"Ishbel McColl," I gulped, and we shook hands. He helped me clean up then we sat on the back doorstep. He was kind and funny and made me laugh. I couldn't help it, Lily, I spilled all my troubles. I told him about Winston who lost his mother on the fateful ship and then, because of my stupidity, lost the little dog that gave him comfort and cheer. I told Joe how my foolish actions caused Bobby to be pushed out in a boat, hours before a storm blew up. He listened and said very little, but I knew by his eyes, he didn't condemn me. Although, heaven knows, I condemn myself. Joe said he'd take a look around for the quilt and I went back to my chores. I had just put the kettle on when a knock came to the door. It was Wild Bill Peyto. Well, that brings me back to the beginnin' of this letter.

I was feelin' down about Bobby but dad says it's always better to lose oneself in action than to wither in despair. So tomorrow (half day off), we're goin' hikin' along the banks of the Bow see if there's any trace of the boat you just never know.

Winter's on its way, Lily. I can feel a nip in the air and the snow is blanketin' the surroundin' mountains. Soon it will cover the little town of Canmore. Miss you lots (and thinkin' of Joe!).

Write soon.
Ishbel

PS: Here is an old Scottish washin' rhyme for your readin' pleasure: 'They that wash on Monday, hae a' the week to dry. They that wash on Tuesday, are no far by. They that wash on Wednesday, get their claes clean; they that wash on Thursday, are no sair to mean. They that wash on Friday, washes for need; but they that wash on Saturday, are dirty daws indeed!'

***

Master Winston Fairfax, Esq.
Duncraig House
35 Duke Street
London
England

Saturday, October 3, 1914

Miss Ishbel McColl, housemaid
c/o The Mine Director
The Mine Director's Cabin
Canmore, Alberta
Canada

Dear Ishbel,

I was very pleased to receive your letter. Nanny Patterson is helping me write this reply. Please know I do not blame you for losing Bobby. Nanny is right. I should have kept a tight hold of his collar when the train was pulling out.

Today it was too cold to go to the park so, instead, I drew a map of Banff from my memories. THE TRAIN STATION where Bobby jumped out of the window. THE PARIS TEA ROOM where Nanny and I ate scones laden with cream and jam. THE MUSEUM with stuffed animals and colourful bird's eggs. THE ZOO where Buddy pulled, clinked and jangled his chain when he saw me. THE CAVE AND BASIN BATHHOUSE where we held our faces to the sun and allowed the minerals to sooth our joints, especially Father's. I also remember going to the pretty church, St. George's-in-the-Pines. Mister Duncan always gave me a wink when I placed my coin in the collection plate. I wish I was still there because all is not well here. German bombers have been spotted over our city. My teacher said if the Zeppelins come, we have to keep indoors, put the lights out, and keep quiet. Every morning we have to start our day by writing in our jotters, 'BRITISH MEANS PLUCK'. Nanny Patterson said we must do things to keep our minds off the war, so next week we are going to the screen début of Charlie Chaplin.

In closing, I would like to thank you and your father for offering to search for Bobby. I have enclosed my map as a token of my appreciation.

Sincerely,
Master Winston Fairfax, Esq.

PS: A song thrush is feeding on a rowan tree. Right now! Outside my window! Tomorrow, Nanny and I are going to fly my kite. I wish I could fly. I would come and help you search for Bobby. And I forgot to tell you Father had a telephone installed in our house. Nanny calls it, 'That Wretched Thing'.

Chapter 4

Morning, November 8, 1914

Mine Director's Cabin

Canmore, Alberta

Henrietta Bloxham pulled the loop of a fresh apron over the salt and pepper hair that framed her rosy face. "Hmm, I see the mistress has partitioned part of her kitchen off?" she uttered, tying the straps behind her generous waist.

"My bed's behind the screen, Mrs Bloxham."

"Oh. So that's where she tucked you." The temporary cook smoothed the skirts of her apron. "Well, it fairly cuts down on the light. Mind you, it was always a bit dark in here. They should have added a second hung sash window when they built it in," she racked her brains. "About five years ago it was. To entertain the important men when they came to visit the mines." Mrs Bloxham spent the rest of the day humming and moving about the kitchen with determined strides. The clock chiming pleasingly, now chimed 8 o'clock. "You can stop polishing the plates, Ishbel. Go change your pinny. We need to start serving."

Ishbel tightened the crossover ties at the back of her waist, "I'm ready, ma'am."

The buxom cook shook her head. "You need to roll down those sleeves of yours. Then hop over to the sink and splash your face with cold water." She handed Ishbel a tea towel to pat her cheeks. "We're all set. Just make sure you've got a good grip on that fancy tureen. If you break it, pickles 'n trifle, we'll be paying 'til we're ready for the grave."

Ishbel followed Mrs Bloxham out of the kitchen, through the tiny hallway and into a sea of stony-faced, heavy-necked, low-browed men. Indeed, the directors of the Canmore Coal Company were a scary-looking bunch. Cook gave Ishbel the nod and she placed the heavy tureen in the centre of the linen-topped credenza. The ornate lid was lifted off and the steam from the thick pea soup rushed to meet the air. Mrs Bloxham was about to give the bowl a wide stir when her pristine cloth fell from the waistband of her apron. She bent down then sprang up with an unrestrained cry that hit the room like a ruptured balloon.

Ishbel's hands flew to her mouth.

Mrs Bloxham, pink from embarrassment, stabbed a finger at the culprit.

The Mine Director tried to kerb his laughter. "Harold, did you just pinch our cook's bum?"

The table of shareholders thought it laugh-out-loud funny. Doe-eyed Harold produced a brash hiccup of despair.

"Perhaps it is best if we serve ourselves," uttered the important man and Mrs Bloxham, her colour higher than ever, fled to the safety of the kitchen and slumped down on the hard chair. "When the mistress is away, the drinking always gets out of hand."

"They're behaving like a bunch of rowdy schoolboys," Ishbel stuttered. "You should tell the mistress what happened."

"Oh, no, Ishbel. 'Tis a man's world," she sniffed, dabbing her moist eyes with the corner of her apron. "My dignity and my self-respect have been injured but I daren't complain. They would say I can't take a bit of fun. I would never be hired back."

"But—"

"But I need the job, Ishbel." The woman smoothed her apron over her generous middle. "Oh, pickles 'n trifle, I've so much to do I'm as touchy as a queen in exile."

The two women carried on, removing the soup plates and lugging in large platters of pork cutlets, grilled mushrooms, braised turkey, and tongue garnished with broccoli. Smaller platters of butter-basted vegetables followed. Finally, Cook carried in her pièce de résistance, four wild ducks in port wine sauce, and was much relieved when the Mine Director informed her they would serve themselves again.

Mrs Bloxham sat down at the kitchen table. "'Tis quiet now. Thankfully, they're taking pleasure from my meal." She dabbed her brow with the tea towel. "Ishbel, you look like you're ready to wilt."

"Oh, Mrs Bloxham, my feet are killin' me."

Cook looked up at the clock. "We've got a bit of time. Sit yourself down, love. I'll fill a basin and you can soak your feet. I saw some Epsom Salts under the sink." Ishbel removed her shoes, unhooked her suspenders and rolled down her stockings. "Now stick your tootsies into this magic mixture," said Mrs Bloxham, "and I'll make us both a cuppa."

They sipped on their tea, nibbled on digestive biscuits and, for a moment, the warmth of the kitchen undercut all their troubles. "I must say, Ishbel, you were a big help to me in there."

"I don't know how you manage to pull it off, Mrs Bloxham. So much food so much *work*."

"Oh, pickles 'n trifle, I can do it with my eyes closed. I've been cookin' for crowds since I was your age."

"So you followed your passion?"

"Oh, heck no. I had more aspirations than that!" She looked into Ishbel's eyes. "Before the dream of my youth crumbled, I planned to be a showgirl in that fabled Parisian cabaret. The Moulin Rouge. I inhaled it all from a fancy magazine in the doctor's waiting room." Mrs Bloxham portrayed a dreamlike expression. "But my mother burst that bubble on the grounds of indecency. She thought the costumes were, well too riské."

"I'm sorry your dream was crushed, Mrs Bloxham."

"Oh, Ishbel, I've long since laid flowers on the grave of my past. If you don't face forward in life. God help you. You'll smack into a tree!" They both laughed out loud.

"My feet feel great." Ishbel quickly put on her stockings and shoes. "I could dance now."

"Dance!" Mrs Bloxham's face lit up. "Then what about a saucy can-can?" The chubby woman sprang from her chair and ran to close the heavy kitchen door.

"But I can't dance the çan-can, Mrs Blox-*ham!*"

Cook pulled Ishbel out of her seat. "Just copy me. First we link arms. Like this like chorus girls. Now. Starting with our right legs. Together one eye-high kick! Ouch! Well maybe not eye-high. Just lower your leg in line with mine. Yes! Again! You've got it! Ta-ra-ra BOOM-DE-AY! *Kick!* Ta-ra-ra BOOM-DE-AY! *Kick!*" They pranced around the table. "Change legs, Ishbel! Ta-ra-ra BOOM-DE-AY! *Kick!*" Hot, sweaty and hooting with laughter, Mrs Bloxham stopped in her tracks and positioned her hands on her knees. "Ishbel." she sucked in a breath. "Enough o' the shenanigans. Time to dance your way to those dirty pots. I'll take them in their puddin'."

The Mine Director pushed himself up in his chair. "By gum, by golly, here comes the Tipsy Cake." A drop of saliva rolled uncontrollably from his mouth. "Is there a full pint of sherry in it, Henrietta?"

"Yes, sir. Just the way you like it, sir. Very moist." She placed the wobbly dessert in the centre of the table and bustled back to the kitchen where Ishbel was soaping her way through a pile of pots and pans. "How's the feet?"

"Much better, thanks."

Mrs Bloxham cocked her thumb at the door. "Heaven have mercy. Just listen to that racket—"

"This Damned War Has Heightened The Need For Coal And Shortened Our Labour Force. But I Will Rot In Hell I Will Shut the Damn Place Down I Will Not Give into the Demands of a Striking Workforce! A Solidarity Rally! Who The *Hell* Do They Think They Are?"

Ishbel's body tensed up at the sound of the shareholders thumping on the mistress's prized table.

The Mine Director continued: "If It Is Not Better Working Conditions They Are After, It Is More Money. Without Us, Those Lazy Sods Would Have No Jobs No Money. How Would They Feed Their Wretched Offspring Then? Damn Fools!"

"Here! Here!" The sound of the mistress's precious china rattling and dancing.

Mrs Bloxham stared at Ishbel over the length of the room. "Do they forget that fifteen miners died because of unsafe working conditions? Some buried where they toiled because it was too dangerous to bring their bodies out."

Ishbel poured a little paraffin oil onto a rag and feverishly scoured the sink.

In the dining room, the air was dense with cigar smoke. The puffy-faced manager stood up, partly to make his case, partly to shake off his languor. He inhaled the invigorating air of ego and entitlement. "We Must Get Those Lazy Sods Back To Work! This Bloody Strike Is Affecting Our Wallets!" He slammed down the lid of his monogrammed cigar box.

"Their wallets, my foot!" Mrs Bloxham was seething. "They say a man's as big as what makes him angry." She screwed up her face. "And as for that dirty cigar smoke! Can't stand it! Blights the brains!"

"I think my dad breathes in worse trying to make a livin'. I wish he wasn't a miner."

The cook's brow crumpled. "You were saying he suffers from black lung, eh. Did he start young?"

"He was hired on at twelve. As a putter."

"Aye, they use the young ones for pushing the tubs so they can develop the strength to cut the coal. Workin' them to the bone. It's a crying shame." Mrs Bloxham opened the hinged trivet and set the kettle upon it. "Do you have a lad, Ishbel?"

"I don't." She gently placed the soup tureen into the basin of soapy water. "Although I met one I *really* liked. I hope we cross paths again."

"What's his name?"

"Joe. Joe Ukrainec. He lives on 6th Street."

Mrs Bloxham staggered backwards. "Get away with you! His mother and I were the best of friends. Stepania was her name. God rest her soul. A fine woman. Knew how to get to the end of the week with very little money." Mrs Bloxham nodded approvingly. "A nice lad is Joe. He and his brother are big up-and-comers in the trade union."

Butterflies churned in Ishbel's stomach. "Are they? He is?"

Cook's face lit up like a beacon. "Ishbel. Next Tuesday, I'm servin' meals at the Canmore Miners' Union Hall. There's a big meeting taking place. I'll bet my first born, Joe Ukrainec will be there."

"My half-day off is Tuesday." Ishbel felt the rush of a sudden blush. "Oh, Mrs Bloxham, do you think you might need a helpin' hand?"

The cook beamed. "Pickles 'n trifle, all love needs is a gentle push."

6:30 pm, November 11, 1914

The Canmore Miners' Union Hall

7th Street, Canmore, Alberta

The atmosphere in the hall was noisy and unnerving. Ishbel McColl stood in the kitchen doorway, drying her rough-red hands on the folds of her pinny, and casually peering at the audience of union representatives from Canmore, Anthracite and Bankhead. Each of them had a similar concern. Their striking members were struggling to support large families on minimal strike pay. The industrial action was dragging on and their men were growing restless.

At last, the burly union leader with the principal book under one arm, leaped onto the stage and a hush befell the assembly: "Good afternoon, men. Welcome to the Canmore Local Union Number 1387, United Mine Workers of America!"

He paused until the bout of cheering subsided. "Men. Trade unions were born in battle. A battle against self-seeking employers and governments which could not comprehend the sufferings of the people. We have made enormous progress. Our funds are protected by law. Commonplace activities of trade unions are acknowledged as legal. Peaceful action cannot be punished. You, the working man, are safeguarded by the shield of the *union!"*

A deafening cheer rose from the striking leaders.

"We all know the story of the bundle of sticks," he continued. "You can break one stick easily, but you cannot break a bundle of sticks tied together with the same ease. One man's demands may go unheard, but the demands of thousands will not." The vociferous organiser punched a powerful fist into the air and cheers and shouts thundered through the hall until he waved for silence. "Lads. Time to take the pressure off." His shoulders relaxed. "In appreciation of your support, we have added a couple of pints to your meal." A keg of beer was rolled across the stage. "Enjoy, lads! Enjoy!"

Ishbel's folded her arms across her chest. "Did you ever see the likes? Beer for 'the lads'. Any spare union money should go to the mothers struggling to feed their bairns."

"I told you, Ishbel." Cook swiftly spooned the stew onto the last row of plates. "It's a man's world. Men do whatever they damn well please, and us womenfolk have to put up with their stupid nonsense."

Ishbel frowned. "Mrs Bloxham, how did women get themselves in this predicament?"

Cook wiped the sweat off her brow with the back of her arm. "Aw, I expect they're all like me, Ishbel. They wanted to change the world but couldn't get a babysitter." The two women burst out laughing. "Now start cutting and platin' those apple charlottes there's a luv."

"How many pieces per pan?"

"Twenty-four."

Ishbel picked up the knife. "I heard they're bringing in prohibition next year. That'll sort them all out."

"Seein' is believin', girl." Mrs Bloxham glanced over Ishbel's shoulder. "Pickles 'n trifle! There's that lad you fancy. Heading this way."

Ishbel McColl
c/o The Mine Director
The Mine Director's Cabin
Canmore, Alberta

Tuesday, November 10, 1914

Miss Lily Saunderson,
The Servant's Quarters
Brett Sanatorium
Spray Avenue
Banff, Alberta

Dear Lily, it's two in the mornin' and I cannae sleep a wink. I think I'm in love with Joe Ukrainec. He came into the union hall yesterday when I was helpin' Mrs Bloxham feed the strikers. When he walked through that door. Oh, Lily. His eyes. His voice. His smile. He's not like the other blokes around here. He looks and acts don't laugh like a knight. Anyway, I cannae believe it he asked me out. We're goin' to the Canmore Hilton. It's a clapboard hotel on Main Street. All the railway workers and miners go there but Joe says the Italian woman who runs the place keeps them in line. Joe says the fiddlers are great and they make the best pie and clapshot in Western Canada. Lily, do you believe in love at first sight? Write back quickly with your answer. Also, I have a bit of a problem. The mistress offered me her old coat. I tried it on. It fitted and I thanked her. Then she told me she was taking the cost of it outta my wages. I don't want to use my hard-earned money for that. I thought it was free. Now I'm scared to tell her I changed my mind. Now, I'm lookin' at the clock. I have three hours before I have to get up and light the fires. Ugh!

Goodnight,
Ishbel

PS: Winston sent me a letter and a lovely map of Banff that he drew from memory he's a clever wee lad.

Miss Lily Saunderson,
The Servant's Quarters
Brett Sanatorium
Spray Avenue
Banff, Alberta

November 14, 1914

Miss Ishbel McColl
c/o The Mine Director
The Mine Director's Cabin
Canmore, Alberta

Dear Ishbel:

Sweet cheeses! Yi got yirself a bloke! That wuz quick.

Problem 1: Fallin' in love at first sight: 'Tis codswallop. Keep yirsel in check.

Problem 2: Stuck with second-hand coat: Be brave. Hand 't back. Yir miserly mistress tried t' hoodwink yi.

So my Peyto signed up. My heart skips a beat picturin' him in his soldier's uniform. Thanks for the poem. From now on, I'll do my washin' on a Monday and I'll have all the week to dry. Ha-ha.

Rushed off ma feet t'day. Wull write as soon as I can.
Miss yi lots, Lily

Evening, November 14, 1914
738 Main Street
Canmore, Alberta

Ishbel shivered like a broken-winged bird outside the cream-coloured clapboard hotel with bright-green trim. 'I really liked him. I thought he liked me.' Large snowflakes swirled around her. She drew her shawl tighter and blew warmth into her woollen mittens. 'Fancy arranging to meet me then not showin' up.' Her heart fell to her shoes. 'What a horrible bloke.'

Canmore was turning ghostly under the moon when Ishbel set off for home so she was glad of the light coming from behind the drawn curtains of the miners' homes. Joe had told her he lived in the small grey cottage on the corner of 6th Street. She couldn't help but glance over. "That must be it. Square and solid. No light showin'. No smoke from the chimney. Maybe he's out? Did he forget about our date? How could he? Maybe he changed his mind? How dare he! I should knock maybe not." Disappointment turning to annoyance, Ishbel found her feet crossing the road, hurrying up the little paved walkway. She took a deep breath. Pulled back her shoulders and wrapped her knuckles matter-of-factly against the brown-plank door.

A shuffling noise came from up the side of the house. Ishbel stretched her neck but she couldn't see anything. Then a voice called out, "Who goes there? Whatta you after?"

Tension tightened in Ishbel's mouth. "I my name is Ishbel McColl. And I'm looking for Joe Ukrainec." Her mind raced over the words. "He lives here. Right?"

Moonlight struck the woman's sunken cheeks. "G'evening, deary," she said, eyeing Ishbel suspiciously. "You have the right house but you won't be seeing him around here for a while."

"How? Where has he gone?"

"He was arrested this afternoon."

"Arrested?!"

"I was minding my own business. Mending my hubby's socks, I was. Dropped my purney when I heard the disturbance and peered through my nets." The woman's waxen fingers gripped the neck of her shawl. "All three of them he, his father and brother all dragged off like common criminals."

The wind whipped at the escaped strands of Ishbel's hair. "You must be mistaken," she cried, pushing it from her eyes.

"Let me tell you something, deary." The woman's breath rattled in her bird-like sternum. "For some time now, a darkness has been spreading far and wide across this country. Some ignored it. Others oblivious to it. Nobody stood against it. Now it's too late we're powerless to escape its vicious hostility."

Ishbel took a step back. "What on earth are you talking about?"

"Oh, you young ones!" She flicked a mottled-brown hand to gesture her annoyance. "If you tried reading the newspapers tried educating yourselves to the goings-on, you'd know our Prime Minister, Sir Robert Borden, applied the War Measures Act. He's ordered all the Ukrainians to register as enemy aliens."

"Enemy aliens! But Joe's not an enemy alien."

"Maybe yes. Maybe no. But I know for a fact that he and his family have to report to the local authorities every single week." Her voice broke like an old twig. "Vladimir Ukrainec was spittin' feathers about it. He thought himself a real Canadian like the rest of us."

Ishbel chewed her thumbnail. "But I am not a real Canadian either."

"More's the pity. Are you Australian, deary?"

"No. Scottish."

The woman took a moment to digest the information. "Well, girl, I wouldn't worry too much. The Canadian government is only hunting down the Ukrainians for the time being. I must admit though, I feel sorry for Vladimir. The poor man worked from dawn 'til dusk in that mine. Twenty-plus years he gave so this country could retrieve its coal, and this is the thanks he gets." The woman shook her head and exhaled. "If you asked me, war hysteria has caused it all. That's what I blame it on war hysteria."

Ishbel stood in numbed silence.

"Oh, don't go upsetting yourself, deary. At least their mother is dead, buried and spared the ordeal of watching her men thrown into a labour camp. It was the flu outbreak that took her. Stepania was her name. Are you new around these parts?"

"Yes. I keep house for the Mine Director. I used to work in the Banff Springs but it closed for the winter."

"The Banff Springs Hotel. Aye, there's real wealth and real deprivation within the Bow Valley." She shivered from the chill breeze. "Well, no point in standing around, girl." They both looked down at her slippered feet. "Best be on your way."

Ishbel, unthinkingly, rested her hand on the woman's arm. "But Joe told me he was rolling up the wash line when he said it he told me he was born in Canada."

The woman exhaled. "Well now. See. That's another part of it. A very shady part if you ask me." She looked directly at Ishbel. "Both brothers were big up-and-comers in that trade union. Riling up the men with their grandiose promises. Giving the big-shots a run for their money. Their surname didn't do them any favours. If you get my meaning."

Every morning in the days that followed, Ishbel waited anxiously for the delivery of the *Calgary Herald*. The Mine Director fizzled with annoyance if his fingers got smudged with newspaper ink so, opportunely, she had to iron it first.

118

Ishbel couldn't believe it. No one in the Bow Valley could believe it. Canadian citizens of Ukrainian descent were being seized all across Canada and thrown into Internment Camps. Their freedom denied. Their property confiscated. She had good reason to believe they had taken Joe and his family to the Cave and Basin camp. It was the closest one. A military base recently converted to house prisoners during the severe winter months. Around town, many folk were asking questions. Some saw past the answers they were given. Canada needed plentiful and cheap labour. The Ukrainian prisoners were plentiful and, at twenty-five cents for a day's work, cheap. Ishbel closed her eyes and prayed hard for the safety of the ill-fated lad. Late at night, if she couldn't sleep, she would light her oil lamp, pick up her pen and paper and write to her best friend.

Dear Lily,

Today I read the Ukrainian prisoners have started to build a roadway between the town of Banff and Lake Louise—

Chapter 5

Early Afternoon, November 14, 1914
The Brewster-Moore Cabin
Corner of Banff Avenue and Fox Street
Banff, Alberta

It was a square log building. Not the prettiest home in the neighbourhood but it was sturdy and snug, had indoor plumbing, and suited Pearl to a T. When Wild Bill Peyto arrived, light was filtering through a large aspen popular, dappling the brazen blue shutters, all steadfastly closed against the morning glare. He rested his kitbag on the stone step, adjusted his little dog under one arm, and rapped twice on the solid door. The tall balsam firs, white birch trees, and thickets of wolf willow swayed in the wind. He knocked again. This time, the door flew wide open and two squealing boys shot passed his feet.

"Look at this mess! You two come *back* here this very minute!" yelled Pearl, catching sight of Peyto. "What are you doin' here? Come away in." She dried her hands on her apron and tucked a strand of hair behind her ear. "What brings you here today?"

The mountain man hid a flash of disappointment. "Um, I'm leavin' and—" The words had barely left his lips when the sound of shattering crockery made them turn their heads.

"Auntie Pearl, 'tis him that did it!" the younger lad pointed to the culprit.

"I never broke the plant pot!" cried his brother, hotily.

"Did so! Did so!" He threw a punch at his brother and a contest of strength and speed erupted.

"You two! Break it up!" The outdoorsman interpolated swiftly, grabbing their collars and pulling them apart. "Here. I've got somethin' that'll stick yar jaws together." He dug in his pocket for a handful of toffees wrapped in greaseproof paper.

"Oh! Thanks, mister!"

"Yeah! Thanks, mister!" The brothers popped the sweeties into their mouths and ran off.

Pearl leaned heavily against the door and smiled. "Thanks, mister."

"Ya've got yar hands full, eh."

She looked at him with furrowed brow. "My sister-in-law's upstairs recoverin' from the influenza. I'm in the middle of a big wash. And those two scallywags of hers, as loveable as they are, have been under my feet all mornin'."

Peyto spat out his chew. "It can't be easy with Philip away?"

Pearl smiled bleakly. "I'm getting used to it. If I feel the need of his company, I place his boots in front of the chair and set his hat on the seat. Then I'm fine."

"Have ya heard from him?"

"I got a corny postcard yesterday." Pearl pulled it from her apron pocket and held it up. "A French teapot on the front. See. And I'll read you the back, '*I cannot sit and talk with you, the way I'd like to do. So brew yourself a cup of tea, and I'll think of you, you think of me'.*"

He laughed. "Is he fighting in Europe or on a bloomin' fishin' trip?" Bobby caught sight of the crusty old cat and his little head popped out from under Peyto's grip. Grrrrrr!

"Oh no!" Pearl suddenly remembered, "Peyto, you asked me to find your dog a good home." She turned a perturbed eye to his knapsack. "You're not leavin'? *Now*?"

"I am that. But don't worry." Peyto applied a plastered grin. "The dog's all fixed up."

The woman's shoulders relaxed. "Thank goodness. You'd be in a fine jam if you were relying on me." She reached to stroke the Yorky now resting in the crook of his arm.

Arf!

"Well, better get goin," his tone gentle. "Keep the home fires burnin', Pearl. I'll see ya when the war's over." He adjusted his dog under his arm and threw his knapsack over his shoulder.

She hid her worry behind a smile. "Look after yourself. Come back safe and sound," she said as Edmée and her two little nephews joined her at the front door. They all watched and waved until Peyto turned the corner on the heels of his newly-polished boots.

Arf!

Peyto put Bobby down and the little dog followed close to his ankles as if connected by an invisible thread. "Bobster, my ruddy train leaves in half an hour and I don't have a flippin' home for ya!" He spat out a gob of tobacco.

Rrrrruff!

"No worries, Bobster. I'll figure somethin' out."

Canon Harrison was on the station platform when Peyto and Bobby showed up. "Good day to you, Ebenezer," he said, an evangelical gleam in his eyes.

"Hullo, Rev."

The elderly minister clasped his hands behind his back. "Allow me to introduce you to my temporary replacement, Reverend Tosh. He will be holding the fort while I carry out my duties as army chaplain. Reverend Tosh, this is Ebenezer William Peyto. Otherwise known as Wild Bill."

The young minister's face flushed red as he shook the coarse hand earnestly, "Pleased to meet you, W-Wild Bill," his eyes drawn to the large knapsack. "Our church will miss you on Sundays."

Canon Harrison sucked in his breath. "We only see Ebenezer at weddings and funerals."

Peyto smiled in an unrestrained manner with his mouth open. "And Christmas service too."

"Ahh, the world sees a confident man, Ebenezer, but God sees your vulnerable soul." The minister oozed a simpering smugness. Bobby gazed up at him timorously. "And who owns this little character?" he said, bending down to pat the dog's head.

"Me." Peyto pressed on Bobby's back to make him sit.

"You? But you cannot go gallivanting off to war with a Yorky in tow."

Peyto knelt down to tighten his boot laces and Bobby settled his head on the side of his knee. "Sure I can," he replied, brightly. "He ain't called a terrier for nothing. Grrrrrr!"

Canon Harrison's annoyance bubbled close to the surface. "Do not mess with me."

Wild Bill stood up and leaned against the pole. "I'm not messin' with ya," he said, bending his knee and striking a match up the sole of his boot. "I never mess with the clergy."

"Oh, for the love of mankind!" Canon Harrison's jaw tightened. "As a dog owner," his eyes were drawn to the flame circling around the bowl of Peyto's pipe. "You had a responsibility to find him a home a good home."

"Rev, no word of a lie I tried." Peyto puffed lightly. The tobacco lit. He removed the pipe from his mouth and smiled his gentle, lazy smile. "Any chance you can ask the good Lord to provide. I'd do it myself but I think he likes you better."

Canon Harrison felt the heat spread from his face to his chest. "Ebenezer William Peyto your manner is insolent and you are downright downright *negligent!*" He turned to face his replacement. "Reverend Tosh," he hoped God was not watching, "I almost forgot to mention that St. George's-in-the-Pines dutifully cares for a dog."

The new minister's pupils dilated. "I I am afraid I it is *our* church's responsibility?"

"Yes. Yes. Because—"

"Because he's no ordinary dog." Wild Bill pressed down the smouldering tobacco with his thumb. "He's Bobby of Banff. The town's mascot. That's why your church looks after him. Isn't that right, Rev?"

Canon Harrison expelled air from his lungs with a sudden sharp sound.

Peyto picked up his dog. "Reverend Tosh, would ya mind holdin' out yar arms?" he said with a crooked smile.

Bobby sensed his fate was in the balance. He fixed his pleading eyes on the young minister and leaped.

"*A-choo* but I am allergic to *ah-choo!*"

A surge of warm air hit everyone. Followed by the eruption of the train's arrival. Reverend Tosh tried to juggle the dog while fumbling in his pockets for his handkerchief. "When I t-took this posting. Nothing in the job description—" He dabbed his watery eyes. "I did not expect t-to *ah-choo ah-choo!*"

The stationmaster blasted his whistle. "LAST CALL! ALL ABOARD!"

Wild Bill Peyto handed over the crumpled leash then stepped back to allow flushed-faced Canon Harrison to board first. The engine hissed. The smoke belched. The wheels began turning and the chugging sound increased.

The young minister clutched the dog like a child with a toy, and a rush of air from the parting train blew into his face and flattened his puzzled frown. In no time at all, the snake of carriages disappeared into the distance. *"Ah-choo!"* He put the dog down. "Oh, what a difficult conundrum." He untangled the knotted leash and clipped it to the Yorky's collar. *"Ah-choo!"*

The evening sun still had some warmth in it when they reached the front door of St. George's-in-the-Pines. Bobby looked up with trust in his eyes and the minister's expression softened. "What is your name? *Ah-choo!"* Bobby of Banff?"

Arf!

"Alright, Bobby of Banff. For the time being *ah-choo!* This will be your home."

Woof!

"I am g-glad you approve." Reverend Tosh removed the stiff-starched band around his neck. "Now, little d-doggy, I have a very busy day ahead of me. I have to s-study the instruction booklet for the church bells. Ah-choo! We will eat at five."

Bobby jumped onto the polished back pew, turned around three times then settled into a ball to dream. Stained-glass windows. Thick stone walls. St. George's-in-the-Pines on the corner of Buffalo and Beaver. Perfect.

Miss Lily Saunderson,
The Servant's Quarters
Brett Sanatorium
Spray Avenue
Banff, Alberta

November 21, 1914

Miss Ishbel McColl
c/o The Mine Director
The Mine Director's Cabin
Canmore, Alberta

Dear Ishbel:

Let me tell yi, this has been a week and a half! Missus Brett told us t' wash her parlour windows first thing this mornin'. So, I wuz about t' dip my cloth int' the bucket when Ethel noticed the Ukrainian prisoners marchin' past the window (they're comin' down from the Cave and Basin internment camp). She stopped workin' and began fluffin' up her hair. Then she started wavin' at them!!! I told her t' stop it it wuz inappropriate they're prisoners! She told me to shut my gob then she dipped her hand int' the bucket and flicked soapy water int' my face! Sweet cheeses, I'll hang for her. She's a daily threat t' my survival!

Anyway, talkin' about the Ukrainian prisoners. Somebody's makin' a fast buck coz they're usin' them t' dig the foundation for the Banff Springs Hotel's new golf course. And they're also drainin' a large swamp on the south side for the hotel's new tennis court. 'Tis true what they say: the rich get richer and the poor have children.

Anyhow, that's not the only dire news. Yesterday, Mrs Brett told me t' take an overfilled donation bag t' St. George's-in-the-Pines. On my way there, I wuz polkadodged by Ethel. She wanted t' look inside t' see if there wuz anythin' for her brother (who's a fisherman in Newfoundland). She grabbed it off me and spilled the contents all over the grass: bizness suits, white shirts, fancy ties. The only thing of interest t' her wuz a pair of red long johns. She rolled them up and stuck them inside her coat. Then hopped off leavin' me t' pick everythin' up and put it back in the bag!!!

Anyway, I wuz about t' cross the road when I heard the sound of thunderin' hooves. I swung around. It wuz Lady Clementine Corrinwallis (the one searchin' for her suitor). "Clear the way!" she cried from behind the veil of her black ridin' hat. The horse came stormin' out of the park gates, gallopin' towards me. I dropped the donations and jumped out of the way. The hooves burst the bag wide open and the clothes scattered in every direction. Torn and caked in mud they were. Her Ladyship didn't look back. "Giddy up!" she cried and disappeared down Banff Avenue.

Ishbel, I wuz knocked for six. Then out of the blue, a woman and a girl came rushin' towards me. They asked if I wuz alright but my words wouldn't come out, so they put the clothes back in the torn bag the best they could. The woman said I needed a strong cup of tea. We had t' gather our skirts and draw them t' one side 'cause the road wuz so muddy. But the Paris Tea Room wuz so warm and cosy. They know what t' do with a scone and don't skip on the butter.

When I got my senses back, I said I wuz sorry for puttin' them out. The woman wuz so matter-of-fact. She said her name wuz Pearl Brewster-Moore and she wuz glad of the company 'cause her husband is away fightin' in the trenches.

Anyway, she kindly offered t' take the donation bag t' St. George's-in-the-Pines for me. She said she knew the church cleaner and between them they would fix the problem. The girl wuz so excited t' go t' the church coz the new minister's got a dog. And wait 'till yi read this he's allergic t' it! So all the parishioners have t' take turns lookin' after it. Have yi ever heard the likes?

Well, that's all my news for now, except t' say I wuz readin' a poem about life bein' like a Ferris wheel in a fair ground. One minute yir on top of the world and the views are great and everythin' is wonderful. Then it goes down and there are no views and life is full of broken eggs. Makes perfect sense t' me.
I bet yir dad's glad the strike's over. No sign of Bobby yet?

Miss yi lots.
Lily

PS: Outside my window, the dried seed heads of hogweed are coated with frosty snow. They look very speshul.

The sun. The snow. The bitter cold. A glare of brilliance dancing on the walls of the vestry, illuminating the stain glass windows. *"Ah-choo!"* Reverend Tosh sat down on the bench and pulled on a pair of cable socks, a present from an elderly parishioner. "Next week is Stir-Up Sunday, Bobby. Our lady p-parishioners will be making their Christmas p-puds and stirring in their wishes. A lovely t-time of year if it would warm up. This cold weather is k-keeping my flock from attending Sunday Service." The little Yorky began licking the young minister's long skinny fingers as he tied his bootlaces. "But it won't k-keep us from visiting that inhospitable internment camp. Will it, Bobby?"

Ruff!

"Now where did my other boot g-go? Oh, you're chewing on it you little scallywag!" He gently wrestled it from the dog's mouth then stood up to peer out of the crystallised window. "Oh, the world has t-turned to white, filling me with delight," he crooned, layering his black overcoat over his thick jacket then adding his woolly hat, scarf and gloves. "Now I am dressed like Captain Scott of the Antarctic." He picked up his little dog and tucked him inside his jacket. "And you, Bobby, are c-closer to my heart for the journey ahead."

Frost crunched under Reverend Tosh's feet, hymns hummed in his head, and the skirt of his black coat flapped about his legs. Through the loopy stitches of his woolly hat, he absorbed the beauty of a landscape. It reminded him of a miniaturised scene in a snow globe. "We have already completed one t-tenth of our journey, Bobby," he chattered through blue lips, his mild sense of accomplishment rapidly diminishing.

Bobby's little face popped out and a nippy tickle filled the minister's nose. "Aaaaaah-CHOO Aaaaaah-CHOO!" Fluffy white particles flew from his nostrils and the Yorky slipped down the inside of his jacket, vanishing into a cavernous snow bank.

"Oh, dear Lord in h-heaven." The colour seeped from the young minister's cheeks. "Bobby, Bobby!" He delved into the frosty white mound.

Woof! The small furry head popped up and shook off the snow.

"Oh, God b-bless you, Bobby!" The minister's face radiated relief. "For a t-terrible moment, I I—" He turned his head at the sound of heavy rumbling behind him. A cumbersome wagon with sleigh-runners was being pulled by a large horse. He quickly slipped Bobby back in his coat.

The driver pulled alongside and touched his hat with his whip. "I am afraid you won't get much further without a pair of snowshoes. Can I offer you a ride?"

The minister felt such a sense of relief the snow was kissing his knees. He narrowed his eyes against the harsh winter sun. "I I am Reverend Tosh, the n-new minister of St. George's in the Pines. This is my f-first Alberta winter. I I am trying to make my way to the Cave and Basin Internment Camp," he said, his owlish eyeglasses frosting with tiny sparking crystals."

A small grin flashed across the man's face. "I'm Luxton Norman Luxton. Climb on up. I'll be happy to take you."

Reverend Tosh settled down on the wagon's spring seat.

Arf!

"Oh! And this is Bobby of Banff." Bobby's head immediately sprung out.

"Howdy, Bobby." Luxton picked up the reins, clicked his tongue, and the horse began trekking through the snow-covered landscape.

"Have you always l-lived in Banff, Mr Luxton?"

"I came to Banff in my twenties." Luxton handled the reins as if he was lightly squeezing a sponge. "I was recuperating after an accident."

"An accident?"

"It's a long story."

"Do t-tell me."

"Well, a friend and I decided to sail around the world in a 100-year-old Nootka dugout canoe. The Tilikum."

"Good g-gracious. Why on earth would you d-do such a thing?"

"Because a Vancouver newspaper was offering us $5000 if we completed the journey." He laughed at the memory. "I was young and naively enthusiastic and my friend was an eccentric sea captain. At the time it seemed an opportunity too good to miss. So we set off from Victoria, BC, and headed west to London."

"A good publicity stunt for the n-newspaper, I would say."

A gust of wind blew Reverend Tosh's hat off and his hair stood on end until he caught it and returned it to his head. Luxton kept his lips closed and laughed inwardly. "Anyhow, after ten thousand miles and five months on the Pacific Ocean, we hit a reef and I ended up in an Australian hospital. I had to abandon the trip. I headed back to Calgary in the hopes of being hired back by the *Calgary Herald.* No such luck so I came to Banff. I landed a job as an agent for a haberdashery shop and on my days off," he chuckled to himself, "I chased wild horses."

Reverend Tosh's words came slow, "Wild h-horses?"

"Yes, through the passes in the Rockies," he replied matter-of-factly. "Then one morning, when the surrounding mountains were still cloaked in a dawn mist, I decided to take a chance. I bought a little Gordon Press and a box of type that was gathering dust in one of the offices I visited. My father was a printer so I knew how to set type. On a wing and a prayer, I started up the *Crag & Canyon*. Shortly after, I met and married Georgie."

"This little town has been g-good to you, Mister Luxton."

"Indeed it has, Reverend Tosh. Banff gave me a start. It's full of opportunity for anyone wanting to expand their horizons."

By the time the two men approached the heavily guarded gates, they decided they liked each other.

Arf!

"He's a good-looking Yorky. Where did you get him?"

"This *this* is Bobby of Banff." Reverend Tosh gave Luxton an old-fashioned look over the top of his glasses. "The town mascot."

"Sorry. What did you say?"

"The town mascot. Bobby of Banff. Dutifully c-cared for by St. George's-in-the-Pines Anglican Church. I thought you, being the publisher of our local n-newspaper, would have m-made his acquaintance already?"

Luxton's eyebrows contracted. "I wasn't aware the town of Banff had a Yorkshire terrier for a mascot. Whoa!" He pulled back on the reins and stopped outside the camp gates. Through the threatening barbed-wire fence, about two hundred Ukrainian men were milling around. A few faces, blank and uncomprehending, stared back at them.

The minister bowed his head in prayer. "Psalm 69:33: *'For the Lord hears the needy and does not despise his own p-people who are p-prisoners.'*" As the words hit the cold air, tiny particles of water and ice formed in front of his mouth, blurring his face as he turned to Luxton. "These s-souls emigrated from countries that are now allied with Germany. That that is why they are branded enemy aliens' and herded into p-places like this."

"I know. Sir Wilfred Laurier spoke out against their incarceration and the Ukrainian Church is up in arms. A month ago, the YMCA sent a jeremiad that was completely ignored," he answered dismally. "This crackdown—"

"AAAAAHHH-CHOO! Indeed, it is a d-disgrace." He shook Luxton's hand and stepped down. "Very nice to have m-made your acquaintance. Thank you for the ride and the m-most enjoyable company."

It was Luxton who now said, "If you are free tomorrow night, Reverend, come for dinner. I'd like you to meet my family. My good friend, Paddy Nolan, will be there too."

"Thank you," said the minister, his head bobbing, "your invitation is very m-much appreciated."

"Good. I live at 206 Beaver Street."

"206 Beaver Street we are p-practically neighbours."

"Oh, just a minute," said Luxton, twisting around to pull a pair of snowshoes from behind his seat. "Here, take these. You'll need them to get home."

Trembling with fear inside the minister's jacket, Bobby kept silent and hidden as they moved along the fence line, passing the chained-up, snarling dogs that growled and bared their teeth. Once inside the menacing gates, Reverend Tosh felt the coldest he had all day. He took his eyes on a tour around the discipline factory: a series of numbered, colourless, wheel less boxcars; an administration building, depressingly grey; a frost-polished watch tower; armed guards here, there and everywhere. The whole shebang wrapped in a grave silence, broken only by the sound of hacking coughs. He braced himself when a prisoner scurried towards him. "Pleasche," a cloud of frigid air escaped the man's mouth and obscured his face, "pleasche, hev you anyzing to eat?"

"I I am so s-sorry." The minister's heart crumpled. "The n-next time I come," he began, but the prisoner tucked his gloveless hands under his armpits and hurried away.

The young minister moved towards a huddle of greyish figures. A sunken-eyed man looked up as he approached. "Pleasche, vee are hungry as dogs. Hev you anyzing in your pocket. "

The minister shook his head. "I am so s-sorry. I will b-bring food the next time I come. Please, go inside. It is f-far too cold to be standing out here."

The prisoner used his sleeve to erase a drip from the end of his bulbous nose. "Vee stays healzier outside."

His heart was in his mouth. "I will pray for you. I will pray for you all."

"Do not vaste your prayers on us." The man jerked his head towards a far-off building. "Valk down zer. Down at de end Sched number 58."

Reverend Tosh's hopes were up. "Shed number 58? Does someone n-need me there?"

The prisoner coughed and nodded. "I tink so."

Outside the dismal structure, the sound of heartfelt sobs. Reverend Tosh squinted into the dark opening; hesitated when he saw a hunched figure. "Son, I am here here to h-help you," he said, gripping the metal sides, hoisting himself into the boxcar.

Arf!

Without warning, Bobby flew from the neck of the minister's coat. The lad jolted back and his grubby grey blanket fell to the floor.

"Good Lord!" the minister's stomach lurched, "What h-happened to your face?"

The prisoner didn't reply. He pulled his cover back, huddling under it in the hopes of gaining some warmth.

"I I am Reverend Tosh from St George's-in-the-Pines." He joined the lad on a floor carpeted with coal dust. "And this is m-my charge, Bobby of Banff."

Arf!

"What is your n-name, lad?"

Silence.

"Can I ask f-for your n-name, lad?"

Disruption cursed through the youth. "Joe, Joe Ukrainec," he snapped, pulling out a splayed hand, cut and bloodied. The little dog crept forward and licked his fingers. The youth's face softened.

Reverend Tosh's shoulders relaxed. "He is a very special dog. He is the town of Banff's mascot," he added, standing up to unbutton his jacket. "You must take this." He pulled the sweater over his head. "You have insufficient clothing for this p-penetrating cold."

The prisoner felt the warmth across his shoulders. He squeezed his eyes. They felt like grit. "We, we are not of the same church."

Reverend Tosh's pulse quickened. "I am sure God will not mind a bit if you use a minister from a different church on a p-path to the same heaven."

They sat in silence for a few long minutes then Joe said, "My father, Vladimir Ukrainec passed away two days ago." The young prisoner wiped his sleeve over his wet cheeks. "I have a brother, John. I don't know where they have taken him. Or if he is alive. Can you," he looked straight into the minister's eyes, "I would be grateful if you could say a prayer for both of them."

"It would be an honour," answered Reverend Tosh. "Let us bow our h-heads."

The young minister continued his work until lockdown then he tucked Bobby inside his jacket and made his way back to the front gates, passing the snarling dogs, alert and waiting. The sky was as black as pitch. Thankfully Luxton's snowshoes were still propped against the metal fencing. He brushed off the fresh snow, fastened them to his boots and began walking, heavily and firmly. Bobby snuggled into his chest and with each step, the minister drew strength from the little warm body.

The next morning, Joe Ukrainec opened his eyes to the crunch of heavy boots outside. Alarm etched on his face and he quickly rose to his feet, scuttling into a condition of readiness. Other prisoners swiftly lined up on either side. Panic began to rise. Fists clenched by his sides, Joe took a deep breath to calm his debilitating fear: the clang and shrill of the metal bar and bolt; the high-pitched noise of the sliding doors parting. Then, for a moment, the comforting warmth of the morning sun falling on his face.

"You goddamn filthy hunky move it *move* it! Inside!" The guard jabbed at the prisoner's shoulder blades with the butt of his rifle. "Filthy-stupid hunky," he complained violently under his breath. The prisoner whimpered, his face a sheen of sweat and dust. He grabbed at the metal siding. Hoisted himself up. Lost his grip and fell back on the ground with a thump. "Dammit!" The burley guard grabbed the dazed man by the collar and dragged him to his feet. Another guard approached and together they lifted him up and threw him forcefully into the container. The heavy doors closed as abruptly as they had opened.

Joe grasped the elbow of the crumpled figure and helped him to his feet. "Take this blanket," he said, his eyes drawn to the gaunt face. Familiar. Obvious. His heart swelled. "John?"

The man stirred. He let out a piercing whisper, "Joe?"

A rush of clarity. Joe could hardly draw breath. "Where? Where the hell have you been?"

"Castle M-Mountain," he gurgled.

The brothers clung to each other until John's wet clothing seeped through to Joe's. "Castle Mountain?" He pulled back. "I thought they shut that hole down for the winter?"

"They kept a handful of us back for building repairs. The cold. Joe, we could hardly move our fingers. The night before last, part of the roof caved in. They they brought us here this morning."

"John, there are hundreds in this camp now they could have put you anywhere."

"How's that for a stroke of luck." He grinned and his face nipped. "How's it in here?"

Joe's fist curled tight. "We've got this this crazy guard. The idiot has had it in for me since day one."

132

"What's making him pick on you?"

"How the heck should I know?"

John placed a quieting hand on his brother's shoulder. "Maybe his girlfriend dumped him and she looks a helluva lot like you."

The youth struggled to submerge his first laughter since he arrived in the hellish place. "Find your own flipping blanket," he hollered, whipping it off his big brother's shoulders.

Flames from the crackling logs in the hearth danced a likeness on the ceiling and evening light filtered through the small pane of glass, exaggerating the darkness and deepening the shadows. Georgina Luxton's pale dress reached mid-calf, exposing a lightly-patterned pair of silk stockings. Her hair fashionably bobbed. She reached across her table to light the candles and the power of the flickering glow illuminated her white-linen tablecloth and lent a sparkle to her wedding china.

Reverend Tosh's eyes scanned the table set for six and his nostrils inhaled the smell of roast beef drizzled in oil and seasoned well with salt and pepper. He tucked the corner of his napkin into his white band and adjusted the remainder over the front his black cardigan. "One of life's p-pleasures is being invited to d-dinner," he proclaimed.

Norman Luxton was at the head of the table, opposite his wife. "Nothing better than sharing a meal with interesting folk."

Patrick Nolan and George Luxton, both dressed in their 'Sunday best' sat opposite Reverend Tosh and the eight-year-old daughter of the house, Eleanor, who looked pretty-as-a-picture in her sailor's frock.

Patrick adjusted the knot of his pleasing tie. "Oi heard yer new ter town, Reverend Tosh?"

"Yes, Mister Nolan. I am f-filling in for Canon Harrison. I am here to take good care of his congregation and the town's p-precious mascot Bobby of Banff."

"Oi wus not aware dat Banff 'ad a mascot. Waaat is it?"

"It is a Yorkshire t-terrier, Mister Nolan."

"A Yorkshire terrier," echoed Patrick Nolan with a puzzled expression. "Never heard av it. Luxton, ye nu Banff 'ad a Yorkshire terrier for a mascot?"

"Er, no." Luxton picked up the carving set, the handles made from deer antlers. He carved the first slice of roast beef and placed it on the blue and white china plate.

Reverend Tosh smiled at George who was a bit heavier than Luxton but shared the family resemblance. "Mister Luxton tells me you are new to town t-too. May I ask what brought you here?"

George smiled when their eyes met. "I have come to manage my brother's theatre."

"Can I interrupt?" said Luxton. "Another slice, Reverend Tosh?"

"Just a s-smidgeon," he replied before returning to the conversation. "A theatre how exciting!"

Luxton passed the plate to the young minister. "In May, I opened a theatre in the King Edward. It turned out to be too much work for one so George has come from Manitoba to lend a hand."

George glanced at his brother and said, "You've done well for yourself, Norman. You've got several strings to your bow now: the newspaper, the hotel, the theatre, and two trading posts."

"All I can say is Banff has been good to me."

"You are too modest, Norman." His brother leaned back in his chair. "From now on, I'm going to call you Mister Banff."

Peals of laughter rose from the table. Eleanor, small for her age, sat with her spine against the chair. "You must come to our theatre, Reverend Tosh! We have a giant velvet curtain and when it rises, the newsreel comes on, followed by a cartoon, then the double feature."

"A double feature. What is that?"

"Two films for the price of one. Have you heard of Charlie Chaplin?"

"Yes, I I think s-so. He has a toothbrush moustache and wears a billycock."

"And he dangles from buildings and slips on banana peels. I laughed so hard when he was pummelled in the face with a big cream pie."

"Slapstick comedy. Very entertaining. I must go t-to your daddy's theatre."

"Oh, it is so beautiful and cosy. And we have real opera seats. They came all the way from Chicago on the train," she cried, her shiny-brown ringlets bouncing off her shoulders, "and we have a Victrola machine."

"A Victrola machine! How very modern."

Eleanor nodded. "We play vinyl records when the reels are being changed. Have you heard of Mary Pickford, Reverend Tosh?"

"Yes. I I think so. Is she an actress?"

"The most beautiful actress! I got her autograph when she was vacationing at the Banff Springs Hotel."

134

"My g-goodness, how exciting."

"Mary Pickford's latest silent movie, Hearts Adrift, is playing in Daddy's theatre right now."

"Elean-or," Georgina flashed her daughter 'a look', "I am sure Reverend Tosh doesn't care to—"

"On the c-contrary, Mrs Luxton. It all sounds w-wonderful." Reverend Tosh held up the platter of peas. "Do you want me to p-put a spoonful on your p-plate, Eleanor?"

"No thank you. I can manage." The child took the dish of peas with confidence.

Reverend Tosh couldn't help but admire the beaded buckskin cuff wrapped around her tiny wrist. "What a p-pretty bracelet, Eleanor."

"It was a gift from the Nakoda tribe."

"I know of the Stoney t-tribe. Do the Nakoda live in these p-parts too?"

"They are one and the same," the girl replied.

Heat rose in Reverend Tosh's cheeks.

Eleanor continued, "They call themselves Nakoda. It was the white explorers who named them the Stoneys."

Reverend Tosh looked at his hand slicing the beef. "I w-wonder why?" he said absentmindedly.

"The Nakoda use fire-heated stones to boil broth in rawhide bowls. That is why they named them the Stoneys."

Reverend Tosh put his knife down. "By gosh. By golly. Eleanor, you d-do know a lot about the Indians."

"A chip av de auld block, I'd say." Patrick Nolan swallowed a forkful of mashed potatoes before adding, "Luxton, tell de Reverend Tosh aboyt yer grand days as an apprentice clerk ter an Indian agent in Ontario."

Luxton laughed and shook his head. "Another time, Paddy."

"Naw, tell him now! Reverend Tosh needs a gran' laugh. Isn't dat roi, Reverend Tosh?"

The young minister moved in his seat, making the walnut legs of the dining chair squeak. "Er, n-nothing quite like a g-grand laugh."

Luxton let out a breath and rested his fork and knife on his plate. "When I was a lad of 16, Reverend Tosh, I had a job accompanying an Indian on treaty paying trips. We travelled in an eight-man canoe. I was in charge of the money so I sat in the middle of the boat with a buckle and strap around my neck attaching me to the cash box. The theory was if the boat tipped, I would float up and they could find the currency. I'm not sure why Paddy continues to find that story highly entertaining."

Patrick Nolan roared with laughter. "'Tis the visual I get, Luxton."

Reverend Tosh patted his mouth with his napkin. "I h-hope the Indians did not treat you cruelly, Mister Luxton?"

It was Luxton's turn to laugh. "Quite the opposite, Reverend. I made a lot of good pals distributing the Treaty money. I have always had a good rapport with the native people. Georgie has too."

"My Mommy speaks fluent Cree."

Georgina smiled. "My father, David McDougall, is a missionary. I grew up with the Indians. Both Norman and I are advocates for aboriginal rights."

Reverend Tosh looked at Patrick. "And you, Mister Nolan, may I ask how you m-met Mister Luxton?"

Patrick Nolan took a sip of water. "Oi worked as a criminal lawyer in an office above Luxton's whaen he worked for de Calgary Herald. After a 'ard day, we'd drown our sorrows in a barley water an' Scotch an' share a grand laugh." Patrick Nolan turned to his host. "Luxton, talking aboyt another gran' laugh, oi read that corny advert av yers in a copy of '50 Switzerlands in One - Banff the Beautiful'."

"Paddy, corny brands it catchy." He grinned cheerfully. "Here is another one for you: 'A beautiful lake. A sunset view. A dandy fish dinner. Built for two.'"

"Luxton, what's dat al' aboyt? Are ye sellin' fish suppers *now*?"

"And Coca-Cola and Orange Crush in my chalet on the north shore of Devil's Lake."

"Cum again?"

"Well, Paddy, when I get my wood-burning steam boat up and running, my customers are bound to get a little peckish. Yes?"

Georgina stared at her husband and he turned to her and said, "What?"

"George is right," she grinned, "I married Mister Banff."

When it was time to clear the table, mother and daughter stood up and moved the cutlery and dishes to the bottom shelf of a walnut tea wagon. Georgina asked if anyone wanted steamed pudding and custard. No one did. The meal had satisfied everyone's appetite. The dirty plates were wheeled towards a saffron-painted door, two feet behind Luxton's chair. Georgina and Eleanor squeezed by and departed to the kitchen.

Luxton pulled out a plain cedar box. "Gentlemen, who wants a *seegar*?"

George and Patrick reached for one.

"Er, n-not for me," stated Reverend Tosh.

"Ye *must* 'ave a stogie, Reverend. De ancient Mayans smoked cigars for religious purposes, so they did."

"For religious p-purposes?"

"Indeed they did, Reverend. Indeed they did."

"Well perhaps maybe. Oh, thank you, Patrick."

Miss Lily Saunderson,
The Servant's Quarters
Brett Sanatorium
Spray Avenue
Banff, Alberta

December 15, 1914

Miss Ishbel McColl
c/o Mine Director
Mine Director's Cabin
Canmore, Alberta

Dear Ishbel:

Sweet cheeses, I haven't heard from yi for nearly 3 weeks???

'Tis my half day off t'day so I thought I'd write yi another one coz the plot is thickenin' with Lady Clementine (the snotty-nosed American searchin' for her suiter.) Well, the suiter has gone and got himself married! And guess who to that nice woman who helped me with the torn donation bag, Pearl Brewster Moore. 'Tis a small world, eh.

Ethel said Lady Clementine wuz furious. She asked Doctor Brett if Pearl wuz from old money, related t' Count and Countess Brewster of Angus, Scotland NO. She asked if Pearl wuz from new money, the upper class of New York City NO. She asked what finishin' schools Pearl had attended. Doctor Brett said as far as he knew, Pearl didn't go t' a finishin' school coz she had t' help her dad deliver the milk.

Lady Clementine shrieked, "No! No! No! A workin'-class woman cannot possibly such a friendship cannot be tolerated!" Then she fainted. Fell against the sideboard, she did. Landed a whoppin' great shiner. Now she refuses t' come out of her room. And here comes the best bit Ethel wuz picked t' answer her beck and call!"

Ethel said when she showed up on her first mornin', Lady Clementine wuz inspectin' her bruised eye in a hand-held mirror. Without lookin' up, she said in her la-de-da voice, 'Tell me Ester, Emma, Emily whatever your name is, are you honest, sober and noiseless in your movements.'

'Yes M'Lady. And my name is Ethel.'

'Are snuff taking and alcohol drinking two of your habits?'

'No, M'Lady.'

'Do you say your prayers at night?'

Ethel said her eyes glazed over with boredom. 'Yes, M'Lady,' she said. And, sweet cheeses, the next thing she knew, she wuz Lady Clementine Corrinwallis's handmaiden. Now she has t' run and fetch all day long for that puffed-up woman who spends most of the day in bed, titivatin' with her hair and face, and callin' out for her heart's desire!

Poor Ethel. (Did I write that?) Anyway, she's met her match. Ha-ha.

I can hardly believe it is almost Christmas. The cook wuz makin' mince pies this morning. She said she uses 3 spices (cinnamun, cloves and nutmeg) t' represent the 3 wise men. Also, a 12-foot tree wuz delivered yesterday. We are all stoppin' work at 2 pm t' decorate it. I bought yi a raffle ticket for the Christmas hamper (t' raise money for the needy). The draw is this afternoon so keepin' my fingers crossed.

That's all my news for now. Write soon.

Lily

PS: Every night I say a little prayer for Joe and Bobby.

***

Ishbel McColl
c/o The Mine Director
The Mine Director's Cabin
Canmore, Alberta

Sunday, December 20, 1914

Miss Lily Saunderson,
The Servant's Quarters
Brett Sanatorium
Spray Avenue
Banff, Alberta

Dear Lily,

Sorry it has taken me so long to write back. My dad caught pneumonia and I've been tryin' to make his dinners and keep his fire goin' before and after my shifts. Thankfully, he's getting' better. On top of that, I've been rushed off my feet, helpin' Mrs Bloxham with the Mine Director's Christmas parties. I think the important man has wined and dined every blinkin' shareholder in Western Canada.

I dropped a line to Joe Ukrainec, tellin' him that I met his neighbour and she told me what happened. I offered him a rain check for our first date I thought that would make him laugh. Alas, he didn't get my note. It was returned unopened from the Cave and Basin Internment Camp. On top of that, yesterday's newspaper said Ukrainian women and children are bein' arrested in some parts of Canada. Terrible. Lily, I hope it doesn't happen here.

Changing the subject. Thank goodness you escaped bein' run over by that horse. It's a shame about the donation bag burstin' with all those business clothes likely belonged to an old gentleman who died up at the Sanatorium. No one wears that paraphernalia (had to look up the spelling) around here. Anyway, that was good of Mrs Brewster-Moore offerin' to mend and clean them. (I think it's great she pinched Lady Clementine's suitor). So did the snotty-nosed socialite don her veiled-hat and go home?

Changin' the subject again, these days, I'm gettin' a bit down about Bobby. My search is turnin' into a big damp squib. If he was here, Lily, surely I would have found him by now.

The mine director and his family are spendin' the Christmas week in Calgary so I'm here by myself. I don't mind. The cabin darkens when the mistress is here. I hate to say it, but she's as mean as a muck-worm, constantly lookin' over my shoulder in the hopes of findin' me dishonest or idle. Ugh!

On the upside, the Mine Director said I can eat the leftovers from his parties. And I have a beautiful Christmas tree. The place is warm and smells great how I wish I could invite you over. Anyway, I enclosed your Christmas present. I hope you enjoy wearin' it as much as I enjoyed makin' it to keep you snug.

Merry Christmas.
Ishbel

PS: I saw the picture in the Crag & Canyon Ethel Finch standin' in the Sanatorium kitchen, wearin' a big fat grin. Trust her to win the Christmas hamper.

Lily slipped into the little stone church on the corner of Buffalo and Beaver. It was packed to the gunnels with toffs, servants, and town's folk, their faith and dedication symbolised in the glimmer of flames dancing on the wicks of pure beeswax candles. A cough, a murmur, someone clearing their throat. Rows of hard-as-rock pews gleaming from years of buffing. A stack of hymn sheets for those who came to sing. A heap of musty bibles for those who came without. A congregation waiting and wondering.

Reverend Tosh, bursting with Christmas spirit, stood at the door of his church to greet each arrival. "Welcome to St. George's in the Pines." He grasped the visitor's gloved hand and shook it with earnest. "Welcome to our Christmas-Eve service."

"I think it rather odd." Lady Corrinwallis extracted her fingers. "Your bells are silent on this momentous occasion?"

The minister immediately reddened.

The woman removed her silver-fox fur and passed it to her personal maid. "If you agree bells equate to atmosphere, Reverend, pray tell me why you have none."

"Oh, atmosphere!" he exclaimed in delight. "We have p-plenty of *that* in St. George's-in-the-Pines. Do step inside, madam. Allow yourself to be touched by the h-holiness of this h-humble church and the spirituality of its congregation."

He pointed to the jewel-coloured panels. "And gaze in wonder at the scene before us! The interpretative beauty of our stained-glass window!"

The rich-looking lady leaned forward to take a closer look and quickly drew back. "A hiker? A skier? A bighorn sheep?!"

The minister gripped his bible and his emotions. "Of course, madam, we have conventional representations too." He raised his hand to the opposite wall. "Look! The Good Lord has a *whole* window to himself. And Saint George does too! And and if you wish, madam, I will be delighted to play a Canadian song on our church's eleven b-bells."

"A Canadian song!" The woman lifted her chin with the purpose of being properly haughty. "A preposterous suggestion. It is not not Christmassy."

"Regrettably." Reverend Tosh did not want to admit he only knew one tune. "Not Christmassy m-madam," he said with a twinge of unease, "but the bells have levers with notes so chosen that the Canadian song can be played p-perfectly."

A thin hysterical giggle rose from inside Lady Clementine's chest. She turned and made her way to the cushioned-front pew.

Carrying his bible slightly in front, Reverend Tosh walked briskly to the church alter, genuflected then turned to scan the expectant faces. The elderly church organist took that as a cue to hit the keys and the sound from the wheezing instrument linked with the children's voices, rousing them to sing with hearty enthusiasm. *'O Come, All Ye Faithful'* rose higher and higher until its effect became soul-stirring. At that point, Reverend Tosh opened his Good Book and read the Christmas story, his voice hooking his congregation so completely even the toughest of his flock became misty-eyed. The children's' choir returned to lead the church praise with *'Joy to the World'* and the worshipers listened, only vaguely disturbed by the long-poled collection-ladles moving up and down the pews. Ethel dropped two coins into the church coffer and smiled up at old Donald Duncan who gave her a wink before pushing the stick forward for the benefit of the rich-looking lady.

"Repeat the sounding joy
Repeat, repeat the sounding joy"

Lady Clementine drew her brows together and gazed down at the green baize-lined box. "At this time of year, I prefer to dispense with the vulgarities of money," she heralded, and no one could tell from old Donald's goggle-eyed expression if he was appalled or amused.

The young minister glanced down at his notes. He had worked long and hard on preparing and practicing his words for the Christmas creed. Finally, the time had come for him to deliver and he was more than ready. "Welcome. Welcome everyone to this celebration of Our Lord's birth." Candlelight illuminated the secretive stained-glass windows, brightened the muted tapestries, and dappled the pale plastered walls. Parishioners bowed their heads, worshiped and prayed through a ritual, hallowed and sacred.

When the service was over, Reverend Tosh plucked up his courage and made the announcement. "In a few minutes I will attempt to play a Canadian song on our church's eleven bells to honour our own soldiers so far from home tonight. I did not take easily or naturally to bell ringing," he admitted, "so please forgive me if it is less than perfect." A great bustle of excitement enveloped the church. Reverend Tosh made his way down the centre aisle, turned left, and ascended the tower steps two at a time. He stood at the top in the buffeting draft. "Oh Dear Lord, please help me with this." His fingers hovered over the leavers his lips lingered over the count. Deliberately and determinedly, he struck the batons and pressed the pedal clavier. The bells in the tower began to ring out juddering the night air soaring high above the church spire whirling around a mountain of spruce and pine all the way across a snow-covered valley towards an internment camp where lowly prisoners huddled for warmth.

Joe Ukrainec leaned back against the prison wall and pulled his knees to his chest. "Oh, Caaan-ada! Our fathers' land of old unless he was a Ukrainian then you're out in the cold."

The laughter from his fellow prisoners was rough, noisy and tinged with bitterness.

"Chrischtmas," Andriy, the oldest prisoner, rested his chin in his hands, "and no schpider. No veb. And no Chrischtmas tree."

Joe put a fist up to his mouth to hide his laughter. "Why the heck do Ukrainians hang spiders and webs on Christmas trees anyway?"

Andriy stretched his legs. "The schtory goes that a poor vidow couldn't afford to decorate her tree. Vhen she and her children voke on Chrischtmas morning, they found a schpider and a glittering veb which later turned into real gold and schilver, rescuing them from poverty."

Joe removed his thin grey blanket and wrapped it twice around his legs and feet. "Well, Andriy, if the spider shows up tonight," he joked, "make sure you wake me up, eh."

The inmates erupted in laughter.

The old Ukrainian retorted, "And vhat would you do with the gold and schilver?"

"Ah! Well. I'd start by buying my way outta this godforsaken prison, get as far away as I could from this miserable country and everything it stands for."

John stared through the misty gloom at the face of his brother. "Joe, stop that talk." His words took them all by surprise. "Misguided politicians and greedy businessmen are not Canada. Men with money and no integrity have wheeled and dealed their way into power positions. That's why we sit here, huddled like a herd of cattle."

"If that's so," said Joe, trying to keep his voice even, "we should expect a helluva an act of contrition when this war's over."

The detainees hollered their agreement and banged their tin cups on the floor.

A passing guard thumped on the side of the locked boxcar. "Keep It Down, Hunkies!"

The prisoners waited until his tread ceased to be heard. Andriy leaned towards his best friend, Danilo. "Vhy are John and Joe prischoners? Dey ver bos born in Canada."

Danilo looked at the lugubrious brothers, sitting side by side and hunched against the wall. He attempted to lighten the mood, "Your fazer ant ich ver the same age as you two vhen ve came to Canada."

Joe pulled himself up. "What made you come?"

Laughter lines formed over Danilo's thin cheeks. "De decischion vas made on a photograph and a promische."

Joe looked at him with eyes wide open. "A photograph and a promise?"

Danilo nodded, "Tventy years ago, Archduke Franz Ferdinand, visited de rapidly-growing Vancouver area. De schtory vas all over the European nevschpapers, *'Heir to the Austro-Hungarian throne looks schplendid in his ostrich-feathered hat and vax mustache as he schteps onto Canadian schoil.'* Beschide it, a big vant advertischment, 'LABOURERS NEEDED IN CANADA'. Our interescht vas peaked. Vladimir, Andriy and I talked to our vives. Canada held a promische a chance for usch to get ahead."

John spoke, "So you said goodbye to everything you knew."

Danilo was silent for a moment. "Ve schaid goodbye to our families and friends and together, Vladimir and Stepania, Andriy and Katrya, my vife, Anya, and I, began de long and dangerous dzhourney by boat, wagon and train. Vee vas out of money by de time vee reached de prairies. Vee had to build a schod house before the vinter came and John vas born. The following year, Joe vas born. Vee loved you bos like our own. My Anya, schhe could not hev children."

"I remember that sod house in Winnipeg." John glanced at Joe, "Do you remember it?"

Joe laughed. "I remember the two-hour walk to school and back."

A gangly man about the same age as Joe and John sat bolt upright. "At least you two could speak the language. When I came from Hungary, I couldn't understand the teacher."

"But you were clever, Ivan," said John. "Once you picked it up, you shot to the top of the class."

Ivan pushed his cap back and scratched his forehead. His sparse hair drooped over his bald crown. "For all the good it did me, eh."

"Vee is proud of you, Ivan." Danilo put a hand on the young man's shoulder. "You became de school teacher you schpeaken de perfect English. Our accents ver a handicap. Two thirds of Vinnipeg vas barred and bolted againscht Ukrainians, Poles and Jews. If you could beat det accent, you could caschually change your name and apply for vork anyvhere. But Vladimir, Andriy and I could not get our tongues around de English vords scho ve ver left vith rough manual labour. Vhen det dried up, vee valked ze schtreets of Manatoba looking for vork but there vasn't a job for love nor money zen ve heard the Hudschon Bay Company was hiring Ukrainians in Edmonton ve headed zer but the jobs ver all gone. Zen vord came zat Coalmine #1 in Canmore vas hiring Ukrainians scho ve headed down schouth." Danilo smiled. "Vladimir, Andriy and I ver hired on de day vee arrived. Vee schent for our families. Schuch happy memories. Scho long ago. Vladimir and Stepania both gone. Andriy and ich both vidowers now."

Joe looked, first at Danilo then at all of them. "Canada's National policy drew Ukrainian families here. Our people worked hard. They gave their lives to build this country. Look around you. This is how they treat us."

John's voice was clear and strong. "When the war is over, Canada will recognise we have suffered a fierce injustice."

"How can you be scho schure?" Danilo foamed wounded pride and spitting-mad rage.

"Because Canada belongs to its people, Danilo. It belongs to us all not the head of the nation, a military unit or a political party."

The prison fell into an eerie silence. The church bells rose up again. John drew his knees to his chest, rested his brow on his folded arms, and listened to the tune of his nation

"O Caaan-ada! Our fathers' land of old
Thy brow is crown'd with leaves of red and gold"

Reverend Tosh's congregation rose as one and began to sing.

Lady Clementine crossed her legs and dangled one foot. "Kindly avert your eyes," she snapped to all those in earshot. "I am not a Canadian. I am an American and I do not have to stand for your English adaptation of the Chant National which I might add is not official."

"Official or no, M'Lady, 'tis a matter o' respect ter stand for the patriotic song of the nation yar visitin'."

"Gadzooks! If the army wasn't pilfering all the servants are you happy now?"

Reverend Tosh positioned himself at the door so he could wish all his parishioners a goodnight and a Merry Christmas. One by one they filed past, each taking a moment to shake his hand.

"Reverend, both the service and the bells were magnificent."

"I am so thankful for your support."

"Reverend, we are so lucky to have you as our new parish minister."

"You are most kind."

"Reverend, the playing of 'O' Canada at your Christmas service was uplifting."

His spirit rose in triumph

"Actually. I thought the whole thing rather biz-*arre*." Lady Clementine, hands in front, pushed him aside and stepped out of the picturesque place of worship into a starry night where snowflakes twirled against an ink-blue sky. Ethel hurried to catch up.

Reverend Tosh squeezed the handkerchief in his pocket and closed the church doors. He was about to turn the heavy key in the lock when he heard scratching on the vestry door. "Hold your h-horses I am coming! I had to lock you in because you cannot jump on our p-parishioners' laps. Nor lick their f-faces. No. No." He turned the handle and the Yorkshire terrier shot into this waiting arms. "Ah-choo! And a very m-merry Christmas to you too, Bobby of Banff."

A rattling kitchen window frame in the Mine Directors cabin. Ishbel pulled back the little lace curtain and light was thrown onto the roof of an icy shed. A cloud passed between her and the full moon; its colour becoming so bright, it almost hurt her eyes. Somewhere, close by, a dog was barking. Further away, the sound of a train. For a fleeting moment the sound of footsteps. Then a faint tapping on the back door. She eyed the mantle clock. Almost midnight. Heart racing, she called through the letterbox, "Who goes there?"

"Brightly shone the moon that night—"

"Dad!" Ishbel dismantled the double-bolt lock and threw the door wide open. "Dad! You scared me witless! Come in! Come *in!"*

Mister McColl caught a whiff of pine and wax polish. "That's the snow comin' on," he said, handing his daughter a covered plate. He glanced around the room: a fur pelt draped across a buckskin chesterfield; an oil-burning chandelier bouncing light off a plein-air painting; a glittering Christmas tree tucked in a corner. "So this is how the other half live," he said, pulling off his brown toque, exposing a touch of grey at his temples.

"As fine as it is, Dad, it's nothin' compared to the Banff Springs Hotel." She put the plate down. "Nobody knows what luxury is until they step inside *that* place."

"Well, I'll have to take your word it," he said with a half-laugh, "I don't see them lettin' a lowly miner walk through their front doors anytime soon." He covered his mouth with the fabric to muffle a rumbling cough.

Ishbel took a few sticks from the basket and put them on the fire. "Oh, Dad, it gladdens my heart to see you." She drew a chair closer to the hearth. "Hand me your coat. Come. Warm yourself by the fire." She pumped up a flattened cushion. "Sit down. Sit down."

Mister McColl wiped his rheumy eyes and chose the winged chair by the fireplace. "Blimey, Ishbel, I must be barkin' mad." He lowered his curved spine into the seat. "If the Mine Director walks in and catches me sittin' in his fancy chair—"

Ishbel hesitated, then brushed the thought from her mind. "The big man's in Calgary, Dad, and likely drunk as a skunk on his Christmas port. We're safe enough." She placed a cushion at his back and reached down for his steel-toed boot. Mister McColl involuntarily lifted a leg.

"You're right, lass. If that old braggart had his way, we'd each be sittin' alone on Christmas Eve." He lifted his other foot. "Sure, we're doin' no harm, eh?"

"No harm at all." She turned her attention to the fire; reached for the coal scuttle; tipped on few pieces. One puff of the bellows and the flame rekindled straight away.

Mister McColl inhaled noisily then lurched forward into a violent bout of coughing.

"Dad! Are you alright?"

"I'm fine, lass." He wiped his whole face with his handkerchief. "I'm fine."

Ishbel forced a smile. "I was given permission to eat the leftovers from the Mine Director's parties. You sit and watch the fire spit. I'll go and get you somethin' tasty—"

Soon, Mister McColl put his knees together to make a lap for his plate. "Oh, lass, you've given me too much," he said, gazing at a big slice of roast goose and a square of buttered fruit cake. "I just don't have the appetite."

"Da-*aad,* it will do you good."

"Have mercy on my stomach, lass. 'Tis the middle of the night."

The fire crackled in the hearth. "I made you a Christmas present," she said, pressing a soft parcel into his rough palms. She watched him untie the string and carefully unfold the brown paper. "You have to bundle up for this Alberta winter," she said, hoping he'd like it.

"Aaah, just what I needed!" He wound the chunky brown scarf twice around his neck. "What a grand present. Thank you, Ishbel. And now 'tis your turn." He reached over to remove the pot lid. "SurPRISE!" he announced with great flourish.

"What!" Ishbel was flabbergasted. "Indulgence and extravagance! I haven't seen one of these since we left Scotland."

His eyes twinkled. "Macaroon bars the next best thing to havin' the wee dug pop outta the pot."

Seconds passed before Ishbel nodded. "Where did you get the recipe?"

"From dear old Mrs Storrie."

Ishbel looked up. "Not Mrs Storrie who worked in the shop with the open fire and creakin' floorboards?"

"One and the same. It was inside her Christmas card," he said brightly. "I took a bash at makin' them this mornin'. Bet you didn't know there's mashed potatoes in them."

"Of course I did." She regarded him through narrow eyes. "Dad. Everyone knows that."

"Everyone but the folks around here," he sighed, drawing a sharp breath and clenching his jaw.

A silence fell between them until Ishbel spoke, "Dad, you look like you're carryin' the cares of the world on your shoulders." She ran her fingers over her father's calloused hands, hoping the warmth would cheer him but a gloom, like a weight, lay deep inside him. "Dad, say your piece."

"Ishbel, sometimes I worry. I cannae help worryin' these days."

"About what?"

"Everythin'. Och, I wish I could send the world back in time. To when your mother placed you in my arms." His eyes grew pools. "And your tiny fingers reached out and curled around my thumb. You were my little kipper and I held you safe then. But now you're all grown up and I'm tellin' myself." His heart churned in his chest. "It was a rubbish idea."

"A rubbish idea?" Ishbel, pinked cheeked and wide eyed. "What?"

Daniel McColl took a deep breath and came right out with it. "Bringin' you to Canada." He turned his eyes towards the flames, crackling and popping. "We were solidly embedded in Scotland. Our roots ran deep in a country we've both known since birth."

Ishbel looked at him. "Daa-*ad*." She took his hand and squeezed warmth into it, "Dad, Canada is our home now."

"Is it?"

"Yes. We are a pair of hardy plants. We can bloom wherever we're planted. Remember?" Her heart hammering. "Dad, do you do you not think that anymore?"

Silence.

He glanced up at her perplexed expression and immediately regretted his honesty for he knew in his heart it was too late for doubt. "Och, lass, 'tis Christmas; I'm drenched in nostalgia." He lifted up his voice. "No more lookin' back 'tis no the way we're goin'."

Relief brought a smile to her lips. "And I'll always be your little kipper." Content with her corner of the world, she scrambled to her feet to draw the lace curtains. "Oh Dad. Come and look at this moon. It's like a giant Christmas bobble dangling above the mountain tops."

They both smiled up at the sky. "Gold. The colour of hope." He turned to face his daughter. "Ishbel, besides findin' that wee dug, what would you be wishin' for this comin' year?"

A moment later she replied, "I wish they would dismantle the internment camps. The Ukrainian's came here for a better life. Like we did."

"Aye, 'tis a big concern. Especially when one of them is Joe Ukrainec."

Ishbel's fingers flew to her lips. "How do you do you know him? How do you know that I know him?"

Mister McColl lowered his eyebrows. "I harboured a curiosity so I made it my business to check him out. For your mother's sake, God bless her soul."

"Check him out! *Daa-ad!* How could you!"

"Oh, keep your hair on," he replied with a guttural laugh. "Joe Ukrainec was my apprentice. I already knew him."

"Your apprentice! I didn't know he didn't know. Did he know?"

Mister McColl shook his head and gave a ghost of a chuckle. "Neither of us knew, at first. But 'tis hard chippin' away at a coal seam with a laughin' hyena warblin' beside you. I asked him what was so funny. Well. As soon as he mentioned the girl throwin' pots and pans at a bear, I put two and two together. And promptly reminded him you are only fifteen."

"Daa-*ad!* I'm nearly sixteen! What what did he say when he found out you were my dad?"

"Och, he began blabberin' at the mouth. A bit embarrassed he was. Well, I'd best get goin', Ishbel. Pass my boots, lass. Save me gettin' up twice."

"Dad. There, there was a bit in the newspaper sayin' a formal complaint was sent to London," she said, tensely. "To protest the ill treatment of the Ukrainian prisoners in the Cave & Basin Internment Camp."

Her father, a conciliatory and calm man, could not hide the fury in his eyes as he pulled on his boots. "You cannae burden yourself with those thoughts, lass," he said, his voice tight and hard. "Joe Ukrainec has a good head on his shoulders. He'll know to work hard; keep his head down; keep from bein' noticed. None of this can go on forever. 'Tis just a matter of getting' through it." He gently squeezed his daughter's hand. "And he'll get through it."

He walked towards the door, pulling on his knitted cap, covering the hair above his far-seeing grey eyes.

"Dad, are you warm enough?" She unwound then rewound his scarf, tucking the ends inside his jacket.

"Stop fussin', lass. I'll be home in fifteen minutes," he said, careful of his footing on the three slick stone steps.

Ishbel stood in the doorway, breathed in the smell of pine, and watched her dad trudging through the snow like Good King Wenceslas. She laughed inwardly and yelled after him, "Daa-*aad!* Watch out for the wildlife! And the locomotive on Engine Bridge!"

Mister McColl turned around as the Mine Director's Cabin blew a spiral of smoke into the air. "Don't worry, lass." He backed up the road. "Rudolph and his pals are prancin' across the rooftops and the Old Goat doesn't haul coal on Christmas day." He coughed into his handkerchief and continued on his way, happiness lifting his every step.

"I love you, dad," she whispered and was about to close the door when she caught sight of a shooting star flashing across the universe, its silvery trail stirring through the darkness. "'Star light, star bright, the shootin' star I see tonight, I wish I may, I wish I might, have three wishes I wish tonight'"

Miss Lily Saunderson,
The Servant's Quarters
Brett Sanatorium
Spray Avenue
Banff, Alberta

December 30, 1914

Miss Ishbel McColl
c/o Mine Director
Mine Director's Cabin
Canmore, Alberta

Dear Ishbel:

This mornin', I woke t' whurlin' flakes of snow outside my window. Thanks for the pretty scarf I love that pale green colour. I tried embroiderin' a handkerchief with yir initials but it turned out like a dog's dinner. So, when yi get back, I'm treatin' yi t' a cream tea at the Paris Tea Room. Ethel's mistress calls it 'a most quintessenshul English meal'.

Well, it wuz quiet around here durin' the Christmas week. Most of the patients and their families went home so, sweet cheeses, I got a bit of a break. Now. Get comfy. 'Tis time for:

<u>*The Continuin' Saga of Lady Clementine and Ethel the Maid*</u>

Ethel said she duzn't want t' be a personal maid t' a puffer fish who blows up at the least thing and spurts poisonous venum everywhere. So she asked for her old job back (workin' with me). But they said no. Sweet cheeses, she wuz hoppin' mad. She kicked a bucket from one end of the scullery t' the other. Our cook says Lady Clementine may have a temper unequal t' anyone so well-bred, but she's met her match with Ethel and that's the real reason they're not movin' her.

Anyway, continuin' on with the story: Lady Clementine wuz sittin' up in bed, nibblin' on a chocolate croissant when, out of the blue, she called for her Italian-leather journal and her lusterous-gold fountain pen. "When one is privileged,

Ethel, one is expected t' champion a charity. A bally nuisance but essential for social advancement. Pick a worthy cause and be quick about it."

Ethel thought for a moment. "What about care packages for our soldiers?"

"Hmm, that will do," she replied.

So, t' cut a long story short, Lady Clementine is goin' t' hold a Hat Auction and Tea Party at the Lake Agnes Teahouse. Ethel told her 'tis on top of a mountain and the train duzn't go up there. But Her Ladyship said the teahouse is named after the wife of Canada's first Prime Minister, Agnes MacDonald, who happens t' own property in Banff. She said if little Agnes attends, it will attract the big newspapers and the large amount of publicity will get her off the fundraising hook for years. "Positively wizard!" she exclaimed, pouring herself a large gin (she calls it juniper water). Ethel told her she will slip down the slippery-slope if she keeps drinkin' 'fore noon and Lady Clementine snapped back, "Ethel, as a person of your class would say slippery-slope my arse!"

Changin' the subject. The Ukrainian prisoners are growin' in numbers. Now hundreds are marchin' past our windows twice a day. Ethel waves and winks at them. Ugh!

I'm glad yir dad's feelin' better.

Oh, I almost forgot t' tell yi. An American guest left me a jar of Ponds varnishin' cream. I'm goin' t' put some on right now and jump int' bed.

Goodnight from Lily.

PS: If Bobby's not in Canmore, maybe he wuz picked up before he got there. I wish we'd asked Wild Bill Peyto 'fore he left t' fight in the war. His Park Warden job took him all over that area.

PSS: Ethel wuz talkin' t' the charlady who cleans Earnscliffe Cottage (Lady Agnes McDonald's house in Banff). She says Canada's retired first lady likes ridin' on cowcatchers and carvin' poems int' the walls of her home! Sweet cheeses, between her and our government arrestin' Ukrainian women and children, I think this country's goin' t' hell in a handbag.

***

Ishbel McColl
c/o Mine Director
Mine Director's Cabin
Canmore, Alberta

January 6, 1915

Miss Lily Saunderson,
The Servant's Quarters
Brett Sanatorium
Spray Avenue
Banff, Alberta

Dear Lily,

Happy New Year! I got a stitch in my side from laughin' at your letter. I'm surprised Ethel hasn't taken to the bottle too. Ha-ha. I really liked her idea though care packages for our soldiers. I wish I could make up a care package for Joe in the internment camp. Lookin' forward to my cream tea at the Paris Tea Room. Just the thought of it makes my mouth water.

Oh, Lily, I could kick myself for not askin' Peyto to look out for Bobby you're right, he knows everybody around these parts. Anyway, no time to write, the mistress wants the Christmas tree down today. She says if we don't have it down by Epiphany then to avoid bad luck we have to wait until Candlemas Day on February 2ⁿᵈ It's sheddin' its needles as I write. Corny joke: Why are Christmas trees so bad at sewing? 'Cause they always drop their needles. Anyway, better get goin'.

Take care,
Ishbel

PS: The mistress told me today to count my blessings. The brass cheek of it. I think she would take a lot longer than me if she was to count her own.

The Break of Day, February 28, 1915
Boxcar Cell
Cave & Basin Internment Camp
Banff, Alberta

A cruel wind thrashed against the sides of the boxcar, rattling the heavy-duty latch; jingling the links on the unwieldy chain. John rested his aching head in the crook of his arm and with his body supported by the wall, watched the morning rays filter through a lonely crack. Reason and memory flourished. Feelings of agitation afflicted his mind. He stared blankly at his wretched socks hanging forlornly from a nail on the mushroom-coloured wall and willed them to dry. The potent stench of sweaty bodies. Prisoners on their backs snoring loudly, mouths wide open. Others lying like corpses. All of it added to the discomfort of his painful joints. He looked across at the sleeping face of his brother. "Why is that swine of a guard picking on you? Is it your strong Ukrainian features the brow ridge the concave nose? *What?*" Through a muffled cough he made the decision. "There's no way around it. I have to get Joe out of his hellhole the sooner the better." Pulling a makeshift calendar from his breast pocket, he scribbled, 'February 28, 1915'. Above him, the sound of a bird walking across the tin roof. "What is it? A clay-coloured sparrow? A short-billed dowitcher? A three-toed woodpecker?" In his mind he watched all three take to the skies to greet the coming day.

Later that day, Reverend Tosh and his dog came to visit. Joe was huddled in a corner, a thin shaft of light illuminating his face. "Look what one of my industrious p-parishioners made especially for you!" The fledgling minister unfolded the colourful quilt and shook it out. The young prisoner wanted to show his appreciation but his stomach hurt and face ached when he tried to smile.

John scrambled to his feet. "Reverend, with all due respect, my brother needs time to rest. That crazy guard had another go at him this morning."

"No! Not again! I have written two two formal letters of complaint." He arranged the colourful quilt across Joe's knees. "I do not understand why why it is taking so l-long."

Joe lurched forward and the sudden movement caused a burst of coughing. John crouched down and fastened his arms around his brother's shoulders. "Joe, spit into this," he held up a rag and helped him expel the blood that swirled in his swollen mouth. "Now, lie back," he said with heavy heart. "Try to get some rest."

"Yes, you need to rest, Joe. Let me make that quilt into a pillow for your head." Reverend Tosh reached to retrieve the coverlet and fell across the dog.

Yelp!

"Oh, I almost flattened my little doggy! Sorry Bobby. Now shoo away, you you little fidget. No! No! No! Leave Joe alone! He does not want a volley of l-licks!" No! No! No!"

John scrambled to his feet, his emotions boiling over. "Get that animal the hell-away from my brother!" He grasped the minister by the elbow and hauled him towards the opening. "Reverend, it's time you left." The minister jumped down from the boxcar and John went back to pluck the dog from his brother's chest but a dangling piece of metal, inscribed with a tiny coat of arms, had kindled Joe's eyes and he was trying to get up.

"The *dog*—" he gurgled before the energy went out of him.

"Lie back, Joe. It's okay." He gently pushed on his brother's shoulders. "Close your eyes." John picked up the animal and carried it to the opening. "Here! Take your dog," he said, dropping Bobby into the minister's waiting arms.

Achoo! The sliding door rolled to a close in front of Reverend Tosh's nose.

The prison was dark and quiet. John banked down his anger and sat at his brother's feet. "Look what they're doing to you to us. Mark my words, Joe. This country will carry a black stain on its history books forever."

Joe's swollen eyes flickered. Everything in his body hurt. Dizziness came to cloud his mind; envelop his consciousness. All of a sudden, he was floating atop a colourful quilt over mountains, hills and slopes a tranquil glade; a turquoise lake white cotton sheets flapping in the breeze a grizzly watching from afar the fleeting vision of a pretty girl holding her face to the sun.

Chapter 6

Edmée Brewster Moore knelt on the kitchen chair, spreading the pages of the *Crag & Canyon* across the pickled oak table. "Mummy, Mummy. Come take a look. Daddy's picture is in the newspaper!"

"In the newspaper?" Pearl dried her hands and glanced over her daughter's shoulder at a youthful-looking picture of her husband. "What on earth is this about?"

ATTENTION: LADIES OF BANFF, ALBERTA

Lady Clementine Victoria Cornwallis

Takes great pleasure in announcing her Tea Party and Hat Auction to be held

On March 14, 1915
From 2 pm to 4 pm
At the Lake Agnes Teahouse, Lake Louise

To solely provide for the purchase and distribution of deluxe care packages for the Banff soldiers fighting overseas.
If you wish to actively support this honourable cause, please come prepared to donate a good-quality hat and bring along enough funds to excite a crowd when bidding.

Take Note:

Free admission to those wearing a suffragette ribbon.

Edmée looked questioningly at her mother. "Why is Daddy's picture in the paper?"

"Um, I'm not quite sure perhaps the editor wanted to draw attention to this announcement so he placed a photograph of a Banff soldier above it."

"But Daddy's not wearing his soldier's uniform."

"Hmm. Odd, I grant you. But there it is. The important thing is to support this fundraiser so all our soldiers can have a care package."

"But we don't have a hat to donate, Mummy."

"Oh, but we do! We have a *very* posh one in the attic. Come with me. We'll haul it down now and take a look."

The girl blew the dust off the circular lid and removed peels of tissue paper with great ceremony. "Oh, Mummy, 'tis lovely!"

"It belonged to Great Granny Brewster. She made it by herself for her wedding day. Try it on be careful how you handle it though. 'Tis old and delicate. Came half way across the world."

Edmée rushed to the mirror. "Oh, I look like a real lady! Mummy, I don't want to give this hat away."

"I don't either, Edmée, but we don't have anything else. And if we keep it, the moths will eventually eat it. Better we put it to good use." Pearl looked at her daughter. "What on earth are you doin'?"

"I'm talking to Great Granny Brewster in heaven. She wants to know who Lady Clementine Victoria Cornwallis is."

Pearl laughed. "Oh, Edmée."

"Who is she?"

Pearl put the hat back in its box. "Well her title tells us she is a woman of superior social position."

"And kind because she is helping our soldiers."

"Yes, very kind and thoughtful."

"Do you have a suffragette ribbon?"

"I believe in the cause, Edmée, but I'm always working the ranch when they have their meetings. One day."

"Do you think she is a mountain climber like Mary Schaffer?"

Pearl laughed. "Probably. Why else would she host a tea party and hat auction on top of a mountain?" She furrowed her brow. "In March it can be very icy and muddy up there. Let's hope for a good snow fall so we can all wear our snowshoes. Otherwise, it will be difficult for the elderly women to walk."

"Maybe they can ride their horse to the top."

"Good thinking, Edmée, but the route for the supply horses is practically vertical in places, so that wouldn't be safe for most riders. Not to worry, we are Brewster girls, eh? We'll put our heads down and crack on."

"Mummy. I think the important lady is carefree."

Pearl picked up the hat box and walked towards her bedroom. "More clueless than carefree," she muttered under her breath. "A hat auction on top of a mountain at this time of year the woman's a few pints short of a milk churn."

Miss Lily Saunderson
The Servants' Quarters
The Brett Sanatorium
Spray Avenue
Banff

March 16, 1915
Miss Ishbel McColl
c/o The Mine Director
The Mine Director's Cabin
Canmore, Alberta

Dear Ishbel:

I hope yi had a good week. Get cosy. Here's the next chapter of:

Lady Clementine and Ethel the Maid

The large bell suspended over the train engine clanged as it approached Laggan Station, a rustic log building constructed to accommodate the tourist trade. Lady Clementine leaned forward in her seat, "Indeed, I am giddy with excitement. Only one more stop until we reach the Lake Agnes Teahouse." Ethel rolled her eyes. She had given up tellin' her mistress the train didn't go up the mountainside. The porter's ears picked up. "I am afraid the train does not go up the mountainside, madam. You must get off at the Laggan Station and take the Tallyho to the Chateau Lake Louise. Walk through the covered platform and turn left. The mountain trail begins at the back of the hotel. One has to hike up."

"How utterly inconvenient! I demand to know the name of the blundering idiot who built this railroad."

The porter's face turned bright red. "William Cornelius Van Horne, madam."

"A complete dullard."

"Er," he swallowed hard, "Queen Victoria knighted him for building it from one end of Canada to the other."

"Really? Knighted for professional incompetence? Picks, shovels and a few hundred peasants would have taken this rail track to the Lake Agnes Teahouse." She rose from her seat. "I wish to disembark. Come along, Ethel." Ethel hurried

after her mistress, trying not to bang the big hatbox, the medium hat box and the little hat stand off the sides of seated passenger's heads.

On the station platform, Lady Clementine's chapeau fluttered in the breeze. "Tell the Tallyho driver to make brisker, Ethel."

The man jumped into action. "Where to, M'Lady?"

"To the Lake Agnes Teahouse. And be quick about it."

"Sorry M'Lady. One has to hike up." He looked down at her feet. "The Chateau has a mountain guide shop where one can rent hiking boots and snow shoes." The colour drained from Lady Clementine's face *'tis a wonder she boarded his Tallyho. Anyway they began the short journey and Ethel said the Victoria Glacier and Lake Louise looked out of this world, and the Chateau looked very grand. They pulled up outside a little shop with a window full of heavy boots and snowshoes. "Ugh! They all look positively ghastly!" cried Lady Clementine.*

"They're practical, M'Lady, not fashionable," said Ethel. "Let's go inside and try them on."

Lady Clementine slipped her foot into the first boot. "Enough! The Hat Auction and Tea Party are cancelled."

The shop assistant lifted her head. "Oh, no, madam. The fundraiser to help our soldiers endure the trenches is not cancelled. We had a good snowfall last night. Look some ladies are passing the window as we speak all carrying their hatboxes and wearing their snowshoes. Now, if madam is comfortable in these sturdy boots, I will bring out the snowshoes for you and your maid. The quicker you start on the trail the better I believe it starts at 2pm."

A single syrupy tear ran down Lady Clementine's cheek. "I fear my fundraiser is marred by buffoonery."

Well, that's all the story for now. Yi'll have t' wait a few days t' see whut happened next coz I'm workin' split shifts for the rest of the week. Goodnight.

Lily

Miss Lily Saunderson
The Servants' Quarters
The Brett Sanatorium
Spray Avenue
Banff, Alberta

March 24, 1915
Miss Ishbel McColl
c/o The Mine Director
The Mine Director's Cabin
Canmore, Alberta

Dear Ishbel:

I haven't heard from yi this week? Anyway, as promised, here is the next chapter of the story:

Lady Clementine and Ethel the Maid

"Sally forth!" cried Ethel and they set off along a trail that followed a steady incline. They had travelled about half a mile when Her Ladyship suddenly stopped in her tracks. She brushed the snow off a rock and plonked herself down. "I am frightfully cold and this appalling footwear is staggeringly ugly. It is giving me a headache. If only I had a palanquin," she pined.

Ethel screwed up her face. "A pallawhat?"

"A pal-an-quin, Ethel. It is a covered chair carried on two horizontal poles by four bearers."

"Ter carry slothful and sluggish women up hills?"

"No! Of course not!" Lady Clementine picked up a handful of snow, pressed it int' a ball and hurled it at Ethel. It smashed against her shoulder.

"Ouch!"

The retaliation wuz halted by the voice of the supply man ploddin' up the mountainside with his donkey. "Hullo ladies. Everything alright?"

Her Ladyship stared openly at him. "You do not actually expect us to say yes. Do you?"

So the supply man helped Lady Clementine onto his donkey and she sat side-saddle on top of the flour bag strapped to its back. Then he took the two hat boxes from Ethel and fastened them to the beast's sides. Ethel wuz glad she only had the hat stand t' carry. They all continued up the mountain side until they came upon a teal-coloured lake. "This is Mirror Lake," said the supply man. "When the wild animals drink from it, they admire themselves in its reflectin' surface. That's how it got its name."

"G'wan!" said Ethel.

Hee-haw! Ethel patted the ass consolingly on the snout. "Hey, what did the donkey say when he got a sore throat?"

"Whut?" asked the supply man.

"Oh do tell us," said Her Ladyship.

"I'm a little hoarse!" grinned Ethel.

Suddenly, without warnin', a large squirrel shot across their path. The supply man sprang t' restrain his frightened animal. Alas, not swiftly enough. Lady Clementine went flying through the air, narrowly missin' a pile of horse dung well, not, absolutely, completely and totally. Ha-ha. Anyway, after utterin' a few posh profanities, she got back on the donkey and adjusted her hat.

"Well, carry on, man," she said. "And stop whistling it is vulgar."

Finally they reached the rustic landmark. "There is no place like this place. Anywhere near this place. So this must be the place," said Lady Clementine.

"Yes. This is the Lake Agnes Teahouse," replied the supply man.

Outside the front door, a girl wuz playin' with a Yorkshire terrier that belongs t' the minister. Ethel says yi should buy it orff him and ship 't t' Winston!"

Next came the BIG surprise. The donkey man stepped forward, opened the door for Lady Clementine, and over a hundred women rose t' their feet. They were all wearin' green, white, and purple ribbons and they were all clappin' and cheerin'. The feathers on Lady Clementine's hat wuz limp, her face wuz streaked with dirt, and her frock wuz covered in muck, but none of that mattered on that afternoon coz she wuz their heroine. And by gum, did she ever revel in the adoration.

"Ladies," her face a wreath of smiles. "You are here today because I am passionate about what I do. Please be seated." Then she took her place in the middle of the head table. Standing tall, she faced her audience. "I, Lady Clementine Victoria Corrinwallis, in honour of your courageous husbands, sons, and brothers, take great pleasure in opening my inaugural Tea Party and Hat Auction. History will record its true worth. Now, may I ask the most honourable *person at each table to stand and pour the tea." And with that public declaration, she lifted the handle and tipped the spout.*

In due course, the fine teas were drained from the teapots, and the dainty treats disappeared from the tiered cake stands. Now it wuz time for action at the auction. Her Ladyship's gaze swept across three large tables of beautiful bonnets and she became quite emotional. "I do believe my hat has stolen centre stage," she hummed. The auctioneer rose from his seat took his rightful place behind the podium cleared his throat in preparation for action. Oh, Ishbel, yi'll never guess what happened next but yi have t' write t' me FIRST!

Goodnight.
Lily

PS: Hope yir dad's feelin' better?

***

Miss Ishbel McColl
c/o The Mine Director
The Mine Director's Cabin
Canmore, Alberta

Tuesday, March 30, 1915

Miss Lily Saunderson
The Servants' Quarters
The Brett Sanatorium
Spray Avenue
Banff, Alberta

Dear Lily:

My dad's a lot better and grateful to be back at work. It's been a tough go stretchin' out the strike pay.

I nearly killed myself laughin' at your Clementine and Ethel story better than Lady Audley's Secret. Hurry up and tell me the rest. And tell me again what the colours stand for on the suffragette ribbon. I forgot.

Must go! Up to my ears in spring cleanin'.

Miss you lots, Ishbel

PS: That Ethel Finch has a dodgy moral compass fancy suggestin' I pass the minister's dog off as Bobby.

***

Miss Lily Saunderson
The Servants' Quarters
The Brett Sanatorium
Spray Avenue
Banff

April 8, 1915

Miss Ishbel McColl
c/o The Mine Director
The Mine Director's Cabin
Canmore, Alberta

Dear Ishbel:

Glad yir dad's recovered. Suffragette ribbon: White stripe PURITY. Green stripe HOPE. Purple stripe DIGNITY. Her Ladyship told Ethel there's a good chance Alberta women, twenty-one and older, will get the vote next year. Lady Clementine is delighted she will come of age on such a momentous year (no comment).

I think Lady Clementine would eat Lady Audley for breakfast. Anyway, here's the final chapter for yir readin' pleasure:

<u>Lady Clementine and Ethel the Maid</u>

Ethel said the auction was like a theatrical production and Mister Jolly was the leadin' man. He wuz about t' grab everyone's attention when Lady Clementine rose from her seat. She pointed t' a table where a girl wuz holdin' a Yorky on her lap. "Children are a disTRACTION and dogs cause disEASE. Remove both from the room at once."

Then the girl's mother stood up. "Just a minute now! This is my daughter, and the daughter of a brave soldier," she said and everyone cheered. Ethel said she could see a nettly sense of irritation washing over Lady Clementine but, before she could reply, the mother continued. "If you didn't want children and dogs at your auction, you should have stated that in your newspaper notice."

Colour rose in Her Ladyship's cheeks. "Do you know who you are talking to?" she snapped, and the gap between them widened.

"Hmmm, Lady Lady," the mother tapped her chin. "What'syourname again?"

"Lady Clementine Victoria Corrinwallis!"

"Oh, I remember now. You're the one who organised this fundraiser on top of a flippin' snow-covered mountain."

The room erupted in laughter.

Her Ladyship pulled her shoulders back like she wuz preparin' for gladitoriul combat. "Cross swords with me at your peril," she spat. Then her facial expression changed. Ethel thinks she saw the following day's headlines in her mind's eye, "Big Brawl Breaks Out at Lady Clementine's Hat Auction and Tea Party." Coz she plastered on a smile and said, "Due to potential inclement weather, the child and dog may remain inside the Lady Agnes Teahouse."

A big cheer went up. The girl's mother sat down and an elderly lady reached across the table and patted her hand. "Good for you holdin' your own, dearly," she said. "That Lady Clementine is a snotty-nosed New Yorker came to Banff to reconnect with a rich gentleman suitor. Now she acts like she owns the place."

"Well, all I can say is, heaven help the poor bloke."

The auctioneer called for order. "Good afternoon, ladies. My name is Mister Jolly." He fiddled with his spectacles. "Before I begin, I would like to welcome Lady Agnes MacDonald, the wife of Canada's first Prime Minister who is gracing us today with her presence."

A little voice perked up, "She is in the back room smoking her cigarettes."

Gasps of shock encompassed the tearoom. Mister Jolly coughed into his fist. "Well, it is a modern practice. And why not? I say, why not? Now, let us get back to business." He checked his notes. "As some of you know, I am more used to auctioning off farm animals not ladies' hats." He looked at his audience. "Hats. Hogs. Hogs. Hats. All the same to me. Let us start with the first pretty bonnet."

Ethel said a straw cloche wuz placed on the table and the action began: "One dollar bid now two now two. Will you give me two? Two-dollar bid now three now three. Will you give me three? Three-dollar bid—"

The pace quickened and a storm of bids rolled in, fuellin' an auction that raged on like a house on fire. By the time half the hats were sold, the money collected had exceeded all expectations. The next item, a magnificent work of art, wuz brought forward. "Ooohs!" and "Aaahs!" abounded as Lady Clementine's Paris Couture (a filmy organza hat with crushed silk millinery roses) wuz placed on the auction block.

The biddin' began again. The price rose higher. And higher.

Suddenly, an overpowerin' terror befell Lady Clementine. She burst out, "That hat is not a charitable object. It was created by the renowned, Madame Virot! Sir," she raised her hand. "I have made a frightful blunder. I cannot possibly donate—"

"Going once. Going twice." Mister Jolly brought down the hammer. "Felicitations to Lady Clementine Corrinwallis. You are now the proud owner of this beautiful hat."

Lady Clementine stood up. "I did not nod! I did not bid! I am certainly not going to buy a hat that I already own!"

"Madam, you gesticulated."

"I did not!"

"You raised your hand, madam."

"But but," she stamped her foot. "Oh, how positively unfair!"

"The vicissitudes of life!" Mister Jolly's smile wuz wide. "All for a good cause, madam."

Lady Clementine begrudgingly opened her purse, "For Pete's sake," she shrieked, "Let us move along with this this travesty!"

Finally, the last hat wuz placed on the auction block.

Mister Jolly cleared his throat. "Not only has it been a very successful auction, it has been a delightful afternoon. My heart swells with pride as I gaze around at all you beautiful mothers, daughters and sisters who, without complaint, hiked to the top of a snowy mountain to raise funds that will bring hope and cheer to your brave Banff soldiers.

A bout of hearty clappin' filled the room.

Mister Jolly waited then held up a quietin' arm. "Before we auction off the last hat, I would like to thank Lady Clementine Victoria Corrinwallis for organising this wonderful event." Lady Clementine stood up and for several long minutes gave a queenly wave.

Mister Jolly said, "And now we are down to the very last hat." He burled a drum-roll sound-effect that made everyone laugh. "The very last hat!" Up went a massive cheer from all. "I say last but not least. Because the owner of this hat has the privilege of naming the soldier she was thinking of when she donated her bonnet. May I ask that lady to stand now?"

Now, wait for the bombshell

The mother of the girl stood up, adjusted the Yorky under her arm and reached for her daughter's hand. "My name is Pearl Brewster Moore. I was thinking of my husband and Edmée was thinking of her dad when we donated Granny Brewster's bonnet in honour of our soldier Major Philip Moore."

Well, to cut a long story short, Lady Clementine had a flippin' kitten. She cried out, "A working-class woman cannot have connubial harmony with an upper-class gentleman! No! No! No! It would never be tolerated in more settled parts of Canada!"

"Why ever not?" asked Mister Jolly.

"You dullard she is not from the right stock!"

Pandemonium broke loose. Ethel gulped down her cake and cajoled her mistress out of the Lake Agnes Teahouse as fast as she could. By the time they boarded the train back t' Banff, a pale sun wuz strugglin' through the rain clouds. "M'Lady, don't worry. There's plenty more fish in the sea," said Ethel.

"I do not want a stupid fish!" cried Lady Clementine. "I want a man with elevated qualities. I want a man with an impeccable pedigree. And furthermore, I intend to get him back!"

Ethel took a shocked breath. She thought her mistress had scruples. "But M'Lady it's too late," she said. "Whatever he was before, he's now the husband of another."

Lady Clementine twirled a ringlet around her finger. "Ethel, I will get him back because I can have the moon on a stick if I want," she said, grinning like a Cheshire cat.

"Oh, M'Lady, let's focus on June, eh. We're on the countdown now."

"June. What is so special about June?"

"Oh me nerves." Ethel squeezed the hat stand. "The season begins, M'Lady. Mister Dimbleby will turn that big key in the door of the Banff Springs Hotel and the gloomy town of Banff will be transformed into a hive of gaiety. We'll move out of the Brett Sanatorium into the grand hotel. There'll be lots of wonderful dinners. And balls in the evening, beginnin' at nine. In no time at all, ya'll be surrounded by admirers vyin' for yar heart."

"Hmm, an abundance of rich dandified gentlemen." Lady Clementine ran her fingers along her necklace. "I suppose I can play the voluptuous temptress of Mount Stephen Hall and kiss a knot of wealthy frogs while I wait for my handsome prince to return from war." Lady Clementine closed her eyes and rested her head against the CPR embroidered linen protector. "Oh behold

among the waters on an evening in spring the loveliest castle, as thus be held, in the whole world'"

"I beg yar pardon, M'Lady?"

"Oh do be quiet, Ethel. I am endeavouring to recall a poem by Lord Conway."

THE END

No more muck in Banff's muddy pits of scandal. At least for now. Sweet cheeses, I can't believe 'tis only three weeks 'til we're back at the Banff Springs. Can't wait t' see yi. We'll have so much t' natter about.

Lily

The weak spring sunlight filtered through the pane casting a yellow sheen on the glass doors of the china cabinet. Ishbel took a step back to check the display. Lined up on three shelves precise, crisp, and opulent a dozen crystal wine glasses, a dozen crystal flutes, and a dozen crystal water glasses. She looked up at the clock. Three minutes to go. Swivelled on her heels and made a beeline through the dining room to the tiny square hall with the long case clock flanked by two doors. One minute to go. She waited. The timepiece struck the hour with a sombre dingdong toll. Ishbel knocked hesitantly on the door of the Mine Director's small office.

"Come in," cried the voice from inside.

Ishbel cautiously opened the door. "You asked to come at noon, ma'am."

"Yes," said the Mine Director's wife then returned to her ledger. Ishbel waited, allowing her eyes to travel around the low-ceilinged space, cosy and tight. A petite drum table amassed with objects: an alabaster bust, an ashtray, and a pile of leather-bound books. Her mistress perched on her husband's leather chair, a cushion at her back, its fabric spiked with great splashy blooms. "Ishbel," Her mistress placed the fountain pen in its holder. "I have tallied up your wages. I deducted the cost of your room and board, the three dollars remuneration you were advanced in the fall, and the purchase you made. That leaves a grand total of fifteen dollars and nine cents. If you value a good reference, do not let your new-found wealth go to your head," she said, opening the cash box, counting out the money, placing it in a buff-coloured envelope. She reached for the fountain pen, dipped it into the inkwell, and handed it to Ishbel. "Sign right *there*," she said with pointed finger.

With the scent from a bowl of oranges wafting up her nose and her heart beating wildly for fear of making an ink splotch, Ishbel, slowly and carefully wrote her name in her very-best handwriting. She was handed the wage packet.

"Thank you, ma'am." Ishbel curtsied, took five backward steps, turned, and closed the door behind her. She strode steadfastly back through the cabin, towards the kitchen and her little settle bed tucked behind the three-panel folding screen. Dejected, dispirited and discouraged, she pushed the little packet of money under her mattress. "All that searchin' and I'm leavin' Canmore without wee Bobby."

Chapter 7

Reverend Tosh had Bobby firmly clipped to the end of his leash when they crossed over Banff's Bow River Bridge. The light was glimmering on the rushing waters, large clumps of broken-loose ice were swirling down the river, and the heat of the sun was gratifying on his shoulders. The young minister breathed in the crisp mountain air, allowing its freshness to nourish his body and soul. "It is g-good to be alive, Bobby. If only the men we are about to visit f-felt the same." He turned right at Spray Avenue and continued straight until he reached the Cave and Basin Internment Camp. His mood slipped toward despair. He picked Bobby up, hiding him inside his jacket until they were passed the chained-up snarling dogs that growled and bared their teeth. Reverend Tosh presented his identification papers, passed through the intimidating gates and trudged through the sludge until he reached the familiar murky container, Shed number 58. He took a deep breath and used both hands to pry apart the heavy sliding doors. As soon as the crack was wide enough, Bobby escaped from the neck of his jacket and wiggled through.

Joe was half-sleeping, huddled against the wall but the corners of his mouth turned up when he saw the little dog scuttling towards him. "Hullo, pal," he gurgled, his pale hand emerging from the blanket to stroke the excited animal. "Reverend, the crest on Bobby's tag. What does it represent?"

"Not sure. I will have to ask Canon Harrison. But he is in France." Reverend Tosh lowered himself onto the floor beside the young prisoner. "You look so much b-better, Joe. Has your s-situation improved?" He tried to adjust himself into a comfortable position.

Joe shook his head. His face showed no signs of emotion.

The minister wrung his hands in anguish. "Never mind. I brought you a p-present." He pulled a brown woollen hat from his coat pocket. "It is an official Red Cross b-balaclava. Knitted especially for you by one of my p-parishioners. Try it on, Joe."

172

The lad obligingly pulled the hood over his head and face until only his eyes and nose were visible.

Reverend Tosh laughed and his breath clouded like steam. "I will t-tell her it suits you."

Joe pulled it off as fast as he had put it on. "Reverend, I need to talk to you in private."

The minister heaved himself onto his feet and clipped Bobby to his leash. "Let us w-walk Bobby to the end of the exercise y-yard and back, like we did last week."

When they reached the barbed wire fence at the far corner of the yard, Reverend Tosh glanced back. "Hmm, another building under construction."

Joe ran his fingers through a shock of his dust-coloured hair. "Reverend, I might as well get to the point five of us are planning to escape in the next week or so. We've been clearing a route under the sheds and the wheelless railcars so we can move in and out quickly when the time comes."

The blood drained from the face of the young minister. He leaned against a metal pillar. "You c-could be shhhot," he breathed.

"Reverend Tosh, it's a living hell for me in here. I need to get out while I still have the chance."

"But but I wrote two l-letters to London. And and things will get b-better here soon."

"No. I can't afford to wait for any crazed notion of justice." Joe rubbed his coarse sleeve across his forehead. "I we want to leave Banff as soon as possible," his eyes searched the minister's face. "But we need false identification papers and money for our train tickets. Reverend Tosh. If you can help us, I promise you'll be paid back every single penny."

The minister pulled out his big handkerchief and dabbed his clammy brow. "You c-cannot escape. Your efforts would p-prove no m-match for the authorities."

Joe's brow creased. "Are, are you trying to say you can't help us?"

"Oh dear, I—" The young minister's voice broke. He tried again. "I want to h-help." His knuckles were turning white from clutching his bible too hard. "But. It it is too d-dangerous."

Joe waited. Finally he said, "Reverend Tosh, please forget we had this conversation."

"No! Wait, Joe." The young minister grasped his sleeve. "You knocked the w-wind out of me. I I just need time to think. Who is attempting to escape with y-you?"

"John, Danilo, Andriy and Ivan."

"Oh, g-good Lord in h-h-heaven." The Reverend's brow tensed and flexed.

A parade of new internees, their heavy boots splashing up dirty puddle water, marched across their path. Reverend Tosh stopped to pick up his little dog. "Joe, t-tell me everything I n-need to know. And and I will do everything in my p-power to help you."

The Banff newspaper office was filled with organised clutter. Luxton picked up a chair and moved it closer to his own. "This is a nice surprise, Reverend Tosh. Have a seat. Ignore the mess. It is conductive to my inspiration," he joked. Daylight spilled through the window and onto the two men as they sat down together. "A social visit? Or business?" asked Luxton.

"*N-N-Neither!*" The words gathering in Reverend Tosh's throat gushed out, "*The the young p-prisoner. He is just seventeen years old. He will not survive much l-longer in that camp that c-crazy guard will b-beat him to d-death! There there are f-five of them f-five p-prisoners.*"

"Reverend Tosh, I—"

"*Indeed, the thought m-makes me nauseous. They have courage; I will say that for them. They've p-prepared a route; each took a t-turn while the others slept. And and they know how to get p-passed that barbed wire f-fence.*"

"Reverend Tosh—"

"*When when John was w-working in Castle Mountain, he attached a pair of h-heavy duty wire c-cutters to the underside of the c-cart that travels back and forth between the camps he has used them already he has m-made the discrete c-cuts.*"

"Reverend Tosh—"

"*They they will h-head to Sooke. Ivan has a c-cousin there who owns a steam-powered s-sawmill. His wood is loaded onto vessels l-leaving f-for San Francisco, Valparaiso, Australia. With the shortage of m-men, ships will be hiring crews. There's a chance to learn a t-trade: sealing, whaling.*" The Reverend drew in a long, slow breath. "*They say they say, fortune favours those who are p-prepared. That is what they s-say d-don't they?*"

Luxton sprang from the chair and pushed back his hair with both hands. "Would you like a brandy? It'll take the edge off your nerves."

A screaming wind swirled around the walls of Shed number 58 and pummelling rain beat mercilessly on its metal roof. Inside, five prisoners sat in a circle, pounding hearts, quickening breaths, they listened intently. The clang of the heavy metal bar. The rattle of the heavy chain. The snap of the brass core inside the padlock. Then silence. A chill froze the back of John's neck. He unfolded Reverend Tosh's paper and the words, 'Modus Operandi' sprang from the page.

"What does it mean?" asked Joe in a hoarse whisper.

"It's a Latin phrase." Ivan pushed his cap back and scratched his forehead. "Means 'method of operation'."

A feeling of ease soothed Joe's mind. "Reverend Tosh came through for us."

"He certainly did," said John.

"One day vee five Canadian Cossacks vill repay him," said Danilo, and Andriy and Ivan closed their fists and extended their thumbs up.

John leaned in. "Now. Pay attention so we're all cottoned on. Once we're through the fence, we'll split up according to this plan." He passed around the visual explanation: part map, part text. Everyone understood. "Good." He folded the paper and shoved it back in his pocket. "Time to make a move," he said, picking up the wooden crate, revealing a cut square of timber in the floorboards. He knelt down, pried it out with a flat stick then looked up at his brother. "Okay, Joe. You go first. Then Danilo. Then Andriy. Then you, Ivan. Keep your calm, now."

Joe's heart picked up speed and a flush of heat reddened his face. He lowered himself feet first, slithering onto the lumpy ground, rotating his body until he obtained a level of physical ease. A tingling smell of fresh air. Beads of sweat surfacing on his brow. He looked up at the undercarriage anchored on heavy concrete blocks and waited. The sound of the guard's boots coming regular and heavy then nothing. He turned his head to one side and a steely terror rushed through his body. The backs of the sentry's boots were a few feet away. The wind howled. A great-horned owl hoot-hooted. A match fell between the guard's feet. Pulverised by a forceful heel. Joe breathed deeply to keep himself from shaking. Finally, the cigarette butt followed suit. The heavy repetitive treading began again. Joe signalled to Danilo before rolling from his cranny. He ran like

175

the wind through the dark and sleet, crouching under the window sills, keeping close to the billets. He reached the safety of the next boxcar. Dropped onto his stomach and, with the determination of a burrowing mole, pushed away the debris and slithered into the protection of the prepared cavity. Took more deep breaths. 'Only 50 feet. Only 50 feet,' he told himself. The words calmed his mind. He removed his glove and was about to lift a trembling hand to his mouth to wipe the bitter taste of dirt from his tongue when he heard a throaty rasping sound. Danilo. Joe nippily pulled on his glove and willed himself to run again.

Now John was alone in Shed number 58. Pummelling rain beating mercilessly on its metal roof. He hoped Joe had made it to the barbed-wire fence. Sweat trickled down his back. He had never known fear. Until now. He lowered himself feet first, slithering onto the lumpy ground. He reached up with a flat palm and patted the edge of the square-cut of timber. Alert to the wooden crate balancing atop of it, he slowly and cautiously, tapped it back into place one sweet snap and the hole was covered. The sound of the guard's boots coming regular and heavy the sound of the guard's boots going. Chill night air filled his lungs and fuelled his energy. He rolled from his hiding spot

Cloud covered the perilous moon and made the heavens mercifully dark. Joe crouched beside the barbed-wire fence, removed his glove and, with his heart thrumming against his rib cage, ran his hand across the icy woven wire in search of the cut. One hefty push and the large square dropped into the slimy mud, soft as pudding. Joe scrambled though the hole as quickly as he was able and dragged his body close to the ground towards a clump of shrubs. Freedom echoed in his mind. He drew his limbs up to his torso and shivered with excitement.

One after the other, the prisoners came out of the shadows. Danilo. Andriy. Then Ivan. Joe's confidence swelled. At last, a pair of eyes alight in a dirt-covered face. Joe reached for his brother's hand. "So far so good, John," he whispered, a cough coming to his lips.

For a few minutes they lay together, spitting bits of grime, wiping muck from their tongues, savouring the airs of the night: winter pine, wood smoke, horses. John brushed a dead leaf from his neck. "Time to split." He felt their fear. "Go go!"

The escaped prisoners scarpered off with steely determination, down icy paths between the massive tree trunks. Leaping over narrow drainage channels. Sliding down snow-covered slopes, patterned with tracks of ground squirrels and snowshoe hares. They ran past the stables. Ran behind a row of workers' cabins that was Cave Avenue. Bursting with high spirits and energy, John followed in their wake. "A good start," he breathed, his legs going like pistons. "God willing, we'll all meet at daybreak."

In the wee small hours of the mist-covered morning Ivan, Danilo and Andriy, fists by their sides, gathered at the back entrance to the little store. Ivan pushed his cap back and scratched his forehead. Then he drew a sharp breath and creaked open the back door of the Sign-of-the-Goat-Curio Shop. A broom clattered to the ground. Ivan cursed and put it back up. In the absence of visible light Danilo stretched forth a hand pulled it back quickly. "Schomthing furry and schtuffed." Andriy covered his mouth to muffle his nervous laughter. Ivan waved them to silence and struck a match. He spotted the kitbags and blew it out. "Over here."

Like excited children opening their Christmas sacks, the three Ukrainian prisoners, flushed and trembling, dug into their bags. They wolfed down sandwiches and pulled out cowboy hats, jackets, shirts, trousers and socks. Danilo drew an envelope marked, 'IMPORTANT' and handed it to Ivan who tore it open. Andriy lit a match so they could read the contents:

I have enclosed three 'British birth certificates': DANIEL MORGAN for Danilo Melnyk. ANDREW BOYD for Andriy Boiko. IAN SHEFFIELD for Ivan Shevchenko. Also enclosed: Three train tickets to Vancouver and $9 cash that came out of my church's collection plates. Please return it as soon as you can. Train leaves station at 5:30 am. May the good Lord go with you. Reverend Tosh.

Rested, fed and disguised, the group of three headed towards the train station.

"Vat if vee are schtopped?"

Ivan glanced at the wiry old man. "If asked, say your name slowly and clearly, 'A-n-d-r-e-w B-o-y-d'. But let me do the rest of the talking."

"Underschtood," he replied turning to face Danilo. "Are you payen sie attention, Danilo? You not to schpeaken either. Just say, 'D-a-n-i-e-l M-o-r-g-a-n'. Schlowly and clearly. Underschtood?"

"Of coursche underschtood! You make mountain out of molehill."

It was twenty minutes after five in the morning when the train blew into the Banff station, breathing steam and blowing flames. Apprehensively and separately, the Ukrainian prisoners watched the carriage doors open. Weary passengers poured out. Picked up their luggage. Hurried away before the sun broke the horizon. Edgy, excited and nervous, Ivan stole a glance at Danilo and

Andriy. They were boarding separate carriages. He thought he saw John and Joe. Steam hissed. The guard blew the whistle. He jumped the train. The piston started to move. Speeded up. Freedom filled his nostrils.

"Tickets Please! Tickets Please!" The conductor made his way through each carriage, punching triangles into buff-coloured vouchers. Ivan stared out of the window. The train passed through the Selkirk and Monashee mountain range. Reduced to a crawl at Kicking Horse Pass, Rogers Pass and Eagle Pass. He turned his attention to the woman opposite, a black Polish shawl covering her head and a stone jar warming her feet. She smiled back at him.

"My name is Mrs Grabowski," she said.

Ivan returned her smile. "Ian. Ian Sheffield," he replied with confidence.

The woman patted the cloth-covered bowl on her lap. "Fermenting bread starter, the stink always brings tears to Mister Grabowski's eyes."

Ivan pushed his cap back and scratched his forehead. "Mine too," he smiled, "I think I'll stretch my legs."

Andriy and Danilo were sitting opposite each other in the next dust-coated carriage. "Hallo!" said Andriy, elbows resting on the table, looking remarkably pleased with himself. "Have you scheen de brothers? Danilo and I did not schee dem at de schtation."

Ivan bent down to them. Quietly, he said, "John and Joe are probably disguised so well, even we didn't recognise them. I'll walk the train and bring them back here." Twenty minutes passed before Ivan returned, his expression grave. "They didn't make it."

"If dey are not on de train—"

"Den ver de hell are dey?"

Ivan looked from Danilo to Andriy in stunned silence. Pushed back his hat and rubbed his head. "Wherever John and Joe are, let's pray they're well hidden." He chewed his lip. "Right now, the guards are probably running around Banff like prairie hens with their heads cut off."

Afternoon, April 28, 1915
The Vestry in St. George-in-the-Pines
100 Beaver Street,
Banff, Alberta

Reverend Tosh, nauseous, tense and weak, paced the floor. Stopped abruptly in his tracks. Stared down at the two brothers facing each other across his table, their brows furrowed, their eyes fearful. "You t-two had every *every* opportunity t-to escape this morning," his voice harsh and out of character. "But you did not t-take it. Now I f-fear f-for your safety and m-my safety."

John stood up. "Reverend, you have done more than enough for us." He thrust his arm into the sleeve of his jacket and turned to Joe. "Come on! Let's get out of here."

The young minister flew to the door, turned and spread his arms wide to block their exit. "Do not l-leave! I n-need to know why you s-stayed when all logic told you to g-go."

John's hands drew into fists. "I won't apologise for any of it."

"Just just t-tell me," begged Reverend Tosh. "What s-stopped you both from boarding the train?"

John boiled inside with a powerless rage. "I took a newspaper from the stand." He gripped the back of the chair. The headline: *'Government Seizes Ukrainian Property'*."

"Oh, John—" began the minister.

"Let me finish, Reverend." His knuckles turning whiter. "Our father's house was lying empty anger coursed through my veins I told Joe they wouldn't get it without a fight."

A knock at the door. The two escaped prisoners exchanged looks. Reverent Tosh's eyes flashed with fear. "Oh dear Lord," he prayed in a splattered whisper. "Where can I possibly hide them?"

"Reverend," a voice called from behind the door. "It's Luxton."

Elation roused in the minister's chest and the tension dropped from his face. With fumbling fingers he dismantled the lock and opened the door. A surge of icy air filled the space.

"Excuse me," said Luxton, "I wasn't aware you were conducting ecclesiastical business."

The Reverend's ears turned bright pink. "I we I. They are not c-clergy. They are p-prisoners!"

Luxton drew in a long breath and after a moment said, "I'll get to the point without the preamble there was a suspicious note found on the station platform. The camp officials will be paying you a visit."

The minister's hands flew to his mouth. "How d-do you know this?"

"My reporter was having a pint in the King Edward when an off-duty guard spilled the beans."

"Goodness g-gracious," he muttered, almost inaudibly. "How foolish of me to sign my name."

The colour drained from John's face. "Reverend Tosh, I'm sorry we involved you."

The minister stared at him, his eyes blazing. "That b-bears little solace now! You did involve me and I did everything in my p-power to help you. Now you are r-running off to Canmore to defend an an empty house! Use your head for heaven's s-sake!" His anger took him by surprise. "What can a nineteen-year-old do to fix this monumental m-madness?"

A heavy silence hung in the air.

John's words came from deep within his throat, almost a howl, as he said, "If it wasn't for me, Joe, you would be on your way to the safety of Ivan's cousin."

Joe shrugged. "If it makes you feel any better, I'd more than one reason to want to go to Canmore."

"Like what?"

"Well nothin'."

"It's that girl."

Joe leaned back, balancing the chair onto two legs. "I don't know what you're on about."

"Fine! We'll join the army then."

"We can't." The chair's front legs thumped down. "Our Ukrainian surnames will land us back in that hole."

John cuffed his brother's ear. "We've got fake names now. Fake papers."

"You reckon they'll work?"

"Only one way to find out." He pulled a newspaper from his inside pocket. "Take a look at this," he said with pointed finger. *"Now Recruiting. 245th Overseas Battalion, Canadian Grenadier Guards. Apply at the Windsor Arcade Building, 149 Peel Street, Montreal.'* And down here," John pointed, *'Merchant ships are being turned into troopships at Montreal then proceeding down the river to Quebec to embark the troops'."*

"I turn eighteen in two weeks."

"I know. So we can enlist together." He turned to face Reverend Tosh. "Can I ask you to change our tickets? We won't be following Ivan, Andriy and Danilo to Vancouver Island."

Reverend Tosh nodded. "Two tickets to Montreal it is."

"Better make it three," said Luxton. "You need to get out of here while the going's good." He looked at his watch. "The next one leaves in two hours. Nine-thirty tonight."

From out of nowhere, it began to sleet. The noise against the window pane made John concerned about the actual doing. "Because of the note we can't disguise ourselves as ministers now."

"N-No of course not." Buds of sweat appeared on Reverend Tosh's forehead.

"What about businessmen?" Joe pulled his chair in and the legs squealed. "I read the Imperial Bank of Canada are expanding their premises on the corner of Banff Avenue and Buffalo Street. If asked, we can say we're representatives returning to our head office in Toronto, changing trains at Montreal."

John shook his head. "We'd need fancy suits and shirts to pull that one off."

"Good Lord!" Reverend Tosh shot from his seat.

"What?" John said cannily.

"The Good Lord has provided providential c-care for all of us!" His mouth slightly open. "About a month ago, one of my p-parishioners, a Mrs Brewster-Moore, brought in a big donation bag full of expensive-looking suits, shirts, and t-ties. Apparently, they had fallen into the mud and were trampled on by by a horse. Mrs Brewster-Moore and Mrs Daily, my housekeeper, set about repairing, cleaning, and p-pressing them. A lot of work. None of it sold." His smile widened. "Now I know why. God had p-plans for those clothes."

Luxton looked out of the frost-covered window. "It's freezing. You'll look odd without overcoats."

"I I have an extra black woollen coat for you, Joe," said Reverend Tosh, "and I will b-borrow one of Canon Harrison's for John. It it maybe a b-bit loose."

Arf!

"Oh dear! What about Bobby of Banff?"

"I'll take him until your replacement gets here," said Luxton.

Successfully disguised as a smart businessman, John leaned forward and rested his clasped hands on the table. "You have a bruise on your cheek, Joe."

Joe adjusted his tie and replied with confidence. "I accidently tripped over a box of bank files, sir."

"How terribly unfortunate."

They laughed one last time, so loudly Reverend Tosh showed his disapproval by raising an eyebrow.

Under a flickering star in a lucid night sky, a full moon gleamed above a shadowy mountain. All forms of life settling down for the night except for a chirruping black-billed cuckoo dropping cones on the heads of the three men hurrying down the path. "A g-good omen," muttered Reverend Tosh when one struck his forehead.

"Quick as you can," pressed Luxton, holding the reigns in place with his thumbs and forefingers. Joe, John and Reverend Tosh clambered aboard his wagon, shuffling along the narrow bench until they were sitting four abreast, their backs supported by a rail that separated them from oil-coated tools. One bone-jarring jolt and they were off to the train station. Joe covered his mouth to muffle a sneeze.

Luxton pulled up outside the entrance and a couple of mice scurried across a ring of light formed by the goldenrod glow of a gas lamp. They slinked into the shadows as he jumped down from his wagon. "I'll be as quick as I can."

"God b-bless you," whispered Reverend Tosh.

Luxton moved quickly through the gates to join a queue forming in front of a kiosk, a sign above, 'TICKETS TO MONTREAL & TORONTO'. His eyes were drawn to a chalked sandwich-board: *The 9:30 From Vancouver Running 20 Minutes Late.* When he reached the front of the line, he asked what the hold-up was.

"Snow drifting across the line at Roger's Pass."

Luxton nodded. "I would like to exchange these two tickets, please." He slid them though the gap in the ticket window. "For three to Montreal."

He opened his wallet. The clerk pushed three printed vouchers back. "You'll need to wait for your change," he said, managing a smile, "they're switching out the cash boxes."

Old Donald Duncan drove the hotel's horse and buggy along a dark band of road until he found a vacant spot enshrouded with a goldenrod glow of a gas lamp. He edged his way in behind a wagon. "Oh Mister Duncan," Ishbel's face on fire. "What'll I do if I've lost six-months' worth of hard-earned money!?"

"Let's retrace your steps 'fore we start worryin'." His faded blue eyes settled on her. "Now. You said you felt your wage packet in your coat pocket when you got off the train at 7 pm."

"Yes," heart thumping. "I didn't know there was a hole in the pocket. I bought it from my mistress."

Old Donald took charge. "Here. Hold onto this. It'll keep you calm." He tossed Ishbel his lucky pebble. "And remember to examine all parts of the pavement as you walk into the station, just in case. If you've no luck, go ask at the Lost & Found counter."

Donald straightened his back and turned up his collar against the dark night. Five minutes passed before he realised the trap up front belonged to Luxton. He put his smokes back in his pocket and was about to step down when Ishbel bounded out of the building. "I've got it! I've got *it!*" Donald reached down a calloused hand. Ishbel put her own into it and was hauled up like she weighed a feather. "Mister Duncan, there wasn't even a penny missing."

Donald's chest heaved twice. "Next time. Put your problems in the pocket with the hole. No the wage packet. Now give back my pebble." The little stone slipped from Ishbel's hand, ricocheted off her shoe and spat at her leg before it landed on the floor of the cart. She picked it up and passed it back to Donald. He popped it back into his pocket and flicked the reigns. As the wagon pulled out, he looked across at the three silhouettes sitting on the bench of Luxton's cart. "Can't make out who they all are. Might as well be neighbourly," he said, tipping his hat. "Now, let's get you back to your home-away-from-home. Lily is bursting to see you. Six months is a long time."

"Oh, I can't wait to see her. We wrote back and forth but it's not the same." Ishbel glanced sideways at the old man. "Mister Duncan, tell me about your lucky charm. Is it very old?"

"Older than the Magna Carta," he replied with a grin and a wink.

"Oh, you're having me on." She pulled her shawl up and over her head. "I think we're in for the Gowk's Storm."

"Aye. When nature jerks out of her winter slumber in the Bow Valley, an untimely fall of snow is part and parcel of it."

"It happens in Scotland too. It's associated with the arrival of the cuckoo."

"Is it now?"

"Aye." Ishbel fiddled with the envelope lying in her lap. "If there was a chill in the spring air, me and my friends would sing the cuckoo song on the way home from school."

Donald shivered. "I wouldn't mind a little song right now."

She chuckled. "Then allow me to give you a spirited rendition." Ishbel took an exaggerated breath. '*The cuckoo is a bonnie bird, he sings as he flies; he brings us good tidings he tells us no lies. He drinks the cold water to keep his voice clear; and he'll come again in the spring of'"* The night wind dissolved the sound of her voice and the racket of wheels in icy ruts.

Luxton folded back his cuff and checked his watch. "Soon," he said, passing out the tickets. "Better to hang here until it comes in." A swift blast of cold air whipped about their shoulders. Reverend Tosh sighed in desperation. Bobby crawled onto his bent arm and nestled in the crook. "Ah-choo! Oh, I will m-miss you d-dearly," he said, stroking the soft Yorky coat. The minutes ticked by. Joe and John sat in silence, focusing their gaze on the slice of concrete platform visible to them through the large, partially-opened gates.

A thundering noise. Screeching metal. Hissing steam. The engineer climbed down from the glimmering beast. A porter walked up the platform, opening one heavy door after another. A flood of passengers poured off the train. Bags boxes suitcases children. John's eyes scanned the shadows between the gates and the waiting train. *"Now, Joe!"*

Joe jumped down from the wagon and walked briskly through the gates. He was part-way across the platform when he was hit by a wave of nausea. The bully-guard, eyes the colour of a hawk's wing, was trudging through the crowd, his great neck cranking every which way. Joe swung around on his heels and made a bee-line back to the wagon. "The the guard," he breathed, clambering back up, taking back his seat, lifting the collar of his coat to hide his face.

"I see him." There was a heavy disappointment in John's chest.

A forceful slam. Then another.

"Oh, d-dear me," muttered Reverend Tosh, "the porter is closing all the d-doors."

In that instance, a little chipmunk popped its head out from under the wagon. John had a sudden thought. He plucked the terrier from the minister's clutches and held him above the striped-rodent. Bobby's tail beat the air and the demon inside him rushed to the surface. The frightened chipmunk tore off and the Yorky shot from John's hands through the gates barking ferociously, trailing his leash, raising a ruckus on the crowded platform.

"Who owns that dog!?" hollered the porter.

The stationmaster sounded the first whistle. The steam engine hissed. The bells clanged.

John looked at his brother. "If we're going to do it, we need to do it now."

Joe bit his lip.

184

The blood drained from the minister's face. "What about the g-guard?" he cried.

They all turned their heads at a sharp explosive cry. Gaped in horror. Bobby, chasing the chipmunk, had wrapped his leash around the bully-guard's ankles. The man's face curdling with feverish fury. A volume of obscenities pouring from his mouth. Bobby jerked back. The leash tightened. The guard, neck pulsating, struggled to catch his balance.

"Ooh my dear Lord in h-h-heaven," wailed the Reverend.

"What are we waiting for?" John spat.

All three men, their minds stirred by the looming evil, pain and peril, jumped down from the wagon. Sweat surfaced under their crisp-white collars. They gripped their borrowed briefcases and walked smartly across the platform. One after the other, the 'bank employees' leaped aboard the waiting train. The porter slammed the last door shut.

A blast of a whistle pierced the frosty air. The heavy wheels began to turn.

"Excuse me! Excuse me!" cried Reverend Tosh, stumbling over the feet of settled passengers in a quest to reach a window seat. He pulled out his handkerchief and rubbed a big circle in the foggy pane and, as the train chugged out of the station, Luxton lifted his hat in a farewell greeting. The young minister responded with the same. Their gestures speaking louder than words ever could.

The minute the bully-guard freed himself from the leash, Bobby shot towards Luxton who snatched him up and turned on his heels. "Not So Fast!" cried a voice of thunder. A sudden grip on his shoulder and Luxton swung around, a second later the defenceless animal was swatted up and out of his arms. The injured Yorky crawled a little then collapsed.

"Bobby!"

Horrified screams rose up from the bystanders when the gun-wielding guard booted the little dog across the platform. Bobby rolled over like a piece of fur caught up in the wind. A panicked porter put his whistle to his lips. He blew and blew until his cheeks turned beat-red. Another porter joined in. Then another. Soon, all the porters were blowing their whistles and the shrill was loud, harsh and high. The noise caught the tormentor by surprise and his eyes, etched with bitterness, darted left and right. That's when a burly bystander dived at him, knocking him to the ground. Others rushed to help: snatching away the menacing gun, pummelling him into submission, tying his hands behind his back. A loud cheer rose from the crowd.

A shudder ran through Luxton's frame. He knelt down beside the lifeless animal. Bobby's tongue dangling from the side of his mouth, blood trickling from his tiny nose. The pit of Luxton's stomach tightened *"Bobby,"* he whispered tensely but there was no response so he scrambled to his feet, scooped up the little dog, and elbowed his way through the swarms of people. In the stillness of the night, underneath the goldenrod glow of the gas lamp he cradled the dying animal in his arms. Then suddenly it came to him. He flicked the reigns and drove his horse and wagon as fast he could.

Chapter 8

The rusty hinges shrilled on the metal gate. Luxton hurried up the path supporting the failing dog in one arm. He balled his fist and rapped on the door. Precious moments passed. No answer. He knocked again before remembering there was a bell on the wall. Reaching in, he tugged on a cord that was buried behind a bush and the bell began to jangle. Footsteps. The clink of the latch. The creak of the door. The old doctor, mossy beard yellow in the moonlight, looked up at Luxton before his eyes were drawn to the blood-smeared bundle of fur in his arms. "Bring the wee mite inside," he said straight away.

Luxton followed the old man through the dimly lit lobby, thick with stags' heads and portraits of Scottish kings and Scottish clansmen. Stacks of books alternating high and low were lined up against one wall. The plaque above read, 'A room without books is like a body without a soul.'

A sudden crash made the old man turn his head. He looked down at the broken cast of a fossil then up at Luxton's startled expression. "Are ye tryin' tae wreck ma hoose, laddie?"

"Er, Doctor Macpherson, I think you knocked it over with your elbow."

"Och, dinny worry aboot it. The damage is done noo. Bring yer wee dug in here."

Luxton walked crablike through a cornucopia of items cluttering a doorway that opened onto an equally untidy area. From a large painting that hung above the fireplace, a highland cow stared out from mist-covered moorland. Symbols of male aptitude: sporting trophies, professional certificates and a coat-of-arms filled the walls, indicating the man's wide range of interests and education. The old doctor pushed away the newspapers, coin folders and stamp albums that cluttered the examination table then signalled to Luxton to lay the dog down. "Gently, now," he said then put an ear to Bobby's chest. "Och, yer a poor wee beastie. What on earth happened tae ye?"

Luxton paused then said, "He was chasing a rodent through the station and tripped up a guard." He wanted to face the doctor but there was a gradual encroachment of floor space by taxidermy. After a few turns and twists he found breathing and leg room. "The man unleashed his anger and—"

"And the wee dug took the brunt o' it." Doctor Macpherson's eyebrows abruptly met in the middle. "If yer going tae staund there, laddie, stop footerin' aboot. Ah need peace and quiet tae carry oot ma work."

"Of course. Sorry." Luxton pulled out his handkerchief and wiped the sweat from his face.

After what seem like an eternity, Doctor Macpherson took off his small metal-rimmed glasses and rubbed his eyes. "Yir wee Yorky took a guid beatin'," he said, clearing his throat. "Twa broken ribs, a broken front leg and a wee crushed paw on the back leg." He bent down to whisper in the little dog's ear, "Dinny worry, Bobby. Ah'll put ye back taegether. Indeed, ah'll dae that fir ye."

"I'm mighty relieved to hear that."

"Ah hope ye dinny mind me askin'. Did ye hae Bobby on a leash?"

Luxton hesitated. "Er…no."

"Then yer partly responsible, laddie. It's the nature of a wee dug tae run after vermin."

Heat rose in Luxton's face. "But—"

"Don't ye argy-bargy wi' me! *Ye* have been told!"

Luxton shut his mouth and took a deep breath. No one could help Bobby more than Doctor McPherson. Of that he was sure.

It was a full minute before the old man spoke again, "He's a gallous wee dug tae have gotten through that brutal attack. Ah like Yorkies. Skye terriers hae spunk tae. Greyfriars Bobby wiz a Skye terrier. After his master died, the wee dug sat on the auld man's grave fir years. Only leavin' him once a day when the one o'clock gun wiz fired from Edinburgh castle. That wiz the wee dug's signal tae go tae the bakers 'n get his bun, Broxton."

"Er, my name is Luxton."

The old man chuckled. "Just checking tae see if yer payin' attention tae ma story."

Luxton looked fixedly at the old man. "I'm Norman Luxton. I don't know if you remember me. Georgina is my wife." For a minute they stood in silence. "You delivered our daughter."

"Och, yer no Broxton. Yir Lux-*ton*. Ah didnae recognise ye. Yer wife is Georgina?"

"Yes. Georgina."

A little memory flitted across his mind. "Och, I remember the night the stork delivered baby Eleanor. Quite a performance that wiz. But we managed, eh."

"Yes. And I will forever be in your debt." Luxton shook his hand over the top of the furry patient for longer than was necessary and the corners of the old man's mouth turned up and exposed his teeth.

"Noo, stop yer bletherin'. Get away home. Ye can come back and see Bobby in the morning." They walked back along the dimly lit lobby, thick with stags' heads and portraits of Scottish kings and Scottish clansmen. Doctor Mcpherson patted Luxton's back then gently pushed him out the door.

He returned to the examination room, covered the sleeping dog with a cosy coverlet then dragged his big armchair across the floor, shoving it up against the sleeping dog. "First, ah'll help maself tae a wee nightcap," he said, turning the key of the polished-wood cabinet and opening the glass-panelled door. The top four shelves were packed solid with tribal artifax and rare books. The bottom shelf had a horn snuffbox with the inscription, 'Presented to Doctor Macpherson, a friend who enjoys his dram. T.D.' The old man stretched his arm behind it, retrieved his bottle of whisky, thooped the cork, and filled his glass. Keeping a steady hand, he sank into the soft warmth of the seat and turned to face the sleeping dog. "It's grand tae hae a wee bit o' company aboot the hoose, Bobby." He took a hearty whiff and a substantial sip. "Ahh, Dewer's White Label the drink recommended by doctors." He turned to look at the dog again. "Tommy Dewer 'n ah grew up taegether. We wiz best pals, Bobby. Ah became an exceptional doctor 'n he became an exceptional whisky maker knighted by King Edward V11 on December 18, 1902. Oh, whut a grand day that wiz. We drove tae the palace in his automobile. Did ah mention he wiz the third man in the sovereign state o' Great Britain tae buy one? Anyhow, tae cut a long story short—"

Afternoon, April 29, 1915
The Paris Tea Room
Banff Avenue,
Banff, Alberta

Under the low ceiling, ornate tables and bentwood chairs ranked close together and wafts of freshly-baked bread and brewed tea fused with noisy chatter and clinking cups. The two friends sat down at the little round table by the window. Lily touched the 'Reserved' tent-shaped place marker, fingered the hem of the white starched tablecloth then declared across the top of the bone-china sugar bowl, "'Tis all bright and perfect!"

"Oh, everything's just lovely, Lily," Ishbel responded. "I imagine they call it the Paris Tea Room because this is what they have in Paris, France, eh?"

"No, 'tis owned by Mr and Mrs Paris."

They were still laughing when the waitress approached with verve. She removed the pencil from behind her ear. "A pot of tea for two, ladies?" Notepad at the ready.

"A big pot of steaming tea for three, pleez. We'd like t' top 't up," said Lily.

"And what kind of cakes would you like?"

"Whut have yi got?"

"Oh, we've got all sorts in the Paris Tea Room. Why don't you take a look in our display case?" She nodded in the direction of the counter then slipped her pencil behind her ear. "I'll get your tea, ladies."

Lily's grin was wide. "She called us ladies."

Ishbel pushed a wayward strand of damp hair from her forehead and looked across at her. "I failed. Pure and simple."

"Yi didn't fail. Don't be daunted by yir first hurdle."

Hope rose in Ishbel. "So you still think there's still a chance I'll find Bobby?"

"Yir good luck helped yi find yir wage packet. Didn't it?"

The waitress interrupted. Cups and saucers. Plates and pastry forks. A pot of steaming tea.

"I've got Mister Duncan to thank for that. The minute I knew I lost it, he turned right around and drove me back to the station. He told me to put my problems in my holey pocket not my wage packet."

Lily chuckled then said, "So yi bought yir mistress's coat after all?"

"Aye. But I like it. I'll sew up the pocket and sing the latest Fanny Brice song." Their laughter made an embarrassing amount of din.

Lily caught her breath. "I've got a comfy bed this year. Whut about you?"

"Yeah. Good. You know why one should always have a comfy bed and comfy pair of shoes?"

"Why?"

"If you're not in one, you're in the other."

"Oh, Ishbel," Lily laughed. "'Tis good t' have yi back. Hey, whut do yi think of Ethel comin' back t' Banff Springs as Clementine-the-Serpentine's personal maid?"

"Oh, tatties o'wer the side!"

"Yir bloody right! Disaster strikes!"

The bevelled-glass display case on the rosewood countertop groaned with every kind of cake from Battenberg to Cream Horns to Vanilla Slices with generous fillings. Lily appeared, grinning cheerfully at the waitress. "I'll take that Thunder 'n Lightnin', pleez," she said with pointed finger.

"Good choice." The server picked up her tongs. "The crust is baked to perfection today. Do you want honey or treacle?"

"Treacle, pleez. And just a bit of clotted cream. I'm watchin' my figure."

The woman turned to Ishbel, saying, "And you, Miss. What would you like?"

"Oh figures be damned. I'm havin' one of them gastronomical monstrosities," she announced, steering her to a row of choux dough pastries, filled with cream and topped with icing.

"Oh, never mind my Thunder 'n Lightnin'. Gimme one of them too, pleez."

When they left the tea shop, it was coming up to four o'clock and a southwest wind was coming up. "'Tis too cold to be spring," droned Lily as they walked at a brisk clip up Banff Avenue.

Ishbel pulled her shawl tighter. "Thanks for that lip-smacking cream tea."

"Better late than never, eh. Oh, and I meant t' tell yi. I put yir muther's hat box under yir AAARGH!" The blood drained from their faces and screams tore through them like great fragments of ice. Pulses quickening, hearts thumping. A huge bull-moose, with five-foot twiggy antlers, rubbernecking from behind the railings of Rundle Memorial United Church.

"Oh, sweet cheeses, I nearly wet my knickers!" gasped Lily, trying to keep the tremor out of her voice.

"Crikey, Lily! He must weigh a thousand pounds!"

The animal ignored their boorish comments and pulled back to munch on the leaves of a gnarled tree.

Ishbel's eyes wandered to the notice board fluttering with Parish news. "Is this the church you wrote to me about? The one where the minister owns the Yorky that Ethel suggested I pass off as Bobby?"

"'Taint. 'Tis the one up the road. Follow me."

Stained-glass windows. Thick stone walls. St. George's-in-the-Pines Anglican Church surrounded by pine trees on the corner of Buffalo and Beaver. Ishbel pressed down on the handle of the church door. "Aren't churches supposed to be open for prayer during the day?"

"S'pose t' be." Lily followed Ishbel up the side of the church, pushing past sodden bushes and a large wet fir tree. "Oh, sweet cheeses," she moaned.

"Lily! Lily! Come *quickly*!" Ishbel's heart thundered. "Oh. My. Lord! Lily, somebody's broken the door down!" She shambled further into the rubble. "Hello?" Nobody answered. He-*llo?* Anyone there?" She listened: Mumbling. Unintelligible words. Then an elderly woman with a small topknot high on her head, came into view. "I'm Mrs Daily. The church cleaner." Her face pale and her voice faint, "Can I help you?"

Ishbel enquired with caution, "What happened here?"

The woman shook her head. "When I came in this mornin', I didn't know what to think," she lifted the hem of her cross-strap apron to dab the corner of her eyes. "Thank thank goodness the man who lives over the back was waitin' for me. He told me the church was broken into last night by the guards the guards from the internment camp. He said they were searching for Reverend Tosh."

"Oh sweet cheeses! Where's the minister?"

The cleaner forced herself to say, "Reverend Tosh, he's, he's gone. Even his little Yorky is gone."

Ishbel bit her lip. "His little Yorky?"

"Yes. Bobby of Banff he calls him."

"Bobby." Ishbel swallowed hard. "The dog's name is is Bobby?"

"It is."

"Mrs Daily. I know this is a bad time to ask. Does does the dog have a tag on his collar?"

"Yes, as a matter of fact he does, dear. It has the strangest little emblem on it."

Ishbel caught her breath. "Bobby's alive!" She threw her arms around the startled cleaner then pulled back. "Where did Reverend Tosh find him? Was he stuck in the Bow River reeds? Did he make it all the way to Canmore?"

"I'm not understanding you, dear. "

"I'm sorry. It doesn't matter now. The main thing is, Bobby will be reunited with rightful owner, Winston."

"Winston?"

"A London lad who lost his mother when the Titanic went down."

"Oh how sad. Well. I'm not sure at all then. Better you clear it with Reverend Tosh, dear." The woman's brow wrinkled. "But I've no idea why he fled. Our young minister's not a Ukrainian."

Ishbel could not help herself. "What if he never comes back?"

Her answer was, "I I expect they'll have to send for another minister."

"Do you know who's in charge of all that?" She bit her thumbnail.

"That would be the Anglican Diocese of Montreal, dear."

Ishbel, flushed with energy and optimism, couldn't get her words out fast enough, "Can can you give me that address so I can write and ask the whereabouts of Reverend Tosh he would have to contact them to get another posting."

Lily raised her eyebrows. "By gum, by golly! Sherlock Holmes has nothin' on yi, Ishbel McColl."

Early Morning, April 30, 1915
Servants' Quarters, Banff Springs Hotel
Banff, Alberta

"My my hat's *gone!* "

"Whut?"

"Look!" Ishbel showed Lily the inside of the circular box. "It's empty!"

Lily's face reddened. "But but I kept 't safe! I never once opened yir box! I brought it straight from the Sanatorium yesterday and put it right under yir bed!"

Ishbel narrowed her eyes. "That Ethel Finch needed a fancy hat to get into the Tea Party and Hat Auction."

"Yi duzn't think she took it?"

"Of course I do, Lily. Who else would pinch my mum's hat?"

"Come t' think of it, the hatbox did feel lighter. I must have moved't 'fore she had the chance t' put it back."

Ishbel's colour returned to normal. "I'll go to the Brett Sanatorium after the assembly catch her on her break." She paused then said, "You don't think she donated it to the hat auction? Do you?"

193

"Oh Ishbel, oh jeez. No." Lily looked up at the clock. "Sweet cheeses, Ishbel! We're late for Dimbleby's sermon."

Mister Dimbleby, stiff-backed and stern, stood centre stage, watching his army of domestic servants file into the Cascade ballroom. His hotel was about to open for the season and a large chunk of his reputation lay in the hands of these women. The cleaning ladies. He placed one hand inside his jacket like a Canadian Napoleon, smiled down at their expectant faces, and began his motivational speech.

"And as commander in chief of the grandest hotel in the entire world, I expect the highest standard of comfort and cleanliness. A single hair found in a bath can implant itself upon a guest's memory and undermine our credibility. An ugly stain on a carpet can eclipse expensive marble floors and priceless antique furniture. Therefore, I count on you. My industrious and receptive maids. My ubiquitous domestic soldiers. My angelic warriors." He shouted over the starched-capped heads, *"Will you swath our guests with the freshest of linens?"*

"YES!"

"Sweet cheeses. Bossy-pants Dimbleby's turnin' int' a domineerin' dictator."

Ishbel shushed Lily with a wave.

"Will you polish our furniture to reflect the light?"

"YES!"

"Will you clean our fine rugs so so," he struggled to think of something. *"So we imagine we are stepping on art?"*

"YES!"

"Then allow me to salute you, the maids of the Banff Springs Hotel. Your spotless characters and devoted service uphold a prosperous domestic state in this great and grand hotel! In an exclamation of congratulations, I call for a huge cheer: Hip! Hip!"

"HORRAY!"

Mister Dimbleby smiled and held out a quieting hand. *"Now go in the knowledge that you will be serving the richest, most demanding clients in the entire world."*

Ishbel and Lily entered the Brett Sanatorium by the tradesman's entrance and walked along the buttermilk-painted hallway until they reached the clatter and hum of the hospital canteen. A pithy smell of disinfectant, pea soup, and strong tea. A densely packed crowd of nurses, visitors, and members of religious orders. Lily pointed to the far corner. "There she is!"

"Wassgoin'on?" Ethel, agog with curiosity, put her fork down. "Come for a yarn have ya?"

Ishbel's fists were tucked inside her cardigan pockets. "No. I've come for my hat." The words slipped out smooth as oil. "I know you took it. So you might as well own up to it! *No* pokies!"

A muddle of words, "Whatta ya talkin' about? I never touched yar blinkin' hat."

Under her calm, Ishbel was seething. "Don't try to fob me off, Ethel Finch," she spurted hotily. "You took my hat. I *know* you did."

Ethel's face fell briefly. "I needed a bloomin' hat ter get inside the Lake Agnes Tearoom?"

"So you should have *asked*. I brought that hat all the way from Scotland it belonged to my late mother."

"I made the decision to ask for forgiveness instead of permission so I wouldn't be up the creek without a paddle so ter speak."

"Go and get her hat," Lily demanded.

Ethel's face knitted. "I can't. I haven't got the blinkin' bonnet." A stiff chill blew through the room. She picked up her fork and drew a line in her mashed potatoes. "I used to have a handle on life but, um, it broke off."

Lily moved her eyes around in a circle. "What a load of drivel."

Ishbel emitted a short cry. "Did did you donate it to the hat auction?"

"No. But I'll tell you the solemn God's truth, Ishbel."

"Oh, enough of your hooptedoodle what happened to it?"

"Oh me nerves." Ethel turned down the corners of her mouth. "Well it was me industrial-strength corset. It was givin' me jip. And yar mudder's hat was itchin' me noggin. Oh, I was as uncomfortable as sin. So I took off the blinkin' hat and put it in a safe spot a table in the corner. I was enjoyin' me slice of cake when a big hullabaloo broke out between me mistress and a woman with a Yorkshire dog. Lard dien' dumpin', I thought she was goin' ter knock Lady Clementine's block off. I had ter get Her Ladyship outta that teahouse as fast as I could. Well, we were halfway down the ridge when I remembered I had forgotten the bloomin' hat. I immediately turned around and ran all the way back. Up the bloody mountainside! Sweat pourin' down me back! Ya'd think I'd been hauled through a knot hole by the time I reached the corner table in the Lake Agnes Teahouse. Then. Oh. Me. Nerves. My heart sank. It. Was. Gone."

"Gone?"

"Aye. I yelled out, 'Who Lifted Me Bloomin' Hat?' But everybody had left, except the woman cleanin' tables. She said she gave it ter Mister Jolly. He thought it had been mistakenly left out of the auction so he approached a group of ladies standin' by the door and asked if anyone wanted ter buy it. One lady did. She put a donation inter the soldiers' box and took yar mudder's hat. Alas, the cleaner didn't know her name." Ethel forked her way through the cabbage and talked around it, barely. "Jeez. It was a humdinger of a hat if I say so meself. When it was on top of me noggin, everyone but everyone admired it."

Ishbel looked fit to burst. "Ethel, hand on heart, you're only alive 'cause 'cause it's illegal to kill you!"

"Ouch!" Ethel's hands flew to her waistband. "Ya made me burst a bone in me corset!" She located the break. "Jeez, it's a good job I keep bits and bobs from me old pairs." She gave an impatient little wriggle and looked up. Thankfully, they were gone.

The Banff Springs Hotel was casting a pool of colour, light and shape against an afternoon of dull and drizzle. Ishbel opened the back door to the servant's quarters and Lily hurried to take it from her. "'Tis orful. 'Tis terrible. Yir mum's beautiful hat. 'Taint fair."

Ishbel was unbuttoning her coat when a childhood memory welled up inside her, overwhelming her anger.

"Yir getting' yir colour back. Are yi feelin' better?" Lily asked in doubtful tones.

She heaved a sigh, *"Never cry over anything that cannae cry over you."*

The Ladies Writing Room, a little sanctuary in the heart of the Banff Springs Hotel, was adorned with grapevine-design wood mouldings and dappled in ruby red, amethyst and emerald from its stained-glass window.

"Oh, how I *wish* I wuz a real lady."

"Oh, Lily, don't start that again," said Ishbel, keeping her hand steady until the brass inkwell was full.

"I would lounge around here all mornin'." A dreamlike expression floated across her face. "And I'd write letters t' my friends in Rome, New York and Paris."

"And you would help me fill all the inkpots."

Lily's brow creased. "No. I wouldn't! Yir the maid! But I'd be very kind t' yi."

Miss Pidgeon, abruptly and disconcertingly appeared in the doorway. "Stop what you're doing this instant, and take this to the Sign of the Goat Curio Shop on Cave Avenue." She flounced across the Persian carpet and shoved an envelope into Ishbel's chest.

"What is it?"

"Banff Indian Days."

"What's that?"

"You've never heard of—" Miss Pidgeon took deep breath, "it is a festival of sports, rodeo and dancing. This envelope contains the names of our guests who wish to ride a horse in the parade. It always starts with a parade."

Lily looked up, a bottle of burgundy ink in her hand. "Can I go too?"

"Have plenty of spare time, do you?" Miss Pidgeon asked.

"No. But I deserves a break."

"It doesn't take two maids to carry a letter to a store." Saying this, she left the room.

"Thorny cow," slipped from Lily's lips.

The Sign of the Goat Curio Shop, indeed a curious place, filled to the rafters with Indian artifax and ephemera, broad and encompassing.

Eleanor Luxton stood on her tippy-toes to dust uncommon treasures that stirred her imagination: chalk figures of Indian Braves; wood-engraved coyote heads; grass baskets with spinning green, maroon and orange circles. "Daddy, why do people call our shop a trading post?"

"Well, it was originally opened to give the Stoney Tribe a place to sell their wares. Over time, it developed into a well-known trading post partly due to your hard work, Eleanor."

"And yours too, Daddy."

"Indeed, mine too. Now, how's that dusting coming along?"

"Well, I gave the leather stool in front of the mukluk shelves a quick clean so our customers can sit down. Then I dusted the quillwork moccasins." The girl pointed to the wall. "And *that* big Indian head dress. And those handcrafted saddles. And those cherry wood bows."

"Hmmm, what about the display cabinet?" he asked as the shop bell jingled above the door.

"Good morning, Miss."

"Good morning," Ishbel responded with a grin. "I've been sent down from the big house with a list of guests who want to ride a horse in the Indian Days' parade. I've to give it to the owner of this shop."

"That's me," replied Luxton, extending a hand. "You are from where? The big house?"

"The Banff Springs Hotel." Ishbel's eyes twinkled. "When my granny worked in Balmoral Castle, the villagers called it the 'big hoose'. It reminds me of that. Sort of." She turned her attention to the chock-full display case. "Oh, what lovely things you've got in here." She pointed to a little willow hoop covered in loosely woven net. "What's that?"

Eleanor peered into the cabinet and her lips curled. "Oh, that's a dreamcatcher. We carry them in different sizes and colours."

"I like the turquoise beads on this one. Is it guaranteed to catch a dream?" she asked with a sceptical grin.

The little girl nodded vigorously. "It's a charm to protect a sleeping child from bad dreams. You hang it above his or her bed."

How much is it?"

Eleanor's face lit up like the sun showing its first rays. "One dime."

Ishbel reached into her skirt pocket for the coin. "I'll take it, please."

"Would you like anything else?" asked Eleanor eagerly, hip-hopping about the shelves. "We have dance fans, beaded belts, medicine wheels, shakers, peace pipes, and *very* scary masks."

"Not today, thanks."

The girl's small hands flew, wrapping the object in tissue paper. "There you go," she said, handing over the little parcel in exchange for the silver coin.

Ishbel merrily smiled her thanks. "I'd better get goin' before they send out a search party."

The girl rushed ahead to turn the door knob. "Goodbye. See you next time," she said, smiling up at her customer.

"Cheerio for now," said Ishbel, closing the door behind her.

Eleanor looked at her dad, her brow wrinkling.

Luxton laughed. "Cheerio. It's a British term. Means, keep up the good cheer until we meet again. Now, sit yourself down on that pile of Indian blankets and take a rest."

"But Daddy, the customers might think I'm for sale too."

Luxton suppressed his laughter. "Oh, if I sold you, Eleanor, your mother would pin my head on the taxidermy wall with the stuffed mountain beasts."

"Da-*ddy!*"

"Yes, Eleanor?"

"Why do the tourists buy the heads of our mountain beasts?"

"Well, when they venture into the Canadian wilderness, they expect to shoot a wild animal. If their hunt is unsuccessful, they often buy a bear, moose or elk head."

"And pretend they caught it. Umm, I think that's called lying."

The bell above the door jingled. "I'll serve this gentleman, Eleanor. Kindly finish your dusting."

Back in London, England, the butler of Duncraig House ascended the wide, brightly-carpeted stairway, each step enhanced by a shiny-brass runner rod. Sunshine filtered through the elaborate, Victorian, stained-glass windows and bounced off the small silver platter resting on the butler's white-gloved palm. He used his other hand to clutch the mahogany handrail for stability and support until he reached the top landing where portraits of Fairfax ancestors adorned the walls and an Azerbaijani runner ran down the centre of a gleaming-wood floor. The scent of polish hit his wide nostrils, forcing him to pull out his spotless handkerchief and blow his nose. He stuffed the rumpled linen back into his pocket and knocked on the young Master Fairfax's door. As usual, the one opposite flew wide open

"Yes. Webster?" Nanny Patterson's voice was curt.

The chief manservant raised the little silver tray, an envelope peeking over its edge. "This came for Winston in the last post."

The door creaked open. The boy stuck his head out and pushed up his glasses. "A letter! For me?"

Webster smiled down at the fresh-faced child. "Quite so, Master Fairfax. And the postmark tells me it might be another from that young maid in Canada."

Winston sprang from the doorway and plucked the envelope from the platter. "Oh, thank you, Webster," he cried, picking up the silver letter opener; breaking the seal:

Miss Ishbel McColl
c/o Servants' Quarters
Banff Springs Hotel
Spray Avenue

Banff, Alberta
Canada

May 5, 1915

Master Winston N. A. Fairfax
Duncraig House
35 Duke Street
London
England

Dear Winston:

I hope this letter finds you well and happy. I am writing to tell you I have some good news and some bad news. The good news: Bobby is alive and well. Reverend Tosh of St. George's-in-the-Pines found and adopted him. We were looking everywhere and he was right under our noses, living in the church down the street from Banff Springs Hotel. The bad news: Reverend Tosh has left town with your dog (he has no idea it is your dog). As yet, I have not been able to track them down but I am sure it is just a matter of time until I do.

Enclosed is a wee present from me. It is called a dreamcatcher. It was made by a member of the Stoney Tribe. They say if you hang it above your bed, good dreams slip through the hole in the middle and glide down the feathers while you're sleeping. Any bad dreams get caught up in the web and expire when the first rays of sunlight strike them. Hope you like it.

Take care, Winston. I will write as soon as I have more news.
Miss Ishbel McColl

Enclosed: A clipping of an Alberta bush pilot standing beside his aeroplane. Lily cut it out of the Banff Crag and Canyon for you.

Winston held up his dreamcatcher for Nanny Patterson's inspection

"Ugh! A pagan relic," she declared with a dubious eyebrow. "It has dead bird's feathers on it!"

"No, Nanny. It is beautiful." He cradled it in the palm of his hand. "Look at the tiny arrowhead."

"Oh, shoo away with it!" she cried, hotly. "Put the ghastly trinket into the rubbish bin. Immediately!"

A look of horror etched Winston's face. He drew himself up. "That that would be the height of bad manners," he said, pushing his spectacles over the bridge of his nose. He rummaged inside his desk drawer for a box of drawing pins, climbed onto his bed and boldly attached his dreamcatcher and the newspaper clipping to the wall above his headboard. "Jolly nice of Ishbel and Lily to think of me. Wouldn't you say so, Nanny Patterson?"

His governess was temporarily deprived of speech.

Chapter 9

Morning, June 10, 1915
Room 525, Banff Springs Hotel
Banff, Alberta

The crisp morning air from pine-covered mountains flowed across the sloping lawns and up through an open window on the south-east side of the grand hotel. "Ethel!" An ear-shattering, teeth-jarring yell. "You are making me late for the Welcome-to-the-Season Breakfast! Ouch! *Your* clumsy sausage fingers!"

"Oops! Sorry, M'Lady!" Ethel mumbled with a pin between her teeth. "Blinkin' waistband!" She moved her weight from one knee to the other. "These bloomin' folds are pissin' me off."

Lady Clementine puffed with rage. "*Ethel*, I insist you not use that frightful language! A lady's maid in New York, Newport or Boston would never ouch!"

"Oops! Darn these clumsy sausage fingers." Ethel clambered to her feet. "There ya go, M'Lady. Yar good ter go."

"Finally! Now, where are the matching hat and gloves? Ethel! You should have them ready and waiting!"

"But, M'Lady, yar no goin' outside. Are ya?"

"A hat and a pair of gloves, Ethel, are obligatory for all meals served before 6pm." Lady Clementine sucked in a calming breath and waited.

"Here ya go," puffed Ethel. "Now yar all coiffed and clad, I need ter take me tea break."

"Your tea break!?" she cackled like a kookaburra. "Fetch my outfit diary immediately. Now. Record today's date. Add the function: Banff Springs Welcome-to-the-Season Breakfast. Note what I am wearing: The gas-blue sublime chemise with a matching hat and three-quarter-length gloves. And do not forget my multi-strapped Astoria shoes." Lady Clementine sniffed the air. "History may repeat itself, Ethel. My outfits do not."

The Alhambra Room's tall sculptural doors opened setting forth a stream of light onto a sweeping-carpeted staircase. At the top, Lady Clementine Corrinwallis was preparing to strike a rehearsed pose when a hearty flagging of a handkerchief from below caught her attention. "Alexis Wutherspoon!" she exclaimed, her eyes lighting up as she descended the flight of steps.

"Clemy, darling, heavenly to see you." The woman's black-bobbed haircut was striking against her ivory complexion. She puckered her ruby-red lips and gave Lady Clementine a 'mwah' kiss. "Frightfully sorry if I spoiled your dramatic entrance. Are you on the Grand Tour thing?"

"Err…no. I came by myself for the love of travel."

"By *yourself!* How terribly brave." She took Lady Clementine by the hand. "Then I positively insist you join my table. There is obviously much to hear and much to tell." They walked further into the room, passing a line of mahogany tables covered with fresh-flower displays and silver dishes with revolving lids. Delicious smells of steak sausages, devilled kidneys and scrambled eggs fused with wafts of freshly-baked bread, buttered toast and coffee. Amidst the clink of the cups and the clank of cutlery on plates, a waiter pulled out their seats then placed crisp-white napkins across their laps. Alexis looked at the smiling faces across the table. "Clemy, darling, allow me to introduce you to my delightful breakfast companions, Marie Imandt and Bessie Maxwell." Both women stretched forth, connecting with firm handshakes that demonstrated the integrity of their bones. "Marie. Bessie. Meet my dearest, sweetest friend, Lady Clementine Victoria Corrinwallis." The morning sun spilled through a large partially-open window and the scents of the garden wafted in. "Clemy, Marie and Bessie are lady correspondents from Scotland."

"Yes," beamed Marie. "We are known as the two intrepid ladies from the city of jute, jam, and journalism bonnie Dundee."

"We were hired by D C Thomson to take the traditional Cook's Tour route," Bessie added with spirit. "And we are travelling eastwards from Europe. Twenty-six thousand miles. Ten countries. Reporting back on women's issues."

Lady Clementine tinkled the silver table bell. "And you are hoping to catch billionaire-oligarchs along the way."

Bessie felt a flush rising up in her neck. "Our main focus, Lady Clementine, is our mission work." There was a small silence as Bessie gathered her thoughts. "We are also covering art, culture, fashion, religion and architecture."

"How interesting. And what do you plan on doing while you are in this neck of the woods?"

A waiter approached proffering a large tray of fresh fruit. Beverages began moving around the table in the opposite direction of the food but at the same time. Bessie held her teacup and saucer at chest level. "Well, yesterday, we visited the Sarcee Reservation."

"Oh, did you see Hiawatha? Or was he off in his birch canoe with Minnehaha? Ha-ha."

Bessie's forehead crumpled. "We saw a residential school, M'Lady. And we learned the Sarcee's numbers have dropped since they were placed on the reservation, after signing a treaty to give up their hunting grounds." She returned her cup to its saucer then said, "May I mention Hiawatha is not from the Sarcee tribe. He was a leader of the Mohawk tribe. In the 1500s."

"Oh curling smoke of wigwams," snapped Lady Clementine. "Kill the Indian! Save the man!"

Bessie's tea caught in her throat. "I *beg* your pardon?"

Alexis leaned in. "Lady Clementine is quoting Canada's slogan, darling," she said, offering her tuppence worth. "It is a motto to encapsulate the belief and ideal of this new country. Indians are under the protection of the government. By forcibly removing the children from their families and placing them in residential schools, they hope to restore a fatigued and dwindling people."

Marie grimaced. "What an abominable idea."

"An atrocious crime," Bessie added. "How dare those Anglo-Saxon politicians meddle in Indian affairs."

"Ladies, it is called progress."

"Sounds more like a self-serving ploy to me," said Marie.

Lady Clementine touched her forehead with her handkerchief. "Ladies. The object of polite female conversation is to entertain and amuse."

Sip.

Swallow.

Smirk.

Bessie broke the silence. "If women are to keep their talk as light as their meal, Lady Clementine, I doubt any of us will have a decent conversation."

"It is nice to feel important, Miss Maxwell. But more important to be nice. Entertain and amuse, darling, and leave the men to take care of important matters. They always do the right thing."

Sip.

Swallow.

Smirk.

"Like building the Titanic?"

Lady Clementine hands curled into tight fists. "Are you quite finished, Miss Maxwell?"

"I am not quite sure. What do you think, Marie?"

"I think if a woman had been involved in the ship's decision-making process, there would have been enough lifeboats for the children, at least."

Lady Clementine's heart fluttered with annoyance. "Women and children *always* board the lifeboats first. Why? Because. They. Do. Not. Make. Decisions."

"And that needs to change," said Bessie, "We need to reel in these middle-aged white men who are wheedling their way into power positions then totally running amok. Take that monstrous railroad for example. Built by the Chinese who were paid a third or less of a white-man's wage. That was exactly the reverse of right."

Lady Clementine laughed without humour. "Nobody forced them to take the work."

"Golly gumdrops!" Marie exhaled and pulled herself up in the chair. "If the Chinese didn't suffer greatly in those harsh and dangerous conditions: typhoid fever, blasting accidents, scurvy, Canada could not have afforded it. There would be no railroad running from one end of this country to the other. There would be no Banff Springs Hotel. And we would not be sipping tea in a place that was once remote and inaccessible."

Bessie frowned. "And all the while the greedy Dominion Government remained far from grateful. Aware a Chinese worker was dying for every mile of track laid, they upped the target to 10 miles a day." Her face flushed red. "But worst of all, they patiently waited until the railroad was complete before imposing an exorbitant head tax which made it practically impossible for a Chinese family to settle here."

"Self-serving and morally unjust!" cried Marie.

"Stop." Lady Clementine held up her hand. "Canada was simply protecting itself from a surge of immigrants with tiny feet and pigtails who, given half the chance, would murder us in our beds."

Marie gripped the table. "Lady Clementine, Bessie and I have travelled to several parts of China and we found the Chinese a family-orientated, courteous and affable race."

Bessie nodded her agreement. "Not to mention the speed and quality of their work is second to none. I had an evening gown made by a Chinese tailor in Shanghai. We stumbled across him working in a curious little shop with a spiral joss stick wafting incense above his front door. I showed him a photograph of a dress in a magazine. 'How muchee to make?' I asked in my pigeon English and he replied, 'four dollar'. I purchased the most wonderful fabric and it took him two days to make the most scrumptious gown. I cannot wait to wear it to the Mount Stephen Hall banquet." Bessie clasped her hands in delight. "The apotheosis of my vacation."

Lady Clementine sniggered behind her hand.

"What is it, Lady Clementine? Is it something I said?"

"A four-dollar gown? How terribly inappropriate," she spat. "It is not a black-tie event. It is a white-tie event. Very rare. Extremely formal. Ball gowns. Tiaras. Everyone must be dressed to the same superior degree as 1st Baron Mount Stephen. He is a person of consideration. It is imperative that you are suitably attired in his presence."

"Puffery!" cried Alexis. "George Stephen began life as a barefoot stable boy!"

"What?"

"The son of a carpenter."

"What!?"

"Yes, darling. He is a mere mortal." She turned to face Bessie. "So your four-dollar gown will be perfectly acceptable."

Lady Clementine's face turned a mask of disapproval. "I cannot believe he is a *Monsieur Tout-le-monde!*" Her knees shook under the table. "Drats! What a waste of effort on my part."

Bessie smiled. "Surely, Lady Clementine, you would not dress down for an important self-made man?"

"I am not a snob, Miss Maxwell."

Bessie's mind struggled for a change of topic. "M'Lady, have you and Alexis known each other long?"

"We met at the Institute Chateau Mont Choisi in Switzerland."

"That is quite an elite finishing school."

"And very intense. We had to balance hard-covered books on our heads for poise and posture."

"And we learned how to yodel in a tea house in a mountain hut. Like this—" Alexis cupped a hand to her mouth. "Yodelay-hee-*hoooooo!*"

Everyone laughed then Bessie placed her crumpled napkin on the table. "Any plans for the rest of the day, ladies?"

"Yes. Alexis and I are off to observe some cowboys on their bucking broncos."

"Bucking broncos?"

"Bucking," said Alexis, "is when the horse puts his four feet together and, in a run of jumps, endeavours to unseat the cowboy."

Lady Corrinwallis nodded. "Most of the horse-breakers are inherently good-looking frightfully handsome. Up until the moment blood gushes from their mouths and noses. They say they have short lives."

Bessie stood up from the table. "Too much information for me," she said.

"Me too." Marie smiled and pushed back her chair. "Enjoy the rest of your day."

Lady Clementine offered a queenly wave. "Goodbye insipid ladies."

"*I-n-t-r-e-p-i-d* ladies." Alexis corrected her in hushed tones. "Fearless dauntless as in 'intrepid explorer'."

"Oh, whatever. Now. Tell me. What have you been up to since we last met?"

Alexis's face lit up. "Oh, Clemy, mother was quite upset but I decided to do it anyway. I got a job deep breath a *real* job!"

Lady Clementine selected a strawberry from the silver fruit dish. "Twaddle! If you want a respectable position in society, you cannot possibly accept payment for work. There is a vast social, educational and financial gap between middle-class women and us. The insipid ladies are getting away with it because they are lower mortals."

"Do not call them that. They are women with oomph doing something interesting with their lives. What are we supposed to put our minds to?"

"Finding wealthy and well-bred husbands."

"And be shackled by convention. Tethered to a 'suitable' male most likely a shallow-minded half-wit." Alexis looked her in the eye. "Clemy, love is fickle and wedding vows last too long. In my mind, the whole thing is scary biscuits."

"Then you are doomed to spinsterhood. Looked upon with pity and scorn."

"Better than becoming a wife and coping with his drinking, extravagance, and affairs. Or worse still becoming someone's mother."

"I agree children can spoil one's figure and ruin one's looks," Lady Clementine's voice was touched by fright, "and they bring ghastly things into one's house, like like spiders and small rodents. But the problem is not insurmountable." She rubbed the pain in her temple. "Is it?"

"Oh, Clemy, I do not have the time or energy to work out the logistics, because," she smiled brightly, "the New York Times hired me last week. They are of the understanding that I will be a reasonably proficient journalist."

"Hmm. Scribbling down what exactly?"

She met her stare. "I do not scribble. I write. For Tittle Tattle."

"Tittle Tattle." Lady Clementine screwed up her nose. "What on earth is that?"

"A new gossip column. Can you imagine?! New York Times! My job is to draw passion, drama, and gossip from the rich and famous and put it into full sentences."

Lady Clementine examined her fingernails. "And now you are going to tell me you no longer have thwarted goals or unsatisfied desires."

"Precisely. I have found my calling and I am here on my very first assignment. And I can assure you, there is no hotbed of gossip equivalent to the Banff Springs Hotel." Alexis used her knife to place a little kedgeree on her fork. "Enough about me. Why are you here? For the love of travel?"

"Actually, I am on a long arduous journey to find my long-lost gentleman suitor." Lady Clementine's smile hung on her face like a mask.

Alexis jaw dropped. "And who would that be?"

"Philip Moore. And please refrain from pontificating."

"Who?"

"You *know*. The athletic one who won the pole vault …before he took that silly horse trip out west with Hussey."

"Oh, Clemy, that was positively years ago out of sight out of mind."

"Actually. Absence makes the heart grow fonder. The problem now is—"

"What?"

"Damn cruel fate. He married another."

"Oh, how perfectly horrid. Of course you accepted the news with dignity and grace?"

"Indeed, I did not." Lady Clementine's chin jutted defiantly. "The woman is of the wrong sort a damn commoner! I am hardly going to let a scheming milkmaid block my road to true happiness."

"A milkmaid?"

"Yes, Pearl Brewster. Another ghastly Brewster. Most likely related to those horrid Brewster boys."

"Brewster boys?"

"The two toughies who sweet-talked Philip and Hussey into taking the trip out west."

Alexis crumpled her napkin to her mouth to stifle her giggles. "Forgive me, Clemy, but I cannot comprehend it. Philip proposing to a girl who milks cows when he never-*ever* proposed to you."

Lady Clementine shot to her feet. "How dare you! I shan't speak to you ever again!"

Alexis sprang from her seat. "Clemy *wait—"*

Lady Clementine swung around. "What do you want now?"

Alexis fought to catch her breath. "I I want to offer a profuse apology it was a horribly mean thing to say *please* forgive me." She gave Lady Clementine a peck on the cheek.

"Alexis, I had great expectations that have been horrifically dashed!" A shiver ran down her spine. "It is impossible to imagine he married a working-class woman."

"But Prince Charming married Cinderella and Princess Jasmine married Aladdin." Alexis sank her chin into her collar. "Sorry. I, um. Damn."

Sharp squares of light from the stained-glass window fell upon Lady Clementine's face. "That that shameless Jezebel will not be an obstacle to my happiness. Alexis, prove you are a true friend. Help me get rid of her."

Goosebumps prickled Alexis' skin. "Kill her off?"

"No, you silly goose. Write one of your salacious tales for that widely read newspaper column, *Tittle Tattle*. Reveal the wicked dairymaid's real character and intentions which are disreputable and dishonourable. Tell the world what a heartless gold-digger she is a shabby little nobody! That should embarrass Philip to a considerable degree and, when he is in the depths of despair, I will pat his head and tell him all is forgiven." A twist of excitement stirred in Lady Clementine. "And do not forget to tell your readers how gracious Lady

Clementine Victoria Corrinwallis was in giving the major a second chance due to the war."

Alexis' eyes glistened with excitement. "Clemy, with my natural ability to write and your impressive pedigree, the world will spin with this story."

Chapter 10

Ishbel rifled through a ring of weighty keys until she found the right one. All the rooms on the 5th Floor were grand but this one, with Chinese lacquer panels and splendid antiques, was especially so. She walked to the casement and drew back the heavy-lined drapes. A gentle fog was veiling the mountains but the sharp peaks were poking out and she gazed in awe as she hoisted up the the heavy pane. The chill morning air came rushing in with the sound of a gruff voice, *"Move!* Lazy sonofabitch!"

A surge of fear engulfed Ishbel. She wrapped the cord around the brass hook and leaned out of the window. A burly guard was shoving a young prisoner who was shuffling along on shackled feet. Her stomach clenched. She yearned to scream her protest. Withdrawing from the window, she threw herself into her work: stripping the bed, beating the mattress, flapping on a crisp-white sheet. Crafting neat hospital-corners, filling freshly-laundered pillowcases, grappling with the long-fat bolster that refused to be encased. A top sheet, a woollen blanket, a lavish counterpane rippling over everything and extending to the floor in graceful folds. Ishbel drew a chafed hand along the bottom of the pillow bulge then smoothed and shaped the well-made bed. Then she took an energising breath. Looped up the heavy drapes. Pinned up the bed valance. Opened up a jar of well-squeezed tea leaves mixed with freshly chopped grass. She sprinkled the concoction over the thick rug and vigorously brushed it off. Replaced the white vinegar in two concealed bowls to neutralise the cigar-smoke odour. Wiped around the inside of the large mahogany wardrobe to deter the months. Removed the ostrich-feather thingamajig from her cart and dusted around the English porcelain, the French drop-front desk, and the 18th Century English corner cabinet.

Drained of physical resources, Ishbel picked up her box of paraphernalia, gave herself a shake, and entered the large marble bathroom. She was half-way through buffing the brass taps on the roll-top tub when she heard someone enter the room. "Hey! I thought you're shift didn't start 'til noon?"

Lily stood clutching a brown-paper parcel. "Ishbel, Mister Ross wuz goin' t' tell yi." She looked beside herself. "But I thought 't better if yi heard the orful news from me."

Ishbel right away knew in her heart of hearts. "Is it my dad?"

Lily, half hidden in the shadow of the bathroom door, nodded. "His workmates went t' his house this mornin'. They couldn't wake him." She involuntary squeezed the bundle.

"Mister Ross told Donald t' fetch the pony-cart right now and drive yi t' Canmore."

Ishbel was still and silent. "That, that was good of him," she said, holding the bridge of her nose tightly to contain her tears and hide her fluster.

"And Miss Pigeon wants t' loan yi this." Lily held out the parcel tied with string.

"What is it?"

"'Tis, 'tis her mournin' shawl and bonnet for the funeral, she said."

Jarred by the answer, Ishbel's lungs tightened. "I I need to finish up this job."

"I'll finish 't for yi."

"I need a minute to myself, Lily." Ishbel sucked in her breath and looked her friend. "I'm glad it was you who told me."

Lily acknowledge her with a nod of the head and picked up an armful of rumpled linen. "At least let me get rid of this trolley," she said, picking up the bath towels and throwing them in with the sheets. "I'll go tell Donald yir comin'."

A shiver ran up Ishbel's spine. She moved stiff and drained into the deserted hallway. Locked the door, picked up the box of cleaning supplies and, with heavy thoughts occupying her mind, reached for the broom resting against the wall. That's when Miss Pigeon's parcel slid from under her arm and she lost her grip on the long-handled brush at the very moment two hotel guests were sprinting around the corner. The violent collision sent the contents of the cleaning kit flying, and all three women sprawling across the hallway, arms and legs spread out, ungainly and awkwardly.

Alexis was the first to surface. "Clemy," she stretched forth a hand and pulled her friend from the floor. "Your partial disappearance was very dramatic," she said, hooting with laughter.

212

Lady Clementine's cold angry eyes rested on the maid's face. "You *you* clumsy-stupid chambermaid!" She kicked a box of Borax at Ishbel as she scrambled to her feet. "You stupid little brat!" She shoved her with a sudden thrust. "Straighten your badge of servitude when I am talking to you!"

For a moment the world stopped turning. "Ma'am, I I don't understand my badge of." She needed this job more than ever.

"Your cap! Your silly-looking cap! Straighten it *immediately!*"

Alexis wrung her hands. "Oh Clemy, enough of your draconian ways." She took hold of Lady Clementine's elbow. "Come come now, darling. Let us go outside. Let us indulge in a wonderful game of croquet."

Lady Clementine shook off her touch. "I have no intention whatsoever of whacking a beastly ball in this swan-bill corset."

"Then take off the impractical contraption."

"I rather think not!" Eyebrows up and curved. "Removing my corset would bring vulgarity to the game."

"Hmm. Well, let us venture to the Rotunda Conservatory for a slice of Scotch Lawn Tennis cake. It will help us recover from the shock."

"Oh very well. But first I must change out of this crushed dress."

The cleaning cupboard with its pungent odour of green soap and bleach was barely big enough for Ishbel to fit into but she succeeded in closing the door. A moment of stillness. Then she removed the package string and peeled back the paper. Astoundingly, it became real. Her tears welled up, blurring the crape-trimmed mourning cape and a black-silk spoon bonnet. She rested her brow against the cold metal shelving and, for a few heartbeats, allowed the raw devouring grief to engulf her. Then she rewrapped the parcel, wiped the backs of her hands across her wet cheeks, and made her way downstairs.

Dressed in their flimsy afternoon dresses and voluptuous shady hats, Lady Clementine and Alexis Wutherspoon drifted into the Rotunda Conservatory, a large highly-detailed structure attached to the hotel and built around a fountain of dark green marble. A blaze of natural light filled the airy and elaborate space. Gilt bamboo jardinières, bursting with petunias, graced the walls. Tall palm trees offered privacy between groups of guests sitting at white-wicker tables. Alexis breathed in the hazy perfume from the vases of fresh-cut flowers and looked up at the two pumpkin-orange cheeked cockatiels, singing their hearts out from a highly-ornamented bird cage. "This summerhouse is quite splendid. The juxtaposition of the tropical plants with the view of pine-covered mountains adds interest. Where would you like to sit, Lady Clementine?"

"Far away as possible from those horrid birds."

Lady Clementine leaned across the octagonal shaped tea table with scalloped edges. "Syrupy scandal, according to Henry Fielding, is the best sweetener of tea." She picked up the silver teapot. "So now we are sitting comfortably, darling, tell me who is disgracing and offending the moral sensibilities of the Banff Springs Hotel. This week."

Alexis tapped her chin with her index finger. Then her face brightened. "Remember that terribly handsome gentleman we met yesterday. At breakfast. The one with a bit of *je ne sais quoi*?"

"Yes. Frankie something-or-other—"

"Franklin Roosevelt. He is the assistant secretary of the United States Navy."

"Hmm, his wife is rather plain."

"Er, ye-*es*. But her personality has a touch of flamboyance," replied Alexis. "And so do her hats. She was wearing a striking one when she checked-out of the hotel yesterday. Anyway the scandal is," she leaned in, "his witty and ravishing mistress checked-in today. That is her." They glanced over. "The one reading a book by the potted fern."

Lady Clementine's eyes turned bulging and inquisitive. "I am surprised and entertained in equal measure. Who is she?"

"A flibbertigibbet." Alexis fingered her pearl necklace again. "One of those ghastly flirtatious types. Of course, she is visibly persona non grata in his social circle. There now. That is all my undiluted gossip."

"Hmm, not a lot, darling," said Lady Clementine, accusingly. "If you want to keep your precious little job, you will have to pull up your precious little socks."

Alexis' demeanour changed. "You are right. I have to sharpen up this week," she moaned. "My editor wants stories on suffragettes, soldiers and servants. Thankfully, I have the Major and Dairymaid story. Pity you are not a suffragette, Clemy."

Lady Clementine's eyes popped with indignation. "I will have you know. Alexis Wutherspoon. I offered free admission to all those wearing a suffragette ribbon at my Hat Auction and Tea Party."

"Commendable. But not militant suffrage activism Alice Paul Emmeline Pankhurst." She lit up again. "Clemy, in the name of equal rights, would you consider tying yourself to the railings of the Banff Springs Hotel?"

"Certainly not," spluttered Lady Clementine. "I prefer to talk about my perfect high-society wedding. It will be frighteningly fun eagerly watched my many."

Alexis looked puzzled. "I hate to shatter your illusions but Philip is wed to the dairymaid. Remember?"

"Oh, stop splitting hairs. My gentleman suitor is only indulging in a bit of hanky-panky. Nothing more. As soon as this war is over, I will eradicate that conniving peasant woman."

"Hmm. Talking of hanky-panky, my mother says, 'A man who gets free milk never buys a cow'."

"Hmm. My maid, Ethel, says, 'One does not have to wed the entire fat pig for the pleasure of his little sausage'."

The bout of hysterical laughter caused fellow guests to glare disapproving but the two socialites did not notice because the sun had moved from behind the clouds. "Alexis, let us venture to the fresh-water pool. I want to show off my fabulous new swimwear a short dress and matching bloomers in the loudest of silk."

"But Clemy! You will have all the men ogling you from the North Wing windows!"

Eyelids fluttering. "I shall hide my blushes under my devilishly-cute bathing cap with the upstanding bow."

Chapter 11

Afternoon, August 27, 1915

In the Wilderness, Among the Wildlife, By a Glacial-Fed Lake

Alberta, Canada

"Bobby!" Doctor Macpherson bellowed at the little Yorky who was yelping a sharp objection at the antics of a squirrel high up in the branches of a gnarled Oak. "Bobby!"

Arf! The little dog did his rounding ritual then lay down with one paw underneath his body, thumping his short tail in the air.

"That's better," uttered the old man as he hunkered down to inspect his still. "If the authorities catch us making moonshine in the depth o' nature, they'll throw us in jail." Doctor Macpherson adjusted the tap over his bucket. "Fermentation. Distillation. Practice. Plenty o' practice."

Woof!

Aye, Bobby, there are shysters oot there who give us a' a bad name. They use hog feed instead o' corn. But genuine moonshiners, like maself, only use the very best o' corn, ground by hand."

Yip! Yip!

"Yes, Bobby, ah use an aluminium still. Some say they cause blindness but that's a load o' havers. Ah'm no spending good money on a copper one when even Tommy Dewar uses an aluminium one."

Bobby shot towards a cinnamon-breasted bird foraging on the ground and it fluttered away. He lay down again and thumped his tail.

"Tommy Dewar only does one distillation. That's normal around the world. But ah do two distillations. Moonshine always needs two," he said, turning to face his little dog. "Bobby, did ah tell ye Tommy and ah grew up taegether in the auld grey toon o' Aberfeldy?"

Woof!

"Aye, we didnae hae much. Washing wiz strung oot tae dry across the streets the bairns played in. Fir a penny piece, the butcher gave us a pig's bladder and we'd blow it up like a balloon. Oh, it made a grand fitba. We'd kick it up the road on the way tae school. Who knew then wee Tommy Dewar would end up a big millionaire." Doctor Macpherson laughed and shook his head. "Dewar's White Label purchased by the White Hoose fir the American President. And ah can safely say." A feeling of deep satisfaction puffed Doctor Macpherson's chest. "Mine is better."

Bobby flew back to the tree where the squirrel was kuking and quaasing. A wave ran through the rodent's tail and it disappeared inside the branches. Macpherson lowered his brow. "Away and lie doon, Bobby. Ye've no got a snowballs chance in hell o' catching it."

Woof! Woof!

"Och, woof-woof *my* granny. Try a bit o' variation. Like the German WUFF WUFF! Or the Japanese WAN WAN! Or the French OUAH OUAH! Or the Spanish GUAN GUAN! Or the Russian GAV GAV! So what one dae ye like the best?"

WOOF! WOOF!

Doctor Macpherson laughed inwardly and removed a screw-top jar from his bag. "Bobby, ah used tae tak' pleasure in letting ma mind wander back tae the auld days tae the faces fae ma past. But noo the passage o' time is beginning tae mist ma memory. I'm havin' difficulty seeing Tommy's face in ma heid." The old man stifled a giggle. "Och, Tommy's got a big ugly mug. Ah dinny need tae be remembering' whut it looks like. Enough o' the melancholy. Where wiz I? Och, ah remember. Ah wiz adding the malt," he muttered. "Ah'll wait until the starch converts tae sugar before ah add the yeast." He stirred the mash and stoked the coal furnace beneath. "Bobby, ah feel so duty-bound tae carry oot this idea. Ah think ah'm turning intae a ideopraxist."

Ruff!

"Aye. It's a big word, Bobby. Ah can remember the big words but ah cannae remember where ah put ma spoon." He lowered himself onto a flat rock and unbuttoned his too-tight waistcoat. "Dae ye fancy partaking in a wee dram?" He ruffled Bobby's fur. Poured a small amount into the tin cup. Slid it under his dog's nose. "Inspiration through fermentation. Sup it up, Bobby, 'n we'll hae a wee sing-song. Ah've a good one fir ye written by the bard himself. Robert Burns. It's called, 'The Birks o' Aberfeldy.' Ah'm sure Robbie'll no mind if we change it tae the Barks o' Aberfeldy. Noo stand up ye always have tae stand up tae sing a Scottish song. Och, ma back's giving me jip ah'm up noo on ma feet. One, two, three

Bonnie lassie, will ye go,
Will ye go, will ye go,
Bonnie lassie, will ye go
To the BARKS of Aberfeldy!—"

Woof! Woof!

Doctor Macpherson fell about laughing. "Bobby, it's a pity ye cannae clap yer paws." He sat down, settled his back between the stump sprouts of a cut tree and raised his cup to the twinkling stars, "Sláinte mhath!" The smoky and smooth liquor slithered down his throat; his head fell back, and the early spring leaves rustled above the violent onslaught of his snoring.

SQUAWK!

"Whatsat?" Doctor Macpherson woke abruptly from his happy snooze. "Oh, for the love o' mankind, ah mustadozedoff."

SQUAWK!

Chilled and stiff, he stared up at the tree. "Och, ye big stupid raven," he cried, heaving himself up. Stretching the cramps out of his legs. Looking around for his little dog. Then he perceived with the eyes. "In the *name* o' the wee man just look at the state o' ye!" He placed his hand on Bobby's heart. Breathed a sigh of relief. "If yer no used tae the moonshine it can knock the stuffing oot o' ye." Doctor Macpherson sucked air deep into his lungs, picked up his little Yorky, and set off for home. "Ye've nothing tae be ashamed o', Bobby. According tae the Oxford Medical Journal, at any one time, around seven percent o' the world's population is inebriated and that's no counting the wee dugs." He giggled. "'As long as ye dinny grow feathers on yer chest we should be alright."

Cupping a bowl of soup in both hands, Doctor Macpherson shuffled his slippered feet across the kitchen floor. "This Scotch broth will bring ye back tae life, Bobby," he said, bending down to position it under the Yorky's nose. "Sup it up noo, while it's still warm."

The dog's head was still in the bowl but he wagged his tail which prompted the old man to sit down and begin another story: "Her name was Queenie, Bobby. She was a bonnie barmaid in the tavern across fae the university. Funnily enough, the more I drank, the bonnier she got." He giggled. "Nevertheless, I was convinced she was the 'one' so I gave her a luckenbooth brooch and vowed tae love her forever but, sadly, she turned me down for a man wi the brains o' a kipper." He was silent for a long moment. "Ma muther disagreed. She said I wiz the only one wi the brains o' a kipper."

The little dog lifted his head and gave a pointed look in Doctor Macpherson's direction.

Heat rose in the old man's cheeks. "Err, it wiz her luckenbooth brooch."

Ruff!

"Aye, it wiz rough." He smiled down at Bobby. "Mind you, some men say marriage is the most expensive way o' getting yer laundry done, but sometimes ah wish ah had a wee wife. Or even a big one. But women dinny appreciate pipe smoking in their living rooms, nor the smell o' whisky on a man's breath. Ah'd have gotten a telling off every day fir ma untidiness. Och, Bobby, ah'm recalling desires that are long oot o' season."

The little dog came to sit by the old man's feet, licked his paws then rested his chin on the soft slippers.

"Ah agree, Bobby. Without wife, without strife. Especially now. Women are no longer bowing tae male authority." He laughed inwardly. "Ah mind when ah wiz in Dundee, ah witnessed the suffragette, Ethel Moorhead, throwing a raw egg at the young Winston Churchill." The old doctor's body rocked with amusement. "Oh, the look on his face it was doonright funny."

Yip!

"Aye, Bobby, we'll grow old together a privilege denied tae many." Doctor Macpherson poured himself another drink. "Just ye 'n me unless that Norman Luxton comes back trying tae reclaim ye." He sat up straight with his chin jutting out. "If he does, ah'll show him ah mean business ah'll roar, *'Judging by Bobby's tag, ah severely doubt he belongs tae ye!'*" There was a slight pause. "Och, ah'll just say it flat oot, *'Yer no getting yer wee dug back!'*"

Afternoon, August 30, 1915
A Scullery in the Banff Springs Hotel
Banff, Alberta

Lily sat down at the big bulky table shielded in yesterday's newspapers. The smelly cleaning liquid pinched at her nostrils and the pile of oxidised soup ladles nipped at her spirit. "I hate this orful job! 'Tis a bluddy pain!" She was rubbing the tarnished utensil with her capable hands when a shadow passed the patterned-glass of the kitchen window and the back door opened.

"Ishbel!" The cleaning cloth dropped from Lily's hands and, having no qualms about showing emotion, she ran to scoop up her friend in a huge embrace. Then drew away. "How are yi feelin'? Come. Sit down. Duz yi want a cup of tea? Of course yi does. I'll put the kettle on." A bench of maids shuffled up the seat to make room for Ishbel. "It'll be ready in a jiffy," said Lily, spooning the leaves into the big Brown Betty. "I'll never forgive Dimbleby for not lettin' me off for the funeral family only he said. Never mind yi had none." Lily added the steaming water, the ceramic lid, and the knitted cosy. "A cup of tea and a quiet day. That is whut yi need now."

Ishbel put her elbows on the table and chin in her hands. "So like my dad to die in his sleep not wanting to give anyone any trouble," she said, the chill of her sorrow still apparent in her pinched features. She gazed around the table of young faces, gentle and attentive. "Thank you for the wreath," she said. "When I read your names on the little card, it lifted my spirits."

Lily handed her the cup of tea and seated herself across the table. Outside, the wind shivered through the branches of a young silver birch. Inside, the clock ticked languorously, its pendulum moving back and forth. Ishbel nursed her cup of tea: scalding and comforting; richly coloured and flavourful. It calmed her mind and soothed her soul until the clock struggled and clanked and sounded the hour. All the maids stood up at once. Glimmering silver pieces stacked onto rolling carts. Tarnished silver relinquished to cardboard boxes. Bottles of polish, capped, wiped and shelved. Stained newspapers crunched and binned. Lily wiped down the table then took the empty cup from Ishbel's limp grip. "Ishbel, yi must be gettin' hungry?" she asked, the quick click of her heels resounding sharply as she returned to the sink to rinse it out.

"No, not really."

"Come with us, anyway." Lily rested her weight on the metal lid of the box that held the rags, snapped it shut then shoved it under the sink. "Maybe yi'll feel like somethin' when we get t' the canteen eh?"

"Lily, I'm fine. Thanks for making me tea." She stood up, graceful, venerable, fragile, and pulled her shawl tighter. "I'm just a bit tired. I'll see you all in the morning."

A dignified silence befell the kitchen.

Ishbel plucked unconsciously at the strands of her blanket. Stared mindlessly at the raindrops lopping down the window-pane. Pulled out the note tucked under her pillow. Now suddenly drowsy, she read it again:

Dear Ishbel, I hoped in earnest that my health would last long enough to see you settled. Alas, it is not to be and I lie here now, my mind in a jumble, wondering what words I could write to help you when I am gone.

If ever there comes a time in life when your road gets tough and you feel you can't go on, look up at your Cascade Mountain, Ishbel, and let its strength comfort you. Remember that summer's day we climbed it together and recall the number of times we wanted to give up. But we pushed on. And before we knew it, the struggle was over and we were looking down on a captivating world, awash in soft pinks and yellows. As you read this, my dearest lass, know deep in your heart I haven't left you. I'm well. I'm fine. I'm out there somewhere. Countless wonderful days lie ahead of you, Ishbel. That I know for sure. Your loving father, Daniel McColl.

She turned her face towards the door. Behind her burning eyelids, she could see his grin. In her aching head she could hear his voice. Events of the past marched through her weary brain. But he was gone. Nevermore. The room grew darker as the sun dropped lower behind the bronzed mountain. Drained. Wearied. Spent. She flung herself onto her back and covered her face with her hands.

Early Morning, August 31, 1915
A Queen Anne style house on Lynx Street
Banff Alberta

Doctor Macpherson lifted the kitchen curtain up at its corner to peek through a gap in the wind-swayed trees. "It's dreich upon dreich oot there. Reminds me o' a good Scottish summer rain stoating off the ground. Bobby, ah think it's a day fir a comfy armchair 'n a good book."

The Yorky expressed his emotions with a playful growl.

"Ye want tae go ootside? Alright. But first ah need tae find ma auld Barbour wi the hairy-cloth lining." Doctor Macpherson rummaged inside his wardrobe. "Ah remember waxing it fir foul-weather conditions. Och, here it is!" He looked down at his terrier. "Whut about a trip tae Devil's Lake? The fish come tae the surface on days like this."

The little dog yelped his approval, shot between his feet and tore around the table.

The big sky uncurled, the day brightened, and the mountain air turned sweet as it always did after a rainfall. Doctor Macpherson dismounted Tilly at a snail's pace. "Och, ah'm gettin' too auld tae ride a horse."

Neigh!

The old doctor untied his Yorky and gently lifted him out of the satchel. "It's a tad breezy," he said, looking across Devil's Lake soaking in the sunshine. "But the scenery is breath-taking so ah think we'll bide here." He patted the Yorky's tousled head. "Wi ma robust approach tae fishing we'll hae our supper in—" Suddenly, without warning, the sound of a hand bell ringing vehemently over the peaceful sounds of nature. Doctor Macpherson looked over his shoulder and his face folded into a hundred lines.

"Tallyho!" cried an upper-crust voice from an open carriage where silver-handled parasols twirled above the heads of merry passengers. The driver tightened the leather straps and the whole shebang halted right behind Doctor Macpherson. "Och, what a scunner," he blubbered. "They're invading ma fishing spot."

The driver alighted the coach. "Allow me to assist you, Madam." He held up a white-gloved hand and, one by one, the ladies in lavish hats, muslin dresses and dainty shoes, stepped down from the carriage. The gentlemen in striped flannel-sack coats and flat-straw boaters followed and they all gathered in a circle, chatting indulgently and laughing hysterically.

Then the real disruption started. Folding-chairs were pulled from the back of the Tallyho and set up along the lakefront with tackle boxes, split-cane fishing rods, and woollen blankets embossed with C.P.R. Next came the table the folding legs coaxed, forced and extracted. Then a heavy damask tablecloth was spread and centred. Toggles on wicker hampers unbuttoned. Glasses. Plates. Nibbles and bites. Macpherson swallowed a humph, "Members o' the landed gentry being waited on hand and foot."

The driver changed out of his carriage-coat into his waiter's jacket. He draped a freshly-laundered tea-towel over one arm and made himself available. "Would sir care for an alcoholic beverage?"

"A gin and tonic for me."

"Certainly, sir."

"Would madam care for an alcoholic beverage?"

"I will have a Milady's Fancy."

"Certainly, madam."

The old doctor watched from the corner of one eye "Fir Pete's sake," he harrumphed. "Are they settling in fir the week noo?"

An English voice perked up, "I beg your paaardon, old chap?"

Doctor Macpherson was caught completely off guard. "Och, er, dinny mind me. Ah'm only doing a wee bit o' fishing."

"Are you Scottish, sir?" An American accent.

"Ah am indeed," replied the old doctor, trying not to engage further.

"My deaaar chap, I positively insist you join us for drinks," uttered the Englishman. "And bring your little doggie toohh."

Doctor Macpherson adjusted his reel. "Thank ye kindly, but ah'll no bother ye all taeday. Just carry on as ye are."

"Nonsense, dear chap," declared the Englishman. "Come! Sit on this taaartan blanket and tell us what clan it belongs to."

Doctor Macpherson glanced down at the coverlet. "Aye, well. That wud be the Hunting Macpherson tartan. Which, since the truce o' 1606, ye are entitled tae sit on as long as ye dinny disturb a man who's trying tae fish."

Laughter bubbled up at his answer. "And we thought the Scots were friendly," said the American.

The old doctor, not wanting to be thought of as aloof and dour, put down his fishing gear and ambled over to introduce himself

"Doctor Macphersohn, hoh delightful to make your acquaintance. Meay I introduce Herbert Asquith, 1st Earl of Oxford and Asquith and his chaaarming wife, Margot, Countess of Oxford and Asquith; Franklin Roohsevelt, Secretary of the United States Navy and his secretary Lucy Mercah; Ross Thompson, err—"

Ross Thompson grinned and extended his hand. "They call me a rag to riches cowboy, doc. And this is my best gal, Abigail Stellarton."

"Precisely." The English face stiffened. "And continuing down the line with my introductions, this is my chaaarming wife, Lady Beatrice and, of course, one's self, Lord Chaaarles Proby." He smiled, exposing good, strong teeth. "We aaare all vacationing at the remaaarkable Banff Springs Hotel."

Doctor Macpherson shook hands with the remaining distinguished-looking men before turning to acknowledge the ladies. "Ouch!" He felt a twinge in his back. "Och, ah wanted tae charm ye a' wi' a sweeping bow but ah might get stuck doon there. So ah'll give ye all a wee wave instead."

The ladies giggled and sank into graceful curtsies.

The waiter approached. "Would you care for a drink, sir?"

Macpherson's eyes lit up. "That would be very much appreciated."

"May I suggest this fine silky Scotch, sir?" The manservant held out a bottle of Glenfiddich Single Malt. "This beautiful amber and gold whisky is a medal winner the world's most awarded."

"Thank you kindly." Macpherson could hardly believe his luck. "Ah'll take a wee nip o' that."

"Sir," said the waiter, opening the bottle. "I am not familiar with the precise measurement of a 'wee nip'."

"Och, laddie, it's the same as a wee drop fill it tae the rim."

Herbert Asquith raised his glass in the air. "Well, since we all have ah lashing in our hands, let us toast King and Country." The English raised their glasses to eye level, *"To King and Country!"*

Clink! Clink! Clink!

They downed their drinks. The waiter stepped forth to refill their tumblers.

"Caaare to make ah toast, Macphersohn.?"

"I would indeed." Doctor Macpherson raised his glass high in the air. "To the Scottish stonemasons who built the Banff Springs Hotel! *"*

Confused glances.

Awkward smiles.

Bobby snapping at a blow fly buzzing around his head.

Franklin grinned, the old doctor was an amusement to him. He held up his glass. "To the Scottish stonemasons who built the Banff Springs Hotel!"

Macpherson caught his eye and gave him wink. Then the whisky slipped down his throat and filled his chest with a warm glow. "Ah'm flummoxed at yer brazenness," he said, waving a hand over the bottles of liquor glinting in the sun. "Wi a' this oot in the open, are none o' ye worried Constable Lawson will show up? Ah heard he nabbed the Italian bottling king up in Red Deer."

Lord Proby raised a single eyebrow, a talent he had perfected over the years. "Not at all, old bean. The justice system turns a blind eye to our kind. We stimulate your fledgling econohmy so we do not have to conceal flasks of illicit liquor in our boot tops. Bwuhuhuhaha!" He looked down at Macpherson's feet. "Rather uncomfortable is it? Bwuhuhuhaha!"

224

Macpherson took a sudden dislike to the man. "Och, ye big stupid sassanach, away 'n bile yer heid!"

Lord Proby immediately rose from his chair. "I I beg your paaardon!"

"Let me translate it fir ye." He adopted a posh nasal accent. "Away and boil your head. You big—"

Franklin Roosevelt quickly intervened. "Macpherson, are you an accomplished fisherman?"

"Aye. Ah'm no bad."

"In that case, would you care to participate in our fishing derby? We'll see who can catch the fish with the greatest poundage."

"Whut? An old Scot single-handedly takin' on the Americans and the English?" He stared intently, first at Franklin then at Lord Proby. "Och, shouldnae be a problem."

Franklin laughed and picked up his rod. "Let the competition begin!"

"Doctor Macpherson, I have a question." Abigail absentmindedly twirled the handle of her pretty parasol. "How did Devil's Lake get its rather strange name?"

The old Scot held the rod at waist level, the stem of the reel felt natural between his arthritic fingers. "Och, lassie, ah expect a wee devil lives at the bottom o' it," he giggled.

The sun broke through the clouds and the afternoon turned glorious. Everyone caught a fish. None a decent size. Perched around the lake front, the fishermen waited good-naturedly. The whizz and buzz of the reels. The densely packed trees. The glimmering lake. All beautiful, but the mountains more so. Each rod flexing differently. A big fish would appear. At some point.

Macpherson's curiosity peaked. "Hey, Franklin, any relationship tae Teddy Roosevelt?"

"My fifth cousin."

"Is that so." Doctor Macpherson adjusted his reel. "It's a pity they could nae remove that bullet in his chest."

"Says he doesn't mind it any more than if it was in his waistcoat pocket." Franklin chuckled inwardly. "He gave up his boxing though. Writes a lot these days."

"Aye, he's a brave and accomplished man; made a fine president. Dae ye like the chap ye've got in noo?"

"Woodrow Wilson. I like he pledged to keep America out of the war."

He turned his head to stare at Franklin. "That's a mere matter o' opinion."

A ray of sunlight gilded the lake. The old Scot flicked a bluebottle fly off his arm. "Dae ye hae any other hobbies? Besides the fishing."

"I do indeed, Macpherson. I am an inveterate stamp collector. Yourself?"

"Ah like collecting stamps tae. How many hae ye got?"

"About forty albums, around twenty-five thousand."

"*Twenty-five* thousand stamps! In the name o' the wee man!"

Bobby woke from his nap and gave himself a hearty shake.

"You've got a fine-looking dog there."

"Aye. Bobby's a grand wee pal. Yersel?"

"No dog. One day perhaps."

"Ah can see ye wi a Scottish Terrier, Franklin. A black one. That wid suit ye."

Ross Thompson agitatedly chewed on the end of his cigar. "Man, where have all the good fish gone?"

Macpherson chuckled. "Maybe the wee devil ate them." He pulled the rod back above his head. The tip swept across his dominant shoulder then came forward swiftly. The second it hit the water there was a pull on the reel. "Hey Proby!" Macpherson cried over his shoulder. "Get Ready Tae Encounter Defeat."

"To quote Shakespeare, old boy," replied Lord Proby, his voice enormously deep, "A lot of sound and fury signifies nothing."

Macpherson turned to Franklin, "Ye must be getting worried, laddie? We all know the Americans hate losing."

Franklin laughed tolerantly. "You've yet to impress me, Macpherson."

"I'm no here tae impress ye I'm here tae slaughter ye!" he giggled, pulling back, unsteadily rising to his feet. "Och, in the name o' the wee man, ah cannae reel in this massive fish."

Bobby's ears stood to attention. Woof! Woof!

"Och, haud yer wheesht, Bobby!"

Lord Proby strode forth. "Old chap, allow me to assist you."

"Ye'll need a' yer strength, laddie." The two men exerted themselves tugging and pulling with all their might. "Oh! For the love o' the wee man, it's putting up a fight! *Oh jings!* Here it comes." All of a sudden, the rod and catch shot headlong into the sky and Proby and Macpherson were propelled through the air.

"AaaaaahhhhhhhHHHHHHHHH!" cried Lady Beatrice.

The Countess of Oxford pressed her hands over her eyes.

"Everyone! Take Covah!" Herbert Asquith marched towards the catch with pointed pistol.

The ravens screeched.

The breeze drummed.

They positioned themselves in a wide circle around the four-foot, slate-coloured fish with a head of a monkey. Its skeletal arms, jutting out awkwardly, displayed thorn-like claws with long-pointy nails.

Lucy stared, unblinking. "What. On. Earth. Is. It?"

Lady Beatrice looked askance at the creature. "A a grotesque abomination!" Her voice frigid.

Franklin focused his mental effort. "A mythical lake critter?"

"It looks like it died in great agony," Lucy added quietly.

An uneasy expression clamped Ross Thompson's features. He picked up a broken branch and gently rolled it back and forth. A nobly spine running from a skull covered in sparse fur to a tail of skin and scales. Ribs exceedingly prominent.

"Give it anuhthah jab, Thompsohn," demanded Asquith. "One has one's colt automatic at the ready. Don't you know?"

A voice piped up from behind, "Sir, it looks like a Monster Merman. According to legend, they roamed these mountains, lakes and streams thousands of years ago. Made their nests in the underwater caves." Everyone turned to look at the manservant who was balancing a tray of brimming glasses.

"Absolute nonsense," stated Herbert Asquith.

"Dinny be so quick tae judge," Doctor Macpherson retorted. "It might be worthy o' consideration. Many onlookers have witnessed the Loch Ness Monster. And we all know about the Kelpies."

Abigail's face showed puzzled amusement. "I don't."

"Lassie, a Kelpie is a water spirit that lives in lochs. It shifts between horse and human form."

She giggled. "Well, I'm going to be extremely brave and take a closer look at our little monstrosity." She lifted the hem of her puffy skirt, tip-toed towards it. "Ugh! It has a dreadful pong."

"I say, I say. Stand back, everyone." Asquith pointed his gun. "Allow one to shoot the frightening catch to smithereens."

Doctor Macpherson scrambled to his feet. "Ye'll do nae such thing!" He hobbled across the grass, stood in front of the quiescent creature and folded his arms boldly and defyingly across his chest.

"Sir," the manservant called to him, "It would be wise to allow the 1st Earl of Oxford to shoot it."

Herbert Asquith quickly regained his balance and took aim.

The old Scot waved him away with a show of irritation. Then he bent down to pat the beast's monkey-shaped head. "Dinny fret. Ah'll no let them hurt ye," he said, and it opened its rheumy eyes, akin to a pair of stuffed olives set in two egg yolks.

"Eeeks!" cried Lady Beatrice. "How can you bear to touch the horrid thing?!"

"Och, hush yer wheesht, woman. It canny help how it looks." He drew his brows together and looked around. "Has anyone seen ma wee dug?"

"Over there," Lucy pointed to the table and laughed adoringly. "He's polishing off our treats."

"Bobby!" Doctor Macpherson scrambled to his feet. "Time to go!"

"Macpherson," Franklin strode towards him. "Since you caught the part-fish creature with the most poundage, I think we all agree you won the derby!" He extended his hand. "Let me be the first to congratulate you you dogmatic old Scot!"

The others applauded heartily.

Doctor Macpherson laughed generously. "Ah'm no a stickler fir rules, either," he replied, grasping Franklin's hand.

Ross Thompson flicked his Hathaway. "So what's your plans for the trophy catch, Macpherson?"

He gave it a moment's thought. "Ah suppose ah could donate it tae Banff zoo." He shook his head. "Nah. They palaeontologists will arrive from Ottawa 'n have it dissected in nae time."

Silence.

A glint came to Macpherson's eye. "Mister Banff."

"Mister Banff?" echoed the cowboy.

The old Scot pointed to a pinprick across the sparkly lake. "He's got a shack on the north shore sells fish suppers."

"Fish suppers!" Lady Beatrice shrieked, all aquiver.

"Och, woman, ah'm no suggestin' he fries it up. He'd likely keep the wee monster as a tourist attraction in a cage for safety of course." Macpherson smiled at his new-found friends. "Ah'd be much obliged if one o' ye could wrap up the sleepy critter fir me so ah can drop him off on ma way home."

Lady Beatrice wrinkled her nose. "Wrap him up in what, exactly?"

The Banff Springs' damask tablecloth was removed from the picnic table and the slimy creature was swaddled tightly. Then Franklin strapped Bobby into the saddlebag. "Now you're good to go, Macpherson," he said, handing him the fishy bundle.

The old doctor shifted into the centre and closed his legs on Tilly's sides. As the horse trotted away, he twisted around in his bulky waterproof jacket. "Roosevelt," he called over his shoulder, "keep up yer efficient working methods 'n ye'll go far in life."

Late Afternoon, August 31, 1915
A Fish Shack on the North Shore of Devil's Lake
Alberta

A day's worth of sun had warmed the plastered walls of the simple wood structure. Luxton pulled down the metal screen, severing the reek of fish and chips from the fragrant summer breezes. He was just about to flip his 'OPEN' sign to 'CLOSED' when the sound of a barking dog made him look through the small square of glass in his door. "Macpherson!" He opened it wide.

The old horse stopped, snorted and began eating the grass. The old doctor clutched his parcel and slid off his mare. "A nice location ye have here," he said, looking around.

"It's the closest as I can get to my tourist boat." Luxton untied the straps and lifted Bobby out of the satchel. "Thanks a million, Macpherson. It's good to see him looking so well. How much do I owe you?" he asked, holding Bobby up, allowing his paws to run in mid-air.

The colour drained from the old man's face. "Och, ah'm no here tae return Bobby!" he snapped. "He's still recuperating."

"Really?" Luxton's brow creased. "He looks great to me."

"Put him doon *noo*! He's no a hundred percent."

"Well. If you say so." He put the dog down and stared at the napery-covered bundle. "What have you got there?"

Doctor Macpherson suppressed a giggle. "Let's open it up inside yer shop." He carried the bulky bundle ceremoniously through the door and set it down on the long counter underneath the window. Luxton watched with interest as the old man peeled back the tablecloth. There was only one moist fold left. "Are ye ready fir yer big surprise, laddie?"

"I am indeed," Luxton replied with a good-natured grin.

"Well, he-*eer* it is!" Doctor Macpherson whipped back the cover.

Luxton staggered back until his head hit the shelf of condiments. "What the heck is it!" he bawled.

"A big scary beastie!" He turned to Luxton and beamed. "He's called a Monster Merman. Ah fished him oot o' Devil's Lake when ah wiz hobnobbing with an earl from England and a prominent American politician who collects stamps like maself he's got twenty-five thousand!"

He didn't hear Macpherson.

"Laddie. Are ye feeling alright?"

Luxton's expression enigmatical. "It's dead. Right?"

"No. His heart and breathing rate are so low it makes him appear dead." Doctor Macpherson rubbed his chin. "Ah'm thinking he might open his eyes any minute."

Luxton touched the creature's nobly spine. "I've never seen a living thing that looks so hideous."

"Och, Luxton, yi can handle it remember that lassie ye courted in college?"

"Mac-pherson!"

"Och, we're only having a wee laugh." The old doctor crouched down to inspect the creature further. "Ye being an enterprising man, ah thought ye might like tae keep him in yer shop. Of course, ye'll need a roomy cage and a basin o' water fir him tae loll in."

"Are you sure you want to part with him?"

"As Shakespeare said, 'Things won are done.' He's all yours."

"Thanks very much. I'm sure the townsfolk will find him intriguing. When he wakes up, what do you suggest I feed him?"

"Och, he'll likely be a ravenous beastie." Doctor Macpherson scratched his head. "Ye can try him wi some porridge and milk."

Bobby raised his head. Alert. A prick in his ears. Grrrrrr.

"Och, haud yer wheesht, Bobby." Doctor Macpherson's eyes moved to an advertisement board nailed to the wall, 'EVERY DAY ORANGE CRUSH. GOOD FOR THIRST'. "If ye dinny mind, Luxton. Ah'll hae one o' them."

Early Morning, August 31, 1915
Servant's Quarters, Banff Springs Hotel
Banff, Alberta

Ishbel brushed her hair into a flat coil and drew it onto her crown. "I canny believe we actually have the same day off!"

"Me neither. So duz yi fancy goin' down t'the Bow. We can buy ice creams and go for a paddle."

"All right, but I wouldn't mind droppin' into the post office on the way. It's been five weeks since I wrote to the Anglican Diocese of Montreal asking them to forward my letter to Reverend Tosh." She secured her bun with a Bakelite comb. "Maybe there's a letter for me."

"Or maybe not."

She looked at Lily. "What do you mean?"

"Well maybe he's no goin' t' write back t' yi. Maybe he duzn't want t' part with Bobby," Lily mused. "Or maybe he thinks yir letter's a trick."

"A trick?"

Lily sat up in the bed and the springs sagged. "Yeah. Maybe he thinks yir letter's a ruse t' capture him coz he helped the Ukrainians escape."

"Oh, Lily, you've got a great big imagination. I'm sure I'll hear from him any day now."

"And if yi don't, yi know why. He's sittin' tight 'til this war's over."

Ishbel turned the door handle and the jangle of the bell made the postmistress look up. "Ah, Miss McColl. You have a letter. I'll just go get it."

A rush of relief swept over Ishbel. "*See.* Told you, Lily."

"Here you go, Miss. I hope it's the one you've been waiting for."

Lily smiled at the woman behind the counter. "Ishbel's tryin' t' get a dog that's livin' in Montreal back t' its rightful and grateful owner in London, England."

The postmistress nodded her support. "Well, the best of luck with that," she said, returning to her ledger.

Ishbel slipped the envelope into her skirt pocket and they headed towards Bow River taking longer strides than usual. "'Taint often we get the same day off." Lily caught sight of the scarlet and white-striped awning. "Duz yi want a 99?"

"Oh, I wouldn't say no to that."

Lily smiled up at the apron-clad ice-cream man. "Two 99's pleez," she said. "And how come yi calls them that?"

"Well, ladies," he said, lifting a cornet out of tin box. "A long time ago. In the kingdom of Italy. The King had a cream-of-the-crop guard consisting of 99 soldiers." The girls watched as he dolloped on a hefty scoop of ice cream. "After that, anything really special was called a 99." He added the chocolate flake. "Now. Who gets the first one?"

Lily polished off the ice cream melting in the sun then licked her sticky fingers. "Are yi goin' t' read yir letter?" she asked, clasping her hands behind her head and stretching out on the spiky turf.

A black-billed magpie soared above Ishbel's head as she reached inside her pocked and pulled out her letter. "That's odd," she screwed up her eyes, "this envelope's addressed to, '*Care of the Mine Director*'. And it was forwarded here."

"Sweet cheeses, Ishbel. Hurry up and read the blinkin' thing."

"Oh, hold your horses." She unfolded the letter. '*Dear Ishbel, I hope this letter reaches you. It feels like a million miles away and a century ago since we chased Aahhh!*"

"Whut?" Lily, shaded her eyes against the sun.

"It's—" she burbled. "*It's—*"

"'Tis whut?"

Her light-grey eyes lifting from the page, staring at Lily. "It's from Joe." She hugged the letter to her chest, disbelief on her face. "It's from Joe Ukrainec!"

"Whut!" Lily bolted upright.

Ishbel, a little wary, gazed down at the note. "Oh, where am I." '*Since we chased a grizzly with a quilt over its head! As I write this letter, the thought is making me laugh out loud.*' She looked up from the letter, her back soaking up the sun. "Oh, Lily, this is like is like a splash of summer rain in my face."

Lily hugged her knees tightly to her chest. "Um, yir face is still red as a beet."

Ishbel fought to steady her hands. "*I have no doubt you heard of the five prisoners who escaped from the Cave and Basin Internment Camp. Did you know John and I were two of them?*"

"WHAT!"

"WHUT!"

Ishbel was open-mouthed. She rose to her feet and stood on a patch of grass, the sky brusque blue and a solitary cloud. She greedily began the rest of the letter, *"Anyway, to cut a long story short, would you believe I ran into Reverend Tosh in the Liverpool Street Station in London a great, dusty, lonely echoing place. He was at the edge of a crowd watching Lieutenant Colebourn's bear, Winnie. (She's a mascot to the Veterinary Corps.) I was overjoyed to see a familiar face. Unfortunately, we only had a couple of minutes to talk. He asked if I remembered Banff's mascot. I did. Bobby of Banff always accompanied him when he visited me at the Cave and Basin Internment Camp. Seems a million years ago now.*

Anyway, that night, I had a flashback. I dreamt of the Cave and Basin. I saw Bobby's nametag dangling in front of my nose it was inscribed with an emblem I had forgotten all about that. Then I remembered you were looking for a Yorky wearing a tag engraved with a coat of arms. If it's the same dog, Ishbel, he's found himself a job as the local mascot ha-ha!

This isn't the only reason I am writing to you. Tomorrow, my brigade is making the channel crossing. We are heading to the battlefields of France. Before I go, I wanted to tell you I think of you often. Keep safe. God willing we will meet again in happier times. Joe Ukrainec."

Lily did a little dance of jubilation. *"Joe and Ishbel sittin' in a tree K-I-S-S-I-N-G. First comes—"*

"Oh, stop it, Lily!" Happiness shining out of her eyes. "Oh, I can't believe he wrote me a letter. The battlefields of France. Oh please God keep him safe." Ishbel held the letter as long as she could then kissed it, folded it, and put it back in her pocket. "And and the bit where he says Bobby belongs to the town," she bit her lip. "Is it possible?"

Lily scrambled to her feet and brushed the grass from her skirt. "Only one way t' find out. Let's go ask."

The administrator gave the merest hint of a raised eyebrow. "I am afraid the town of Banff does not have a local mascot. If it did, I can assure you, it would not be a Yorkshire terrier. It would be something indigenous to the area, like a bear or a beaver." He rubbed his forehead. "Or a duck."

Chapter 12

Afternoon, September 6, 1915

Spray Avenue,

Banff Alberta

A white-rumped sandpiper took wing from a clump of grass as Lady Clementine and Alexis Wutherspoon whizzed by on their rented sit-up-and-beg bicycles. "Weeehoo!" Alexis's divided skirt allowed her the freedom to peddle faster. She overtook her friend, calling over her shoulder, "Clemy! Did you read about that bizarre creature they found in Devil's Lake?"

The graceful pleats in Lady Clementine's wheeling outfit rippled in the breeze as she peddled to catch her up. "A deceitful ploy by the *Crag & Canyon* to boost the town's revenue,"

"Oh no, darling," Alexis quavered. "It actually does exist. In fact they have it on display. Over there." She nodded to the Sign of the Goat Curio Shop. "Oh Clemy, I am extremely curious. Do let us stop and take a peek."

Lady Clementine squeezed the handlebars. "I have no intention of stopping until I have crossed the bridge."

"And now. You have missed your chance to kiss it."

She started. "But it is not a frog prince."

"Oh right. And we don't want to catch salmonella." Alexis straightened her back. "Changing the subject, Clemy. My *Major and Dairymaid* story is turning out to be a rip-roaring success it was picked up by the London press! Let's hope it makes it to the Wipers Times."

"Wipers Times?" Agog. "I have never heard of that."

"It is a trench newspaper humorous, satirical and subversive. Published by the soldiers fighting on the front line. If they print it, you can be sure Philip will see it."

She sat up in the saddle, suddenly more alert. "He will be positively flabbergasted and utterly enraged." She squealed with delight. "Alexis, when we get back to the hotel, I insist you telegram the London press make sure they forward it to the Wipers Times. It is positively crucial this last sentence be added, *'The merciful Lady Clementine Victoria Corrinwallis has understandably forgiven her brave soldier in these trying times.'"*

Morning, September 19, 1915
The Brewster-Moore Cabin
Corner of Banff Avenue and Fox Street
Banff, Alberta

Edmée shifted her legs on the rag rug in front of the fireplace. "I see another picture of Daddy," she cried unfolding the newspaper, spreading it across the floor. "Mummy, can you help me read the words?"

Pearl pushed a strand of hair from her cheek and poured another splotch of Gold Dust cleaner onto her scorched pot. "I need to finish this job, love," she called from the kitchen. "Try reading the title sound out the words."

"A c-r-u-e-l a-n-d c-o-n-n-i-v-i-n-g d-a-i-r-y-m-a-i-d h-a-s r-u-i-n-e-d t-h-e l-i-f-e o-f—"

Pearl bit her lip to stop herself from laughing. "Oh luv, I'm coming." She quickly dried her hands and knelt down beside her daughter. Her eyes skimmed across the article. "*What* in heaven's name," she choked.

Edmée reached out. "What's the matter, Mummy?"

Pearl removed her daughter's arm, kissed it, and clambered to her feet. "Edmée go go and get your new jigsaw puzzle. It's it's on the dresser." She grabbed the broom from the cupboard, her head whirling, her mind deliberating. 'Philip was twenty-seven when I met him. Of course he courted other women. But if *their* love was so so 'special'. She put all her strength, effort and energy into sweeping the floor.

"Mummy, why is your face all red?"

She came to a startled halt. "I've a cold coming on have you finished that puzzle?"

"Mummy. How could I? I'm just opening the lid." A sudden breeze made masses of larkspur rap at the living room window. Then came a sudden loud clattering at the front door knocker. For a moment she thought her legs would not carry her.

The telegram boy looked up at her. "Are you Missus Moore?"

Pearl furrowed her brow. "Yes. I have a cold."

"I have a telegram. From England. Can you please sign my book?"

The day darkened. The floor swayed. She reached for the boy's pen and with mounting dread, wrote her name. The lad reached into his canvas satchel. "Missus Moore, your long-distance message—"

Pearl took the buff-coloured envelope and closed the door. Hands trembling on edge of the casing. Puzzle box tipping upside down. Cardboard pieces scattering everywhere. Life poised to turn. 'Oh dear God, please don't make me a widow.' She opened and read it in agony of confusion:

1/16890 17 SEPTEMBER MRS P MOORE FOX STREET/BANFF AVENUE = REGARDING NEWSPAPER ARTICLE STOP STORY IS NONSENSE STOP CLEMENTINE SELF-INDULGENT PEST STOP PLAGUED MY YOUTH STOP YOU ARE TRUE BREWSTER STOP ARE YOU UP TO RUNNING HER OUT OF TOWN STOP LOVE PHILIP STOP

Stiffness fell from Pearl's neck and back. She loosened her grip on the paper and slid her back down the wall until she was crouched beside Edmée who was lost in the world of play. The airy stalks of blue blossoms were still tapping on the window.

"Larkspur is a symbol of an open heart, Mummy."

"It is? Where did you learn that?"

"Daddy told me when we were planting the seeds. He said true love has no boundaries and if we plant them there, they will grow tall and tap on our window. I miss Daddy so much."

"Me too, Edmée."

"Mummy, I have something to tell you."

Pearl put her arm around her daughter, warm and secure. "I'm listening."

The girl's small brow creased. "Eleanor said her daddy has a little monster in his shop. She said everyone screams when they see it."

"A monster?" Pearl wondered what exotic creature Luxton was harbouring now. She stretched her legs into the expanse of the rug in front of her. "We Brewster girls aren't afraid of monsters. Are we?"

"Not us, Mummy. We're warriors."

Pearl couldn't help laughing. "A pair of warriors in wrap-over aprons, eh?" She cuddled her daughter close.

The Next Morning
Sign-of-the-Goat-Curio Shop
Cave Avenue, Banff, Alberta

The sun was peeking out from behind a swirl of cloud when Ishbel and Lily came out of the busy little shop, passing Pearl and her daughter who were going in. "Oh, Mrs Brewster-Moore," Lily called out. "Duz yi remember me?"

A surprised expression. Then the smile in her eyes catching the one in her voice, "Lily the burst donation bag, Lily."

"That's me! Burst-donation-bag Lily."

Pearl laughed. "Oh, I didn't—"

"Oh, I know what yi meant," she said then added, "Mrs Brewster-Moore I'm no sure if I should say I seen yir picture 'n read that orful story in the Crag 'n Canyon."

Pearl groaned. "Oh, don't get me started."

"But I have t' say I need t' say it!" That *that* horrible socialite 'n her pal are jealous, spoilt-rotten snobs. Yir husband's away fightin' in the trenches and their makin' up stories 'cause yi pinched one from their class. So good on yi, I say!" She turned to her friend, "This is Ishbel. We came t' see the Monster Merman 'fore our shifts start. 'Tis worth seein'."

"Is it? Well, Edmée's dyin' to see it too. So I'll get goin'. Nice meetin' ya."

Luxton felt guilty and a little uneasy when Pearl entered his shop. "Er, good morning, Mrs Brewster-Moore." He pushed up the sleeve garters on his solid white shirt. "I was planning on paying you a visit to apologise for that ridiculous story that ran in my newspaper. You see, I was tied up on a project and my new editor—"

"Luxton," Pearl cut in sharply. "Everybody in town reads your *Crag & Canyon* but most are clever enough to know half of it is rubbish. So don't bother explainin' yarself. We've only come to see the little monster."

"Right." Luxton, somewhat relieved. "Well, he's over there."

"Mum-*eeee*! Come! Look!"

Pearl's head jerked back. "Holy smokes! That's one helluva creepy critter!"

"I love his eyes, Mummy!"

Luxton walked over to join them. "That's the thing about monsters. They can be as ugly as sin but you still want to stroke them."

Pearl snickered. "A fair point, but I'll pass."

"So how's your father doing?" Luxtion asked. "I haven't seen him around."

"Oh, still working away on his ranch in Kananaskis. He had a visit from the Remount Service purchaser last week. A snippety little English fellow."

"How did that go?"

"Oh, it was heart-breaking, Luxton. Our finest and most beloved horses, relinquished to the government. We watched helplessly as they were loaded onto the trains." Pearl's voice lowered. "They use them to pull heavy guns through brutal artillery fire. It's a crime. At least our soldiers know what they're there for."

Luxton's lips pinched together. "Did they take Whiskey?"

Her eyes went to his face. "No. Thank goodness. My brother, Jim, kept him well hidden."

He gave a faint smile. "I see Jim from time to time. He was saying he was teaching the Duke of Connaught to fish when the war was announced."

"Yeah. A bit of history that." She glanced down at the Monster Merman and the two of them stood there, watching it in silence until she said, "I think he needs a bigger container. That basin of water's not givin' him much room."

"All taken care of, thanks to Donald Duncan. Before you got here, two maids came down from the hotel with a message. Apparently, our old friend's found some left-over materials from building the fossil-display case, so he's going to have his carpenters build a fancy monster house." He laughed and added, "With an attached pool."

"His carpenters?"

"All on their own time, of course."

Pearl made a face. "All on their own time my granny! It's a good job Dimbleby doesn't know the half of it."

"Anyhow, I've got my orders to drop the Monster Merman off at the hotel workshop so they can make it to fit his size, wants and needs."

Ishbel and Lily reached the back end of the Banff Spring Hotel and were climbing the grassy slope when Lily said, "Ishbel, I wish I wuz able t' do somethin' that would make Peyto sit up 'n take notice of me. Somethin' t' impress him when he gets back from war. I'm sick of him seein' me as the girl with the mop and bucket."

"Well, I could teach you to knit. Then you could make him a heavy Aran jumper with a ribbin', diamonds, and raised cables."

"Oh, sweet cheeses, Ishbel! No. I wuz thinkin' of getting' him somethin' speshul, like like his fossil."

"His fossil! But it's under lock and key. And it's in the middle of the busiest lobby on the continent! Oh, no! That's a daft idea."

"'Taint! For a woman in love, nothin's daft."

"But it weights a ton! It would take three folk to lift it."

"I've got three: Mister Duncan 'cause he feels responsible. Ethel 'cause she likes stirin' the pot." She smiled broadly at Ishbel. "'N *yi*."

"What? No! Keep me out of it."

"Sweet cheeses, are yi sayin' yir no goin' t' help me?"

"Yeah."

"But yir my bestie! 'N I helped yi with Bobby. 'N didn't yi say, yi wished yi'd taken my advice?"

"Er, yeah."

"Well, there yi are then."

"Oh, *Lily*. Even if we managed it, where would we store it? It may be a good-long while 'fore Peyto returns from war."

"I'll take care of the storage part, if yi help me with the move. Of course, it'll have t' be durin' the night when the lobby's empty."

"But the nightshift concierge is *always* around!" Ishbel stood on the doorstep of the kitchen and was about to turn the handle when it came to her. She turned and beamed at Lily, "And he, just so, happens to fancy you."

Lily turned pink. "Bloody pest." The door swung open and the sun retreated behind a swirl of cloud.

Evening, September 25, 1915
Mount Stephen Hall
Banff Springs Hotel

Under the gothic replica architecture, in a whirling circle of colour and movement, ladies in extravagant gowns twirled with gentlemen in formal attire to an orchestra playing elegantly and well. Lady Clementine sat down at a large table with throne-like chairs; fluffed the skirt of her scarlet taffeta gown, and gazed around Mount Stephen Hall. "Hmm, apparently, the grandest chamber on the entire continent."

"Yes, fit for a princess in a romance novel." Alexis took a sip from her ruby-stemmed flute. "Oh, I do *hope* someone behaves badly at this soiree. I am so in need of titbits for my column."

"Luck is on your side, darling. Here comes that champagne swigging and chandelier swinging couple, Lady Marjory what'shername and her shipping magnet husband."

She swung around. "Where?"

"Over there. She-of-the-large-bottom is dressed in a vulgar, carrot-coloured gown." Lady Clementine gave a short, half-suppressed laugh. "And behind them, the Duke of Kent flaunting another gorgeous-looking lover. I am sure he does it on purpose to shock the gossips."

"Clemy, the great and good of the world are gathering as we speak."

Sip.

Smile.

Bow.

Stand.

Curtsy.

Sit.

Raise a glass.

Clink.

"My-oh-my. Look who's emerging from the undergrowth. That poet person. *'Deep-hearted, pure, with scented dew still wet'.*"

Alexis twisted in her chair. "Which one?"

"The curly-black bob." Lady Clementine's plastered grin caught the woman's smile. "Dorothy Par-*ker*. Charmed I am sure."

"Oh, the element of surprise!" the woman stopped at their table. "Are you having a jolly evening?"

"Of course."

"Excusez-moi." A waiter in a light-coloured jacket proffered a tray of drinks. "Ladies, would you care for a summer cocktail?"

"No thank you." Dorothy pointed her ivory cigarette-holder upwards. "I only have two at the very most."

"Because three she's under the table," hooted Alexis.

"And four she's under the host!" whooped Lady Clementine.

Their eyes followed the poet's departure. "Did we *say* something?"

Lady Clementine brayed with laughter then glanced around the room. "I wonder if Puffy and Saggy are here."

"Who?"

"The dull and predictable duo from Scotland. Speak of the devil. Here comes the younger one in a painfully picturesque ensemble."

Flounces of ballerina tulle peaked from the hem of Marie Imandt's filmy pink dress as she approached with vigour. "Hello, I say. Because I am polite like that," she uttered with a hiccup then gulped a mouthful from a glass in hand. "Do teeny happy bubbles of champagne go to your head as they do mine?" She covered her mouth with a silk palm to suppress a nervy giggle.

Lady Clementine's gaze travelled up Marie's dress. "Where is your friend? I am eager to view her four-dollar gown."

Marie placed her empty glass on the waiter's tray then tugged at her soiree gloves, smooth and extending to the elbows. "Bessie is not coming to this most magically spiffing event because—"

"Not coming?!" An expression of horrified astonishment. "But I wait to view the prolific talents of the Chinaman." Noises of disappointment and annoyance. "How appallingly unsocial of her. I thought this was the apotheosis of her vacation?"

"It was," Marie suffered another hiccup. "Until her romantic encounter with a dashing Mountie."

"You are jok-*ing*?"

"No. Candlelit dinners and similar other things have swept Bessie off her feet. Did you not miss seeing her around? Hiccup!"

A truculent sneer. "No."

"Well, tonight they are off on an invigorating horse-drawn jaunt, over the river and through the forest." Marie straightened her embroidered bandeaux. "He is going to show her a magical spot where they can indulge in a picnic under the full moon. I must say, he looked devilishly handsome in his Stetson campaign hat and red serge tunic. Hiccup! And when he clapped eyes on Bessie this evening his jaw dropped!" She took a breath. "Oh, I wish you both could have seen her you would have swooned."

Lady Clementine squirmed uneasily. "She will freeze out there."

"Oh don't fret," Marie replied, grinning cheerfully. "Bessie's striking Mountie wrapped her up in a cosy Hudson Bay blanket after he tucked a love poem into the palm of her glove."

"What!? That is a made-up story!"

"It is not!"

"You. Miss Imandt. Have a thrasonical disposition." Lady Clementine's voice rang with nastiness. "Your friend is a homely woman of a certain age. Dull as dishwater. Which makes it unfeasible she would lead a racy and exciting life."

Marie gave Lady Clementine a horrified stare, retreated a step then stood her ground. "Lady Clementine, I find your remarks. Hiccup! Extremely hurtful!" She turned her back and stomped off in her strappy high-heeled shoes.

Lady Clementine stared at Alexis. "All of it. Absolute nonsense! Pass the wine."

"Darling," Alexis lifted the bulbous decanter. "Marie was only trying to fit in. Try to put yourself in her shoes."

"What? And try to fit in?" Her eyes grew wide. "I was born to stand out, Alexis. Why in heaven's name would I try to fit in?"

Chapter 13

Standing outside the heavy-panelled door to Miss Pidgeon's office made Ishbel nervous. "This is folly pure folly." She chewed her thumbnail. "I canny believe I was talked into this."

Lily and Ethel stepped inside the small room: a small secretary desk with ball and claw feet; a pigeon-blood painted filing cabinet; two floor-to-ceiling bookshelves. "The safety key-box is over there," Lily whispered, pointing to the flowery-patterned wall. "On the left of the rolling ladder that I dust dutifully and faithfully every day." Expectation hung in the air. The lock was incapable of turning. The lock was immobile. Fingers fumbling. The useless key wasn't turning. The little door flew wide open. Heart pumping, Lily ran her index finger down the list of names and room numbers adjacent to the emergency keys. "Sweet cheeses. I duzn't see it?"

Ethel looked over her shoulder and a deep silence followed until she hissed, "There it is, ya dummy! Beside Room 525 Fossil Display Case."

"Mind who you're callin' dummy." Lily lifted off the brass key, closed the door of the little wall box, and her initial trepidation and hesitation was replaced by a feeling of mild accomplishment.

Outside, the sudden sound of rapid footsteps. Ishbel's heart fell to the soles of her shoes. She opened the door a tiny crack. "Pssst! Come out now!" she beckoned. "Or or I'll have to lock the pair of you in."

The concierge placed the envelope atop a silver salver and snapped his fingers at the fresh-faced bellboy. "Take this, at once, to Lady Clementine Corrinwallis in Mount Stephen Hall."

"Shall I not take it to her room when she gets back like I do the other guests?"

"No. She demands her mail the minute it arrives. And we're in the business of being agreeable so," a smile clamped to his features. "Chop-chop!"

The lad set off for the grand hall. Bolted up the marble staircase. Darted along the carpeted passageway. Dashed around the flock-wallpapered corner. Arrived at the limestone steps, leading down to Mount Stephen Hall. The air was stiff with formality, contentment and perfume. Crystal. Silver. Salmanazar bottles of wine. Waiters in jackets with piping, balancing gleaming salvers laden with exquisitely-prepared fare: Oysters á la Russe, Quail Eggs in Aspic with Caviar, Poached Salmon with Mousseline Sauce. "Attention to detail is the core of our flawless service," proclaimed the maître d' to his charges as soft music from musicians in bow ties merged with a hum of cultured voices.

The bellhop stopped in front of the head waiter and raised his platter. "An urgent message for Lady Clementine Corrinwallis."

The chief attendant nodded towards a table where the volubility of one guest was igniting peals of laughter. "The lady in the scarlet gown sitting with the Count," he informed him.

The lad gave him a cheeky grin. "The Count of Monte Cristo?"

"I am not amused, boy."

The flushed bellboy walked towards the table. Corks popping. Glasses tinkling. Plates of dainty canapes travelling around the table. "Excuse me, Lady Corrinwallis." He bowed from the neck and offered the silver platter. "An urgent message for you."

"An urgent message how incredibly interesting," she uttered with a spurt of malice.

Alexis read the bellboy's face. "Clemy," she waved her spoon left to right over her soup plate. "If you take the pressing communication, the boy can return to his work."

Lady Clementine shook herself free of the Count's kiss drafting along her arm. Snatched the envelope from the little platter, and opened it:

Dear Lady Corrinwallis:

I am writing this in regards to Alexis Wutherspoon's article, The Major and Dairymaid Story, published in a recent copy of the Wipers Times. I must admit our Hellenistic romance came as quite a surprise, considering we have not had contact for ten or more years! The entertaining tale of you, the chaste heroine and I, a love-struck warrior under the spell of a wicked dairymaid, no doubt brought tears of laughter to hordes of readers, but not to me.

Since we last met, Lady Clementine, not only have I accomplished much, I have achieved the thing we all wish for most, to be happy and content. This is largely due to what I consider to be my greatest achievement; my ability to convince my beautiful wife, Pearl Brewster, to marry me.

So, dear woman, I would be much obliged if you pack your bags, don one of your outrageous hats, and catch the next train out of town. Regards, Philip

Blood rushed to Lady Clementine's head. Her mouth opened and a bizarre burble escaped, "Ecchhh Acchhh Hrrrh."

"Clemy. What is the matter?"

"Ecchhh Acchhh Hrrrh!"

Alexis's voice faltered and strained. "Clemy! Are you? Oh holy jumping mother of Moses your face is souring from blue to plum! Help. Someone. Help!"

Eyes spinning. Tears welling. Lady Corrinwallis dug her bright-red nails into the hem of the tablecloth. "Ecchhh Acchhh Hrrrh Hack—"

The maître d' flew to assist. "Stand back, everyone," he ordered. Stretching his arms. Flexing his hands. A kowtowing group of waiters, anxious to learn the skill, quickly gathered around him. "First, we reassure madam." He patted her shoulder. "Then we explain to Madam what is about to happen." He stepped behind Lady Clementine's chair and whispered in her ear. "I am going to, matter-of-factly, place my cupped hands below your bosom."

"HACK HRRRRK!" she gagged and choked.

"Now. I make a nice fist by bending my fingers in toward my palm and holding there tightly—"

Red-faced and panting, "AHGKAGKAHH!"

"And *here* we go. Bringing up the fist inwards and upwards quick and forceful inwards and upwards. Do one's damnedest not to pull madam off her seat."

"AHHHOCHUGH!" A morsel of turtle meat spurted from Lady Clementine's windpipe. She drew a frantic lifesaving breath and, amid a sea of concerned faces and clapping waiters, she was up and out of her seat. She flew out of the grand hall, the skirts of her gown streaming behind her like scarlet wraithlike wings. She did not stop until she reached the elevator lobby. One after the other, she pressed a fifth-floor button on all five elevators. She waited, and waited, and waited. "Damn stupid pulleys!"

Puffing and panting, Alexis arrived on the scene. "Oh, Clemy! I took the liberty of reading that horrid letter. How dare he tell you to leave town!"

"How *dare* he call my hats outrageous!" she emitted in a long, loud, doleful cry.

Alexis shushed her with a wave. "Everyone is staring at us, Clemy." She gently took her by the elbow. "Let's walk down to the privacy of the Oak Room. No one ever goes in there."

"Drats!" Lady Clementine fingered her earlobe and winced. "*Now,* I've lost my precious diamond and black-opal eardrop!"

"Let's retrace your steps immediately."

"Are you mad?" I cannot possibly go back into Mount Stephen Hall after what happened. You must go and search for me. I will wait in the Oak Room until you return."

"Oh, I am not leaving you here by *yourself*!"

"Why ever not?"

"Because this room is haunted by the ghost-bride of the Banff Springs Hotel!"

"You are talking absolute nonsense! Run and fetch my earring before some unprincipled person puts it in their pocket."

By the time Alexis returned to the Oak Room, a dwindling sun had turned the western wall of the Banff Springs Hotel a mawkish yellow. She put her head around the door. "I found your earring, Clemy!" she heralded. But the room was empty. "Hmm, I expect she got bored staring at the four walls."

The Following Evening
The Banff Springs Hotel Balcony
Banff, Alberta

The Banff Springs Hotel was resplendent under the moonlight when Mister Dimbleby emerged onto the balcony. The crowd below fell silent when he raised his voice to speak, "I Have Summoned You Here For A Purpose." He rested his hands on the balustrade. "Lady Clementine Victoria Corrinwallis Has Been Missing For 24 Hours." The crowd mumbled their alarm. "As We All Know, the Dangers That Lie Beyond These Walls At Night Are Many. Treacherous Rocks. Cougars. Bears. Now The Weather is Barrelling In, We Have Little Time To Waste. So I Say One and All Collect Your Lamps And Let Our Search Begin!"

Brandishing their lanterns and with the pressure of wind on their faces, the volunteers spread out to cover the rugged slopes and ledges. Their cries going unheard. The night wearing on. The temperature dropping significantly. From his window, Mister Dimbleby watched the bobbing lights weaving a circle of white on the distant mountain. The sound of Miss Pidgeon's shoes click-clacking across the polished floor made him turn his head.

"Sir," she said in a softer tone of voice. "Mr Luxton from the Craig and Canyon called. I took the liberty of telling him you were unavailable for comment."

Dawn broke over the valley. The morning air crisp and clear and every crevice and cavity in the surrounding mountains perceptible to the eye. That was when Mister Dimbleby received the good news. He returned to the balcony to make the announcement. "Lady Clementine Victoria Corrinwallis Has Been Found Alive And Well!"

A tremendous cheer rose up from the crowd below.

Alexis removed the half-empty glass of juniper water from Lady Clementine's bedside table. "Now close your eyes, darling, and try to rest." She smoothed the quilt over the spread, glanced up at the mantle clock and fizzled with annoyance. "Where is that wretched doctor?"

A knock at the door.

"At last. Inherently consoling."

"Good day, lassie. Ma name is Doctor Macpherson 'n ah've come tae see yer patient."

Arf!

His smile was wide. "And this is ma wee dug, Bobby."

"Ugh!" Lady Clementine's profusion of hair shot from her fat pillow. "Out with that animal before I catch Rocky Mountain spotted fever!"

The lines on the old doctor's brow knitted. "Noo look here, lassie," he tucked Bobby under one arm. "Ah left ma sugared tea tae come up here."

Lady Clementine's fragile tolerance evaporated. "Then you jolly-well wasted your time. I summoned a doctor. *Not* a veterinarian!"

"Ah'm no a veterinarian! Ah'm a medical doctor. The only one in town. The rest went tae Calgary fir a meeting."

"Even fuddy-duddy Doctor Brett?"

"Ah beg yir pardon?"

Alexis rolled her eyes. "Just give Lady Clementine some barbiturate salts and be on your way, man."

Macpherson's feelings were nettled. "Ah wiz called oot tae see an ailing Lady. No a pair o' spielt besoms!"

Perplexed and confused, Lady Clementine and Alex Wutherspoon looked at each then at Doctor Macpherson whose face had taken on a thoughtful expression. "Maybe that wiz a bit harsh. Ah'll give it one more try." His smile wide and winning. "Good day, lassies. Ma name is Doctor Macpherson and ah've come tae see the patient."

Lady Clementine clutched the collar of her lace bed jacket. "I am the patient, Lady Clementine Victoria Corrinwallis, and you were summoned here because I am bedridden. I have suffered a personal crisis and I am in need of medical help." She couldn't fathom why she was being so cordial.

The old doctor drew a chair close to the King Louis XIV's canopied bed and, looking directly into her pale face, said. "Tell me aboot yer deep personal crisis."

"I cannot."

"Why not?" His voice full of kindness.

"Because your tweed jacket smells of pipe smoke."

"Oh, fir the love o' mankind," he muttered under his breath and Bobby jumped down to settle at his feet. The old doctor pulled out his clean handkerchief and picked up the bottle of lavender water from the bedside table. "Pit this across yer snout," he said, saturating the fabric before handing it to Lady Clementine. She covered her face below her eyes then fell back on her sateen pillow.

"Noo, lassie. Help me. Help you—"

Lady Clementine talked through the wet handkerchief. "An unmitigated disaster," she whaled. "I am utterly mortified! My dignity and self-respect are ruined!" Her voice shuddered and the cloth blew up. "Yesterday evening, at Lord Mount Stephen's banquet, I choked on a morsel of turtle meat." The conductor dropped his baton. The orchestra squealed to a halt. And an elderly military gentleman cried out from the back of the hall, "What is that ghastly garrotting noise? Are the Germans attacking? Then captains, princes and politicians all gathered around to gawp and goggle while a pesky little waiter aggressively resuscitated me!"

"A pesky little waiter?" Doctor Macpherson's eyebrows met in the middle. "The clever man saved yir life, lassie."

"I would have preferred to die. Everyone is now laughing behind my back."

The old doctor raised his shoulders as a gesture of indifference. "Och, dae ye know what happens tae females who spend their time minding deeply what others think?"

248

The blood drained from Lady Clementine's face. "No." She looked intently at Macpherson. "What happens to them?"

"They leave a' their happiness in another's keeping. All that matters, is whut ye think o' yerself." He patted the back of her hand and stood up. "Noo, stay in yer bed. Warm and cosy. By tomorrow morning, ye'll be as right as rain."

Lady Clementine fixed her eyes on him and a single syrupy tear trickled down her cheek.

"Och, ah've a feeling there's more tae this story than meets the eye." The old doctor sat back down. "Lass, begin at the beginning." "Ye were attending the Lord Mount Stephen's banquet when—"

"When, when I was presented with a a horrid letter!"

"A horrid letter?" He gave her arm a gentle squeeze.

"From my sweetheart. The written words were so wounding, I began to choke on my soup," she told him from her pillow. "When I finally took a lifesaving breath, a sea of nosey-parker faces and cheering waiters, made me jump out of my seat. A cold sweat drenched me. I ran from the grand hall. All I wanted was to hide in my room but the stupid elevators were out of order. I was pressing and punching the buttons; trying to ignore the gawping bystanders, when Alexis appeared and suggested we walk downstairs to the Oak Room because because I needed to cry in a private space and it is always empty in there. We were outside the door when I noticed my very expensive diamond and black-opal eardrop was missing! I wanted to retrace my steps, but I could not face going back into Mount Stephen Hall so Alexis left me inside the Oak Room and went back in search of my jewellery." Lady Clementine squeezed her lavender-filled heart-shaped pillow. "Then then—"

"Take a deep breath, lass," urged Doctor Macpherson.

"I I was admiring my reflection in the window, puzzling over why Philip would choose a plain-looking woman over me. And that is when it appeared behind me!"

"What—"

"A ghostly-pale face obscured by a veil!" The garbled words leaked through the fabric and her fingers. "I turned around, and it was *gone*."

Alexis screamed, "The ghost-bride of the Banff Springs Hotel!"

Lady Clementine snatched the cloth from her face and pulled herself up onto her elbows. "No, you foolish woman! It was that conniving prankster Pearl Brewster!"

"It was not!"

"It was."

"It was not!"

"It was! That beastly dairymaid knows full well I have every intention of reclaiming my man, destroying her so-called marriage in the process. *That* is why she pretended to be the ghost to make me flee from Banff!"

"Oh that's insane." Alexis looked at her friend with anxiety in her eyes. "Your suspicious mind is inflamed, Clemy."

A deep line developed between Lady Clementine's eyebrows. "My supposition is not without basis. One: it was *she* who wrote that horrid letter a well-disguised falsehood to cleverly simulate the truth. Two: she assumed I would flee to my room after reading it, so she jammed the elevators knowing, full well, I would have to climb the dimly-lit staircase where she, no doubt, planned to lift her stupid veil and reveal a plastery-white face," she scoffed and a knowing shadow crossed her face. "That beastly dairymaid must have thought she had it in the bag when I ventured into the Oak Room because—" Lady Clementine's laughter echoed off the Chinese lacquer panels. "Apparently, the Ghost Bride resides there!"

Bobby raised himself and let out a couple of barks. Doctor Macpherson patted the little dog consolingly on the shoulder. Then he said to Lady Clementine, "Okay. Tell me how you know Pearl Brewster."

"I know she exists as a brash working-class woman," she blurted out the words, "who frequently forgets her station in life."

The doctor looked over the top of his glasses. "Yer saying folk should not try tae rise above their station?"

"Precisely. The rules keep the world in good order, Doctor Macpherson." Lady Clementine's face tightened. "And Pearl Brewster is not following them!"

Concern replaced his smile. "Go ahead, lass. Finish yer story."

"So I pulled a hairpin from my head. It was ever so sharp. That must have frightened her because the door flew wide open and I went flying across the hallway. Luckily, I am not made of sponge sugar." Lady Clementine jutted out her chin. "I pulled myself to my feet. I was determined she would not get the better of me. I set off through the backdoor of the hotel. Unsure of where to go, I twirled in confusion a heady confection of mountains, forests and waterfalls. Then it came to me. Shivering violently, I stumbled across the meadow dotted with indigo petals and huddles of gold anthers until I came upon a narrow pathway shaded by a verdant tunnel of shrubbery. My breathing laboured. My neck moist. Hock deep in thistles, I staggered, strode and sprinted until my eyes adjusted to the gloom and I saw it in the clearing: the lair of Pearl Brewster a wind-blasted cabin with gaudy-blue shutters and a matching door." Lady Clementine's hands balled into fists. Her voice dropped to a hiss. "I decided to lay in wait for her return, so I could catch her washing the plastery stuff off her ruddy complexion and punch her in the ghost-bride snout!"

Doctor Macpherson shrank back and Bobby cowered under his armpit. "In the name o' the wee man! Yer no in the best o' tempers."

Lady Clementine's eyes grew icy. She turned sideways and looked at him through a curtain of ringlets. "Because I want. I *need*. Syrupy-sweet revenge!"

The old doctor grimaced. "Tae quote Sir Walter Scott, lassie. 'Revenge is the taste o' an ugly morsel o' bread in hell'."

"Oh to hell with Sir Walter Scott! What about me-*ee*? I slipped on a clump of moss and hit my head on a slimy fence post. My knees and the heels of my hands bruised and bloody. Exhausted and heartbroken, I wept for my lost love in a forest silent and fearful. Mist clinging to my hair. Not a fragment of warmth in my body. When I turned my head, I could see the Banff Springs Hotel glowing warmly and welcomingly in the distance but I could not move a muscle. For two nights and one day, my only comfort was a poem resonating in my head: *'Underneath the bearded barley, the reaper, reaping late and early, hears her ever chanting cheerily, like an angel, singing clearly, o'er the stream of Camelot.'"* Lady Clementine shook her head; it was filled with a dull ache.

Doctor Macpherson picked up the next line, *"Piling the sheaves in furrows airy, beneath the moon, the reaper weary listening whispers, ''Tis the fairy, Lady of Shalott.'"*

"You know the ballad?"

"Och, aye. Ah like Tennyson. He wiz a bit like masel'."

"Tennyson. Like you?" Lady Clementine's eyes expressed her amusement.

"Aye, he too dealt with grief, monsters, and death-defying battles."

"Really?"

"Aye. Really."

"Well, Doctor Macpherson, I too can identify with that poem. My heart is captivated by a soldier."

"In that case," the doctor cleared his throat, "let's see if ah can pull another line or two from my ragbag mind o' useless information: *She left the web, she left the loom, she made three paces thro' the room, she saw the water-flower bloom, she saw the helmet and the plume, she look'd down to Camelot.'"*

Lady Clementine continued on, "*'Out flew the web and floated wide; the mirror crack'd from side to side; the curse is come upon me,' cried The Lady of Shalott.*" She looked down at her folded hands, her flourish of rage deflated.

Doctor Macpherson wiped his face with his handkerchief. "Probably wisnae the outcome she wiz hoping fir, eh?"

Lady Clementine punched the bedcovers. "Lord Shalott did not hop off with a dairymaid."

"Wait a minute." Macpherson's voice faltered, "Yer no saying that Pearl Brewster married the soldier who captivated yer heart?"

"Of course *I* am! But that is not important."

"No important! Lassie, let me give ye some sapient counsel. Chasing after another woman's husband will only bring ye distress and anxiety. In fact, it can be downright dangerous."

"But Pearl Brewster is only an entertaining distraction an uncouth, uneducated, penniless dairymaid!" she wailed. "Philip belongs to *my* world! I cannot lose a man such as he!"

Doctor Macpherson reached to pat the woman's hand. "Lassie, love cannot be forced by a mandate written up by one partner." Kindness oozed from his voice. "That lad didnae ask ye tae be his wife. He chose another."

"Why!? Because she tricked him? Because he caught cabin fever? Because he imagined I would grow a turkey wattle like my mother? *What!*?" Lady Clementine's voice convulsed with sobs. "Doctor Macpherson. Tell me. Why would he choose her?" Her cry dwindled to an aloof tremble. "When he could have had me-*ee*?"

The old man's brows met in the middle. "Och, ye silly goose! Ye dinny need me tae state the obvious."

"The obvious? I am afraid the obvious is not apparent to me. I am so much prettier than she is!"

Moisture snaked above Doctor Macpherson's collar. "They two jelled and ye're ye're oot o' the picture."

"If I am out of the picture. Sniff. Then I am no longer relevant. Sniff. I am departed. Sniff. I am a bona fide spin-*ster*." She covered her face with her hands. Her eyes were so full of tears, she could see Doctor Macpherson only dimly through them.

He patted her shoulder. "Alas, what cannot be cured must be endured." He turned to face Alexis. "Are ye a good friend?"

"Of course." She cocked an eyebrow. "I am one of Lady Clementine's closest friends."

"Well, tae avoid nurturing a festering resentment, ah suggest ye take Lady Clementine back tae her family."

Alexis formed her features into a pleased and kind expression. "Of course. Clemy darling, which home would you like to go to?"

Lady Clementine patted her puffy eyes. "Well, definitely not the London one. Father's groaning drives me batty," she blurted out. "Quite frankly, I do not care if the Inland Revenue is charging him twelve pounds and ten shillings for the privilege of keeping five male servants, four carriages and one dog."

"Hmm," said Alexis. "Then what about the New York townhouse?"

"And listen to Mother whine about her fading looks? No thank you!"

"Dae yer parents live on opposite sides o' the pond?" asked Doctor Macpherson.

"Indeed they do. I am the precious daughter of a peppy rich American marrying a penniless member of the English aristocracy. Mother is a real-life Dollar Princess who swapped her American fortune so she could wear a tiara. So, what do you say to that, *dear* Doctor Macpherson?"

"Ah say families can be notoriously complicated." He rubbed his chin. "Is there a place in yer past that made ye happy?"

Alexis voiced a thought. "You were very happy in Paris, Clemy."

"Ahh, the wine. The food. The razzmatazz. I love it all. But I refuse to live in that *that* minuscule pied â terre."

"Well then, how about your uncle's large Italian villa?"

"Too Italian."

"Your grandfather's stately home in Scotland?"

"Too drafty."

Macpherson rolled his eyes. "Yer no thinking o' biding here?"

"And why not?" Lady Clementine poked her head towards him. "I do not have to take your so-called prudent advice."

"Ye dinny." Macpherson tucked Bobby under one arm, stood up and hobbled towards the door. Before he turned the handle, he turned to face his patient and said softly, "If ye liking yer life tae a novel, lassie, ye're stuck inside a chapter. Leaving here noo will give ye a chance tae turn the page."

The door closed.

Lady Clementine threw a pillow at it and sobbed until she could sob no more. The day dawned with brittle brightness.

"Clemy, darling." Alexis called through the keyhole. "I forbid you to suffer defeat. It is so terribly middle class."

"Go away!"

Alexis placed her two hands on the door. "Darling, may I suggest you dispense the *entire* bottle of lavender oils into your bath then close your mind's eye and concentrate on a picture of Janus, the God of gates, doorways and new beginnings."

"Oh stop your prattling nonsense!" wailed Lady Clementine with a convulsive catching of the breath. "And go tell Ethel to start my packing!"

Alexis picked up her skirt and sprang to the adjoining room. "Ethel! Wake up! Wake up and start the packing! Lady Clementine and I are leaving Banff."

"Oh me nerves!" blinked Ethel. "What? Where to?" She pushed an escaped wisp of wiry hair up the front of her night cap. "First, I need ter say goodbye ter my pals."

"No need. You are not going."

"Not goin'? How?"

"Why? Because you are a malapert, Ethel."

"A malapert?" She looked questioningly at her.

"A person who is overly bold in a cheeky and rude way. That type of maid is not tolerated out east." Alexis placed her hands on her hips. "Well. What are you waiting for? Chop-chop!"

Ethel put on a freshly-laundered uniform. "Like anyone gives a bloomin' toss whut happens ter me," she moaned as she walked towards her mistress's dressing room. She was unbuckling the crocodile straps of the barrel-top trunk when the door opened. The lace ruffles on Lady Clementine's portrait collar served to worsen her mottled complexion.

"Ethel, you look decidedly saturnine."

"Are ya coming back, M'Lady?"

"No. I am bidding farewell to Banff so I can *supposedly* turn a page."

"Can I ask where yar goin'?"

"To Newport, Rhode Island. Miss Wutherspoon aspires to further the cause. So we are joining Alva Vanderbilt and her solid bunch of suffragettes in stiff-white shirts to dutifully stuff envelopes. When one is privileged, Ethel, one is expected to champion a cause. A bally nuisance but essential for social advancement."

"S'pose that's that then."

"Yes." Lady Clementine exhaled. "But before I leave, I wish to bestow on you a token of my appreciation."

Ethel was gobsmacked. "A present? For *me*, M'Lady?"

Her Ladyship stepped forward and fastened a sparkling brooch to the bib of Ethel's apron. "You were never proficient in fine-washing, fine-mending, or fine-anything-else for that matter. And you would often set my teeth on edge." A glance flickered between them. "But . . ."

Ethel stared down at the glittery piece of jewellery. "G'wan!"

Lady Clementine drew back her lips. "For your loyalty."

Ethel sniffed quietly, tears threatening to spill from her eyes. "There's a lid for every pot, M'Lady, and mark my words one day ya'll find yar pot." Her voice rose to a screech, "Hell, with a bit o' luck, I'll find mine too, eh!"

The stationmaster enunciated his words through the loud speaker, "Stand Back from the Rails. The Train to Montreal Is Now Approaching."

Lady Clementine Corrinwallis and Alexis Wutherspoon held onto the brims of their hats until the carriage rumbled to a complete stop. "Clemy, one never knows who will be travelling in First Class a king, a prince or a host of industrialists," she said, excitedly.

Lady Clementine gazed at her reflection in the train window. "I am not going with you."

"What? No! Goodness gracious! You cannot stay *here!*" Alexis felt a surge of anxiety. "Darling, Banff is for the uncouth and the uncivilised! You and I, we are pampered socialites. We lead profligate lives. We were born to swirl from New York to Paris in a heady champagne daze."

"But the freshness of this mountain air."

"But the sparkle of Harrods of London."

"Hmm," she exhaled. "I had forgotten all about Harrods. Superior quality whether one is selecting a brassiere or a pot of jam."

"And remember the fun times we had at the Waldorf-Astori!"

A girlish giggle. "Sparkly high-heeled shoes and afternoon tea dances."

"And don't forget Floris."

"Conspicuous consumption at Floris!" Lady Clementine allowed herself a little sigh of gratification. "Oh, I simply adore having my banknotes ironed before change is given on a velvet-covered tray."

"And Banffites care not a whit about ironing a banknote."

"They care not a whit about ironing a shirt!" she scoffed. "Quite scandalous!"

Alexis lifted the skirt of her linen coat above her ankles. "So the time has come for us to shake the dust of this parsimonious town from the soles of our shoes." She stepped onto the train, turning her head to warn her friend. "Careful, darling! I fear Cornelius Van what'shisname's impractical gridiron to be a tripping hazard."

Lady Clementine's voice was touched by fright. "If these horrid parallel bars gobble up my pretty heels, I shall I shall do a lot more than write him a strongly-worded letter!"

Ethel folded her life into one suitcase then took the elevator from the 5th floor of the Banff Springs Hotel to the lower ground floor where she sweet-talked her way into a temporary job as a scullery maid. Now there was only one thing left to do.

The quirky pawnbroker shop was nestled in a quaint street in the heart of Banff. The bell jangled, startlingly loud, as door swung back on its hinges and Ethel stood puffing and panting. "Jeez b'y thought ya'd closed for the day."

"You made it in the nick of time," uttered the lugubrious shop owner, eyeglasses balancing on the end of his nose. "What can I do for you?"

She thrust her hand deep inside her coat pocket. "I want ya ter look at this oh me nerves now the damn thing's caught in the threads." She yanked out the sparkling brooch and plopped it on the counter. "I've not much occasion to wear it. So if we can agree on a price, eh?"

The pawnbroker swapped his eyeglasses for his loupe.

Ethel watched, a lump in her throat.

Then he said, "This is an exceptional piece. Do you mind me asking where you got it?" He didn't want to take stolen merchandise.

"It was a partin' present from me mistress. For me loyalty."

"Your loyalty!? You must be one helluva maid." He gave her a long examination before his eyes were drawn back to the ornamental pin. "I can certainly take it off your hands." He wrote a number on a piece of paper and slid it across the counter.

Ethel picked it up and studied it. "Hmm," she said, her eyes lifting to scan the contents of his shop. Finally, they rested on a champagne stole draped around a tailor's dummy. "Throw in that bit o' fox fur and ya've got yarself a deal."

The pawnbroker nodded his agreement, opened his till and counted out the money. "One moment, please," he said. "I'll go and wrap your fur."

Ethel stuffed the wad of notes into her purse, rested her elbows on the polished surface and hollered towards the back shop. "This cash is gonna buy me a new frock for the summer and a pair of leather boots for when the snow starts blowin'." The man didn't reply so she carried on. "And it'll fix up me brother's boat too! *Bloomin-hell*, I'll even have enough left over for a trip back home ter see me old mudder. I'll have ter buy her a fox fur too. She'll want one when she sees mine. Then we'll go for high tea and a concert afterwards. Oh me nerves," she choked. "It's not every day Morris kills a cow. Is it?"

The man reappeared and handed her the parcel. "Thanks, mister," she said, unable to resist the urge to ruffle his combover. And with that she was gone.

The Next Morning,
Mister Dimbleby's Office
The Banff Springs Hotel
Banff, Alberta

A knock at the door. It opens. "Sir!" Mister Ross took a few deep breaths to find his normal breathing pattern. "Mister Dimbleby. *Sir!* I need to talk to you about about—"

The big boss looked up from his desk. "About exceeding all expectations, I hope."

"No, sir. Well, yes, sir. But. But first, sir—"

"Mister Ross," he tapped his fingers on his cigar box. "Take a seat. I want to talk to you about Lady Clementine and Miss Wutherspoon."

"Yes, Mister Dimbleby. But first—"

"First!" Mister Dimbleby leaned forward. "Let me remind you our hotel attracts the most demanding world-travellers from four corners of the globe because we offer the same quality of service they would enjoy in Singapore or Bombay."

"Yes, Mister Dimbleby. *Sir—*"

"Illustrious travellers, Mister Ross, are roaming all over the Rocky Mountains of Canada. So explain why you allowed two wealthy socialites, too young to worry about losing their looks, their money or their marbles, to flutter away from the Banff Spring Hotel *earlier* than expected!"

"Lady Clementine and Miss Wutherspoon?"

"Off course! Who else?!"

"*Sir*, I cannot talk about that now because—"

The sound of clattering shoes then Miss Pidgeon flew into the room. "Sir, sir," she shrieked. "Pandemonium has broken out on the main floor! Utter mayhem total bedlam! Everyone is checking out of your award-winning hotel! Absolutely *everyone*!"

"What?!" Mister Dimbleby sprang to his feet. Bolted out of the room and down the stairwell with Mister Ross hot on his heels. They both looked over the bannister at the crowd below. Long queues at every check-out desk. An important-looking man thrusting his arm into his jacket sleeve and bellowing, "And you need not forward my bill! I won't be paying a brass farthing!"

His wife tying the ribbons of her hat under her chin. "And I can assure you we will not be returning to the Banff Springs Hotel!"

Mister Dimbleby swallowed hard and his eyes moved to the reception area. Guests in their travelling attire. Piled-high luggage everywhere. Lord Proby perched on the arm of a fully-occupied button-leather sofa. "Are you asking *me* to wait for a ruddy Tallyho?"

"Look, sonny," replied the rich American oilman. "You're not in England now, so your title won't help you jump the queue."

Lord Proby's mouth pursed with righteous indignation. "You cocky so and so!"

"Gentlemen. Order please!" exclaimed the president of Michigan Savings Bank. "We were all given the opportunity to ship our cars. In hindsight, I wish I had brought my Winton Six a cracking automobile. I can start it without leaving my seat. Do you take the wheel, Lord Proby?"

"I have ah chauffah," he replied, adjusting his cravat. "They seay money cannot buy you happiness but I have ah Rolls-Royce that tells ah whole different stohry. Hoh-hoh!"

"I take it you own a Silver Ghost?"

"I doh indeed."

The Michigan Bank president chimed in, "They assure me the horse is here to stay but I would advise any adventuresome motorists to invest further in it." At that very moment, a huge suitcase sprang open and the revolving door jammed, leaving the Tallyho driver trapped inside the cylindrical enclosure, his nose squashed up against the glass.

"Drats!" snapped Lord Proby. "Our driver chappy is stuck." It was then the thought crossed his mind. He took a flying leap and landed on the fifth step of the entrance hall's grand-marble staircase. "Attentiohn Everyone!" he heralded above the heads of guests of every age, shape, and plethora of personalities. "I have ah foregone conclusiohn there is some confusiohn. Meay one suggest we all forgoh the Tallyhoh, link aaarms with our loverly wives, and take ah brisk perambulate to the train station. What doh you seay, ladies and gentlemen?"

"By Jove, an excellent idea!"

"Jolly good suggestion."

"Lead the way, man!"

Guests surged around Ethel like a rippling tide, and streamed out of the side doors.

Panic rose in Mister Dimbleby's chest. He gripped the balcony railings and called down, "Miss Finch, *what*—" he took a deep breath. "What is causing the stir down there?"

Ethel beamed up at him through the leaves of a hanging basket. "It might be this ugly thingamabob in yar display case that's makin' them all flee. Lard dien' dumpin, it's got a face on it only a mudder could love."

Mister Dimbleby hastily descended the staircase despite the rheumatic affliction in his knee. "*Eeek!*" A repulsion stronger than fear yanked him from the cabinet. "What the heck is it? And and where is my beautiful fossil!?"

Ethel wiped the front of the container with the hem of her apron and the little monster sprang to its ducky feet and lunged at the glass. "Since ya don't have yar spectacles on, sir, would ya like me ter read aloud the printed material attached here?"

"Read it out, Miss Finch!"

She brought her face closer to the wording:

"*Attention: Guests of the Banff Springs Hotel.*" She cleared her throat. "*In 1915, Mister Dimbleby, the manager of this prestigious castle hotel, unveiled a wonder-of-the-world a giant fossil. Indeed, it was a huge success. This season, he is proud to present yet another wonder, a Monster Merman.*"

The little beast lunged at the glass, causing them to jump back in horror. Ethel gave her shoulders a shake and picked up where she left off: "*These fascinating beasts were known to have lived in the caves and lakes of Alberta billions of years ago and, until recently, were thought to be extinct. New evidence tells us they are resurfacing in close proximity to our grand hotel. As wildlife ambassadors, naturally we embrace every opportunity to assist them in reproducing offspring and, because we sense our guests have an insatiable curiosity for life, we have created a once-in-a-lifetime opportunity. Beginning today and for one week only, a number of 'Monster' families will be removed from under the nooks and crannies of our surrounding mountains and placed under our fabulous tall-framed beds (wire fencing will be stretched around the base for your protection). This will allow our guests to experience an up-close and personal miracle from the comfort of their own rooms. To mark this momentous time, we are delighted to provide each guest with two memorable keepsakes:*

- *A limited-edition Banff Springs Hotel brass tin containing an ivory nose clip (Monster Merman odours can be sporadic and pungent).*
- *A monogrammed (B.S.H.) velvet pouch containing a pair of pliable wax earplugs (grunting and suckling noises will occur during the night).*

By combining our conservation efforts, we will aid in the revival of these exceptional beasts, allowing them the chance, once again, to roam free in the Rocky Mountains of Canada. If you have any comments, questions or suggestions, please take advantage of our 24-hour world class Concierge professionals who will forward them, on your behalf, to the Alberta Department of Fish & Wildlife.

BSH's Polite
and Dedicated Team
Developing a strong sense of place in the Bow Valley

"Wiiild Biil." Mister Dimbleby's incoherent speech gave way to his unsettling weightlessness, causing his knees to simply fold beneath him.

***

Due to the highly publicised Monster Merman incident offending the moral sensibilities of the time, the elite Banff Springs Hotel was forced to close its doors early that season. It remained closed the following year in a futile attempt to halt the scandal.

Fortunately for Ishbel, Lily and Ethel, Doctor Brett had just expanded his premises to include a School of Nursing which called for the hiring of permanent domestic servants. By the time 1917 rolled around, Mister Dimbleby had recovered from the whole shebang. He set about luring back his most trustworthy and reliable workers by offering initiatives such as attractive new uniforms and off-the-job activities. Soon the Banff Springs Hotel was back in business. To use Mister Dimbleby's own words, "We are up and running like the engine room of a battleship."

***

ATTENTION:
OFF-THE-JOB ACTIVITY FOR EMPLOYEES
Mr Dimbleby is seeking 8 enthusiastic members of his staff
(4 men and 4 women) to represent the Banff Springs Hotel in a display of
Scottish Country Dancing at the
BANFF HIGHLAND GAMES
September 23rd, 1917
Central Park, Banff
Successful applicants will be provided with dance lessons and costumes.
If you are interested, please add your name and job title to the attached sheet.
BSH MANAGEMENT

***

The response was overwhelming. Mister Dimbleby was delighted and hired Miss Stretch, the local dance teacher. Three preliminary competitions were held in order to select the final eight dancers. Outside of the staff canteen, Miss Pidgeon was pinning up the list on the workplace bulletin board:

***

THE BANFF SPRINGS SCOTTISH COUNTRY DANCE GROUP

The following employees have been chosen to represent our grand hotel at the Banff Highland Games:

Miss Abigale Bories, *Laundress*	Mister Thomas Ross, *Junior Manager*
Miss Sarah Pickety, *Kitchen Maid Supervisor*	Mister Nathan Knightingale, *Bellboy*
Miss Polly Clarkson, *Purchaser*	Mister Matthew Abbey, *Groundsman*
Miss Ishbell McColl, *Maid-of-All-Work*	Mister Donald Duncan, *Odd-Job Man*

The successful applicants are requested to meet in the Oak Room, this coming Saturday
8 a.m. sharp

***

Ishbel jockeyed for position. "Lily did we get a place?"

"I'm still tryin' t' get a look in."

Ethel elbowed her way to the front of the crowd. "Oh, me nerves," she said, scrolling her finger down the list in search of her name that wasn't there. Peeved by the nonfulfillment of her hopes and dreams, she stomped off in the huff.

Lily's face lit up. "Ishbel! Yi got picked!"

"*I* did? What about you?"

"No such luck." She hesitated, caution in her voice, "Hey, the stooped and tottery Mister Duncan's yir dance partner. I thought he wuz on his last legs?"

"Oh, no." A smile spread across Ishbel's face. "When the music starts to play, he's as fit as a trout."

The early morning sun flooded the Oak Room turning the beige-wood panelled walls a shade of welcoming blond. Apart from a small piano pushed into a corner and a row of chairs lined up against one wall, all the furniture had been removed. Miss Patricia Stretch stood in the centre of the floor, large, glossy and cool under the balls of her feet. "I am here to awaken your expectations and inspire your love of dance so, without further ado, let us begin."

Ishbel shivered with excitement. "Oh, we're lucky people. This is great."

The dance teacher smoothed down the back of her tweed skirt and sat down on the piano bench. "I would like a longwise set of four couples. Men to the right. Ladies to the left. As viewed from my piano." She began by playing a 6/8 double jig. "I am now calling on the couple closest to me. Take your partner's right hand and whirl around!" Donald reached for Ishbel's hand and the music came to an abrupt stop. Miss Stretch rose from her seat and walked towards him. "We cannot direct the wind but we can adjust the sails," she said, gently yanking on the elderly man's shoulders. "It will be a challenge but I intend to whip you into the finest Scottish Country dancer that Western Canada has ever seen." And so the class began

Promptly at noon, Miss Stretched ended the lesson. "Only seven more Saturdays to go!" she announced. "So practice practice practice your Scottish social dancing."

Old Donald leaned heavily against the wall, catching his breath and his balance. "If that Miss Stretch handed me a pint right now," he wiped his forehead with his square of fabric, "it would definitely make it a bit more social."

Bobby gazed up at Doctor Macpherson, apprehension on his furry face.

"Och, Bobby, I'm no masel this morning," he grumbled, balancing on the edge of his bed with his feet dancing about the floor in search of his slippers. "These baffies are gettin' as tight as ma shoes. Soon ah'll hae nothin' left tae wear on ma feet."

Yip! Yip! Informal and frantic.

"Och, haud yer wheesht, dug! Ah'm hurrying as fast as I can." He shuffled towards the back door. "Oot ye go my bonnie Bobby. Get yersel' some fresh air 'n mind yer manners nae weeing on the leg o' that bird feeder." Macpherson fastened the top button of his tattersall shirt and returned to the kitchen. "Ah used tae love a plate o' fried eggs, back bacon 'n tattie scones but ah've lost ma wholesome appetite. Maybe ah'll try some Scott's Porage Oats." He was reaching for his pot when the sound wafted in through the slightly-open window. "In the name o' the wee man!" His deepest emotions were stirred. "The Banff Highland Games! Ah forgot a' aboot it!" He hurried back to open the door. "Bobby! Come in! The pipes calling all the big hairy clansmen. And us! Wid ye like some porridge before we go?"

Grrrrrrrr!

"Whut? All the hard-working sheepdogs eat porridge. If it's guid enough for them, it's guid enough for ye!"

Knock! Knock!

Woof! Woof! Bobby ran to the door, his tail twitching

"Och, it's ye, Luxton!"

"I hope I'm not too early but," he ruffled Bobby's fur then looked up at Doctor Macpherson. "You told me you wanted to find a good spot before the crowds arrived."

"Aye. Yer a good-hearted laddie. Can ye fetch ma folding-canvas chair? It's leaning against the umbrella stand."

Doctor Macpherson buttoned up his green tweed jacket then turned his attention to Bobby. "Sit doon!" he said, clutching the dog between his knees. "Ye need tae wear yir Macpherson tartan collar fir this grand occasion." He looked up at Luxton, "I wid be much obliged if ye poured ma pot o' tea intae ma flask they're both sitting on the kitchen table beside ma pile o' newspapers and remember tae add plenty o' sugar."

Bolts of fabric. Shelves of patterns. Drawers of lace and thread. Mrs Kilpatrick, her bun the colour of steel wool, called over the top of her Singer sewing machine, "Are you ready, love?"

"Almost!" Ishbel skimmed the frock low over the floor boards and stepped into it, slowly pulling it up over her hips, slipping her arms into its sleeves. She caught sight of herself in the full-length mirror and her breath wedged in her throat. "I should be in my nightgown. I'm surely dreamin' all this."

The elderly seamstress pulled back the pink curtain trimmed with white pom-poms. "Turn around, love." Her nimble fingers fastened the remainder of Ishbel's tight bodice. "I am very happy with the fit. You look lovely, dear."

"Thanks so much, Mrs Kilpatrick. You're a nifty seamstress."

"With a nifty sewing machine. It's a godsend these days," she chuckled. "The tactile practice of hand-stitching is not for the hands and eyes of a person my age."

"Have you always worked here, Mrs Kilpatrick?"

"I was here with the old structure plenty of job security repairs and alterations for hotel guests and making servants' uniforms." She called to the other three dancers to line up beside Ishbel. The hems of the shimmering white taffeta dresses were all the same distance from the floor. "Perfect," uttered Mrs Kilpatrick.

The door opened. Miss Stretch was balancing a precarious pile of shoeboxes. "Help! Take one each!" she cried.

Miss Abigale Bories, Miss Sarah Pickety, Miss Polly Clarkson and Miss Ishbel McColl removed the lids and the crisp white tissue paper. Abigale was the first to pull out her soft-leather gillies. "Hold me down! I think I am goin' to float to the ceiling." Everyone laughed and set about lacing up the eyelets." The elderly seamstress returned with four, freshly-pressed, Alberta tartan sashes. Green, gold, blue, black and pink plaid silk swathed across her outstretched arms. "The finishing touch," she declared.

"What shoulder do I drape it over?" Polly asked.

"The right shoulder," Sarah replied. "The wife of the Clan Chief wears it on her left shoulder."

"And the members of the Royal family," Mrs Kilpatrick added. "Now watch me, ladies." Little bubbles of excitement rose in her. "First, fold your sash, like this.

"That's right. One side should be slightly shorter than the other. Now, concertina it at the top." She held up the example. "Should resemble this. Now place it on top of your right shoulder so it drapes down your back." She held out a small bowl. "When you are ready, help yourself to a little brooch and secure the fabric to your shoulder. One last step, catch the longer end of your sash and bring it around to your hip." A tap on the back made Mrs Kilpatrick turn.

"I am looking for Miss Stretch," said Miss Pidgeon.

"Yoo-hoo! I am over here!"

MEMO TO: Miss Stretch. FROM: Mister Dimbleby. For today only staff members in dance costumes have permission to use the front entrance of the Banff Springs Hotel. The male dancers have been instructed to wait for their partners in the front lobby (by the stuffed and mounted parakeet in the glass dome).

It was time to leave the sewing room. Miss Stretch led the four pretty dancers up the narrow and steep steps and opened the discrete door that led onto the main level. They walked across the plush-patterned carpet, drawing polite admiring glances from the passing guests. Turned the corner. Stopped and gasped. The four male dancers were outfitted in the peacock splendour of Highland dress.

Nathan the bellboy was the first to spot the girls. "Holy moly!" he cried. "You're a bunch of bobby-dazzlers!" And all they could do was laugh.

Ishbel made a beeline for old Donald. "Mister Duncan, I wanted to give you this. It being a special day and all."

The old man's eyes lit up. He carefully unfolded the crisp, white linen handkerchief and fingered the embroidered letters, D.D."

"I made it myself. I hope you like it?"

"You made it for me? What a fine present, Ishbel," he said, reaching into his pocket. "And I have something for you too." Donald pressed the pierced pebble into her hand. "It being a special day and all."

She stared at it in silent homage. "But Mister Duncan, I cannae take your lucky pebble."

"Put it in your pocket."

Dimbleby approached with vim and vigour. "Your dancers look splendid, Miss Stretch."

"Thank you. Only the best is good enough when representing the Banff Springs Hotel, Mister Dimbleby."

"Quite so." He turned to face old Donald. "Mister Duncan, I hope you have a decent handkerchief with you today?"

And that's when Donald Duncan leaped high off the floor: mink sporran flapping and silver-buckled shoes clanking. "Great Chieftain o' Banff Springs Hotel!" He pulled Ishbel's present from his pocket and waved it in front of Mister Dimbleby's nose. "Pray do not humiliate an old, bold warrior who stands alone to defend your castle."

"Good Lord!" cried Mister Dimbleby. "You are about to represent the grandest hotel on the entire continent! Govern yourself accordingly!"

Old Donald gave a sheepish grin and they all hurried out of the door.

The Union Jack was waving from the parapet of the Banff Springs Hotel. "Here they come!" cried Lily and all five maids stopped working and rushed to the south facing windows. "Let me in! Let me in!" cried Ethel, nudging her way to the front. "Oh look at Mister Duncan's knobbly knees."

"Oh, sweet cheeses, Ethel. Shut yir mouth and have a bit of respect."

Miss Stretch took a step back to admire at her troupe. "I cannot pretend there wasn't a few moments when I wondered if I could pull this off. But I look at you now, all polished and primped. Phew! I did it!" She clasped her hands at chest height like an opera singer. "And now, I have a wonderful surprise for you Pipe Major Hosie," she announced with great flourish as a tall man in full-highland regalia walked towards them. He drew the pipes to his lips before the dancers could express their pleasure. "Quickly now!" ordered Miss Stretch. "Form a line behind our piper. Men to the right. Ladies to the left. Now join hands with your partner and elevate slightly above the shoulder. Marvellous! Remember, bagpipe marching is simply walking in time to the music."

With a swish of the kilt, the piper from Medicine Hat turned on his heels and began the fifteen-minute journey to Banff Central Park. The skirl of the bagpipes rich with harmonics stirred Ishbel's innermost being and the soaring lovely sound carried her mind back to her past to the old country to the posy of flowers placed on her mother's grave the day before she and her dad left for Canada to the new country where the moon was the colour of hope. She recalled the voice through the Mine Director's letterbox. Heart racing, *"Who goes there?"* Her dad on Christmas Eve. *"'Twas a rubbish idea coming to Canada!"* he said. Because he was afraid. Making a lap for his plate with his knees. But too sick to eat. Her mind carried her to the mountain top. *'Mas leat an saoghal, is leat daoin' an domhain if the world is yours, the people of the world are yours too.'* Tears welled in her eyes. *'Countless wonderful days lie ahead of you, Ishbel. That I know for sure.'* Dad, are you watching today?"

She turned her head. Old Donald was gaily marching along. He smiled back and gently squeezed her hand. "Ishbel, let's sing along. Keep us all goin'."

> *"High in the misty Highlands,*
> *Out by the purple islands,*
> *Brave are the hearts that beat*
> *Beneath Scottish skies.*
> *Wild are the winds to meet you,*
> *Staunch are the friends that greet you,*
> *Kind as the love that shines*
> *from fair maidens' eyes."*

Chapter14

Afternoon, September 23, 1917

Central Park

Banff, Alberta

The common was circled by a wall of tents erected to honour the various clans. Doctor Macpherson filled his lungs with 'a little bit o' Edinburgh', the peaty smell of a brewery and the dankness of damp grass. Then feasted his eyes on a cornucopia of comings and goings: A ginger-bearded gentlemen brushing his Scotch Collie for the breed completion. A band of yarn-swapping Highlanders recalling old-country tales. A weaver explaining the difference between tartan and plaid to a cluster of well-heeled ladies.

The old doctor settled into his wide canvas chair and poured himself a cup of sugared tea from his trusty flask. "Luxton, ah see the officials are taking their seats noo. The Banff Highland Games must be starting soon." He partly closed both eyes in an attempt to see more clearly. "Is that The Honourable Doctor Brett up there?"

"Yes. He's the guest of honour."

"The guest o' honour!? *He*'s no Scottish." Macpherson took a slurp of the hot liquid. "Och, never mind. They say if ye scratch any Canadian, ye'll find a wee bit o' Scot."

Louise Brett's flowing-flowery skirt moved in the breeze until she took her seat in the covered stand. "How delightful. We will have a splendid view of everything from here."

Doctor Brett lifted his trousers at the knees and sat down beside her. "I find these games quite uplifting."

"It must be your Scottish roots, dear."

"My parents emigrated from Ireland."

Louise touched his elbow. "Robert. The Master of Ceremonies is gesturing to you."

268

"Ladies and Gentlemen. I want you to put your hands together and welcome him to the stage. Our special guest. The Honourable Doctor Robert Brett Lieutenant Governor of Alberta!"

The audience gave him an enthusiastic round of applause.

Then Doctor Brett spoke, "Mister Chairman, Distinguished Participants, Ladies and Gentlemen, good afternoon and welcome to The Banff Highland Games of 1917!" He waited for the whoops and whistles to die down before continuing. "In my name and on behalf of the Government of Alberta, I would like to say a few words on the importance of the Highland Games and its contribution to Canada's rich and diverse society."

And so the games began. Sword dances. Highland flings. Pipes and drums triggering infectious energy of the Scottish spirit. At the opposite end of the park, clan members embarked on a hard-fought struggle for supremacy in a fierce tug-o-war. Their cries drowning out the sound of a busked melody when one team dragged the other across the line.

"Luxton, did ye enjoy the pipe band competition?"

"Very much. The Medicine Hat band was outstanding."

"And what aboot the caber tossin'. Did ye like that?"

"I did. It's a man's sport."

"Ye think? Hurlin' a log?"

Luxton laughed. "To tell you the truth, Macpherson, I didn't quite get it. I saw a lot of powerful throws awarded a low score."

"That's because it's judged on the angle the log lands no the distance. The small end o' the caber should fall directly away if ye liken it tae an hour-hand on a timepiece, the perfect score wid be 12 o'clock."

"Why?"

Macpherson drew his brows together. "Use yer brain, laddie. We cannae defeat the English, if we cannae get the tree trunk across the moat that surrounds their castle." The old Scot settled his spectacles and picked up his program. "Dae ye want me tae tell ye whut's up next?"

"What's next?"

"The Banff Springs Scottish Country Dancers."

Piper Charles Davidson Dunbar, having just won the Beattie Silver Cup, was given the privilege of leading the Banff Springs dance troupe onto the park. A thunderous foot-stomping cheer rose up from the audience. Bobby raised himself up, his ears erect and forward. Doctor Macpherson broke a bit off a tasty biscuit.

"Eat this 'n settle doon." But Bobby remained on alert, producing long, loud, doleful cries. "Och, yer getting oot o' hand noo. Get under ma chair!"

To the delight of the spectators, the piper sounded the first two bars of the reel. The four male dancers bowed to their partners. The four girls dropped graceful curtsies. The drums rolled. The pipes stirred. And they were off like a big sneeze. Skirling. Circling. Clapping. Linking arms. Changing partners. The audience laughed nonstop when Ishbel gave Donald an almighty spin that nearly sent him flying.

"By jings, it's a sight tae behold, Luxton."

"Do you miss the old country, Macpherson?"

The old man's face softened. "Och, sometimes ah let ma mind wander tae the rollin' hills o' Scotland but Canada is ma home noo," he said, reaching inside his jacket for his sporran flask. "Ah wiz born a Scot 'n taken on by Canada both are in ma heart firever."

"Did you come to Canada for a job opportunity?"

"Nae. There wiz more prospects fir me in London. I wiz attending the King's College School o' Medicine. It's one o' the oldest 'n grandest schools in the United Kingdom, ye know."

"So, if it wasn't a job—"

"I wiz kicked oot."

Luxton accidentally spilt his tea down the leg of his trousers. "Kicked out of your country?" he asked, wiping down his clothes.

"Kicked oot o' medical school."

"But why?"

The old man was silent.

"I'm sorry, Doctor Macpherson. I have no business asking."

"Och, ah've telt ye that much, ah might as well finish." The old doctor glanced at Luxton whose eyes were wide with disbelief. "Ye see," he continued, "ah wiz plagued by a couple o' English bullies. It made matters worse when ma Professor told the class ah wiz his rising star." Doctor Macpherson tipped back his hat and scratched his head. "Ah used humour as a buffer between me and ma situation. It kept the bullies at bay but, unfortunately, it also disrupted the class. Ah should have heeded the professor's warnings, but ah went ahead and told the joke anyway." Macpherson put his head in his hands.

"So a joke changed your path in life?"

"Aye, but it wiz a good joke." He straightened up and smiled at Luxton. "Dae ye want tae hear it?"

"Sure."

"See if ah can remember *a golfer is cuppin' his hand tae scoop water from a Highland burn on the St Andrews course. A groundskeeper shouts: 'Dinny drink tha waater! Et's foo o' coo's shite an pish!' The golfer replies: 'My good fellow, I'm from England. Could you repeat that for me, in English!?' The keeper replies: 'I said, use two hands - ye'll spill less that way!"*

Luxton looked at him and started to laugh.

"Aye, the class thought it funny tae, but it didnae go doon well wi the professor. It wiz nae a school that fostered free spirit." He was silent for a moment. "Ah went tae the tavern tae spill ma troubles tae ma sweetheart, Queenie. She handed me a newspaper and pointed tae the advertisement: 'COME TAE CANADA. THE LAND O' OPPORTUNITY'."

"Did Queenie want to go too?"

"Nae. She wiz in love wi a bloke wi the brains o' a kipper but that's another story."

"But what if you—"

The old doctor's voice old, calm and measured, "Luxton, better a life o', oh wells' than what ifs." He turned his attention back to the park. The Scottish Country dancers were still whooping and spinning.

Yip! Yip! Yip!

"Och, fir Pete's sake, whut's wrong wi ye noo?" He reached down for his dog and Bobby shot from his hands, bounding across the park, tail waving like a tiny flag. Macpherson sprang from his seat and hurried after him.

Quicker and quicker the dancers flew. Until Ishbel glanced over her Alberta tartan sash and saw a Yorkshire terrier bouncing up and down beside her. She stopped dead in her tracks and the little dog circled her legs. She didn't dare say it, but the word, Bobby, slipped from her tongue before she could stop it. She dropped to her knees and the Yorky jumped into her waiting arms. Whereupon Donald Duncan fell across both her and the dog and brought down the Junior Manager and the Kitchen Supervisor. The Bellboy tried to avoid joining the heap by sliding across the grass but he forgot to let go of the Purchaser's hand so they joined the tangled pile too. The fiddlers stopped playing. The audience cried with laughter. Miss Stretch threw her hands in the air. Then fainted.

The Groundsman and the Laundress had managed to keep their balance so they helped everyone to their feet.

The Master of Ceremonies, feverish with annoyance, picked up his loud speaker. "Who owns *that* wee dug!?" He sucked in his breath when he saw Doctor Macpherson scurrying across the park.

"He's Winston's!" cried Ishbel, scooping the Yorky up before the old doctor could reach him.

Macpherson folded his arms across his chest and scrutinised her through narrowed eyes. "No. He's ma dug."

The Master of Ceremonies patted his brow and urged the fiddlers to play their music.

A powerful grip of emotion held over Ishbel's brain. "I've been searching for Bobby for years. He belongs to an English boy who lost his mother. I've hung posters all over Banff and Canmore. I've put umpteen printed appeals in the newspapers. I practically gave up hope of ever finding this dog." Bobby was vigorously licking her face so she had to tilt her head to look him in the eye.

"Did you neve*r once* see any of them?"

Doctor Macpherson felt a twinge of guilt. "Ah've a feelin' this is no going tae be the most riant chat," he replied sheepishly.

"I hate to interfere, Miss," said Luxton. "But are you sure you have the right dog? As far as I know, Reverend Tosh of St. George's-in-the-Pines was the original owner."

Ishbel hugged the wriggling Yorky. "Sir, when Reverend Tosh owned Bobby, did he have a tag engraved with a coat of arms?"

Macpherson and Luxton exchanged glances. "Aye," said the old doctor, his voice low. "It's in ma kitchen drawer."

When Miss Stretch surfaced, she demanded the Master of Ceremonies hand over the loud speaker. "Calling *All* Banff Springs Scottish Country Dancers," she hollered through the Tannoy. "Please Take Your Places!"

Doctor Macpherson turned to face Ishbel. "I wid be much obliged if ye allow me tae say ma goodbyes tae Bobby." He nodded towards his canvas chair. "We'll both be sitting there when yer dance is over. Ah promise."

Ishbel passed Bobby over.

To the delight of the spectators, the piper sounded the first two bars of the reel. The four male dancers bowed to their partners and the girls dropped graceful curtsies. The drums rolled. The pipes stirred. And the crowd clapped and whistled like never before

Doctor Macpherson sat down in his canvas chair and stroked his little Yorky under the jaw. "Ah hate tae say it, Bobby. Ah've a dwindling amount o' time left we ye."

Arf.

"Och, ah'm no happy aboot it either." His face clouded. "But, if truth be told, ye were never mine tae keep."

Two boot-button eyes looked up questioningly.

"Ah'll tell ye a wee secret if ye promise tae keep it tae yerself."

Arf!

"God works in mysterious ways." A sad little laugh. "Looking back, ah think he made arrangements fir me tae borrow ye on that dark winter night." Doctor Macpherson hugged the little dog to his chest. "Ah'm ashamed tae say it noo but I wiz so lonesome I wiz aboot tae commit a pusillanimous act ah wiz gettin' ready tae end it a'. Then then oot o' the blue, a knock came tae ma door. It wiz Norman Luxton with ye lying half dead in his arms."

Yelp!

"Aye, that's the truth o' it, Bobby." He pulled out his handkerchief and blew his nose. "One must hae something in life n' ye became ma something. It wiz never an empty hoose wi ye in it. So while ah still hae time, Bobby, allow me tae thank ye fir makin' me a happier and kinder man." He looked up sharply. "Och, here they come noo. The jig must be over." He hugged his little dog again. "Bobby, ah'm gonna miss the silkiness o' yer coat and the warmth o' yer little body. But it's time." He looked up at Ishbel from his seat. "Lassie, ah wiz a foolish auld man. Ah should hae handed Bobby back when ah first saw yer placards but ah wiz blind and selfish. I did nae want tae part wi' the wee dug. Ah hope ye and that English lad can forgive me."

Ishbel knelt down on the grass beside him. "I can see you cared for him very well, Doctor Macpherson. And I thank you for that. Nothing else matters now," she said quietly.

He scrutinised her through narrowed eyes. "Lassie, yer face looks familiar."

Ishbel spoke hesitantly, "Are you the doctor from Aberfeldy?"

"Aye. Ah'm Doctor Macpherson."

"We met a few years back in Dave White's store," she beamed. "You gave me two bottles of Bayer's heroin for my dad."

"Ah remember noo," he chuckled. "That wiz a while ago. How's yer father keeping?"

Ishbel's brow puckered. "My dad passed away."

"Och, that's too bad. How are ye managing?"

"I'm alright now," she replied in a hushed tone. "I'm accepting of the situation."

"Ah'm glad tae hear that. The mind like the body can be moved fae the shade tae the sunshine."

There was a moment of silence then Ishbel spoke. "I can ask my manager, Mister Dimbleby, if Bobby can stay with you until arrangements are made to send him back to England."

A dismal bit of forevermore opened in front of Doctor Macpherson's eyes. "No, lassie. It's best fir both o' us if ye take him noo," he said, blinking away a tear.

Ishbel's tone was tender. "If you're sure," she said, picking Bobby up. "I'll keep an eye on him until he goes."

"Ah wid appreciate that, lass."

Ishbel rested the little dog across her shoulder. "Well, goodbye, Doctor Macpherson."

The old man gripped the elbow-rests of his portable chair and hauled his bulky self up. He took Bobby's furry face in his wrinkled hands, kissed him on the snout, and whispered in his ear, "Good luck and a safe journey tae ye." As if on cue, the pipes rose up with a tune Macpherson had learned a lifetime ago at his mother's knee. His whole body ached but the lyrics kept him rooted to the spot, and he waved a bent hand until the wind stopped carrying the barks and he could no longer see his wee dug in the lengthening shadows.

'O ye'll tak' the high road and I'll tak' the low road'

Late Afternoon, September 23rd, 1917
Command Post of the Banff Springs Hotel
Banff, Alberta

Mister Dimbleby bounded out of his office. "Miss Pigeon! Dispatch a telegram at once to the Fairfax family. The Banff Springs Hotel has recovered their fine pet animal is in good health and highly valued by all of us arrangements are being made for its safe return to London. And make sure you capture all the dog's incidentals on the bill."

"Yes sir." She rose from her chair, "Sir, who is responsible for the dog while arrangements are being made to send him back to England?"

Mister Dimbleby sat down, palms on desk, eyes round and staring. "Why *you*, of course."

"Sir, I am afraid that is not possible." Miss Pigeon sucked in her cheeks. "I I am a cat person."

It was a warm evening with not a breath of wind. Ethel was behind the shed sucking the flame through a cigarette when Ishbel came up the path. "Hoy! Whut ya got there? Another flea-bitten rodent on the end o' a rope?"

Ishbel stopped in her tracks. "It's Bobby. Don't you recognise him?"

"Speak o' the devil! Baby Moses! I wonder if he remembers me." Ethel bend down and looked him in the boot-button eyes. "It was me that saved yar life, eh."

Bobby remained rooted to the ground.

"Jeez b'y! Have ya forgotten yar Auntie Ethel?" She stood up, flicked her cigarette and stared at Ishbel. "Ya look like ya've been hauled through a knot hole!"

"I know." Ishbel brushed down her skirt with her hand. "I was walking him through the forest when he took off into the bushes. When I caught up with him, he was digging up an old still."

"A still," she echoed, her curiosity piqued. "Whut? Like an illegal still?"

"An abandoned one by the looks of it."

They stood in silence until Ethel blew the smoke in Ishbel's direction. "How come ya got the job o' walkin' the mutt?"

"Miss Pidgeon's a cat person. She told Mister Dimbleby I was a dog person."

"'How much are they payin' ya?"

"Nothin'." She picked Bobby up. "I don't need pay for looking after this cute wee Yorky."

A cunning look came into Ethel's eyes. "Would ya like me ter lend a hand with yar God-bless-ya job?"

Ishbel was suspicious of her motives. "He's used to Doctor Macpherson and me. I don't think he'll go with you."

"'Course he will!" Ethel bent down and moved her hand back and forth on the dog's back with pressure. "See! He likes me rub-a-dub-dubs." Bobby shook himself briskly. "Yes! Yar Aunty Ethel's gonna take ya for walkies. Ya'd better not pull on yar leash! I don't want one bloomin' arm longer than the other."

"Sorry, Ethel, I must get going."

"Tooraloo then."

Mister Dimbleby's face contorted with fury. "Look at this!" He tossed the telegram at his secretary. "What does that pompous man think I am running? An animal refuge?"

A look of prickly apprehension crossed Miss Pidgeon's face. She hastily put on her spectacles

1/36870 AUGUST 25 MR DIMBLEBY/ BANFF SPRINGS HOTEL/ SPRAY AVENUE = REGARDING WINSTON'S DOG STOP DO NOT RETURN DOG STOP WINSTON BOARDING AT ETON STOP BANKERS NOTE TO FOLLOW STOP TRUST THIS IS TO YOUR SATISFACTION STOP LORD FAIRFAX STOP

She laid down the telegram. "Oh dear. Can Ishbel not keep it?"

The manager's eyes bulged. "Miss Pidgeon, you know fine and well, pets are forbidden in the servants' domain."

"But the dog is already there," she said bluntly. "And Lord Fairfax is forwarding a banker's note to cover all costs. Of course it would not belong to Ishbel, Sir. It would officially belong to the hotel. Maybe the animal could become a mascot an object of good luck." She gave a half smile. "Maybe maybe we could call it Bobby of Banff Springs Hotel."

The manager hemmed and hawed and scratched his head. "Pah! Give me one more good reason," he said, sinking weak-kneed into his big leather chair.

"Let me think—" She tapped her head with the end of her pencil. "Sir, terriers chase away unwanted things. Like like Monster Mermen."

Chapter 15

Morning, April 1919
Port of Southampton
England

The Great War had long since ended but Canon Harrison was still waiting for a berth on the Olympic heading back to Canada. He opened his newspaper to the headline: 'MILITARY REPATRIATION, THE LARGEST MOVEMENT OF PEOPLE IN CANADIAN HISTORY'. And quickly read the article. '*267,813 troops and approximately 54,000 dependents attempting to return to Canada. Ships responding with spaces for only 50,000 departures per month. Only two large ice-free ports available, one of which is Halifax which remains crippled from the massive maritime disaster that occurred in December 1917. Canadian trains are running at full capacity, accommodating 25,000 passengers per month.*' Canon Harrison closed his eyes and prayed, "Oh, dear Lord in heaven, *please* help me get home." Familiar and dissatisfied with the frustrating and difficult process, he made his way to the public waiting room and squeezed himself in-between two snoozing soldiers supported by a green-leather back rest. His mind wandered back to the past. To the wonderful packages from the ladies of Banff. Their presents had lifted his soldiers' spirits when they had needed it most. He hoped one day to have the honour of meeting the commendable soul who had organised it all, Lady Clementine Corrinwallis. "Ahh, Banff. Such a long time ago." Tumbled images of Ebenezer William Peyto marching off to war with a Yorkshire terrier tucked under one arm made him laugh inwardly. Had Wild Bill survived? Or was he one of the 60,000 Canadians who died. A shiver coursed down his spine. Then there was Reverend Tosh. Young and vulnerable. Had God been watching? He felt a tingle of shame. "Well, how was I supposed to know he was allergic to dogs?"

A month later, Official Port of Entry

Halifax, Nova Scotia

Eastern Canada

Canon Harrison showed his proof of identity and was cleared for entry. He made a mad dash and was lucky enough to catch the Ocean Limited, a train from Halifax to Montreal. Unfortunately, it was hellishly crowded and he did not manage to claim a seat. Clinging onto the roof strap, his round body swaying back and forth, he recalled a letter from the Anglican Diocese of Montreal informing him Reverend Tosh had taken a leave of absence. "Oh, I dearly hope it wasn't because of that Yorkshire terrier. What was its name? Bobby? Yes, Bobby of Banff."

The minute the train pulled into Montreal, Canon Harrison jumped off and hurried towards the mainline track for the through train that would take him to his final destination. Puffing and panting, he plonked himself down on the first available seat; peeled off his coat, and unlaced his shoes. Then he turned to face his fellow passenger, a battle-weary soldier who looked like the life had been sucked out of him.

"Hello. My name is Canon Harrison. I am on my way to Banff, Alberta."

The private roused himself. "Joe Ukrainec," he said, huddling into his jacket. "I'm headin' there too." The two men leaned back in their seats and closed their eyes. Over the next three days, Canon Harrison tried to strike up a conversation; by the time the train crossed into Alberta, he had all but given up. Then Joe opened his eyes and stared up at the moon through carriage window. "No more terror and death lashing down from the sky," he breathed.

"No. Thanks be to God," replied minister.

The young soldier covered his face with his hands, and the sight of his heaving shoulders and the tears leaking through his fingers greatly saddened Canon Harrison. "Joe, the hardest adjustment is that of the mind," he said, quietly. "You have lived through hell, witnessing horrific things that no man should see."

There was a long silence then Joe lifted a face ravaged with grief. "My brother wanted to enlist. I followed. We fought side-by-side in the trenches." Hesitation in his voice. "I did not have time to expect the worst."

"What was his name?"

"John. John Ukrainec. We parted on a lonely ground pitted with shell holes, his blood mingling with the rain and filth."

Canon Harrison drew a deep restorative breath to dispel his anger. "The Great War. A revolting spectre born of the devil."

Joe gazed out of the window. The sky grew enormous as the train travelled through the gentle curves of Alberta. Soon the softness of the rolling foothills was replaced by wild forest and the black shadows of the Rocky Mountains loomed above the railway line.

"Almost home, Joe. Is anyone coming to meet you?"

"A friend." There was a shift in his expression. "She wrote to say she would be at the station."

Through the mist-covered windows, they could see groups of excited families dotted along the platform. The Ladies of Banff launching a fifteen-foot long 'WELCOME HOME BOYS' banner into the air. The ambulance tooting its horn. A group of tykes with dusty boots yelling up and down the platform, "Crag & Canyon! Free Copies to Soldiers in Uniform!"

A coin was placed in a sticky palm. "Thanks mister!"

"Crag & Canyon! Free Copies to Soldiers in Uniform!"

The train ground to a hissing halt. The mayor signalled to the elderly musicians to strike up the band and the energy of the song was conveyed in everyone's singing:

> *'Keep right on to the end of the road,*
> *Keep right on to the end,*
> *Tho the way be long, let your heart be strong,*
> *Keep right on round the bend.'*

Joe stood up and threw his rucksack across one shoulder. "Goodbye, Canon Harrison."

"Goodbye, Joe. I hope to see you around town," he replied, but the soldier was already gone. Before Canon Harrison rose from his seat, he rubbed a circle in the foggy pane. A young woman frantically waving a little Union Jack. Joe running towards her. Scooping her up. Kissing away her tears.

Morning, November 11, 1919
The Norman Luxton's Theatre
Banff Avenue, Banff, Alberta

Major Philip Moore was the first to take the podium, "*At the eleventh hour on the eleventh day of the eleventh month—*" Outside, a flock of birds surged upwards in a fling of flight above the Royal Canadian Legion surrounded by a mass of poppy wreaths and patriotic posters.

Reverend Tosh's fingers hovered over the leavers; his lips lingered over the count. "Dear Lord, the time has come for me to welcome home the soldiers. Please give me the strength to do it well," he prayed, striking the batons and pressing the pedal clavier. The joyous peal from the cast bronze bells juddered the morning air. Above the church spire, the tolls rang repeatedly across the green valley between the mountains of spruce and pine reaching out to a hollow Ukrainian Internment Camp where the ghosts of prisoners past lurked in its shadows.

Under a canopy of coppery larches, a large group of veterans gathered. They wanted to mark the day by staying together so they began their climb up Tunnel Mountain. Crows cawed. Squirrel's squeaked. Boots flattened prickly grass shooting through the snow. Laughing, thinking and weeping, they pushed their hands against the woody bark of aspen trees until they gained their momentum.

Upon reaching the summit enshrouded with fog, they set about building a bonfire. Smoke. Dirt. Decaying leaves. Decaying memories. The flames sparked and crackled. A formidable reminder of their bitter victory.

Late Afternoon, November 11, 1919
The Brewster-Moore Cabin
Corner of Banff Avenue and Fox Street
Banff, Alberta

Philip Moore rose to answer the door as soon as he heard the knock. "Good Lord, man, you took your time getting back!" He reached for the old soldier's rucksack and urged him inside.

Wild Bill Peyto removed his hat and his hair stood up in tufts. "So much for the 'first-out-first-back' rule, eh?" He wiped his boots on the mat before entering the cabin: the old buffalo head, the heavy stone fireplace, and Indian blankets draped over the chairs. It gladdened his heart to see nothing had changed."

"Pey-*to*!" She flew from the kitchen and launched herself into his arms. "Oh Peyto, it's wonderful to have ya back! Come. Sit by the fire." Light from the window drew a chequered pattern on him as he sank into the chair with the wooden-spindle arms. "Ya're limpin' heavily," she said, feeling a dreadful ache.

"Battle of Ypres hit in the leg. No worries," he grinned. "Consider myself lucky."

Pearl returned to the kitchen and Philip pulled his chair closer to his guest. "We suffered terrible losses at that battle the first massive use of poisonous gas."

"Aye, it did more than tickle our throats."

"You men put up a remarkable fight for a small Canadian force."

Peyto chuckled inwardly. "Considerin' most of us lucky bastards were only civilians several months before."

Pearl came out of the kitchen drying her hands. "Edmée's finished settin' the table and my dinner's pretty much ready."

Peyto gazed down at the stately table and precious china inherited from Philip's mother. For some strange reason, it did not look out of place in the sturdy log cabin. "Yar a family of eclectic interest," he chortled, taking his seat. When the meal was over, he leaned back in his chair. "That was a helluva dinner for a woman with a reputation for openin' a tin of ham and dumpin' it on a plate."

Pearl reached across the table and playfully slapped Wild Bill across the head.

"Ouch!" He turned his attention to his empty pipe. Blew in it. Filled it. Tamped it. Made it ready to light.

Pearl stood up to clear away the dishes. "Peyto, are ya comin' with us to the Armistice celebrations tonight? Starts at 8 o'clock. There's gonna be a honk-a-tonk pianist."

"Naw. It'll be packed to the rafters."

"Oh, please come, Mister Peyto." Edmée rose to help her mother. "I've two polkas left on my dance card. One for my daddy." Her smile was wide. "And one for *yooou*."

Wild Bill gave a bellow of a laugh. "Another time, darlin'. I've to rise bright and early tomorrow mornin'."

Philip folded his arms across his chest and leaned back in his chair. "A bit of unfinished business?"

Wild Bill took his pipe out of his mouth. "Yeah, I plan on visitin' that beef-brained twister the bloke that runs the Banff Springs Hotel."

"Mister Dimbleby."

"Yeah. Him. The war's over. Time I reclaimed my fossil."

Pearl's voice turned serious, "Think he'll give it back?"

Peyto's face twisted in an expression of annoyance. "Like hell, he ain't keepin' it." His voice reeling. "I chipped, chiselled and hacked that relic outta the rock and paid a mate to help me carry it down the mountainside."

Pearl put down her tray and walked over to her quilting frame. "Just to recap, Peyto. Tomorrow mornin', on a hopeful wave of optimism," she rested her hand on her work-in-progress, a patchwork quilt draped over wooden bars, "you're gonna ride to the Banff Springs, seek out dough-faced Dimbleby, and punch his lights out. Right?"

"No. I'm gonna gallop to the Banff Springs Hotel. Kick Dimbleby's ass. Punch a hole in his fancy display case and reclaim my property. Yee-*haaa*!"

"Jeez." Pearl whipped back the counterpane, "let me spare ya the trouble—"

Peyto jumped from his chair. "How how," he cried, choking on a mouthful of tea. "How in hell's name?"

"Looks good, eh? Dimbleby had Ishbel and Lily clean it."

"Magnificent!" His fingers reached to explore the dents and curves of his great fossil. "Bloody magnificent!"

Pearl's hands fell to her hips. "I've been hidin' it under my quilting rack for the past two years."

"Two years! How the hell did you manage to get it past the old fart's nose?"

"I was only responsible for storing the blinkin' thing. You'll have to ask Lily. It was her idea and she roped Ethel, Ishbel and Donald into helpin' her. But that's not the funny part." I surprised burst of laughter. "They replaced your relic with another wonder-of-the-world a Monster Merman."

"A whut?"

"A fishy-lookin' creature with a monkey's head that was pulled out of Devil's Lake."

"Yar havin' me on, Pearl."

"*No.* Hand on heart. They put the wee monster in the fossil display case and scared the livin' hell out of all the fancy guests shut down Dimbleby's entire hotel!" She cupped her hands over her mouth and her shoulders shook with laughter. "Lily did it for ya."

"She's a feisty kid who's more than a pretty face, eh?" He laughed softly. "So where's the fishy-monster now?"

"Sign-of-the-Goat-Curio Shop. You should go take a look but before you do, I want this goddamn fossil outta my house."

"I'll go get my cart right now." He threw on his jacket. "I'll stop by Luxton's place and pick up the Bobster on my way back. Reverend Tosh said he left the dog with him."

"Luxton? No, I can't remember him ever having your dog. But I'll tell you who has him now."

"Who?"

"Dimbleby."

"Whu-*ut!*" Peyto's face turned scarlet. "The lily-livered louse! The swag-bellied turd! Whut does that cross-eyed CPR hawk need a Yorkshire terrier for?"

"A mascot. For the Banff Springs Hotel."

"Bobster? A flippin' mascot?"

"Don't look so surprised. According to Canon Harrison, *you* said the dog belonged to the Town of Banff."

Peyto offered a sheepish grin. "I was in a tight spot."

Pearl raised her hands reassuringly. "Anyway. As it turns out, you were only a link in a chain of folks who looked after Bobby. When the war broke out his rightful owner, an English lad, had to leave the Banff Springs Hotel in a hurry and Bobby was accidentally left behind. Ishbel found him huddled in a doorway on Banff Avenue then she lost him. Then, strangely enough, you found him miles away in the forest. Then you gave him to Reverend Tosh who gave him to Luxton who gave him to Doctor Macpherson. When he was finally located, for whatever reason, he could not be returned to England. So the hotel kept him and Dimbleby not one to miss a business opportunity made him 'Bobby of the Banff Springs Hotel'."

Peyto snorted. "He's not turnin' Bobster into a stupid mascot!" He pulled his shoulders back. "I'm off to collect my dog—"

Pearl called over her shoulder as she headed towards the kitchen. "I wouldn't do that if I was you."

"How?"

"Well, Ishbel McColl was given the job of looking after the hotel's mascot. She's devoted to that little dog. You know her father died, eh?"

"No. I didn't."

"She doesn't have a soul in the world, Peyto. It would break her heart if you took the Bobster back now."

Arches of evergreen and the words: YPRES, SANCTUARY WOOD, VIMY RIDGE were strung across the stage and a WELCOME HOME BOYS banner, festooned with ribbons and garlands, hung above the double doors. Ishbel lifted a handful of crepe-paper streamers from a cardboard box and was about to substitute a chair for a ladder, when the double-doors opened.

"Ethel, what are they draggin' in under a blanket?"

"We'd do well ter mind our own beeswax, eh?"

"Ethel, what's under the flippin' blanket?"

She rattled the box of thumbtacks. "A still."

"Not *the* still?"

"I dunno."

"Well, well, well." Ishbel threw the streamers back in the box. "Three ways of spreading news: Telephone. Telegraph. Or tell Ethel Finch!"

"Oh, don't go gettin' yar knickers in a twist! It'll be hidden in the boiler room and only a few of us are 'in-the-know,'" Ethel replied, pulling out her handkerchief and lustily blowing her nose. "Even the bartender doesn't know it's there."

"If a bunch of inebriated fools spoil this party oh finish the decoratin' by yourself!" Ishbel cried, forcefully pulling on her coat.

Ethel rattled the box of thumbtacks and did a cheerful little jig down the hall. *"I's the lass that builds the boat, and I's the lass that sails her. I's the lass that catches the fish, and—"*

The door slammed so hard the snow slid off the broad-gambrel roof.

The dancehall was stuffed to the gizzards with the biggest party that Banff had ever seen. After Patrick Nolan's performance of the Whistling Postman, Ethel Finch took the stage. She adjusted the champagne fox-fur stole draped across her shoulders, rotated her curvy hips and held her pint tumbler high. "A Round of Applause for Our Brave Soldiers!" she cried at the top of her lungs. The dancehall erupted with high-pitched whistles and great shouts. "And Now. Ladies and Gentlemen. Please Welcome My Boyfriend Ter the Stage—"

The powerfully-built man gripped his musical instrument and froze with fear.

"C'mon!" Ethel urged. "Remember what we practiced!"

The reluctant performer, hair slicked back with Macassar oil and pencil moustache neatly clipped, ambled onto the stage. Took a deep breath and a deep bow. "My name is Boris Klumpenbovur and I'm going to to." He looked at Ethel.

"Boris! Hold yar shoulders up and just damn well *do* it!"

The audience quaked at the upsurge of a bizarre deafening sound. Then he got it. "Trill along with me," he cried and everyone joined in:

"Mademoiselle from Armentieres, ParLEY-VOO?
Mademoiselle from Armentieres, ParLEY-VOO?
Mademoiselle from Armentieres,
She hasn't been kissed in forty years,
Hinky, dinky, parley-voo—"

A cowboy shouldered up to the bar and elbowed Wild Bill in the ribs. "Hey Peyto! Remember when you had a banjo ukulele."

"Well, he doesn't now," said old Donald. "And we'll thank you not to ask why."

The cowboy shrugged and ordered a pint.

Peyto was much touched. He smiled down at the old man. "Thought ya'd have grabbed yarself a granny by now?" he said, chuckling at his own wit. "Whut's the hold up? Cataracts? Bad back? Dicky knees?"

Donald cuffed Peyto's nose. "Naw. I'm only 80. I've got bags of time."

"Ya mean ya've lost the knack? Ya fear rejection?"

"Kinda."

"Awe, there's nothin' to it, man." He turned to rest his elbows on the counter. "Pick one and walk over to her. Exude confidence. A faint heart never won a fair lass, eh?"

"Easy for you to say." A silence hung heavily between them until Donald asked, "What about all those questions that come later?"

"What questions?"

"Like like, 'does my bum look big in this frock?'"

"Aw, Donald. Just smile and say, 'Are ya kiddin' me? Ya've never looked so lovely.'"

"What about that other one. 'Do you think that lady's pretty?'"

"Oh, man. That's a dangerous one. Put on a baffled expression." "Whut lady? Ya say."

"Okay. Okay. Should have thought of that myself." The old man scratched his forehead. "Then there's that that other one, 'What are you thinking about?'"

Peyto hooted with laughter. "Oh, ya always stick to the script for that one, Donald. Ya say yar thinkin' of all the ways ya and her can spend the day together. Hell, man, if ya need more help, try rubbin' on yar lucky pebble."

"I can't."

"How come?"

"I gave it away."

"Whut? You've been clinging to that talisman for years."

Donald's shoulders slumped. "It it was a useless object."

"No. It was Duncan's little pacifier." Peyto began tickling the old man under the chin, "Coo chi coo chi coo."

"Stop it!" He smacked his hand off. "Enough of your tomfoolery!"

"Coo chi coo!"

"Do it once more, Peyto, and I'll bash your bloody face in."

Lily appeared on the scene. "Here's t' a night we'll never remember with friends we'll never forget!" she said, melodically.

Peyto flashed her a cheeky grin. "Make it more memorable, Lily, and give old Donald here a dance."

"But first," she removed the beer bottle from Peyto's hand and looked into his eyes; they could be boyishly mischievous or seriously tough. "I want to dance with yoo-*ooou*."

"No! No, Lily," he said, gently removing her hands from his shoulders.

Old Donald sniggered. "Peyto, you've got a nerve handin' out romantic advice when you can't even dance."

"I can dance!"

"Show me!"

Light brightened Lily's face when Peyto took her confidently in his arms. He turned his head to look at Donald, "Um, how does it go again?"

"Nothing to it, lad. Just skip hop prance. No! SKIP! HOP! PRANCE! *Like this!* That's better. Now. One, two, three. ONE! TWO! THREE—" Peyto whisked Lily off her feet and spun her around. Soon they were whirling around the dancehall.

"See! Jigging's easier than makin' Banff Springs' furniture polish!" she giggled.

> *"You might forget the gas and shells. ParLEY-VOO.*
> *You might forget the gas and shells. ParLEY-VOO.*
> *You might forget the groans and yells*
> *But you'll never forget the mademoiselles,*
> *Hinky, dinky, parley-voo—"*

Old Donald turned back to the bar to slurp the dregs of his pint.

"Same again?" asked the barman.

"Might as well." Donald slipped off the barstool and felt his pockets.

"Have you lost somethin'?"

"My lucky charm." A softness came over his face. He hopped back up and curled his toes around the footrest. "Must be goin' senile. Forgot I gave it away."

"You gave away your lucky charm?"

"Aye. The stone had its roots in a touching memory. But it's all in the past now," he said, cheeks flushing.

The barman threw a towel over one shoulder and finished drawing the pint. "If you need to get something off your chest, feel free. I hear it all in this job." He slid the pint of suds across the bar.

"If you hear it all, lad," Donald supped through the froth. "Tell me what you've learned."

"Well," he gave the counter a quick wipe. "I've learned there are two kinds of men. The ones who drink to forget their past and the ones who grow comfortable with themselves, even as time gives them less reason for it."

"I'm not the kind who drinks to forget the past. In fact, I often dive into its long tunnel to face what I don't care to remember. Like like the foundling hospital in Bloomsbury."

"In Bloomsbury?"

"London." Donald looked across the counter. "Give me one of your one-cent wheeling tobies." The server lit the cigar and the old man continued. "It's where destitute mothers seek the haven of charitable pockets. For one full hour every night, they blow out the lamps and candles so heartbroken women can deposit their tiny bundles unseen."

The barman slowly polished the glasses. "If their fortunes improve, can they go back and get them?"

Donald nodded his small white head. "The mothers are allowed to leave a token," he said with a sniff. "By the knowledge of that token, a mother can reclaim her child. Some notch a button. Some disfigure a coin. Some are so poor they tear a bit of cloth from the hem of their skirt for they have little else."

"You know of a baby left there?"

Donald looked slightly alarmed. "I I wasn't a babe in arms. I was about three, maybe four," he said with a forced expression. "I remember being lifted out of the cart and looking up at the big brick building. It was cold and dark and the wind was ruffling my hair. Tears welled up in my mother's eyes and she placed a tiny pebble in my hand. I'd never seen a stone with a hole in it before. She told me she was going to the Dominion of Canada and when she had enough money, she was coming back for me and my sister."

"Did she come back?" he said in a soft, clipped voice.

Old Donald shook his head. "We were abandoned and cared for by a well-supported charity originally founded by three famous men. Coram the sea captain. Hogarth the artist. Handel the composer. Oddly enough, none of them had nippers of their own."

"How was it in there?"

"It got better when I stopped livin' in a fool's paradise. When I accepted the fact my mother wasn't coming back." A shadowy memory wafted across his face. "I never judged her for that. Times were harder than you can imagine, lad. No, the thing that bothers me to this day, is the knowledge she had a babe in arms. She told me it was my sister and she was only three hours old. She said no matter what I was told, I'd to remember I had a sister close by. The Foundling Hospital said I dreamt that up. 'Only one child per family. No exceptions.' I knew they were lying. But it made me feel remote from the world."

"So you came to Canada in the hopes of finding your mother."

"Aye. When I was fourteen, the Matron gave me back the stone with the hole in it and a map with an X on it. She said British workmen were flocking there. Of course, back then it wasn't called Alberta." The old man forced a smile. "Full of excitement, risk and adventure, I tucked the pebble and map into my chest pocket. I worked a plethora of jobs until I saved enough money for the train to Liverpool and the boat to Canada." His face was filled with memory. "On the Acadia to Halifax, I was tossed on the rough and cruel sea. Thick fog. No sight of land. Heck, the sea scared me witless. Then a terrible storm blew up. Giant swells. Sixty-foot waves. And God said, *'Let the waters under the heaven be gathered together unto* one *place, and let the* dry land *appear: and it was so.'* 'Tis the most powerful thing in the world, the sea." There was a long silence, then the sound of jagged breathing. "I lay seasick in the bowels of that steamship for thirteen long days. At last, we reached dry land. I remembering standing on the dock watching my fellow passengers being affectionately greeted by friends and family when one of the sailors bought me a sarsaparilla from an old woman's stand. I was grateful for his kindness and drank the foamy drink with relish. But my troubles were far from over." Donald lifted the jug to his lips and downed half of his pint in one long swallow. "I had another thirteen days of hitchin' and jumpin' freight trains to get across Canada. Sleeping in luggage racks. Knocked in the ribs at every turn."

The barman drew breath at Donald's stream of reminiscence. "Did you find her? Your mother?"

"Never did," the dark words fell from his face. "You know my story now. So, lad, what have you learned?"

The barman hesitated then plunged on.

I learned your overwhelmin' mountain of sorrow became a boulder on your back then a pebble in your pocket. And now you've given it away, sir, you can look to the future." The barman took a cigarette from a packet and a box of matches from his pocket. "Plenty of good-looking women here," he said, nodding towards a table of white-haired ladies in pretty floral frocks with hand-embroidered collars.

Laughter changed the old man's face. "The only thing I'll be cuddlin' tonight, lad, is my hot water bottle."

"Your hot water bottle?!"

"Aye, lad." Donald Duncan stubbed out his cigar; straightened his dicky bow then slipped off the barstool. "I've got cold feet," he added then he was gone.

> *"Mademoiselle from Armentieres, parLEY-VOO?*
> *Mademoiselle from Armentieres, parLEY-VOO?*
> *Just blow your nose, and dry your tears,*
> *We'll all be back in a few short years,*
> *Hinky, dinky, parley-voo."*

The Armistice Day celebrations were over. The crowds spilled from the Cascade Dancehall. The moon was full and the snow-capped mountains were luminous against an indigo sky. Joe reached for Ishbel's hand and took it in his own. "Did you have a good time?"

"I had a grand time, Joe. It's great to see everyone so happy, now the war's over."

"Only the memories left," he said and they walked on in silence.

Behind them, Ethel jabbed Lily in the ribs with her elbow. "Hey, I saw ya helpin' yarself ter a little drinky-winky in the boiler room."

"Hush up! Ishbel will hear."

"So what if she does." Ethel drew her body up and tightened the scarf-knot under her chin. "It was her bloomin' dog that dug up the still bless his little heart."

Lily's voice, wistful as the breeze, "I wunder who it belonged to'."

"Oh, God only knows." Ethel stuffed her hands into her pockets. "But I'll tell ya one thing. Whoever it was, knew what he was doin' 'cause that liquor was no a bath-tub gin. Hell no. It was good enough for the Banff Springs Hotel." She stopped to contemplate. "Hell, it was good enough for the President of American's White House."

Lily laughed indulgently. "Ooh, there'll be a few sore heads in the mornin'."

Ethel gave a vigorous nod. "Ya can say that again. But what a grand night we'll be livin' off the memory for weeks." She looked straight ahead. "Hey! Ya two up front there! Stop yar dawdlin'! Yar holdin' up the crowd!"

Pearl looked back with wrinkled brow. "Are *you* referrin' to us?"

"Yeah! Enough o' yar luvy-duvy hand-holdin'. Put a blinkin' step in it! Yar holdin' up the crowd."

Philip stopped in his tracks and turned to his wife. "If I do this," he said, gazing into her dove-grey eyes with the purest of love, "we will hold up the crowd."

To the hooting of a great-horned owl reflecting the magic of Alberta, Pearl tilted her chin, closed her eyes, and they kissed until Edmée ran towards them, taking their warm hands in her own. Amid the shouting and cheering the little family, veiled in a white mist from the falling snow, bid their farewells and set off down an icy-gravel road towards a cabin with brazen blue shutters and matching door.

With two cents worth of apples and a flask of Dave White's root beer by their side, the young couple gazed down on the random rooftops and church spires of the world below their feet. The air sweet. The breeze subtle. Joe leaned back on his elbows and said, "Everything's the same yet, at the same time, completely different."

"What do you mean?"

"Well, look down there. The rolling terrain of the Banff Springs golf course. See it?" he pointed.

"Yes. It's beautiful."

"Beautiful. Significant. Now force yourself to remember it was built by men with hungry bellies, working ten-hour shifts for twenty-five cents. Men beaten down."

"Joe," she interrupted softly, "those memories belong to another time, another world. You have to step out of the shadows of war."

A lonely cloud drifted by and for a few moments, it cast its shadow across them. "Ishbel, if the war taught me anything, it was to watch my back." His face poker straight. "They say it was the war to end all wars. But there's nothing to stop it from happening again."

"You're wrong, Joe. The world isn't as wicked as it once was. It will never happen again."

The hair on his neck stiffened. "Ishbel, can't you see? The people of Canada are attached to many motherlands France, Italy, China, America, Switzerland, Japan you name it. Under Canada's goddamn War Measures Act, we are all sitting ducks waiting to be thrown into internment camps depending on who we go to war with next."

"Oh, stop it, Joe. Everyone's sick of war. You slew the dragons. You survived." She took his hand. His fingers warm against hers. "You've come home to me. Better things lie ahead for all of us now."

At her touch, all the fight went out of Joe. He looked into her eyes, sparkling with optimism and bit back what he was going to say, replacing his words with, "We may not have it together but together we have it all." He touched her gently on the cheek. "Ishbel McColl, I love you with all my heart and all my soul."

She looked into the eyes that spoke to hers and steadily, unwaveringly, the words tumbled from her mouth, "Joe, with all my heart and all my soul, I love you back."

A slow grin spread across his face. "Say that again," he said, biting into his peach, the juice spurting down his chin.

Ishbel plucked a handful of grass and threw it over Joe's head. It clung to his hair like bits of confetti. "You say it again!" she yelled in delight, and the wind lifted their laughter to carry it high into the air, across the old internment camp, all the way to the mountain tops where it ceased to exist.

Chapter 16

Morning, June 21, 1920

The Servants Quarters

Banff Springs Hotel

Banff Alberta

Ethel took the kirby grip from her teeth and pushed it through the flower stem and into the bun resting on the back of Ishbel's neck. "Keep still!" she exclaimed then patted her masterpiece. "I don't want folks sayin' it's lopsided."

Aarff!

"Oh me nerves. Daft dog. Get from under me feet." She slid Bobby away with the side of her shoe. "Jeez, I can't believe they made him a mascot for the blinkin' hotel."

"Oh, leave him be." Ishbel picked Bobby up, hugged him close and kissed his snout. "Oh, I'll sorely miss you when I move to Canmore. But I'll come and visit you as often as I can."

Yip!

"Oh don't worry, Bobby. Miss Pidgeon told me she has the best person in the world waiting to look after you."

Lily wrinkled her brow. "Who's that then?"

"Oh, I'm tired of asking," said Ishbel. "She won't tell me."

"S'pose yi'll find out soon enough." Lily fluffed the satin ribbon that hugged the stems of Ishbel's tussie-mussie. "Hey, I meant t' ask yi. Have yi heard from Winston?"

"He wrote me a letter from Eton."

"Eton?"

"It's an English boys' boarding school. Winston likes it there," she said, recalling his letter. "Hey, remember that little dreamcatcher I sent him?"

"I duz."

"Well he said it fell apart."

"Oh, sweet cheeses!" Lily gushed. "Accordin' t' Indian folklore, it falls t' pieces when the person doesn't need it anymore."

"Really?" She grinned cheerfully. "Hey, I forgot to tell you, Nanny Patterson passed away peacefully in a cottage on the Fairfax estate. She was found in the early morning in a rocking chair, her hands cupping, of all things, a pierced pebble." Ishbel slipped her hand into her white-cotton purse and pulled a little stone with a hole in it. "Like this one!"

"Funny yi've go the same one."

"I know. Donald Duncan gave it to me for good luck. Anyway, Winston said every time he asked Nanny Patterson about her stone, she would reply, 'A pert and useless question is the germ of vanity and affectation.'" Ishbel rolled her eyes and dropped the pebble back into her wedding purse. "Anyway. I think it a strangely funny that both Nanny Patterson and Donald Duncan cherished identical stones." She tied the white-cord ties.

Lily fluffed her billowy skirt. "Hey, it wuz orful kind of Missus Kilpatrick t' lend us these bridesmaid's frocks."

"And she transformed my Scottish Country dance frock into this lovely weddin' dress." She twirled.

Ethel moved anxiously from foot to foot. "Oh me nerves! I could do with a big gin and tonic right now."

Afternoon, June 21, 1920
St. George's-in-the-Pines Anglican Church
100 Beaver Street
Banff, Alberta

Fragrant pine trees, tall, rustic and thick, enclosed the little church, but the heavy double-doors were wide-open and welcoming. Ishbel, Lily and Ethel stepped into the tiny vestibule, its walls dappled in gentle hues from the Bell-Ringers window. "Here ya go, Lily!" Ethel held Bobby up like a trophy. "He's all yours now."

"But he's *yir* responsibility," said Lily. "Yi told Ishbel yi'd look after Bobby all day, if yi could be her bridesmaid and wear a fancy frock."

"Well I'm no a blinkin' dog minder! And *yar* wearin' a fancy frock, yarself!"

"Sweet cheeses! I'm the important maid-of-honour!" Lily moved closer to Ethel's face. "I hope that's no gum yir chewin'?"

"Bloomin' hell!" Ethel removed her gum, bent her knees, and stuck it under the prayer-book table. "Are ya happy now?"

"And don't swear in the church," hissed Ishbel.

"I'm no swearin'. Hell's a place. Ask Reverend Tosh."

Arf!

"I'll look after the dog." They all turned to see old Donald Duncan, stooped and tottery but suited and booted. He picked Bobby up and tucked him under one arm. "I've a feelin' your dad's here spiritually, Ishbel."

"I feel it too," she replied quietly. Then a thought came to mind. "Mister Duncan, in my dad's absence, would you care to walk me down the aisle?"

"What!? An old bachelor like me?" His heart suddenly grew too big for his chest. "Ishbel McColl, it would indeed be an honour."

Reverend Tosh looked up from his bible, his neck lengthening from the starched banded collar of his crisp white cassock. He signalled to Joe and Luxton to stand, whereupon Mrs Luxton forcefully brought her fingers down on the keys of the church organ and the holy place was filled with a thunderous rendering of Mendelssohn's Wedding March. Old Donald turned to Ishbel. "I know how it's done, you know. I've been watchin' fathers walk brides up the middle of Mount Stephen Hall for decades."

"For decades?"

"Aye, I keep my brushes in the cubby hole on the landing above."

"You need to take my arm. Like this," he chuckled. "Now we step in synchronisation to the music. Left, together. Right, together. Don't hurry. Remember, you're worth waitin' for." Lily and Ethel followed and they all walked up the flagged floor, under the little arched ceiling and past the princely pews. When they reached the altar, old Donald gave the bride a peck on the cheek; shifted the eighteen-pound dog to his other arm then took a big step back.

Joe took a big step forward. "You look beautiful," he whispered, taking Ishbel's hand and kissing it ever-so-gently. Her jitters fell away.

Arf!

"Ah-choo!" Reverend Tosh began the ceremony, "Dearly beloved, we are gathered together here in the sight of God to join together this Man and this Woman—"

And the morning sun cast a golden beam onto the stained-glass window of St George himself.

"I, Joseph Danilo Ukrainec, take Ishbel Jane McColl, to be my lawfully wedded wife, to have and to hold, from this day forward."

Ishbel tightened her fingers in Joe's grasp. "I, Ishbel Jean McColl, take Joseph Danilo Ukrainec, to be my lawfully wedded husband, to have and to hold, from this day forward."

Patterns of soft light danced on the walls and a heavenly illumination of colour and warmth fell upon the young couple, their witnesses, and the little dog. A strong, barely controllable emotion rose in Reverend Tosh's chest but he managed to get his final words out, "And may love, laughter and adventure be under your wings for the rest of your lives." The ceremony was over.

Joe kissed Ishbel with all the passion he barely held in check. Old Donald gently dropped the dog onto the floor and gave his arm a shake. Ethel pulled a hanky from her sleeve and blew her nose with such ferocity it made Lily jump and Bobby bark. "Sorry!" She grinned. "Somethin' in the eyeball."

Georgina Luxton struck up the organ again.

Arms around waists, Joe and Ishbel hugged each other close and headed back up the aisle with Bobby padding behind them. Passed the row of jewel-coloured windows and through the doorway, emerging into the sunlight and an explosion of cheering and the tossing of rice. Ishbel raised her head from a fit of laughter. And that is when she saw it. Her mother's blue-ribboned bonnet.

"Holy doodle! The friggin' hat's surfaced!" cried Ethel. "Hoy! Edmée! How much does ya want for yar hat!?"

The girl screwed up her little face. "I'm not selling my hat to nobody!"

Ishbel began to laugh. "And you shouldn't have to, Edmée. It was the first thing I saw when I came out of the church on my wedding day. That good omen will last me a lifetime."

A smile spread across Ethel's face. "Never sneeze at a good omen, eh."

Ishbel turned around sharply at the sound of the sudden voice. Her eyes scanned all the familiar faces. "Over Here! Your chariot awaits!"

The crowd backed away to give the bride and groom room. A magnificent white horse, attached to a beautiful open buggy, lowered his head so Pearl could reach up and fondle his ears. She turned back to Ishbel, grinning at her baffled expression. "Yours for the day."

"What?" Ishbel gawped at the lavish blooms, brightly coloured ribbon, and the little brass marker inscribed, 'Brewster', on the door and her laughter travelled over all the heads. She lifted the hem of her dress and stepped into a

295

coach fit for a princess. "Oh, I canny believe it!" she cried, bubbling with excitement.

Joe stepped in too and rubbed his chin awkwardly. "Where are we goin'?"

A stout middle-aged man edged forward and closed the short door. "Don't worry, lad. My Henrietta has everything under control."

The face rang a bell. "Your Henrietta's husband. Mr Bloxham."

"The one and only. And she's done a grand job with the cake too."

"Good Lord." Ishbel's hand shifted to her chest. "I have a wedding cake."

"Aye. And 'tis piled three tiers high." The grinning man turned back to Joe. "In yar mother' memory, Henrietta got all the miners' wives together and they've planned a helluva weddin' party. Miners always look after their own, eh."

"I don't know what to say." Joe looked at Ishbel. "You know Mrs Bloxham, don't you?"

Ishbel chuckled. "Of course I do. She set us up."

"She did what?" he asked with a bemused expression.

In that instant, Ethel's big rosy face popped over the side of the coach. "'Fore ya go, I was given me orders ter deliver this." She stood on her toes and dropped Bobby into Ishbel's lap. "Weddin' present from old Napoleon Bonaparte."

"What! He gave us Bobby!?"

"Jeez b'y, take a look at the brand-new tag."

Joe lifted the little gold coin engraved, *'Bobby of Banff'*. It wasn't until he turned it over that their hearts skipped a beat. Inscribed on the back the treasured words, *'This dog belongs to Mr and Mrs Ukrainec'*.

The wedding carriage trundled out of Banff and turned right on its way to the Canmore Miners Union Hall. The sound of church bells now far off and faintly. Ishbel smiled up Cascade Mountain, waterfalls rushing down the sides and the spectacular peak awash in soft pinks and yellows. *'Indeed lass, that's your mountain.'*

Epilogue

Banff, once a camp from which mountaineering expeditions set out, is now a thriving town catering to millions from every corner of the world. If you enter it on the east side, be sure to tip your hat as you drive past Bill Peyto's handsome roadside picture. The legendary pioneer is looking down and he will appreciate your greeting. Don't forget to visit a plaster-copy of his much-loved fossil. It is tucked around a corner on the second floor of the Banff Park Museum. The original is in Ottawa.

When you stroll up Banff Avenue, pick up a copy of Alberta's oldest newspaper, the Crag & Canyon. First published by Norman Luxton in 1902, it later became the Banff Crag & Canyon and now the Bow Valley Crag & Canyon. This weekly newspaper is jam-packed with local news and events. For more information on Mister Banff himself, check out the Luxton museum.

For fun, try counting the number of times you see the Brewster name. Look for it on the sides of luxury motor coaches, gondolas, and mountain pack trains. The family have grown in numbers over the last six generations, which, no doubt, would delight Pearl. You can take a tour inside her cabin, now called the Moore Heritage Home. Standing on the grounds of the Whyte Museum, it still flaunts brazen blue shutters and a matching door.

Numerous places in this book still exist to explore, from St. George-in-the-Pines Church, where the bells still ring out over the mountaintops, to the remains of the Cave & Basin winter internment camp that housed the unfortunate Ukrainian prisoners during the First World War.

The Banff Springs Hotel became a National Historic Site in 1988, and is known today as the Fairmont Banff Springs Resort. You don't have to purchase a room to eye the big iron key that once locked the front door, or look at the amazing mountain view from the Bow Valley Lounge, or gaze in wonder at the stunning panoply of Mount Stephen Hall but you should ask for directions. The Oak Room is close to Mount Stephen Hall. Eighty years would pass before the marble wall was finally torn down. To everyone's astonishment, the sweeping staircase where the bride supposedly tumbled to her death did exist.

And so it came to pass that the Monster Merman breathed its last breath. It was nobody's fault it was exposed to the light. Luxton, a capable taxidermist, prepared the fascinating creature and put it on display in his shop where it remains to this very day. The Sign-of-the-Goat-Curio Shop on the corner of Birch and Cave (now the Banff Indian Trading Post). Dance fans, beaded belts, peace pipes, and the scary beastie that Doctor Macpherson pulled out of Devil's Lake (now Lake Minnewanka). View it for free.

Alas, the dainty china teacups and saucers have disappeared from The Lake Agnes Teahouse but you can still enjoy a beverage and look at the view through the same windows as Lady Agnes MacDonald, Lady Clementine Corrinwallis, and the ladies of the town did when they auctioned their hats for the war effort a century ago. The windows were recycled when the old building was replaced in 1981.

If you visit the nearby town of Canmore, make sure you visit the Miner's Bronze on Main Street. This life size statue is a tribute to the European immigrant mine workers. Perchance an uncanny resemblance to Joe Ukrainec. Right beside it, the newly renovated Canmore Hotel where, on a winter's evening in 1914, Joe intended to treat Ishbel to the best pie and clapshot in Western Canada. Across the road and one block down on 8th Avenue, is the Miners' Union Hall, built plain and practical like the men it served. This building housed many a fiery union meeting and generations of couples, like Joe and Ishbel, shared their first waltz in this quaint, historical place. Continue down another block and turn right on 6th Street. At the end on the left you will see Bridge Road. Nestled on the right at the opposite end of the bridge, the Mine Director's Cabin. Laundry flapping wildly and threateningly in the back garden probably not. But the windows still gleam like they did when Ishbel polished them with vinegar and a crumpled sheet of newspaper.

On May 9, 2008, the Government of Canada formally recognised that the National Internment Operations of 1914 to 1920 were a terrible mistake. Eight thousand, five hundred and seventy-nine 'enemy aliens' interned in twenty-four concentration camps across Canada were finally recognised to have suffered a grave injustice. Unfortunately, none of them has lived long enough to see the day that brought closure to the pain they suffered, the prejudice they felt and the discrimination they endured.

R.M. Clark always loved wild landscapes. She grew up surrounded by the hauntingly beautiful glens of Scotland and eventually settled in the powerful and mysterious mountains of Alberta. "I've always cherished the aspiration to write a novel with a connection to my beloved province, and my inspiration came on a snowy evening when I took shelter in the grande dame of the Canadian Rockies, the Banff Springs Hotel. The Gothic Revival architecture; the astounding view over the valley; the history of the two worlds meeting: servants and guests; British and backcountry. I wandered the great halls of that magnificent building and, in a fortunate stroke of serendipity, came upon my characters frozen in time."

Back cover photograph: Patricia R. Bories
Author photograph: Les Berezowski Photography

CPSIA information can be obtained
at www.ICGtesting.com
Printed in the USA
LVHW080432300821
696386LV00004BA/331